MW01533045

SAVAGE SAINTS MC

THE COMPLETE SERIES

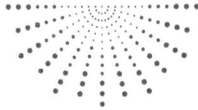

CAMERON HART

Copyright © 2023 by Cameron Hart

All rights reserved.

No part of this book may be reproduced in any form or by any electronic or mechanical means, including information storage and retrieval systems, without written permission from the author, except for the use of brief quotations in a book review.

WANT A FREE BOOK?

Sign up for my newsletter and get your copy of Chasing Stacy.

River: One look at the stunning waitress carrying the weight of the world on her shoulders, and I'm a gonner. I wasn't looking for a sweet little thing with auburn hair and more baggage than I can fit on the back of my bike, but there's no going back now. She's mine. I'll prove to her I'm more than capable of handling her past and making her feel safe again.

CONNECT WITH ME!

Check out my website, cameronhart.net, for sneak previews on my latest projects.

Follow me on social media:

Facebook Page

Facebook Group

TikTok

Instagram

Goodreads

Bookbub

fear, squared her shoulders, and lifted her chin. Pure determination stared back at me, and I knew she would work her ass off to prove herself a worthy hire. She needed life to cut her a break, and I needed a bartender who could start tonight."

I nod, letting his words sink in. A thousand thoughts race through my mind. *Why did she need a break? Why would she ask for a job in a biker bar if she was afraid? Is she in danger?*

"Hawk, are you listening?"

"Huh? Yeah, definitely."

Blade rolls his eyes, then crosses his arms over his chest. He straightens his spine, staring down at me with all the power and authority of the President of Savage Saints MC.

"Be careful with her, Hawk. We take care of our own, and Tessa is part of the family now, understand?"

"Tessa," I repeat, letting her name linger on my tongue. *What the hell is wrong with me?* I've never had these instant, possessive thoughts about someone before, never felt like I was crawling out of my skin every second I wasn't in their presence.

"Jesus, you're already a goner," Blade mutters. "Just be careful. Promise me, Hawk. I'm not sure what her story is, but she deserves a fresh start, just like we did."

I nod, thinking back to my first few years with the club. I stumbled into the Savage Saints bar after hitchhiking my way across the country to put some distance between me and my demons.

"I understand, Prez. I promise to be careful with Tessa," I tell him with all the conviction I have.

"Good. Now, what time is Rider supposed to get here? The man's been locked up for five years. You'd think he'd be on time for his own welcome home party."

I shrug, draining the last of my beer. "Any minute now, I think."

Blade grunts and waves at another member headed his way. He gives me a nod, then strikes up a conversation with the newcomer, leaving me to my devices.

As soon as the focus is off me, I make my way to the bar under the guise of getting another drink. The truth is, I can't stand not knowing what color Tessa's eyes are.

Leaning against the solid oak bar top, I catch Madge's eye. The older woman with gray dreadlocks and a full sleeve of tattoos gives me a warm smile.

"Hawk, I was just talking about you," she says, gathering the empty bottle from my hand and seamlessly replacing it with a fresh one.

"Is that right? Good thing I got here in time to save my reputation," I joke.

"What reputation?" Madge snorts.

She's been the restaurant manager and head bartender here at the Savage Saints clubhouse for longer than I've been a member. Madge has hired a few part-time staff members over the years, but they don't tend to stay around for very long. Once they realize we're not like other MCs who have club bunnies to tend to their every need, sexual or otherwise, they lose interest.

Something tells me Tessa is different.

"So, who's the new hire?" I ask, trying to sound casual.

Madge narrows her eyes at me and shakes her head, though a small smile curls up one corner of her lips. "Subtle," she deadpans.

"The new hire can speak for herself," comes the sweetest, sassiest voice I've ever heard.

I peek around Madge to see Tessa standing right behind her, carrying a dish tub in her hands.

Green. Her eyes are bright green with a golden center. Magical, just like the rest of her.

Her voice may have projected an air of confidence, but

HAWK

A CURVY GIRL/MC ROMANCE

HAWK

The new waitress at the Savage Saints clubhouse is a pretty little package wrapped up in mysteries and filled with secrets. I can't explain the urge to protect her, to reveal whatever she's hiding, whatever is making her so afraid.

Tessa doesn't trust easily, but I've always loved a challenge. I'll win her over one smile at a time, and then I'll find a way to keep her forever.

When the truth finally comes out, I have a decision to make. Trust Tessa and risk losing everything I've worked for, or leave the only woman I've ever cared about for the good of the club.

Time's running out, and so are my options. Should I trust my head or my heart?

What to expect from a Cameron Hart book: Lots of heat, plenty of sweet, and just enough drama to keep things interesting. No cheating, safe, guaranteed HEA!

CHAPTER ONE

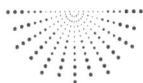

HAWK

"...*A*nd that's when the little shit peed his pants! Can you believe it?" Blade barks out a laugh, the sound rusty and unexpected coming from our usually stoic leader. "Hawk? Did you hear me?" He claps me on the shoulder, and I nod, tipping my beer in his direction.

"Yeah, that's crazy, Prez," I say, trying not to sound as distracted as I am.

"It really was," he replies slowly.

It's no use. As soon as Blade starts talking, my eyes search for her. The new bartender. I've only caught a glimpse of her red ponytail swinging behind her and her full, round hips, but everything in me is drawn to her.

The enchanting woman turns, giving me a side view of her curvy little body. Swallowing thickly, I try to keep my thoughts above board, but she's too much of a temptation. I allow my gaze to drop from her full, flushed cheeks, down the slope of her neck, lower, over the curves of her generous breasts, slightly rounded belly, and wide hips that I have the strongest urge to wrap my hands around.

Snapping my attention back to the conversation at hand,

I realize Blade is waiting for a response from me. "Sorry, what was that?"

The President of my MC, Savage Saints, is staring a hole right through my head. Good thing I have a thick skull.

"How was the last run? Any trouble with the sheriff and his minions?"

"Good. Went smoothly," I answer.

"What's going on with you today? First, I told you the funniest goddamn story anyone has ever heard and don't get so much as a chuckle. Then, I ask for an update on a mission and get brushed off in less than five words."

"Sorry, Prez," I tell him sincerely, barely managing to hold eye contact with him. "Got a lot on my mind recently." It's not a lie. I *do* have a lot on my mind. Mainly, who is the new girl, and how can I learn everything about her in a way that doesn't make me look like an over-eager creep?

"Does this have anything to do with a certain too-young, too-innocent bartender with red hair and enough baggage to fill this entire clubhouse?"

"What kind of baggage?" My mind races with possibilities as I search for her once more. Her back is turned to me again, and this time, I see more of her frame. She holds herself like she's ready to bolt at any moment, and I notice her eyes dart to the available exits every once in a while.

"Did you miss the part where she's too young?"

"She's old enough to work in a bar," I counter, my gaze still trained on my mystery woman.

"Barely. Twenty-one is still too damn young for your thirty-six years," Blade grumbles before taking a swig of his beer. "I wasn't sure about hiring her. She had that deer-in-the-headlights look on her face when she stepped into the clubhouse earlier today asking for a job."

"So, why did you? Hire her?"

"There was a moment when the little lady swallowed her

the look in her eyes tells me a different story. She puts on a good front, but just beneath the surface, she's barely keeping it together. My chest aches with how much pain this woman is carrying. I can feel the weight of her sadness, her fear.

Tessa furrows her brows, her eyes darting between mine and reading me the same way I'm reading her. No, not quite the same. She's assessing if I'm a threat. I try not to think about why she has that response to meeting someone new. If I let my imagination go, I might do something crazy, like find out who put the fear in her eyes and rip their throat out.

"You must be Hawk," she says, the slightest waver in her voice.

My eyebrows lift in surprise as a smile spreads across my face. "I am," I tell her, holding out my hand for her to shake.

She steps up to the counter, her cheeks turning the lightest shade of pink as she briefly brushes her fingers against mine. "Madge was telling me about the *Hawk stare-down*."

"Ah, see, there's my reputation," I say with a wink. Madge rolls her eyes, but I see her grinning at me. Focusing my attention back on Tessa, I try to remember how to put words together to form a sentence. "Hawk stare-down?"

Tessa tries unsuccessfully to hide a little smirk as she nods. It's adorable, and I'm having a hard time keeping my hands to myself. "She warned me about you. Said you got your road name for your attention to detail and intense stare."

"That about sums it up," I confirm, taking a sip from my beer to give my hands something to do. What I really want is to slide my hand into her silky red locks, cup the back of her neck, and pull her into me for what would surely be the single hottest, all-consuming kiss of my life.

Tessa shifts her weight from one foot to the other and chews on her bottom lip. I'm not sure if she's a naturally

7

anxious person or if I make her fidgety, but I don't want to cause her any discomfort.

"Well, it was good to meet you…?"

"Tessa," she answers instantly. I'm glad she gave me her name. It would have come off as a bit too much if I told her I already knew it.

"Tessa," I repeat with a soft smile. Her green eyes linger on mine, and I know she has to feel whatever this is between us. However, I get the sense that she's hesitant to trust anyone. I'll just have to prove to her I'm worth taking a chance on. "I'm sure I'll see you around–"

The front door of the bar swings open, and out of the corner of my eye, I see the familiar, lumbering frame of Rider, our MC brother, who just got out of lockup. The biker bar erupts in cheers and chaos as everyone moves toward Rider to welcome him home.

I hang back, knowing he's already dealing with a lot of people right now. We'll have more quality time to catch up later without the crowd.

Turning back to the bar, I look for Tessa, only she's not there. I lean over the bar top and peer into the back room, but she's not there either. *What the hell?* It's been barely ten seconds since Rider walked in. Where could she have gone?

Then I hear a rustling. Tipping my head down, I'm surprised to see Tessa crouching on the ground, hands over her head as if protecting herself from an earthquake. Jesus, this woman is pulling out every protective instinct inside of me. I have half a mind to jump down there and scoop her into my arms.

Instead, I take a deep breath and try to get these insane urges under control.

"You okay down there?" I ask with what I hope is a light tone.

Tessa pops her head up and looks around as if just realizing where she is. I hate the look of terror in her eyes, though it fades quickly. A testament to how often she's had to mask her fear.

"Yeah! Yeah, totally," she rushes to say. "Just, uh... dropped a... bobby pin!" she exclaims, digging around on the floor and picking up a small hairpin. She stands up and presents it to me as proof. The thing is covered in dirt and grime and has clearly been lying lost and forgotten on the ground for quite some time, but I let it go. The last thing I want is to embarrass her.

I want to wrap her up in my arms and tell her she never has to worry about anything ever again, but I manage to finish my beer and shove my hands in my pockets.

"I better go see the man of the hour," I tell her, nodding toward Rider. "I'm glad you'll be working here," I say sincerely. "I'll see you soon."

Tessa gives me a smile and the cutest little wave. I turn around, forcing myself to walk away. I could stand there all night, staring at her and attempting to flirt. It's been a long damn time since I've been involved with anyone, let alone wanted to impress someone or flirt with them.

With Tessa, though, everything is different. More real. More intense. I don't know what exactly that means, but I can't wait to find out.

CHAPTER TWO

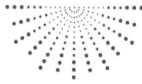

TESSA

I wipe my sweaty palms on my jeans and take a deep breath, remembering what Madge told me about balancing the register before opening. It's my first solo shift at the Savage Saints clubhouse, and thankfully, it's an opening shift. The bar officially opens at two-thirty most afternoons, but we don't get busy until closer to six.

Grabbing the stack of twenties from the drawer, I take my time counting each one before deliberately setting it back in its spot in the register. It shouldn't be this difficult to balance a register or count a stack of bills, but my father's voice echoes in my head, making everything worse.

How stupid are you, Tess? It's a wonder they let you graduate high school. Can't read or do a math problem to save your life. What a waste.

Tears sting my eyes, but I blink them away. He doesn't get the satisfaction of making me cry anymore. And, for the record, I *can* read. It just takes me longer than other people to sound out the words in my head. The math comment is pretty much on point, however. Numbers always gave me more trouble than letters. Not that it made a difference to

10

my dad. He views dyslexia as one thing and one thing only; a shameful blemish on his family line.

Blowing out a determined breath, I focus on the cash in my hand. I can't screw this up. This job is the one thing I have going for me, aside from my bestie, Sutton. Still, I need to earn all the money I can, not only to pay Sutton back for letting me stay with her in her grandma's old house but to save up and eventually leave this awful town filled with awful memories.

I was so close to freedom last year. After spending all of high school and what should have been my college years babysitting and selling my handmade resin jewelry, I finally had enough to buy a car and get the hell out of here... when my stash was discovered by the monster himself, my dad.

I close my eyes against the memory of that day and the resulting trip to the hospital for "falling out of the window."

Shaking those terrible thoughts from my head, I finish counting the drawer, thankful that everything balanced out. Next, I get the coffee going, even though Madge told me we hardly ever serve the stuff. People come here for beer and whiskey, apparently. They sometimes get coffee when they've had too much of the fun stuff, so the quality and freshness don't matter as much. At least, according to Madge.

I'm just finishing pouring in the ground coffee beans when the front door opens.

Shit. I forgot to lock it back up after clocking in for my shift.

Double shit. What if it's my dad?

I spin around, grabbing the nearest thing that could be used for a weapon, and point it directly at... Hawk. Of course it's not my father. He wouldn't come within a mile of this place, let alone waltz right in.

Hawk holds his hands out in front of him, palms up, in a sign of surrender. He has that same easy grin on his handsome face as when I first met him last week. It somehow winds me up and relaxes me at the same time, and I'm not sure what to do about it.

"Woah, there. Easy, killer," he says, taking a few tentative steps forward as if I might use the weapon in my hand. The idea of me scaring this six-foot-tall, muscled Roman god of a man with nothing more than a pair of tongs is laughable. He could snap me in half if he wanted to, even with my extra curves and thick thighs. "Didn't mean to startle you."

"I'm not startled," I say with more confidence than I feel. I've learned that's the key to surviving in this life. Don't give anyone an edge. Don't let them see weaknesses. Don't give into the fear, at least not until you're alone and no one can see you cry.

Hawk raises an eyebrow at me, then looks pointedly at the tongs in my hand.

"Opening this here clubhouse requires many tools and skills," I inform Hawk as I face the coffee machine once more and adjust the pot before hitting the start button.

"I don't doubt that," he replies warmly.

I have my back turned to him, yet I swear I can *feel* his deep voice rumbling through me, his breath on my neck, the ghost of his hands sliding down my body.

Get it together, I shout at myself in my head. So he's hot with a great smile, deep blue eyes, and messy hair I want to glide my fingers through. No big deal. Just because he's being friendly now doesn't mean he won't show his true colors later. My father was able to fool everyone. Still does. They have no idea the hell I grew up with after my mother passed…

"Tessa? Are you okay?"

"Yes," I'm quick to respond. Hawk looks like he doesn't believe me, so I try again. "I'm good," I manage to say with a halfway decent smile. "It's hard to turn down my thoughts sometimes," I admit for some stupid reason. Wasn't I just saying I never show weakness? Less than ten minutes in Hawk's presence, and he's already somehow gotten through my first layer of protection.

"I get that," Hawk replies, his eyes going soft with understanding.

"Why do you do that?" I blurt out, my face instantly heating once the words fall from my lips.

"Do what?"

"Make it impossible to…"

"To…?"

His eyes capture mine, the royal blue depths pulling me under like they did the first day I met him. What is it about this man that makes me want to trust him? Why can't I seem to control my words around him? That's a dangerous game to play, especially with the secrets I hold.

"You make it impossible to ignore you," I tell him, my eyes darting around so I don't have to look at him.

"Then I'm doing something right," he says smoothly.

It should give me the creeps or, at the very least, make me brush him off. Instead, I find myself smiling.

"Cocky, are we?" I tease, grabbing a clean rag and wiping off the handles for the draft beers.

I feel Hawk's shadow before I see it, and I look up, peering into those blue eyes as he towers over me. I'm not intimidated by his size and closeness, though everything in my past tells me I should be. It's the strangest thing. With the massive, tattooed biker leaning over the bar top, his gaze trained on me, I feel safer than I have in a long time. Since before my mom passed away.

"Confident, not cocky," he gently corrects, his voice deep and filled with conviction. "I know what I want when I see it, but I'm a patient man. I'll wait however long it takes for you to feel comfortable around me."

"You don't make me uncomfortable," I say, matching his soft tone. "I'm just… It's complicated. I'm not…"

"No need to explain, beautiful. Like I said, I'm a patient man. And, for the record, I'm not scared off by *complicated* situations."

I blink a few times, not sure how to respond. His steady blue gaze never leaves mine, like he's infusing his strength and confidence directly into my soul.

The front door swings open with a bang, making me jump out of my skin. Hawk looks worried, but I smile at him and shake off the scare. He might think he can handle my complicated life, but he doesn't know my father. Or, rather, he does. And that's the problem.

"It's five o'clock somewhere!" one of the men who just walked in shouts into the empty bar.

"It gets funnier every time you say it," one of his companions says sarcastically.

"Leave him alone. He's just trying to have a good time," a woman says as she stomps into the bar with her six-inch stilettos and bleached blonde hair.

"Yeah, this place is barely open. Save the jabs until happy hour," another man says, his arm wrapped around the Barbie look-alike.

My anxiety kicks in as soon as the four patrons approach, and I look at Hawk for some reason, as if he's going to help. Without missing a beat, he steps around to the other side of the bar and stands next to me without saying a word.

"Hawk!" the woman says loudly as she leans against the bar top. Her cherry-red halter top has a plunging neckline, showcasing her entire cleavage. She bats her eyelashes and smiles at him like he's an ice cream cone she wants to lick.

I stiffen next to Hawk, liking this woman less and less. It shouldn't bother me. Hawk has every right to hang out with whomever he wants. He can even sleep with her for all I care.

As soon as I think it, my heart drops to my stor
not jealous. I'm *not*.

"Brandi," Hawk replies, his voice flat and unintere

"I didn't know you worked in the bar. You can ju
in and do anything, can't you?" she swoons.

"Just helping out the newest bartender while s
used to everything," he says in the same tone.

I peer over at him, surprised to see him looking
me. He winks, making me feel tingly in places I've ne
before.

"All right, babe," the man who came in with her say
ping up behind her. "You tryin' to make me jealous?
isn't looking for a hookup, and neither should yo
when you have me."

He spins the woman around and fuses his lips to
bending her over the counter as he devours her. I blink
times, trying not to be scandalized by the public disp.
affection.

Hawk clears his throat, and the two finally break
"What'll it be, Chains?" he asks.

"Best beer on tap and whatever the lady want
grunts.

"Triple dry martini, top shelf gin, of course," Bran
in a sickly sweet voice. "Think you can handle tha
girl?"

Before I get a chance to answer, Hawk steps in. "S
handle anything."

Brandi rolls her eyes but follows Chains to a bootl
back.

I pour the beer, unsure which one is the best, and :
a tray before working on the martini. There's a reci
around here somewhere, but I don't remember where
said it was. I should have memorized the basics, b
told we don't get many mixed drinks. I should have

omeone would order one during the first ten minutes of my
first solo shift.

Out of the corner of my eye, I see a spiral-bound notebook labeled "mixed drinks."

Thank God.

I open to a section on martinis and squint to read the
handwritten recipe. All the letters merge, some cursive, some
regular, all but obliterating my weak reading skills.

Taking a slow, soothing breath, I close my eyes and focus
on slowing down. When I look at the page again, I try isolating
each word and identifying the sound of each letter. Gin is the
first ingredient, and I know exactly where that bottle is.

As I reach for the top-shelf stuff, Hawk pours another
beer. "Need help with Brandi's drink?" he asks.

"Nope! I got it," I tell him, my voice a little too shrill, even
to my own ears.

Bringing the gin back to my workstation, I look at the
next ingredient. "V-E-R… Mouth?" I whisper. "Vermin. No.
Shit," I mutter under my breath. Maybe I'll recognize the
label once I see it.

Staring at the wall of liquor bottles, I scan the labels,
frowning when I don't see what I'm looking for. Letters
dance in front of my eyes, some vibrating while others flip
backward or upside down.

"Vermouth is up there," Hawk says, pointing to a small,
dark bottle.

"Thanks," I whisper, too embarrassed to look at him.

"Any time. Do you need me to ring everyone up? Or
finish the martini?"

"Umm…" My voice wavers as I process his questions.
Between the recipe, my stupid dyslexia, and thinking about
what Hawk should be doing, it's all too much. I can't fuck
his job up, though. Especially on my first real shift.

I breathe in through my nose, forcing my tears to settle deep in my gut instead of pouring out of my eyes. Swallowing past the lump in my throat, I try to speak again.

"I just, uh, need..." I trail off, racing thoughts clouding my mind.

"You know, I've never had a martini. Do you mind if I make one for Brandi and then one for myself? I'll pay, of course."

I know what he's doing, and I should be upset that he's coddling me. As it is, I swear I could throw my arms around him and kiss him. I don't, of course, but I'm thankful he seems to know what I need, even before I do.

"Y-yeah. That would be good," I say, my voice barely above a whisper. "I can pour the last beer. Pale ale on tap, right?"

"You got it, boss," Hawk replies, giving me his most charming grin and a wink. I try to smile, but I'm too worked up.

Turning on my heel, I grab a beer glass and begin filling it, tipping it to mitigate the foam, just like Madge showed me. My hands grow sweaty, and my breathing becomes more and more shallow.

Do NOT have a panic attack. I repeat, do NOT have a panic attack. Not here. Please, get it together!

The tears from earlier rush to the surface, blurring my vision. I tighten my grip on the beer glass in an attempt not to drop it, but my move has the opposite effect. Instead of securing my hold, the glass slips from my hand, crashing to the floor and breaking into a dozen pieces.

My father's voice booms in my head, and I squeeze my eyes closed, trying to shut out the sound. It's no use.

Clumsy AND stupid? How did I get so goddamn lucky to have a daughter like you?

The table of bikers and Brandi all let out boos and shouts, and my face flames with shame and embarrassment.

"Tessa?" Hawk says softly from behind me.

I jump at his voice, and my foot gets caught in the rubber mat on the floor. Great. Just perfect.

I brace myself to hit the floor, but Hawk wraps his arms around me, pulling me into his chest.

"Hey, now," he whispers. "I've got you. You're safe here, okay, Tessa?"

I shake my head before burying myself further into his embrace. No one has ever held me like this, comforted me in a gentle tone, or come to my rescue so instantly, without a second thought.

"I'm sorry," I say automatically. It's a reflex at this point.

"Nothing to apologize for, beautiful," he soothes. There it is again. *Beautiful.* The way he says it so casually makes me almost believe him. "How about you grab a bottle of water from the back room, and I'll clean up here?"

"What about ringing everyone up? And the last drink since I dropped it and made a mess?"

"I've got it covered. I promise. Just take a few minutes to reset in the back room, okay? I'll be there soon."

"But…"

"Let me help, Tessa. I want to."

"But why?"

Hawk peels me off of his chest, his sapphire eyes capturing mine. "You don't know this yet, but life doesn't have to be this hard. This scary. I think you've dealt with some shit, and you're not sure who to trust. Am I right?"

I shrug, not wanting him to know how on point he is.

"I want to prove to you I'm someone you can rely on with my actions, not just my words. So let me do this for you. Let me help."

"You don't even know me," I counter, our eyes still connected as our bodies press closer together.

Hawk cups my face, his thumb gently brushing over my cheekbone. "But I want to. And this is the first step. Now, go on and take a little break while I finish up out here."

I nod, my throat constricting as I swallow a fresh wave of tears. Why is this man being so kind to me? How does he know exactly what to say to soothe my fears?

Stepping out of his embrace is harder than it should be, but I manage to pull myself away. I head to the back room and grab a bottle of water like Hawk suggested. Pressing the cold bottle to my forehead, I finally take a full breath.

How the hell am I going to explain my freak-out to Hawk?

CHAPTER THREE

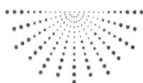

HAWK

*A*fter cleaning up the glass and mopping the floor, I total up the cost of the drinks and charge them to my card. I can't go over to the table and hand those assholes a bill at the moment without yelling at them to shut the fuck up and leave Tessa alone. But I don't want my girl to get in trouble for giving away free drinks.

I roll my shoulders and inhale deeply, preparing myself to go in and check on Tessa. I don't know what she's been through, but seeing the frustrated and defeated tears in her eyes gave me enough of an idea. And the way she apologized, as if I was going to be irate. She hasn't had a lot of love in her life, but all that is about to change.

I head to the back room and knock on the open door so I don't startle Tessa. She's sitting on a folding chair in the corner of the room, and my eyes are immediately drawn to hers. My chest caves in when I see tears streaming down her face.

Closing the distance between us, I kneel in front of her, taking her hands in mine. It's then I notice a cut on the side of her left hand.

"You're hurt," I say, more to myself than to Tessa.

She turns her hand to look at the wound, then shrugs. I'm starting to understand her body language, and I've gathered that shrugging means I'm onto something she doesn't want to talk about or deal with.

While I won't push her to give me more information than she's ready to, I'll have to insist on taking care of her cut. No way in hell am I going to leave this woman bleeding in the back room of the clubhouse.

"I'll be right back with a first aid kit," I tell her. I stand before Tessa has a chance to protest and jog toward a cabinet that I think holds medical supplies. *Jackpot.*

Grabbing bandages, hydrogen peroxide to disinfect, and antibiotic cream, I race back to the beautifully broken angel sitting on the saddest chair in the darkest corner of the room. I get the overwhelming urge to bring her into the light and show her what I see; a warrior. A strong as fuck woman who has battled through hell to get to where she is. A goddess in the flesh with a sassy mouth and kind, vulnerable eyes.

Soon. First, I need to take care of her cut.

"Let me see your hand," I say softly when I get back to Tessa. She hesitates at first, but I kneel in front of her once more, trying to make my massive frame less intimidating.

As the enforcer for Savage Saints, I can't say I've been in many positions where I wanted to make myself smaller. Usually, I use my size to my advantage. With Tessa, however, I need to show her I'd never hurt her. I'll use my strength to protect her, always. She doesn't know it yet, but she officially has me as her bodyguard.

Tessa finally rests her hand on my open palm, and I hiss when I see the wound. It's not deep, and it's already stopped bleeding, but I still hate knowing she is in pain.

"This might sting a little," I warn as I pour a little of the hydrogen peroxide on a cotton ball and lift it to her hand. Tessa nods, her eyes fixed on where our hands are touching. I press the antiseptic liquid over her cut, surprised when she doesn't even flinch. She didn't even blink.

I don't want to think about why she has a high pain tolerance. Not right now. I need to keep my anger and blood pressure under control while I'm still taking care of Tessa. I'll get answers eventually, but she doesn't need to see that side of me right now.

Next, I rub a small amount of the antibiotic cream over the open cut, then wrap her hand with a breathable cotton bandage. Lifting her hand, I press my lips to her knuckles, loving how her green eyes sparkle and her cheeks turn the lightest shade of pink.

"Can you tell me what happened out there?" I ask, adjusting my position so I'm sitting instead of squatting. Something tells me Tessa will respond better if I'm down here and she's sitting up. She needs the high ground, needs to know she's in control. I want to give that to her.

Tessa nibbles her bottom lip, focusing her attention on the opposite corner of the room. I swear I can see her racing thoughts. I can almost hear the internal battle she's having over whether to trust me.

She inhales sharply, then lets out a slow, measured breath. Her eyes lock on mine, and I know she's decided to take the leap. Tessa is ready to trust me, at least a little. I'll make sure she never has a reason to regret it.

"It's... Well, I have... I mean, I..." She huffs a frustrated breath, and I place my hand on her knee without thinking about it. Tessa looks down at where I'm touching her, and I almost yank my hand away. Then, she places her much smaller, softer hand on top of mine.

"Take your time, beautiful," I whisper.

Tessa's eyes find mine, and her fingers curl around my hand in a tighter hold.

"I have dyslexia," she says quietly.

I have to strain to hear her, but once I do, everything snaps into place. The apology, the trouble finding the right bottles, the struggle to read the recipe. No wonder she was stressed out on her very first shift. I'm so glad I decided to come in today.

"That's nothing to be ashamed of, you know that, right?"

Tessa shrugs, looking away from me. My heart aches for her, but I'm so grateful she shared a little piece of herself with me.

"Please don't tell Madge," she begs, her green eyes pleading with me. "I'll do better. I can take pictures of the recipes on my phone and memorize them on my own time so I don't screw up again. I really need this job, and if I get fired…"

"Breathe, sweetheart," I encourage, taking a deep breath so she can follow me. We take some breaths together, each one binding my heart closer to hers. "I won't tell anyone anything you don't want me to. But for the record, Madge wouldn't fire you for something like that. And I can help you with the recipes. We can go through them together before your shifts so you feel more confident."

"Why are you being so nice to me?"

"I hate that you have to even ask," I tell her, bringing my free hand up to hold the side of her face. Brushing my thumb against her soft skin, I feel her relax slightly. I want to kiss her pain away and run my hands up and down her body until she forgets everything bad that's ever happened to her, but I'll settle for this for now.

"I guess I don't have a lot of people in my life who want good things for me just because I'm me, you know?"

Tessa nibbles her bottom lip again, and I gently graze the pad of my thumb across her chin, pulling her poor, abused lip from the grip of her teeth.

"Well, you better get used to it," I say with a grin. I can tell the moment is getting too intense for her, and she already shared more than I thought she would. Hopping up from my position on the floor, I hold out my hand for her to take. "My afternoon is free, and I would love to stick around until the second person comes in for their shift."

"You don't have to do that," Tessa is quick to say. "I don't want to take up your whole day just because Madge made a bad hiring decision."

"Hey, now. I don't want to hear you say mean things about yourself. You're perfectly capable of doing this job."

Tessa looks like she's about to cry again, but she blinks her tears away before I can ask why. Deep down, I know why. No one has ever made her feel like she can do something. I'm guessing her family didn't handle her dyslexia in a healthy or positive way. That shit ends today.

My girl places her hand in mine, letting me pull her out of her chair and into a big bear hug. At first, I think it might be too much, but Tessa sinks into my embrace, burying her face into my chest and wrapping her arms around my waist.

"I'm right here," I soothe, grazing my fingertips up and down her spine in calming strokes. "I'll always be right here."

After soaking up a few moments of peace, Tessa steps out of my arms and squares her shoulders, holding her chin up high like the queen she is. I hope I had a small part to play in giving her back some of her confidence.

"Thank you, Hawk," she says, her eyes conveying gratitude and disbelief in equal measure. One day, she won't be surprised when I want to help. One day, she'll realize she can always rely on me.

Until then, I'm content to stay by her side and show her what a real man acts like when he's found something worth treasuring.

CHAPTER FOUR

TESSA

$\mathcal{I}$ turn on the coffee maker in the clubhouse, waiting until it starts dripping to move on to my next task. It's my second week working as a bartender for the Savage Saints MC, and I've almost gotten this whole opening routine down. Just in time for me to get scheduled for closing shifts, of course.

True to his word, Hawk has been helping me learn different drink recipes before or after my shifts. We finished with the last one two days ago, and I'd be lying if I said I wasn't a little anxious to see if he shows up today. I think he likes spending time with me, but now that there's no reason for him to seek me out, a part of me is worried he'll forget all about me.

Leaning against the counter, I take a final look around the front lobby, ensuring I don't need to sweep or wipe off any tables from the night before. My phone rings, the sound echoing in the nearly empty clubhouse.

I immediately silence it, then look at the screen. A smile lights up my face when I see it's my bestie and new roommate, Sutton.

"Hey, girl, hey!" I answer as I make my way to the back-room. We don't open for another fifteen minutes, which gives me plenty of time for a quick chat.

"Tessa!" Sutton exclaims. She's always surprised and happy when I answer my phone or reply to her texts. After she told me her whole story and the way she grew up, I can understand why. "Sorry to call while you're at work. I hoped to catch you before you started your shift."

"You did, no worries," I assure her. "And you know you can always leave me a voicemail or send a text if I don't answer."

"I don't want to bother you," she replies automatically.

"Sutton," I say gently. "We're friends. I like talking to you. You're not bothering me."

My bestie lets out a sigh. "Thank you for reminding me. I've been free of my parents for three years now, but I guess some things just take time to unlearn."

"Believe me, I get it," I mumble, thinking about all the times I've heard my father's voice in my head the last few weeks.

"Yeah, actually, I wanted to talk to you about your parental unit," she says hesitantly.

Ice runs through my veins, and I start to feel light-headed. "Did he find the house?" I whisper.

"No, no, we're safe at my grandma's old house. No one knew we were related. I have a different last name, and I'm positive my parents haven't so much as picked up the phone to try to figure out where I ran off to. As far as the outside world knows, I just moved here and rented an old house on the outskirts of town."

"Right. I know you're right. I just can't help but feel paranoid."

"That never really goes away, but it fades in time," she whispers.

My heart hurts for everything Sutton has been through in her life. We only met last year, but we're all we have in this world. She's the only one who knows my secrets, and I know I'm the only one she's shared her childhood trauma with.

"Um, so anyway," Sutton continues after clearing her throat. "I was at the grocery store this afternoon and saw two cops in the parking lot, walking out to their squad car."

"Okay, and?" I don't like the cops in this town any more than the Savage Saints, but it's not exactly news that they go to the grocery store.

"And they were having a conversation on one of the guys' walkie-talkie thingies."

"Uh-huh," I urge, though my voice falters.

"Your dad is having them look for you, Tess."

"Well, we knew that would probably happen, right?" My voice is too shrill, but I can't control it right now. Not with the adrenaline ricocheting throughout my body and seeping into my veins. "But we're prepared. He doesn't know you exist, he doesn't know about the house, and he definitely doesn't know about my job."

"Do you really think you're safe there? I know you picked the Savage Saints because it's the one place your father wouldn't look, but are they going to treat you any better?"

"Yes," I answer without hesitation. Hawk's ocean-blue eyes and charming grin pop into my head, followed by the memory of being held by him. "I know I'm safe here. These men might be big, burly bikers, but everyone has treated me with respect."

"Except for the jerks who laughed at you on your first shift," Sutton growls. I love my bestie. She's painfully shy, heartbreakingly self-conscious, and afraid to use her voice in general. And yet when it comes to me, Sutton turns into a mama bear, ready to tear into anyone who upsets me.

I get it. I'm the same way with her.

"*Buuuuuut*, remember how I told you about the nice biker who helped me through the rush?"

"Oh, I remember, all right. I remember how you said his name all breathily," she teases. "*Hawk, Hawk, Hawk!*" Sutton does her best impression of me, then falls apart into a fit of giggles.

"I do *not* sound like that," I hiss, though I'm laughing, too.

Good thing I didn't mention how Hawk patched up my hand, the sweet words he whispered, or the way he held me and said he'd always be there. Sutton also doesn't know about our study sessions. I can only imagine the comments she'd make. All in good fun, of course, but I don't need someone encouraging me in that direction. I'm having enough trouble not falling head over heels for him as it is.

The bell above the front door dings, alerting me to my first customer of the day.

"Hey, my shift is starting," I tell Sutton. "Just got my first customer."

"'Twenty bucks says it's Hawk!"

"I'll take that bet. But how about the loser has to buy pizza instead? I get my first paycheck today, and I need something other than canned soup and stale cereal."

"Ooooh, that sounds great. Since I'm not working today, I'll swing by and pick you up after your shift. We'll cash it and pick up pizza on the way home?"

"I can't wait!"

"Since I'm obviously winning the bet, I'll make sure to order extra toppings."

I laugh and then hang up, a smile still on my face as I make my way to the front. I'm almost certain I know who is sitting out there, but my anxiety is whispering that I'm not good enough for someone like Hawk. Surely he has to know that, too.

My worries fade into nothing when I see Hawk leaning

CAMERON HART

against the bar, his blue eyes fixed on me. I can't help it. My smile grows wider, and my face heats, liking that this powerful, sexy man seems enthralled by me. How is it possible for him to be the hottest man alive and yet so gentle with me? So understanding of my dyslexia without a second thought? My own flesh and blood shamed me for my learning disability, but Hawk sees me just the same as anyone else.

Well, maybe not the same. Is it crazy to think he might want me the way I want him? Not that I would know how to do anything about my wanton desires. Something tells me Hawk would take control and make me love every minute of it.

Shoving those thoughts aside, I take a cleansing breath, hoping my cheeks aren't as blushed as they feel.

"You just made me lose a bet, mister," I inform him as I grab an apron and tie it around my waist. Hawk's eyes are drawn to the movement, his gaze fixed on my hips. Usually, I'd be self-conscious of my extra curves, but Hawk can't seem to get enough of them.

He clears his throat, tearing his eyes away from my torso so he can look at me. "A bet?" he asks, that easy smile stretching across his handsome face. He has a bit of stubble today, and I won't lie, I like the gruffer look. Paired with his kind eyes and charm, Hawk is the total package.

"Yes. About who my first customer would be," I answer as I grab a beer glass. By now, I know Hawk's favorite beer is the IPA on tap.

"Is that right? You didn't think it would be me?" I swear Hawk almost looks offended, as if I was expecting someone else.

"Oh, I knew it would be you," I assure him, though a part of me doubted I'd ever see him again. "I just didn't want my bestie to buy pizza tonight. I'm getting my first paycheck, and I wanted to treat us to a real meal instead of whatever we can find in the pantry. She's already letting me stay with her for free, so it's the least I can do."

Hawk grins when he hears my explanation but then furrows his brow. "Do you two need groceries? We have a stockpile of things here in the clubhouse. Sometimes members crash in the apartments out back, so we keep the essentials on hand and restock once a month."

"Oh, no, that's okay," I rush to say. I don't know how to accept gifts, and I'm still wary of good things. In my experience, they always come with strings attached.

"I can pack up a box of stuff for you to take home after your shift. Seriously, that's what this stuff is here for."

"You don't have to do that. We'll be fine," I tell him, though honestly, having some essentials would be amazing. Then this paycheck could go toward utilities, and I could put a little extra toward my car fund.

"What if I *want to* do it?" I open and close my mouth, unable to come up with a response. "It's your choice, of course. Just remember that kindness doesn't always come with a cost. Some people genuinely want good things for you simply because of who you are."

Blue eyes capture mine, and I find myself swallowing past a lump in my throat. Those were my words from the day Hawk rescued me from my embarrassing panic attack. I can't believe he remembered and that he's showing me with his actions how serious he is about helping me.

A dozen questions flutter around in my brain as I absorb everything about this man. *Why me? What makes me worthy of your attention? When are you going to get tired of me? How can you be so patient?*

Instead of letting any of those thoughts out, I take a deep breath and focus on Hawk. He's been nothing but sweet and understanding. He could have made fun of me or ignored me after I told him about my dyslexia, but instead, he found a way to help me and put me at ease.

I trusted him with one secret, but he still doesn't know everything. Can I really accept kindness from someone who might hate me if they knew the whole truth about who I am?

Yes, yes, yes! My heart chants with every beat. Even though my brain is screaming at me to slow down and be cautious, I find myself leaning into the warm feeling I get whenever Hawk is around.

"Okay," I whisper, wringing my hands together in front of me.

"Okay?" Hawk repeats, his eyes filled with disbelief and excitement. It's kind of adorable. How can I say no to that face?

"Yeah," I say with more of a smile. "Thank you, Hawk. For your kindness. I won't forget it."

He furrows his brow but shakes off the questions I know he has. I don't have the answers he wants, so I'm glad he let it go.

Hawk rests his large hand on both of mine, settling my nervous fidgeting. "Hear me when I say this, Tessa," he murmurs, his voice thick and velvety. "It's my honor to take care of you, and it's not something I take lightly. Thank you for letting me in."

He squeezes my hands and leans further over the bar to brush the lightest kiss on my forehead. *God. Swoon.* Who does stuff like that?

Before I get a chance to ask, Hawk steps away from me and grabs an empty cardboard box from the corner of the room. He takes off toward the back of the clubhouse, and I swoon even harder, knowing he's going grocery shopping for me.

Several hours later, I'm just getting ready to clock out when the front door opens, and Sutton steps inside. I didn't think about how intimidating this place might be with rough-and-tumble bikers hanging around. I should have told her to stay out in the car.

Waving my friend down, I see her eyes fill with relief the moment she recognizes me. My heart twists when I see her trembling slightly, but she hides it well.

"Hey, Sutton, sorry I'm running a few minutes late. You can wait in the car if you want."

"N-no, it's ok-kay," she says with a shaky voice. Sutton clears her throat and tries again. "I don't want to be scared all the time. It's good for me to go out and do new things. Even this. At least at the end of today, I'll be able to say I survived visiting a biker bar, so that should give me a boost of confidence, right?"

I smile at my friend and nod. "Exactly. You just sit right here, and I'll grab my check real quick," I tell her, spinning on my heel. "Oh, and Hawk has some groceries for us," I call over my shoulder.

Grabbing the white envelope with my name on it, I leaf through the stack of twenties. Aside from avoiding my father, the other reason I chose to work at the Savage Saints clubhouse is because they pay in cash, under the table. Perfect for someone who gave a fake last name during her interview.

By the time I get back out to the front, Hawk is sauntering up to the bar with the cardboard box full of food. He grins at me, and dammit, I automatically return it.

A large man stands next to Hawk, and it takes me a second to place him. Rider, I think his name is. I don't know much about him other than he was gone for a few years, and he mostly keeps to himself.

"Hey, beautiful. On your way home?" Hawk asks. Rider gives him some strong side-eye, and I get the sense that Hawk doesn't call a lot of women beautiful. It makes me feel special and wanted, which I suppose is how I always feel around Hawk.

"Yeah, me and my bestie have big plans tonight, right?" I look over at Sutton, who nods.

Rider chokes out a cough, causing all three of us to stare at him. He looks... possessed. Rider is breathing heavily, every muscle in his body tense as he locks eyes with Sutton.

"Rider," he blurts out, shoving his giant hand in Sutton's direction.

My friend stares at his hand, then looks up at the now sweaty and shaky man offering it to her. He must take her shyness for distaste and withdraws his hand before rubbing the back of his neck.

"Uh, good to meet you," he half growls. Rider curses himself under his breath while Hawk grins at his friend.

"Don't mind Rider's manners," Hawk cuts in, clapping his friend on the shoulder. "He hasn't been around people lately. All bark, no bite, really."

Rider grunts and jabs Hawk with his elbow but doesn't say anything else.

"Right," I say with a little laugh, trying to break up the tension. I have no idea what that was all about, but poor Sutton has already had quite the adventure today. "Well, we better get going if we want to pick up the pizza on time, right, Sutton?"

She nods and stands from the bar stool she was perched on. I loop my arm through hers and head out to the parking lot, Hawk hot on my heels with our groceries.

Sutton unlocks the car and hops in the front while I help Hawk get the box settled in the back seat. I close the door, and Sutton starts the car, indicating she's had enough for one day. I get it. Whatever happened with Rider was intense, and she's had too much intensity in her life already. I hope pizza can make up for the unplanned outing today.

"Is she okay?" Hawk asks quietly.

"Yeah," I assure him. "She's a little shy and has some social anxiety."

"And Rider didn't help things, the poor idiot," he says with a chuckle.

"What was up with that? Is he always so…"

"Awkward?" he finishes for me. I nod. "No. Never. Which is why this is going to be so fun to watch."

"What will?"

Hawk smirks at me, his blue eyes shining with good-natured mischief. "You'll have to wait and see."

"You think he has a crush on her?" I whisper-shout.

Hawk laughs. "Something like that." I raise an eyebrow at him, but Hawk just keeps grinning. His hand finds mine, and he squeezes gently. "Thank you for letting me help out with groceries. I know it was a big step."

I tilt my head to the side, trying to figure out why he always says just what I need to hear.

Hawk lifts my hand to his mouth, pressing a soft kiss to my knuckles, just like he did that day in the back room. I know Sutton can see everything, and I *know* she's going to give me crap about Hawk, but I don't care. This is the happiest I've been in a long damn time.

"Have fun tonight, beautiful," he murmurs before opening the passenger door for me. I float down into the seat, smiling like a fool as Hawk closes the door.

"Oh my god, girl," Sutton gushes as soon as we pull out of the parking lot. "You have to spill all of the tea about Hawk over pizza. I knew you were holding out on me!"

I giggle and agree to her demands. I wonder if I'll be asking her for more details soon about Rider…

CHAPTER FIVE

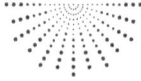

HAWK

"*I*'ll give you one guess as to why I'm calling church this afternoon," Blade says from the front of the room.

I'm surrounded by my MC brothers, each one of us on edge after the prez stormed into the clubhouse and yelled for everyone to come to church ASAP.

"Dirty fucking cops," Rider grunts, leaning forward in his chair next to me.

Blade nods as he squeezes his hands into fists. "There's been a significant rise in drug overdoses among high school kids and young adults in this town and the surrounding communities. Hard shit. Meth. Heroine. Stuff kids shouldn't be able to get their hands on."

Grunts echo around the room, and a few members shake their heads. We might have our hand in several criminal enterprises, but we have rules. Standards. No trafficking, no drugs, no harming women or children. The same can't be said of the local police force.

"What's worse," Blade continues, "is that the kids who don't OD get caught up in a cycle of debt that eventually ends with them getting trafficked or selling drugs for themselves."

"Fuck," Rider mutters. "Things haven't changed at all in the last five years, have they?" he whispers to me. "With Sheriff Huxley in charge, there's no hope for cleaning up this town. Guess he's too busy falsifying evidence and locking up innocent men to deal with the real problems in this town."

Before I get a chance to answer, Blade starts up again.

"It should be the police taking care of this. It should be our elected sheriff coming up with a plan to rid this town of drugs and keep the kids safe. Instead, they are the ones supplying the drugs in the first place."

Silence blankets the room as we absorb this new piece of information.

"How do we know that?" one member asks.

Blade jerks his head in the direction of the voice, his eyes hard and narrow. "Are you doubting me?" he growls.

The man shakes his head and wisely shuts the hell up.

"Since you asked, I know this because I was doing recon after finding out the latest statistics involving minors in our town. Who did I find handing out ungodly amounts of hard drugs to sixteen-year-olds behind the police station? Sheriff Daren Huxley himself."

"Jesus," I say under my breath. The cops weren't always so corrupt, but when Daren Huxley was elected sheriff, all that changed. He overhauled the department, fired anyone who stood up to him and replaced them with cronies and yes men.

In short, Daren Huxley is everything that's wrong in this town, and I can't wait until we get rid of him for good.

"What's the plan, Prez?" Axel, our newest patched member, asks. He's eager to prove himself, and while we like to give him a hard time about it, we're all happy to have him in the family. He's got more energy than the rest of us, and the need to please is written all over his face.

"Surveillance for now. We need hard evidence, proof of the corruption. That's step one."

Heads nod all around the room as the men grow restless. Everyone wants to jump in and get rid of the disease that's plagued the police department for far too long.

"Rider and Hawk," Blade says, cutting through the grumbles around the room. As the road captain and enforcer, I'm sending you to put trackers on the sheriff's car and all the deputy vehicles. Axel will go with you since he knows the most about cars."

"And tech!" Axel chimes in.

Blade rolls his eyes, but there's a good-natured smirk on his face. "Go on then, get out of here and teach these two about cars and tech," he says, nodding at Rider and me.

The three of us stand and head out of the room to discuss the details of our mission. Blade will likely assign more tasks to other members, but we have our orders. It's time to march.

Axel, Rider, and I pile into a cage, aka, a car, much to Rider's dismay.

"Fuckin' cage," he mutters. "I was locked up for years and swore I'd only ever ride my motorcycle once I got out. Need to taste freedom as often as possible."

"It's a car, not a prison, big guy," I tell him, clapping him on the shoulder. "Besides, you know this requires stealth. Our bikes aren't exactly subtle."

Rider grunts but eventually rips the passenger side door open and plops down into the seat with a thud. The nearly seven-foot-tall giant of a man has his arms crossed over his chest and looks like he's pouting. I might comment on it if I didn't think he'd punch me in the gut. As it is, Rider doesn't need me making fun of him. Just yet, anyway.

Axel runs to the driver's side, hopping in and cranking the engine. I fold myself into the backseat, ready to get this mission over with so I can check in on Tessa.

She's been working at the clubhouse for almost a month now, and I'm trying to be patient. As much as I want to throw her over my shoulder and take her back to my place, I have to move at her pace. Tessa has already trusted me with so much, but it's her heart I'm truly after.

"So, uh…" Rider starts, clearing his throat before trying again. "How is, um, Tessa? And her friend? Sutton, I think."

The guy is about as subtle as a bear in an antique shop, but I humor him nonetheless. "Yeah, Sutton," I confirm. "They're good. You could always just talk to Sutton the next time she comes to visit Tessa."

"Why would I do that?" he rushes to say, his tone slightly higher than usual.

"Just a suggestion," I say with a shrug. "Might not be the worst thing in the world for you to make a connection with someone."

From my spot in the back seat, I can see Rider's shoulder slump. I feel for him. He didn't deserve to be sent to prison. Add that to the list of atrocities the cops around here have doled out.

"I royally screwed up our first meeting. How do I recover from that? I think I scared the shit out of her. She was shaking."

"So were you," I point out.

"Not helpful," Rider grunts.

"Just relax. Next time you see her, approach slowly. Ask her about her day. Get her talking; then the focus won't be on you."

"And when did you become an expert on women? As far as I know, you and Tessa aren't together, right?"

"Tessa is mine," I snap, hardly recognizing my harsh tone.

"She just has to get used to the idea. My girl hasn't had an easy go of it, and I don't want to push her into anything she's not ready for."

"So you're all in?" Rider asks. "Dead set on Tessa as your old lady?"

"Hell yeah. Now that I know Tessa exists, I don't want to be with anyone else."

"Damn," my friend murmurs.

"As much as I love getting relationship advice from two single dudes, it's showtime."

Rider jabs Axel with his elbow while I ruffle his hair. The new recruit jumps out of the car and glares at us while we grin. It's all in good fun, and soon, Axel won't be the newest member.

After several hours of monitoring the comings and goings of the police department, the three of us tracked down Sheriff Huxley's car. Axel was the one to secure the tracking device on the underside of the vehicle, and he showed us an app to download so we can have eyes on the tracking device at all times.

We hit up several of the sheriff's closest deputies, then called it a day. We'll be back at it tomorrow, but we have the essential people tagged and tracked.

Besides, it's nearly two in the morning. Tessa should be finishing her closing shift, and I want to be there when she clocks out. I didn't get a chance to stop in for her shift earlier with my assignment, so I want to make sure to see her before she leaves.

I can't help it. I need to be in her presence at least once a day, or I start to get restless. Soon, she'll live with me. I'll fall asleep with Tessa in my arms and wake up to her adorable freckles, emerald eyes, and brilliant smile.

As we pull into the clubhouse to drop off the car and pick up our bikes, I see Tessa locking up the back door, her purse and jacket in hand. I hop out of the backseat before the car stops moving, but I don't give a fuck. I'm that desperate to see her.

"Tessa!" I call out as I jog over to where she is. My girl tenses and gasps, and I hate myself for startling her. When her eyes meet mine, however, she relaxes and rewards me with a smile. "Didn't mean to scare you, beautiful," I say in a quieter tone as I walk up to her.

"Oh, it's fine," she responds, brushing it off like always. "I didn't think I was going to see you today."

"Did you miss me?" I ask, wagging my eyebrows at her.

Tessa blushes and nibbles on her bottom lip. Just like the day I helped her in the bar, I cup her chin and gently pull her lip from her teeth.

She looks up at me, a painful vulnerability shining in her green eyes. "I did," she whispers. "And I'm not sure what to do about it."

A huge grin spreads across my face as I drop my hand from her chin and lace my fingers through hers. "I missed you too. Now, let's get you home so you can rest. I know it was a long shift for you."

I glance around the parking lot, looking for her car, but I only see the club cars and my bike. Axel and Rider must have taken off, leaving just Tessa and me here.

"Where's your car?" I ask, turning my attention back to my girl. Damn, I should already know what she drives, but so far, we've always just met up at the clubhouse while she's working or slightly before her shift.

"Oh, I don't have one. Yet. I'm saving up for one. I just…" she trails off, sighing as she shrugs her shoulders.

"So, how are you getting home?" I'm still holding her hand, and I squeeze it gently, encouraging her to talk to me.

"I can walk just fine," she says, perking up a bit. "I live like half a mile away. It's no big deal."

"And you've been walking home this whole time?" I don't like that one bit. Not in this town.

"Relax, Hawk. I've been on the opening shift for the last month, so I'm walking home in the daylight."

"There's no daylight right now," I grumble, peering around the dimly lit parking lot, then beyond it, to the barely-lit country road leading into town.

"Good eye," Tessa teases. "I'll be fine, I promise."

"Can I at least give you a ride home? I don't feel right leaving you out here in the dark. I wouldn't be able to sleep knowing you're walking alone this late at night. There could be criminals prowling about in the shadows."

"Ironic that you're warning me about delinquents, don't you think?" she replies, arching an eyebrow at me. Dammit, she's adorable, but I have to insist on taking her home. No way in hell is she walking anywhere unprotected ever again.

"I'm serious, Tessa. If anything bad happened to you out here…"

"Evil can be done in broad daylight, too," she mumbles to herself. I almost don't hear it, but something in her tone has every protective instinct in me surging toward the surface.

"What do you mean?" I whisper, matching her volume.

"Nothing. I…" Squeezing her hand again, I silently beg her to trust me with another one of her secrets. "Being a criminal doesn't inherently make you a bad person, just like being a cop doesn't make you a good one."

I reel back a bit, furrowing my brow at her words. I don't disagree, but I'm dying to know why she thinks that. What experiences has she had to give her such a big chip on her shoulder?

"That's true," I say slowly, unsure how to respond. "Still, I'd really like to make sure you get home safely. Will you let me do that? For my own peace of mind?"

Tessa swings our joined hands back and forth, her eyes

locked on where we're touching. I can feel the tension rolling off her, the silent war waging in her mind. As much as I want to lift her and put her on the back of my bike, I need her to make the decision. I get the sense that Tessa hasn't had many choices in her life, and I'm not about to be one more person to take that away from her.

"Okay," she finally whispers.

"Yeah?"

Tessa nods, then finally graces me with the smallest, most precious smile. I'll treasure it forever.

"Thank fuck," I say on an exhale, making Tessa laugh. "Love that sound, beautiful," I tell her, pulling her toward me. She blushes, then surprises me by wrapping her arms around my torso. I hold her close, leaning down slightly to brush a kiss on the top of her head. "Thank you for letting me take care of you."

CHAPTER SIX

TESSA

I'm not sure why I threw myself at Hawk, but he didn't hesitate to wrap me up in his strong arms and cover me with safety. I nuzzle into his chest, loving the way he smells. Leather, mint, and something that's uniquely Hawk.

Untangling myself from the warmest hug ever, I try to get myself under control. I can't be thinking dirty thoughts about Hawk or imagining us touching without any clothes on at all.

As Hawk places a helmet on my head and secures the strap, however, I forget all about protecting my heart. His deep blue eyes find mine, and he grins before winking at me. This man is ruining me with his sweetness.

"Ever been on a bike before?" he asks. I shake my head no. "I'm happy to be your first, then," he says with a wicked grin.

My face burns, but I hope the helmet masks most of my blush. There are a lot of firsts I would like Hawk to have…

He swings his leg over the bike and gets adjusted before instructing me to do the same. "Hold on to me, Tessa. I'll keep you safe."

"I know," I whisper, though I don't think he heard me.

"What's your address?"

I hesitate momentarily, mostly out of habit, but quickly realize he's going to need to know where to take me. I've already given him more pieces of me than I thought possible, so what's one more?

I tell him my address, and Hawk starts up the bike. I squeeze his waist, digging my fingers into his stomach. *Holy crap, this man is cut.* He might be flexing, but still. I can feel the ridges of his muscles, his abs beneath my fingertips, and his chiseled back as it presses against my front.

"Scoot up closer, beautiful," he shouts over the roar of the engine.

I do as he says, moving up as far as possible and spreading my legs wider. My thighs rest on the outside of his, and I can feel the vibrations of the bike roll through him and into me. Gripping onto his waist, I inhale sharply as we take off into the night.

Hawk takes his time winding down the road, which I appreciate. I know he can go faster. I've seen him do it. But right now, he's treating me like I'm some precious cargo. I won't lie, I'm already addicted to the feeling.

The longer I'm on the bike, holding on to Hawk, the freer I feel. I get it now; why people like motorcycles. The wind tangling in my hair and kissing my cheeks, the world passing by in a blur. It's like nothing else matters. Just me, the bike, Hawk, and the open road. Nothing can touch me when I'm on the back of this bike.

Before long, we're pulling into Sutton's grandma's old house. Sutton always corrects me and tells me it's now my place, too, but it doesn't feel right. I'm not paying rent, I'm hiding out, and I plan to leave as soon as I have enough money saved up. Basically, I'm the worst roommate ever, but Sutton doesn't seem to care. She's just happy to have a friend.

Hawk puts the bike in park and turns it off before looking at me over his shoulder. Even in the dark, I can see his boyish grin. He helps me off the motorcycle, keeping a hand securely on my hip as I step down. Good thing, too, since my knees wobble and I nearly lose my balance.

"I've got you," Hawk says, pulling me into him once more. I love being in his arms.

"Thanks, I didn't realize I was still vibrating," I say with a laugh.

"Is Sutton home?" he asks, looking at the dark windows and lack of porch light.

"Oh crap," I mutter under my breath. I forgot Sutton got a call from the bank in her hometown asking about the deed to her grandma's house. She told me it was nothing to worry about, but she would stay there tonight to get things worked out.

"Tessa? Everything okay?"

"Yeah," I lie. "Sutton is out of town tonight. I forgot all about it." Taking in the house in the dark, I never realized how imposing it is. Have those windows always been so large and looming? Anyone could see in. And when was the last time the locks were replaced? They might be old.

"Tessa?" Hawk asks again, stopping my thoughts from spiraling any further.

"It's fine. I mean, obviously, it's fine. I can stay in a house by myself. I'm not scared or whatever," I say in the least convincing voice ever. Hawk isn't going to let me get away with that, however.

"You could come back to my place," he offers. "It's not much, just a little ranch-style home a few blocks from the clubhouse. You'd have your own room and everything."

"No, I couldn't," I insist. I'm not sure if the cops are following the Savage Saints. It wouldn't be the first time, and I don't want to put a target on Hawk's back.

"Then maybe I can stay here? Before you say no, just hear me out. I make a mean omelet, and I know you have the ingredients for it from the clubhouse. I haven't had an excuse to make a good breakfast in a while, and I'd love to make one for you."

"I could protest, but I have a feeling you'll wear me down eventually," I say as I roll my eyes playfully.

"So that's a yes? I can stay?"

Hawk is acting like I just told him he won a million bucks, which is pretty adorable.

I nod in confirmation, then lead Hawk up to the front door and unlock it. As if on instinct, Hawk enters first, scanning the dark entryway and living room for threats. He doesn't know what I've been through, but Hawk is observant enough to figure out I don't feel safe very often.

"All clear," he says, returning to my side.

"Thanks," I say softly. He gives me a supportive smile, and part of me wants to tell him everything. Tell him who I am, who my family is. He'd understand. Right?

Still, I can't bring myself to actually say the words.

"Why don't you go get cleaned up? You had a long day. Just point me in the direction of some blankets, and I'll make up the couch for myself."

I nod, grateful for the chance to have some alone time. Not that I don't want to be around Hawk. It's just that I need to get myself under control. He's getting closer to the truth, and I need to make a decision before he finds out and gets the wrong idea.

Not tonight, though. Hawk is right. I had a long day. I'll have a clearer head tomorrow.

I show him the closet with extra blankets and pillows, then head to the bathroom for a shower.

Fifteen minutes later, I'm feeling refreshed. Or, at least, slightly more human. As I make my way back into the living room, I'm half expecting Hawk to be gone or asleep already. Instead, he surprises me by having a cup of tea prepared for me on the coffee table next to his.

"Hey, gorgeous," Hawk greets me, his eyes roaming up and down my body. I might have chosen a tank top that's slightly too small, showing more cleavage than usual. Is it terrible that I love the attention he gives me? I know I'm playing with fire, but part of me wants to get burned.

"Hey, yourself," I say as I saunter into the living room. Hawk scoots over and pats the seat next to him on the couch. I sink into the old piece of furniture left here by Sutton's grandma, but for once, I don't notice the lumps in the cushions. I'm focused solely on Hawk.

Our eyes meet, and I can't look away. I sway closer to him, feeling the heat radiating off his body. I get the strongest urge to slide my hands up his shirt, feeling his muscles flex beneath my fingers before I take it off completely.

"Tessa," Hawk whispers. "I want to kiss you so damn bad, but I don't want to pressure you into–"

Something takes over my body, and I wrap my arms around his neck, pulling him closer. Our mouths are inches apart, our breaths mingling as we stare at each other.

"Kiss me," I murmur.

"Are you sure? Once I get a taste…" He groans, resting his forehead on mine.

I don't let him doubt me a second longer. My lips find his, a surge of electricity popping and sparking along my nerves. Hawk takes over, his hand cupping the side of my face, angling me so he can kiss me more deeply.

My lips part as Hawk slides his tongue inside my mouth, winding me up with slow, steading strokes. I tangle my fingers in his hair, needing something to hang onto while liquid pleasure pours over my body, threatening to drown me completely.

Hawk slides a hand down my side, gripping my thigh and tugging me so I'm straddling him. God, this feels amazing, having this powerful man consume me and run his hands all over my body.

We finally break apart, gasping for air.

"Best first kiss ever," I whisper, smiling nervously. I don't know why I said that, except that he makes me comfortable saying pretty much anything. I've felt that way since the very first day I met him, even if my heart wasn't ready to believe it yet.

Some deep, gravelly noise bubbles up from Hawk's chest as he tips his head back and takes a deep breath. "Fuck, Tessa. You have no idea what that does to me," he groans almost painfully.

"What?" I ask, genuinely confused.

"Knowing I'm the only one to touch you like this. To see you all disheveled, your lips bruised, your eyes glossed over. It'll only ever be me, love. You understand that, right? There's no going back now. You're mine."

I chew on my bottom lip nervously, wanting his words to be true but having a hard time believing this isn't all a dream. Will he still feel this way about me when he finds out what had me running scared in the first place?

Hawk takes my silence for uncertainty and cups my face so sweetly. "We'll go as slow as you want. I'll never take anything you don't willingly give me."

"I know," I whisper, tilting my head so our lips are inches apart. "It's not you I'm worried about." Hawk furrows his brow, but I don't want to explain. Instead, I brush my lips against his and breathe, "I trust you. With all of me."

With that, I kiss him again, letting him know I want this, I want him more than words can say. Each swipe of his tongue and nip of his teeth open up a need deep inside me. There's a tugging low in my belly, an almost painful throbbing.

"Gotta stop," he grunts into the side of my neck before licking me there and catching the tender skin between his teeth. "I can't hold back much longer, and I don't want to scare you away."

"I'm not scared," I breathe out. "I can't hold back either. I just... I don't know what I'm doing. Can you show me?"

"Fuck," he growls, attacking my lips with more intensity. Hawk tightens his hold on me and stands with me in his arms, setting me down and walking me backward until I'm pressed up against the wall. With his large frame towering over me, his lustful gaze heating me from the inside, I know what I want from this man. And I know he's going to give it to me. "Are you wet for me, Tessa? Is my dirty little angel wet for me?"

I let out a throaty moan and nod. "Will you... Can you... t-touch me there?"

"Fuck, yes," he grits out, cupping my pussy and rubbing my aching center over my jeans. "Goddamn, I feel your heat. Do you need something from me? Does this pretty little kitty need to come?"

His words are so filthy, but they trigger something inside me. This man has reduced me to base urges I didn't think I had until I met him. I nod and roll my hips, trying to get him to touch me deeper, more, more, more...

Hawk nips at my chin, my pulse point, my shoulder, and then slips his hand into my leggings. I know he feels how soaked I am, and it only turns him on more.

"Jesus," he grunts, stroking my pussy and parting my folds over my panties. The fabric scrapes against my sensitive clit, making me shiver and moan.

"More," I beg, gripping his meaty biceps and digging my nails in.

Hawk plays with the waistband of my panties, teasing me and driving me absolutely wild. Finally, *finally*, he touches me where I'm throbbing for him, swiping two fingers up my slit and circling my clit.

"Tessa... so fucking hot for me," he grunts. My pussy contracts at his dirty words, trying to suck him inside. He groans and continues to stroke me up and down, gathering my arousal and massaging my little ball of nerves.

I squeeze my eyes shut and moan, throwing my head back and exposing my neck to his greedy mouth. Hawk sucks on the side of my neck and dips one finger into my tight hole, making me grind down on his hand.

"Oh," I gasp, pulsing around him and releasing even more wetness.

"So tight. You're gonna feel fucking incredible wrapped around my dick, aren't you, love?"

"Mmm..." I nod frantically, shifting my hips and forcing his finger deeper inside me. "Fuck!" I cry out.

Suddenly, Hawk removes his hand, leaving me empty and confused. I open my eyes and see Hawk kneeling in front of me, gliding his hands up and down my thighs. "I need to taste you. Just one taste. Is that okay? Can I make you come on my tongue?"

"God, yes," I whimper. I don't even care that I'm begging him. Hawk practically claws my leggings down my legs along with my soaking panties.

"Jesus, how do you smell so good?" he says more to himself than to me.

Hawk helps me step out of my clothes, staring at my pussy the whole time. I should probably be embarrassed or have at least a few reservations, right? But all I can think about is the ache between my thighs, the pulsing need for Hawk's touch, and his breath tickling my exposed skin.

I tremble as he ghosts his fingers up my legs, guiding one over his shoulder, opening me completely to him.

"Perfect, just like the rest of you," he whispers before parting my lips with his tongue and sucking on my clit. Hard.

I buck my hips and grab his hair, overwhelmed by the sensation of his warm tongue against my sensitive, swollen clit. He growls into my pussy, the vibrations rattling my bones as he devours me.

Hawk spears his tongue into my entrance and swirls his nose around my clit. My breaths come out as short little gasps as my muscles tense and pulse. It's unlike anything I've ever experienced. I feel myself teetering on the edge, close, so close to falling over into total bliss.

A strangled scream is torn from the very depths of me as I explode on his tongue. I jerk in his arms, but Hawk grips me tighter, steadying my movements even as he laps at me and bats my clit around, prolonging my pleasure.

He looks up at me right as I tip my head down to look at him. His eyes are stormy, dark, and feral. I see my juices covering his lips and nose, making me moan. Hawk doesn't give me time to recover before flattening his tongue and licking me from bottom to top.

"Oh, ohmygod, Hawk, I... I can't..."

He grunts and continues to nibble and suck on my folds. The world crashes down around me until all I can focus on are the relentless strokes of his tongue as he pushes me higher and higher, winds me tighter and tighter, increasing the pressure in my core almost unbearably.

I gasp and writhe as he plunges two fingers inside me and curls them up, hitting some spot that makes my nerves light up and burn deliciously beneath my skin. He swirls his tongue around my clit again and again. I can't breathe. My heart thrashes. There's a rushing sensation flooding my body. I feel like I have to twist away, back down from the onslaught of pleasure, but I can't. I'm rooted in place, completely at his mercy.

My whole body gets tight. The pressure builds inside me, through my pelvis, over my skin, in my muscles, and along nerves. Pleasure swells and erupts as I convulse in his arms. He pins me to the wall, mercilessly eating me out with a growl. My sweaty flesh shakes as I jerk and fight my way through my orgasm.

"Yes, Tessa," he growls, lifting his face to stare at me in awe. "You're incredible. Love making this perfect little pussy gush."

I'm floating through space, through bliss, through lust and release. A rhythmic, sharp throbbing between my legs brings me down from my high. I open my eyes and see Hawk slowly licking me up and down, swallowing down all of me, every last drop.

My bones turn to liquid as I slump against the wall, completely wrung out. Hawk helps me get dressed, then stands up, pulling me into his chest. He holds me up and kisses me, letting me taste myself. Hawk groans, and I bury my face in his chest, unsure of what happens next.

"Are you okay, love? You're shaking," he whispers. "Was that too much?"

"It was amazing," I murmur.

"*You're* amazing," he counters.

I open my mouth to tell him how cheesy he is, but a yawn escapes instead.

"Let's get you to bed, love," Hawk says, kissing the top of my head.

I smile at his new pet name for me. As much as being called beautiful made me swoon, I think I like being called *love* most of all. It's what I've been missing in my life, and Hawk wants to make up for it.

"Will you stay with me?" I ask, tilting my head up.

"I wouldn't have it any other way," he assures me.

I untangle myself from his arms, then take his hand in mine, leading him to my room. Hawk pulls back the covers for me, and I climb into bed while he takes his shoes and shirt off. I can't help but gawk at the ink swirling up his arms and over his chest. He's impossibly sexier, and I can't believe he wants me.

"Stop looking at me like that," he groans. "You need rest. Any more of those heated glances, and I'll need to go in for another taste."

"Oh no, that would be *so awful*," I say sarcastically.

Hawk grins at me, then joins me in bed. He rolls me onto my other side, making me giggle, then wraps his body around mine, cocooning me in his strength and warmth.

"I promise we'll do that again. Soon," he whispers into the shell of my ear. A shiver runs down my spine, and I can feel Hawk growing tense behind me. "But for now, we need sleep."

I nod, settling further into Hawk's embrace. He ghosts his lips over my exposed shoulder and neck, placing soft kisses everywhere he can reach. It's the last thing I remember before sleep takes me.

CHAPTER SEVEN

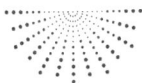

HAWK

I can't keep the grin off my face as I pull into the parking lot of the clubhouse. Tessa's shift is ending soon, and I'm hoping to convince her to come back to my house for the night. For dinner, of course. And if it leads to something more…

I bite back a groan, then park and hop off my bike. I meant it when I said I'd never pressure her into anything or make her uncomfortable. After last night, however, I'm hoping she at least trusts me to take care of her needs. If all we end up doing is falling asleep in each other's arms, that's enough for me.

Stepping inside the clubhouse, my eyes immediately search for Tessa. It's kind of ridiculous how much I've missed her these last few hours. I left her place around eight this morning to finish an assignment with Rider, and it's just past six-thirty now.

"Hawk," Rider calls out. "Figured you'd show up here sooner or later." He nods toward the bar where Tessa is wiping the counter down.

I don't even try to hide my cheesy smile. He's right. I'm here for all of her shifts at some point.

"Before I lose you to your girl, I heard from Axel today about the trackers."

"Yeah? He already has data for us?"

Rider takes a swig of his beer, then chuckles and shakes his head. "I'm pretty sure he stayed up all night observing everything from his set-up in the back room. Blade hasn't shown his face here yet, but Axel wanted to have an update anyway."

I smirk, just picturing Axel sitting in a dark room, staring at a computer screen with a pile of empty Monster energy drink cans next to him and bags of Flaming Cheetos scattered around the desk.

"Sounds about right," I say with a chuckle. "Well, what's the news?"

"We have a lead on what appears to be a run-down cabin up in the hills. Several deputy cars made the trek in the early morning hours."

"Are we thinking it's a stockpile of weapons?"

"Possibly, but Axel thinks it's a meth lab."

"Fuck," I mutter. "That makes sense. A local supplier who has guaranteed sales and immunity from the law. Must be a nice gig."

Rider grunts, then finishes his beer. "One more thing," he says, his voice hushed.

I lean in, wondering what could be more secretive than our mission to track the cops.

"Axel said the Sheriff circled the block around the clubhouse three times around four-thirty this morning."

"What the hell does he want?"

"Checking up on me, maybe? Ready to catch me doing something mundane and then spin it into a web of fucked up lies–"

"Take a breath," I tell him, resting a hand on his shoulder. "You have more reasons than anyone to want Sheriff Huxley out of the picture for good, but rash, impulsive actions won't help. We have to be methodic. Calculated. You can be sure that we're going to take him down, though."

"Goddamn right, we will," he mutters, clenching his fists at his sides.

I catch a glimpse of bright red hair out of the corner of my eye and turn in that direction as if drawn by a string. Tessa is gorgeous as always, but she's even more radiant than usual today. I hope it has something to do with last night. I hope to do it again tonight.

"Go on, I see I've already been shoved to the back burner," Rider teases, elbowing me in the ribs.

I nod and clap his shoulder, though my eyes never leave Tessa. The second she sees me, her face lights up, those freckles standing out even more as her green eyes sparkle.

She surprises the hell out of me by stepping around the bar and walking toward me, her arms looping around my neck seconds before her mouth finds mine. She owns this kiss, her tongue sliding against mine as I lift and hug her into my chest.

We get lost in each other, chasing our pleasure and blocking out the world around us. It's only after Tessa breaks our kiss that I realize everyone is whooping and whistling. My girl buries her face into my chest, but I peel her off me and gently grip her chin. Green eyes meet mine, and though she's a little embarrassed, she's mostly just happy to be with me.

"Looks like the secret's out," I tease.

Tessa's face flashes with panic, her eyes darting from side to side. "What?" she whisper-shouts.

I furrow my brow, wondering what set her off.

"Us," I clarify. "I think making out in public makes us an official couple, don't you?"

"Oh, right," she sighs, relief flooding her features.

Interesting. I'll tuck that little piece of information away for later. I already know Tessa is hiding more of herself than she's letting on, but it doesn't bother me. I can't imagine anything she could say or do that would make me love her less.

Yeah, love. Somewhere between our introduction and having Tessa on the back of my bike, I fell ass over heels in love with her, and I wouldn't have it any other way.

"You're mine now," I murmur, nuzzling into the side of her neck. "Just like I'm yours."

It's not the usual way we Saints announce a claim on our Old Lady, but it's perfect for my Tessa. She wouldn't want a big fuss or to be put in the spotlight. This moment, however, is just as meaningful. Everyone already knew she was my girl, but now it's official.

"Are you officially clocked out yet?" I ask once we take a step apart. "Can I take you back to my place and cook you dinner?"

"Really?"

"Of course," I tell her with a smile. "I have some hidden talents in the kitchen," I say, wagging my eyebrows.

"Is that so?"

"Yup," I confirm, leaning down to nip her jaw and brush my lips and stubble across her neck. Tessa giggles, making me grin. She's fucking adorable and sexy and so *mine* it hurts.

"I clocked you out, Tessa!" Madge shouts from the back room. "Get out of here before you really put on a show," she says, wagging her eyebrows.

Without wasting another second, I grab Tessa's hand and haul her out of the clubhouse. After getting her situated on the bike behind me, I rev the engine and take off toward my home. I can't wait to have her in my space, to have her scent on my sheets.

Having Tessa on the back of my bike solidifies it. She's what I've been missing. I felt it last night. Hell, I felt it the moment our eyes met. But now? Now I'm determined to make her mine. I can't let her go. I won't.

It's hard to concentrate on the road with Tessa's soft curves pressed against my back, and... is she moaning? I feel her rocking her hips slightly, rubbing back and forth on the leather seat.

She's getting off sitting on the back of my bike.

My dick is so hard right now that it's painful.

I speed the rest of the way home and park, putting the kickstand down with the engine still running. I hop off and turn toward her, my lips crushing hers in an all-consuming kiss.

"Did you like being on my bike, love?" I rasp.

"Mmhm..." she moans.

"Fuck, baby, were you getting off just being back there? Did you feel that power vibrating between your legs?"

"Yes..."

I move her sexy ass up on the bike seat and sit behind her. Pulling her close, I start rubbing her pussy through her leggings and panties as she throws her head back onto my shoulder and rocks her hips on the seat, the bike still humming beneath her. I suck on her exposed neck, and she tilts her head to give me better access.

"Oh, God, Hawk. This is... I... *yesss.*"

Tessa reaches her arms over her head and tangles her fingers in my hair. She's stretched out, back arched, rubbing her luscious ass against my rock-hard cock and angling her hips to hit her clit on my fingers.

I move her panties to the side and shove two fingers inside her dripping wet cunt. She cries out and grinds down on my hand. I lick and kiss my way to her shoulder and pull her loose shirt and bra strap down with my teeth before biting down on her soft skin.

"Yes," she moans.

"God*damn*, Tessa, you're so hot. I can't get enough of you."

I reach my free hand up and knead her gorgeous breasts, pinching one nipple through the fabric of her shirt and then the other. She bucks and thrashes in my arms. I press my thumb to her clit, pinch her nipple, and bite her again. She fucking falls apart in my hands.

Tessa screams my name and bows her back, gripping and pulling my hair as she shatters and shakes, her pussy clenching my fingers and gushing on my hand. I continue rubbing lazy circles around her clit. Between my thumb and the bike still vibrating underneath her, her orgasm stretches for so long I think she might pass out.

Finally, her hips slow, and her trembling stops. I shut off the bike and cup her face in my hand, turning her head to kiss her long and deep. I drink up all of her desire as the last of her orgasm ripples through her.

Tessa falls against my chest, breathing hard and totally spent. I pull my fingers from her pussy and bring them to my lips, growling as I suck off her sticky, sweet honey.

"God, Hawk. I love everything you do. I can't... I can't believe we just did that," she admits, her cheeks still flushed from her orgasm.

I kiss the top of her head and sit her up. I hop off the bike and help her down, only to scoop her up in my arms again. Tessa shrieks out a giggle and loops her arms around my neck as I carry her inside.

CHAPTER EIGHT

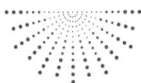

TESSA

*a*s soon as Hawk sets me down on my feet, he backs me against the closed door and fuses his lips to mine. I open up wider for him, loving the way his tongue invades my mouth, taking what he needs and giving me everything back in return.

Hawk drags his lips down my neck, nipping at my sensitive flesh and licking away the sting. I tremble beneath his powerful hands, loving the way they glide over my curves and press me closer to him.

"Tessa," he pants, resting his head in the crook of my neck. "Jesus, woman."

I tilt my head back, resting it against the door. A smile spreads across my face, even as I fight for air. I can't believe he wants me so much that I drive him crazy with desire. It's intoxicating.

"I love everything you do to me," I murmur.

Hawk groans and palms my ass, squeezing and pressing my core against his hard body. "Love your sexy fucking body," he replies, his tone deep and dark.

I get a wicked idea, one I never thought I'd be confident

enough to pull off. But with Hawk? He makes me feel safe and seen, like I could do anything and he'd be right there to catch me if I fell.

I slip out of his embrace, giggling when the six-foot-tall beast pouts. Hawk changes his mood the instant I pull my shirt over my head. Tossing it right at his shocked face, I turn around before unhooking my bra and throwing it behind me.

"You're playing a dangerous game, love," Hawk groans. I take a few steps toward the hallway, where I assume his room is, then peer at him over my shoulder.

His nostrils are flaring, his eyes nearly black with lust. He looks absolutely possessed. I love it.

Without saying anything, I shimmy out of my jeans, leaving them on the floor while I skip down the hall in just my panties. Hawk sounds like he's in pain, so I shake my hips a bit, prolonging the torture.

Peeking into the first door on the right, I'm ninety-nine percent sure it's his room. A huge king-sized bed with dark sheets and a nightstand, but not much more. It smells like Hawk, though, so he must sleep here.

I slip inside the room and quickly take my panties off, waving them outside the door like a toreador antagonizing a bull. Hawk snaps, his feet pounding on the hardwood floor as he prowls forward, his eyes never leaving mine.

When he's right in front of me, Hawk's eyes flash with a dark hunger, telling me he wants me as much as I want him. He drags my bottom lip through his teeth and then plunges his tongue into my mouth, making me moan. His kiss is primal and needy, and I kiss him back, matching every need of his with a need of my own.

"Fuck," he says, breaking our kiss. His hips buck, thrusting his erection up against my core, making me wet and needy.

"I want you, Hawk. I want all of you."

He grows still at my words and leans back to look at me.

"Are you sure, beautiful? Because once we start, I don't know if I'll be able to hold back."

I'm sure that was meant as a warning, but it only makes me hotter for him.

"I'm sure. I ache for you. I feel so empty…"

"Jesus, Tessa. When you say shit like that to me, it makes me want to tear your little pussy apart."

"Then why don't you?"

His eyes darken, and he devours my lips, growling into my mouth and kissing me savagely. Hawk breaks our kiss and presses his lips to my forehead, breathing deeply. It's such a contrast to the way he just made my lips numb from his intensity.

"Not this first time, love," he whispers. "I can't lose control with you."

Hawk scoops me up in his arms and tosses me on the bed. I bounce twice, and then he pounces on me, nuzzling my neck. Hawk rolls on his side, facing me. He reaches out, tucks some hair behind my ear, and pulls me in for a soft kiss.

"Are you sure?" he asks me again. "I never want you to regret anything between us, especially our first time together."

"I'm sure," I tell him. I wish there were stronger words, some way to convince him, but everything I can think of just sounds cliché. "I trust you, Hawk."

I kiss him this time, pouring out everything I can't seem to say.

The next thing I know, Hawk has me on my back, and he's looming over me. At this moment, he looks absolutely possessed, like a wild animal. Underneath, though, I still see the way he cares for me. I know he'd never hurt me, which makes me want to unlock the beast I know he's trying to suppress.

I lean up to kiss him again, but he pulls away. I strain my neck higher, but he pulls back farther, grinning as I pout. He gives me a chaste kiss and gets off the bed.

I follow him off the bed, about to complain, but then I see him take his shirt off, revealing his chest to me. I can't help but lick my lips as my eyes drift over the tattoos swirling over one shoulder and down his chest. Then my eyes drop lower to his six-pack and lower still to those two sculpted lines leading to his massive dick.

When I finally drag my eyes back up to meet his, he's smirking at me.

"I've been thinking about licking your little pussy since the last time I tasted your sweetness," he grunts, his eyes trained on my core.

In one swift movement, Hawk is kneeling in front of me, kissing a trail down my stomach. His large, rough hands skim up the back of my calves, my thighs, my ass, and then he pulls me forward so he can kiss my pussy. My inner muscles clench with desire, and I know he sees my juices dripping down the inside of my thighs.

"Goddamn," he groans before leaning down and licking up my arousal. Hawk dips his tongue inside my slit and then pushes me back on the bed, making me squeal.

He spreads my thighs apart and guides one leg over his shoulder, followed by the other, opening me up for him. Then, Hawk dives into my soaking wet cunt, making me cry out with the feeling of his hot mouth on my most private place.

He begins slowly, with long waves of his tongue that roll up and down inside my pussy. Just when I need more, his thumb finds my clit and rubs circles around the little ball of nerves while he continues to lick me and suck on my folds.

An index finger slides inside me with ease, then a middle finger joins as he pistons in and out of me with his muscular arm, fucking me into the bed. He rotates his fingers and pauses to look up at me, grinning with mischief. Then he curls his fingers up and finds that secret spot, rubbing his fingers against it and watching me tense and moan as he completely destroys me with his fingers.

"Yes, oh yes," I cry out, unable to stop myself.

He growls into my pussy, making my clit vibrate with his voice. Hawk slides and twists and rubs the walls of my pussy with his fingers while his tongue does wicked things to my little bundle of nerves. He licks it, bats it around, and finally sucks it into his mouth and bites down gently, causing my orgasm to rip through me and spill all over his fingers.

I buck my hips as he sticks his tongue in my entrance, lapping up everything I give him.

When I finally come back down to earth, I sink into the mattress. Hawk climbs on top of me, propping himself up on one elbow while his other hand cups my face. He presses gentle kisses all over with featherlight touches of his lips. He tickles my forehead, nose, cheeks, and finally, my mouth. Hawk strokes his tongue inside me slowly, deliberately, while his hand moves from my face and trails down my body, caressing and setting me on fire.

I spread my legs and welcome more of his skin on my skin. At some point, Hawk rid himself of his pants and boxers. I feel his hot, hard cock rubbing against my pussy.

In a sudden surge of confidence, I push against Hawk's chest, urging him to sit up.

"Everything okay?"

"I want to see you," I breathe out, my heart hammering in my chest.

Hawk grins and stands up. I sit on the edge of the bed and take him in for the first time. All of him. Even though I just saw his chest moments ago, I'm still surprised at how muscled and perfect he is. And then there's his thick, glorious cock that I know is going to stretch me and break me in the most exquisite way. I stand up and place my hands on his bare chest, loving the feeling of his warm skin and how his muscles tense and flex underneath my fingers.

Hawk throws his head back and hisses out a breath. "God, your touch, Tessa... It undoes me."

I smile and continue my exploration, trailing my hands over the dips and curves of his sculpted body, followed by my tongue. I can't explain it, but I want to taste him, his sweat, his skin, his essence.

"I'm losing my damn mind, love, but I need to be inside you when I come."

"Yes," I whimper, nodding my head. "Please," I beg.

"Jesus," he· groans, pushing me back on the bed and climbing on top of me again.

Hawk holds himself up with a forearm on either side of my head. I spread my legs once again, welcoming all of him. I feel him rub his dick through my folds, moaning when he hits my clit. I wrap my legs around his hips and try to pull him where I need him most. All of this teasing and dirty talk makes me desperate to finally have him inside me.

My movement has the opposite effect than I want. Instead of entering me, Hawk pulls back and kisses away my protests. "Let me do this, Tessa. Give me control," he whispers into my lips before kissing me sweetly and passionately.

When we pull apart, I feel his right hand slipping between our bodies as he fists his cock and guides it to my entrance.

"Are you ready?"

"Yes," I whimper, excitement and anxiety swirling in my stomach.

Hawk pushes inside me slowly, watching my reaction. I feel myself stretching, almost to the point of pain. It burns a little bit, but I still want more. Hawk is shaking as he tries to restrain himself. He continues his slow invasion of me until I feel him bump up against my barrier.

I gasp and close my eyes, preparing for him to enter me completely.

"Look at me, Tessa. I want to watch you as I claim you for the first time."

My eyes snap open, and Hawk pulls back slightly so he can rub my clit with his thumb. It relaxes me a little bit.

"Mine," he growls as he thrusts all the way inside o me, hitting home.

I feel a pinch deep in my core, and pain ripples out of me, making me cry out.

Hawk doesn't move; he just stays still as I adjust to this new feeling.

"Breathe for me, baby," he whispers before kissing my forehead. "I'm sorry I had to hurt you. It gets better, Tessa. I promise I'll make you feel so good."

I take a deep breath and stare into those beautiful eyes of his. They are full of such emotion, such warmth, and concern. I truly feel like I'm the most important thing in the world to him right now.

"I'm okay," I tell him. "I trust you."

"Can I move?" he grits out, his restraint slipping with each second he's not moving inside me.

I nod my approval.

"Need you to tell me what you want, Tessa."

"I want you to move. Please, God, please, Hawk, I need you," I whimper.

"Fuck," he grunts, pulling out and thrusting into me again.

We both groan when he hits home over and over. I love feeling the thick veins in his cock sliding against the walls of my pussy as he moves in and out of me.

"So goddamn tight. Jesus, you feel so good."

"You… too…" I manage to say in between thrusts. I wrap

67

my arms around his back and grip the taut muscles there, clinging to him while he picks up speed.

Hawk twists his hips slightly, changing up the angle. He hits that spot inside me with his dick, making my whole body jerk in his arms.

"Does that feel good?" he asks.

"Y-yes…" I moan.

I dig my nails into his back to spur him on. Hawk crashes his mouth down on mine as our bodies come together, again and again, flesh meeting flesh, pleasure meeting pleasure. I squeeze my legs around him and clench my pussy to get him deeper inside me.

Hawk thrusts into me harder, faster, each stroke of his dick pushing me closer, closer, hitting that spot over and over, once, twice, again, again, *fuck*, one more time, please, please, I need it, my body trembling and aching for more.

He slams into me one last time, and I scream, shattering around him. My pussy clamps down on his thick cock as all my muscles tense up tightly and then unwind, the orgasm rolling through me in explosive waves.

"That's it, sweetheart. That's so fucking it. Come for me again, Tessa."

Without giving me time to respond, Hawk leans back and sits on his heels, grabbing my hips and fucking himself with my body. The angle is different, deeper, hitting new places that make me shake and moan uncontrollably.

"Oh, God, Hawk. This is…"

I gasp and cry out as his fingers blur over my clit. With one pinch, he has me twisting in his arms, but he won't let me escape the onslaught of sensations as my orgasm claws at me and rips me apart from the inside out. I thrash and scream as Hawk continues to fuck me through it.

"Look at us, Tessa," he demands, his voice gravelly and

desperate. "Look how your pussy stretches and takes my big cock like a good girl. You're fucking incredible."

I open my eyes as my orgasm fades and see him sink into me again and again. It's fucking dirty and hot as hell. His movements become jerky, and I feel his dick swell, growing impossibly larger. He's throbbing and thrusting and working me up into another orgasm, both of us sweating and shaking.

"Fuck, fuck, fuck, Tessa," he groans. "Mine, fucking *mine*."

The feeling of his thick cock sliding in and out, his feral grunts vibrating through me, and his rapid breaths as he thrusts harder and harder has me bowing my back off the bed and climaxing so hard I can't breathe.

This time, I take him with me over the edge. I feel him shoot his load deep inside me, rope after rope, until he is spent.

I must pass out for a second because when I open my eyes, Hawk has me wrapped up in his arms, pressing soft kisses over my face and neck.

"Are you okay?" He sounds panicked, almost.

"What?" I ask in total confusion. "Hawk, that... I don't even know how to describe it. I didn't know I could feel so incredible."

His hands cradle my face as he searches my eyes for the truth. When he's satisfied with what he sees, he closes his eyes and rests his forehead on mine, breathing in deeply.

"Tessa. My precious Tessa," he whispers more to himself than to me. "Fuck, you're perfect, you know that? So perfect."

Hawk strokes my hair and whispers sweet things until my breathing evens out and my heart rate slows. Gently, Hawk repositions us so we're on our sides, my back against his front. My man curls around me, covering me with his strength, warmth, and comforting words.

CHAPTER NINE

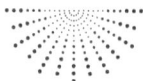

HAWK

I wake up in the middle of the night with an ache only Tessa can satisfy. We're in the same position as when we fell asleep. I bury my face into her soft red hair, breathing her in. Then, I kiss her neck, sucking and nibbling the tender spot where her neck and shoulder meet. She stirs and moans quietly.

I rock against her, letting her feel my need.

"Hawk?" she asks in a half-awake, half-asleep voice.

"Yeah, beautiful. I can't get enough of you."

I nuzzle her shoulder and slip my hand between her legs, finding her clit and massaging the ball of nerves. She's already wet for me, and it makes me impossibly harder.

"Fuck, Tessa, love this dripping pussy. Is this all for me?" I dip a finger into her entrance and slide her slick cum up and down her slit.

She moans again, pressing her ass into my hard cock and grinding against me.

"Are you sore?" I murmur, though it takes all of my willpower to stop.

"I ache," she breathes out.

I'm about to roll away from her and take a cold shower to calm the hell down, but then she finishes her sentence.

"I ache for you."

Growling in satisfaction, I rub her swollen bundle of nerves, loving how her body sparks to life beneath my touch. She's so close, so goddamn close. Her cream drips out of her as she writhes in my arms. I hold her there, keeping her orgasm just beneath the surface. I feel it claw at her insides, making her whimper with each breath.

Right before it hits, I take my hand away, moving it to her ass and spreading her cheeks. Without warning, I line up to her entrance and push her over the edge with one long, powerful thrust. She fucking falls headfirst into her climax, screaming my name and soaking my dick with her release.

I hold still inside her, growling as I feel her orgasm ripple around my cock. Before Tessa has a chance to recover, I begin hammering into her, setting a relentless pace. I grip her breast, using it as leverage to fuck into her harder, hitting her so damn deep with each stroke.

"H-Hawk, yes, yes," she chants over and over.

I drop my hand from her breast and blur my fingers over her clit until her pussy clenches around me and soaks me with another orgasm.

I pull out and flip her on her back, wrenching her legs apart and slamming home. Her back bows off the bed, and her legs wrap around me, holding me close. Tessa digs her heels into my ass and claws my back, leaving her mark on me.

"Jesus, fuck," I snarl before claiming her lips as my own.

I devour her, biting at her lips and spearing my tongue in her eager mouth, licking up every inch and then sucking on her tongue. It's a wild, messy kiss, one that matches the way I'm fucking her like a goddamn animal.

I slide one hand down her body and grip her ass cheek,

changing the angle of her hips and helping her meet me thrust for thrust. My cock scrapes against her most sensitive spot with each fierce stroke.

She's breaking apart for me. I can feel it. Every time I hit the end of her, she cracks a little more, the pressure of her orgasm building and pulsing and pushing her boundaries.

My balls draw up tight as my orgasm gathers in the base of my spine. My rhythm falters slightly as I try to hold on, needing her to come with me. "Get there, love, fuck, please get there. Need one more from you."

She sucks in a huge breath and holds it, her whole body trembling and then freezing. Every damn muscle is pulled tight as she clings to me with everything she has. With one last brutal thrust, we both shatter.

Tessa floods my cock with her release, and I give her everything in return, my cum splashing into her throbbing pussy as she sucks down every last drop. We grunt, shake, and sweat as we ride that high together.

Eventually, Tessa goes limp in my arms. I bury my face into her neck and pump into her twice more before collapsing. I roll to the side and drape my freshly fucked woman over my chest. She breathes out a satisfied sigh, and I press a kiss on her forehead.

"Tell me something about you," she murmurs, lifting her head slightly from where it was lying on my chest. "I feel like I've told you more about myself than almost everyone," she adds quietly before resting her head against me once more.

Tessa glides her fingers over the ink on my skin, tracing my tattoos absentmindedly. She still has secrets, but she's right. She was vulnerable with me the day she told me about her dyslexia, and I need to show her I can be vulnerable with her, too. Maybe then she'll feel more comfortable sharing everything with me.

"I grew up in New York," I start, my fingers finding her

smooth skin and stroking her thigh where it's draped over my leg.

"Really? I can't picture you as a city boy."

"Yeah, well, it didn't suit me," I say with a wry chuckle. "There's a reason I left at eighteen and hitchhiked my way out here to California."

"Didn't have your bike yet?" she teases. I narrow my eyes at her, then tickle her thigh, loving how it makes her giggle.

"No, my sassy girl," I tell her, my hand wandering up her side.

Tessa gasps and stifles another giggle, trying to roll away from me. I push myself up and lean over, pinning her to the mattress. Tessa laughs, her green eyes sparkling with mischief.

Her features turn soft, her eyes scanning mine. She surprises me by placing her hand on my chest, right over my heart. She's not pushing me away. She's just holding her hand there as if she could touch my very soul.

"That must have been scary to do as a teen," she whispers, her gaze remaining thoughtful with a tinge of concern. Can't say anyone has ever cared for me in this way, but it makes sense that Tessa would know just what to say.

I shrug, but Tessa doesn't let me get away with that. She lifts an eyebrow, and I finally nod my head yes.

"It's not my favorite memory, but also not the worst."

Tessa furrows her brow, and I know she wants to ask a million more questions. However, she decides to let it go. I have a sneaking suspicion it's because she doesn't want me to ask prying questions about her life in return.

"However you got here, I'm glad we were in the same place at the same time," she says with a sweet smile.

I lean down, brushing my nose against hers. "Me, too, beautiful," I whisper.

Our lips meet in the softest kiss. Her hand is still on my

heart, and I cover it with mine as I slide my tongue inside her mouth. Giving her long, slow strokes, I drink down everything Tessa offers.

When the kiss ends, I readjust us so I'm spooned around my woman, holding her close and breathing in her sweet scent.

We must have drifted off, though I don't remember exactly when we fell asleep. I suppose after two intense sexual encounters, we were both exhausted.

Rolling over, my heart swells when I see Tessa sound asleep, the sunlight weaving through her hair and making it glow. I brush my knuckles against her porcelain cheek, appreciating every delicate curve and the way she's put together. The perfect little package for me to take care of, love, and protect.

"Are you being a creep right now?" Tessa asks without opening her eyes. "Staring at me while I sleep?"

I chuckle and tuck some hair behind her ear. "Some people might think it's sweet," I whisper, pressing a kiss to her forehead.

Tessa pops open one eye, then the other, scrunching up her nose in the most adorable grumpy face. "Coffee?" she asks, closing her eyes again.

Grinning, I kiss her forehead again before sitting up. "Coming right up," I tell her before throwing on a pair of sweatpants. Apparently, my girl isn't a morning person. One more piece of information about her I'll treasure forever.

After a breakfast of scrambled eggs, bacon, blueberry pancakes, and two pots of coffee, I'm satisfied that Tessa knows I can cook and provide for her. We didn't exactly get around to dinner last night. Not that I'm complaining.

Tessa had to be at the clubhouse early to help with inventory, which worked out perfectly. I dropped her off at the bar a few minutes ago and headed to church.

Blade hardly ever calls church before noon, so this must be serious. It's hard to concentrate on club shit when Tessa is on the other side of the building. I have half a mind to storm out of here and toss my woman over my shoulder, but then the Prez himself steps up to the podium at the front of the room.

Blade is covered in tattoos and hardly cracks a smile, but there's something even darker than usual about him today. When he starts talking, I find out exactly why.

"Goddamn trackers were discovered," he snarls.

Mutters of disappointment and disgust echo around the room.

"What about the lead on the meth lab?" Rider asks. "That had potential. Maybe that was valid info before they found the trackers?"

"It was," Blade confirms. "Until we found one of the trackers at the cabin in question. The place had very obviously been cleared out in a hurry. Smelled like cleaning chemicals, bleach, and shit, but there wasn't anything or anyone to be found."

"Fuck," Rider grunts, shaking his head.

Blade runs through a few of the other missions he handed out, and my mind drifts to what our next move should be. We were obviously onto something; we just weren't fast enough.

"Hawk," someone says, jarring me out of my thoughts. I jerk my head up, looking around for who said my name. I notice for the first time that I'm the only person in the room, aside from Blade, who must have been talking to me.

"Yeah, Prez. Got a little lost in thought."

"Me, too. I didn't want to say this in front of everyone, but…"

He walks over to where I'm sitting and spins a chair around so we're facing each other. "I think we have a rat," he whispers. "The trackers... They weren't destroyed or taken offline; they were removed and placed on random trash cans and park benches around town. The police want us to know they know."

"A rat? Really?"

"No. Maybe. I..." he sighs and runs a hand through his hair. "Honestly, I'm not sure, which is why I'm not telling many people. Just keep an eye out for anything, yeah? Report back to me at the first sign of suspicious behavior."

"Of course, Prez. I can't believe we might have a traitor in the Savage Saints."

"Like I said, I don't know for sure. But if it's true, the fucker better start praying to every god out there that I don't find him. There won't be anything anyone can do to save him once I get my hands around his throat."

I grunt and nod, knowing Blade means every word. We don't take betrayal lightly around here, especially when it puts the lives of our brothers and everyone we love in danger.

Blade claps me on the shoulder and then stands, signaling for me to do the same. Without another word, the Prez walks out, with me close behind. No one is allowed in the church room when Blade isn't there, and I'm no exception.

Even though the meeting was a downer and shit's fucked up with the cops, my mind never strays far from Tessa. As I walk into the lobby area and bar, my eyes are immediately drawn to hers, and I smile when I see her behind the counter, confidently making a mixed drink for Brandi.

My heart squeezes tightly, almost painfully, as I watch my woman. I remember on her first solo shift, she had a bit of a breakdown when the drink recipe was giving her trouble. Now, she's pouring and shaking like a pro. I'm so goddamn proud of her.

Our pre-shift sessions with the recipe book really paid

off. It makes me crazy with anger to think about her parents and why they didn't do anything to help their daughter. She's eager to learn once she moves past the years of indoctrinated shame. I have a feeling her childhood left more scars than I could possibly know, but I'm determined to support her through her healing journey.

Tessa looks up as if sensing my presence. Her face lights up, her green eyes sparkling as a smile stretches across her lips. God, she's incredible. Gorgeous, strong, sassy, sexy as hell, and thankfully, not scared off by bikers.

I can't wait to get her underneath me again. One look at the blush creeping up her cheeks, and I know she's thinking the same thing.

CHAPTER TEN

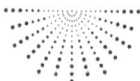

TESSA

"*A*re you sure you don't need me to do anything else before I clock out?" I ask Madge.

The older woman with beaded dreadlocks and a kind smile shakes her head. "You've done plenty, Tessa," she replies. She turns, then pauses before facing me again. "You know you don't have to keep proving yourself, right, hon?"

"Huh?" I tilt my head to the side and furrow my brow. Madge's eyes turn soft, and she rests her hand on my shoulder.

"You're part of the family. You don't have to take on extra tasks or run yourself ragged to get approval. Life doesn't have to be that exhausting."

Tears sting my eyes, but I blink them away. Hawk told me something similar when I first met him. It's still hard to believe, but every day I'm here, the closer I am to accepting their words.

"How did...?" I can't even finish the sentence without more tears clogging my throat. How did she know what I was feeling? And how did she know just what to say?

"I don't have to know the details to know you're battling

demons every damn day. Everyone who passes through the doors of the Savage Saints clubhouse has a story to tell. It's okay to share yours whenever you're ready."

She never breaks eye contact with me as I nod slightly. Madge gives me a sad smile, her eyes filled with understanding.

"I just want you to know you can let your guard down around us," she continues. "We protect our family."

"Thanks," I manage to squeak out.

Madge folds me into a hug, and I squeeze my eyes shut, absorbing every kind word she spoke.

When she lets go, she surprises me by wiping a few tears from her eyes. "Now look what you made me do!" she teases. "You better get on out of here before Hawk comes barging in looking for you."

I laugh and roll my eyes, though Madge is right. Hawk has picked me up before and after every shift this last week.

"I'll just take the garbage out real quick, then I'll leave," I call out, already half turned away from Madge.

"Tessa! What did I tell you about running yourself ragged?"

"I'll stop once I take the trash out one last time," I reply, already tying up the garbage bag and wheeling the massive bin toward the back door.

Madge mutters something about *damn stubborn girl*, but her eyes glow with amusement. She's the closest I've come to having a mom since my own passed away. My stomach churns when I think about disappointing her when my story finally comes out.

Once outside, I drag the garbage bin across the rough ground littered with gravel and random weeds popping up. I briefly consider pulling the weeds and clearing out the rocks but decide to wait. Like Madge said, I don't need to try so hard to prove myself.

Don't you? The voice in the back of my head whispers. *If they knew who your real family was, do you think they'd accept you as one of their own?*

My heart sinks into my stomach like a lead weight. I can feel the heaviness of my secret pulling at my shoulders, but I don't know how to confess. Not after everything Hawk and I have shared. It would kill him.

I open the lid of the dumpster and haul the garbage bin up in my arms, setting it on the lip of the dumpster to use for leverage. The heavy bag slides out and hits the bottom of the dumpster with a satisfying thud.

Setting the bin back on the ground, I lean against the side of the clubhouse, letting the cool brick ground me. Hawk has tried asking about my family a few times over the last several weeks, but I've brushed him off. I wasn't ready to dive into everything, especially knowing the club's history with my father.

And now... now my heart is forever tied to his. I can't lose him. I also can't lie to him anymore, even a lie of omission. Plus, isn't it better for him to hear the truth from me than to find out a different way?

But what if he hates me? I'd lose everything. My job, any hope of making money, and the only man I've ever loved.

The sound of crunching gravel tears me from my spiraling thoughts. I'm used to the roaring motorcycles by now, but this is a different vehicle.

Turning my head toward the noise, my eyes widen, and panic shoots through my veins at what I see. A cop car slowly inches around the corner of the building until it's facing me. But it's not just any cop car.

It's the Sheriff.

AKA, my dad.

"No," I whimper, lifting a trembling hand to cover the sob

threatening to break free. My knees buckle, but I manage to prop myself up against the brick wall.

What is he doing here?

I know I need to move, open the door and run back inside, or hell, jump inside the dumpster and hope he didn't see me. But I can't. I'm frozen with fear, tears streaming down my face as my eyes lock on the driver's side door.

Everything happens at once, and yet in slow motion at the same time. I watch the door open, one foot hitting the ground and then the other. My father stands to his full height, only a hair shorter than Hawk. The brim of his hat shadows his eyes, but I feel his gaze burning through me nonetheless.

My breaths turn shallow as I fight for air with each inhale. Black dots float into the periphery of my vision, but I will them away, not wanting to pass out in front of this monster.

"There you are," my father says, his voice deceptively amiable. I know him better than that, though. Beneath his diplomatic words and even tone, pure evil runs through his veins. "You know, I had my boys running around town looking for you. Didn't think to send them up this way. Then again, I didn't think you'd be stupid enough to run straight into the enemy's lair."

"They're not the en–"

"Oh, she has an opinion," he muses to no one but himself.

My father takes a step closer to me, then another, and another. I press myself against the wall, not caring about the rough brick scratching my skin and ripping at my hair. My dad will do much worse once he gets his hands on me.

"Here's the thing, dear daughter," he says, closing the distance between us. His tone turns sharp, his words slicing into me like razor blades. "I don't give a fuck about your opinion. You made me look like an incompetent fool, losing my daughter like an idiot."

"I'm an adult," I point out.

I hear the slap before I feel it, the familiar sting ricocheting through my skull before I can comprehend what happened.

"You're my daughter, and when I say jump, you jump. When I say clean the goddamn kitchen, you clean it. When I tell you to cook meals so I can work hard and provide for this family, you cook."

"Not anymore," I grit out with more strength than I knew I possessed.

This takes him by surprise. For once, my father is struggling to respond.

"I have a real family now," I continue, wanting to ride this confidence out as long as possible.

My dad's face twists into a deranged smirk, the fire of a fight blazing in his eyes. "Real family? *Real* family?" he scoffs. "I knew you were stupid, but Jesus Christ, Tessa. They won't give a shit about you when they figure out you can't read. You're worthless. Society will never accept you. Your only option is to come back home with me."

"No," I spit out, his lies clashing with everything Hawk has told me these last few weeks. "They do care," I insist.

"Yeah? For how long?"

"Forever." My voice wavers, sounding weak even to my ears.

"Really? Are you sure? I'll always take care of you, Tessa. You're a burden to society, but you can still find purpose in cleaning and cooking and taking care of the house."

"I'm worth more than that," I whisper.

"What? Speak up, Tessa. I can't hear you over the bullshit coming out of your mouth."

"I-I'm worth–"

"You're worth what I tell you you're worth," he says, cutting me off.

"Dad, I–"

"I know it was you who put the trackers on our cars," he hisses.

I blink at him a few times, unsure where the change in topic came from.

"What? Trackers?"

"What were they for? Giving our coordinates to your new *family*?"

"I don't know what you're talking about," I tell him, though I don't expect him to believe me.

"I *will* get the truth from you, even if I have to wring it out of you with my bare hands," he growls.

As if to prove his point, my father wraps his right hand around my throat, pulling me forward until all I see are his dark pupils and sinister smile. His fingers tighten around my neck, each movement sparking a twisted joy in his eyes.

I open my mouth to scream for Hawk or Madge or anyone nearby, but then I'm shoved backward by the hand on my neck, a sickening crack reverberating in my skull as it slams against the brick wall.

"I wouldn't do that if I were you," my dad warns. "I can make life for your *new family* very difficult. Wouldn't be the first time I threw a Savage Saint into the slammer for getting in the way. Which one did you go and spread your legs for? The first man to smile at you?"

I blink away my tears, but I can't keep up. My father's face blurs in front of me, his last words echoing in my mind. *The first man to smile at me...*

Hawk was the first man to treat me with any amount of respect, but that doesn't mean what we have isn't real... right?

"Of course you did," he scoffs. "I'll never understand how

I got such a pathetically stupid child. Well, I suppose it was from your mother. She checked out before you were in school, so she never had to deal with all of your bullshit."

My dad mutters something under his breath that sounds like *Probably knew you were defective.* It wouldn't be the first time he's told me that.

I struggle to breathe through his grip on my throat, each inhale burning my lungs. My head throbs painfully in time with my heartbeat, each passing second draining me of hope.

Just when I think I'm going to pass out, my father releases his grip on my throat and takes a step back. I choke out a cough, my hands automatically covering what I'm sure will be bruises around my neck by tomorrow.

Without wasting another second, my dad loops his fingers around my wrist and tugs me toward his car. I refuse to move at first, but he jerks me forward, making me stumble.

"Don't make this more difficult than it needs to be," he says sternly. "Any shit you give me will be repaid tenfold to the Savage Saints."

"They're not afraid of you," I whisper, dragging my feet on the gravel.

"No? They should be. Never know when a leaky gas pipe or faulty wiring will cause a tragic fire. Would be a shame if this clubhouse had an accident like that, wouldn't it?"

I'm not sure if my father is actually capable of blowing up the Savage Saints clubhouse, but now is not the time to call his bluff. If I can get him away from here, I'll be taking the danger with me. It hurts beyond words to think about leaving Hawk and everyone I've met here, but if I can protect them from my dad's wrath, that's what I'll do.

"Fine," I grit out, hoping to sound tougher than I feel. "But you promise you'll leave them alone? No *accidents* or throwing people in jail who don't deserve it?"

My father stops in front of the passenger door, opening it before turning to face me. "You're in no position to bargain, Tessa. I'll leave everyone alone for today, but only if you come with me right now. The rest will have to be earned."

I'm about to ask what I have to do to be free of him for good, but the back door to the clubhouse swings open. My heart stutters in my chest when I turn and see Hawk stepping outside.

"Tessa?" Hawk asks, lifting his hand to his brow to shield his eyes from the sun.

"This him?" my dad asks, stepping up behind me and nodding in Hawk's direction.

"Dad, don't…"

"Dad?" Hawk echoes, his features morphing from shocked to betrayed and, finally, stone cold.

"It's not what you think," I start, taking a step in his direction. I'm sandwiched between the open car door in front of me and my father behind me, his hold on my wrist excruciatingly tight.

"Time's ticking, Tess," my dad says under his breath. "You don't want to find out what happens when it's up."

"You're the rat," Hawk states, his tone flat and detached.

"No, I…"

"This is perfect," my father whispers.

"Hawk," I try again.

"Tell me he's not your father," Hawk says slowly.

"I… Yes, he's my father, but–"

Hawk growls then wipes a hand down his face. "Tell me this is some mistake. Some misunderstanding. Tell me anything, Tessa."

What can I possibly say? I know this looks bad. It *is* bad. But it's not what he thinks.

"Come on, daughter," my dad says in a deep, authoritarian voice. "Your work here is done."

He shoves me into the car and slams the door shut, his hand resting on his gun as he walks to the driver's side. He looks directly at Hawk, a demented smirk twisting up his features.

My beastly biker trains his eyes on me and then my father. When he turns his back on me, my heart shatters. I deserve this. I didn't tell him the truth. I betrayed his trust, and now the love of my life, the most patient and generous man I've ever met, hates me.

"Looks like prince charming won't be any help," my father sneers.

Please turn around, I silently beg. *Please, Hawk. Believe me. Save me. Please...*

CHAPTER ELEVEN

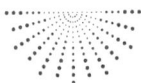

HAWK

*M*y head is spinning with the image of Tessa in a cop car with the goddamn Sheriff. He's her father, for Christ's sake. Why didn't I make that connection? How the fuck did I miss such an important detail?

That's not like me. I got my road name for a reason, after all. I notice things others don't, thanks to being a product of the foster care system. Growing up, I was always on edge, always vigilant, always sizing people up and assessing their words.

One look from Tessa and all of that went out the window.

She ruined me. Broke me. Betrayed the trust I so freely gave her. Did it all mean nothing to her? I was too caught up in getting her to trust me to determine if she was worthy of my trust. My heart thuds painfully in my chest, not liking the accusation against Tessa. Even now, my heart belongs to her. I'm fucked.

Staggering down the gravel ally, I'm finding it hard to breathe through the pain of reality crashing down around me. I rub the heel of my hand over my chest to try and ease the ache there. It's no use. There's a void where my heart used to be, and it's threatening to consume me completely.

Images of Tessa's curvy body beneath mine take over my thoughts, and I remember the exact moment I filled her completely. She was a virgin, for Christ's sake. Surely she didn't give a gift like that away just to fulfill her father's orders. That's not the Tessa I know. The Tessa I spent the last month obsessing over and wooing.

Then again, I apparently don't know the real Tessa at all.

Never thought I'd be one of those idiots who threw everything out the window for a pretty face. I spent my life watching the ugliness of my various foster parents' marriages, swearing to myself that I'd never get messed up with someone who lies.

I didn't have many good examples of relationships aside from Titan's mom and dad. When they passed unexpectedly, it nearly ruined my friend. I know he still carries guilt about the accident, even though it wasn't his fault.

The engine roars behind me, pulling me from my racing thoughts. Gravel crackles under the tires as the Sheriff backs out of his spot. I try not to look over my shoulder, but I'm only so strong. I must enjoy torturing myself. If Tessa is going to rip my fucking heart out, I want to sear the image of her into my brain. Maybe then I'll remember the price of love.

I spin on my heel, scowling at Tessa... and then I see her face.

I freeze, watching tears stream down her cheeks, her right hand splayed out on the window as if she's reaching for me. I stumble forward, confused as hell but needing to be near her. Even now, I can't stand to see her cry.

The car is almost out of the parking lot, and I finally find my footing, racing forward to get to Tessa. Her father grabs a fistful of her hair and yanks her head backward before slamming it against the window.

A rabid snarl leaves my lips, adrenaline and rage pumping through my body as I sprint after the vehicle. *What the fuck?*

My mind races with a million thoughts, each one slipping away before I can grasp it. *Her father was the asshole who made her so jumpy. Did he blackmail her into spying on us? Threaten her? Is she even involved with this at all? If not, why did she come to the Savage Saints for a job? Why did she confide in me about her insecurities?*

The car peels out, speeding down the road and off into the distance. I follow it for as long as I can, roaring at the top of my lungs when I finally accept that I can't catch it.

"What the hell is going on?" Blade hollers from the door to the clubhouse.

I hear his footsteps getting closer, followed by a second set of footsteps. Without looking, I know Blade and Rider are right next to me.

"Was that Sheriff Huxley?" Rider asks, his distaste for the man obvious from his tone.

I grunt and nod, unable to form words at the moment.

"What the fuck did he want?"

I choke out a growl, then try clearing my throat. If I'm going to fix what I fucked up and save the woman I love, I'm going to need the help of my MC brothers.

"Tessa," I rasp, trying to slow my deafening heartbeat. "He took Tessa."

"He *what*?" Blade roars. "I knew he was a corrupt mother fucker, but kidnapping?"

"He's her father," I tell him, the words tasting bitter in my mouth. I can feel Blade staring at me, fury and confusion radiating from him. "I don't know much more than that, but Tessa didn't want to go with him. He…" I shake my head, hardly able to say the words without going into a blinding rage. "He laid his hands on her. Hurt my girl. Needs to die."

"Okay, killer," Blade says, clapping a hand on my shoulder. "This is a complicated situation. We can't go offing the Sheriff." I glare at him, and the Prez crosses his arms over his chest. "Yet," he clarifies. "Something like this requires strategy."

"Fuck strategy," I growl. "Tessa is in pain."

"Hawk–"

"I got it," Rider suddenly says. He's been quiet nearly the whole time, calculating and observing like always. As our road captain, Rider is particularly skilled at seeing the bigger picture and getting things done efficiently.

Blade and I turn to him, waiting for his plan.

"The cabin. The one we pegged for a meth lab. It's the perfect place to keep a hostage."

"He knows we know about that place, though," I counter.

"Which is exactly why he won't expect us to figure it out," Blade says, nodding at Rider. "You and Hawk head in that direction. I'll take a few men to Sheriff Huxley's house, send a few to stake out the station, and have everyone else patrol the town."

I nod, grateful for Blade as our president. I know he'll have questions for Tessa and me later, but he knows what's important - getting Tessa to safety.

Fifteen minutes later, Rider and I cut our engines and walk our bikes along the narrow, overgrown road leading to the cabin in question. Without a word, Rider points to a large oak tree, indicating we should hide our bikes behind it.

I follow his lead, both of us careful not to make too much noise. We squat behind a nearby bush with a view of the front door and two windows, assessing our surroundings before coming up with a plan.

Just then, the front door swings open, and the devil

himself steps onto the porch. Rider and I freeze, both on high alert as we stare at Sheriff Huxley. He pulls out his phone and taps the screen before lifting it to his ear.

"Found her," he grunts. "Yeah, the little bitch holed up with some Savage Saint fucker. Probably thought I'd never come looking for her there."

I tense, ready to jump out and beat this man to a bloody pulp, but Rider steadies me with a hand on my shoulder. Snapping my head in his direction, I'm about to shove him off me when he points to the side of the cabin. I squint, finally noticing what appears to be an open window. He nods for me to head in that direction, letting me know he'll stay here and ensure the Sheriff is occupied.

He paces back and forth on the porch, and I wait until he turns and starts another lap before half crawling, half running to the side of the cabin. I press my back against the wall and inch toward the window, peering in when I get close enough.

I grit my teeth at what I see, tensing my jaw so damn hard I'm sure I'm about to crack a tooth.

Tessa is tied to the bed with a piece of Duct tape pressed across her mouth. Blood trickles down the left side of her head from the wound her father inflicted on her in the car. Jesus, I want to claw my heart out for letting the Sheriff drive off with her. Had I known…. Shit, had I trusted her, I never would have let him take her. This is my fault.

Swallowing down my shame, I focus on rescuing my girl. I can worry about groveling and apologizing later.

"Tessa, beautiful, can you hear me?" I whisper against the screen of the open window. She stirs, wincing as she faces the light. My heart twists and sinks to my stomach at the sight. "That's it. I'm here, love. I'm so sorry."

She makes a muffled sound that kills me yet spurs me on. I rattle the flimsy screen, managing to rip it off of the frame with hardly any effort. Hoisting myself up, I slip through the window and am next to Tessa in the next instant.

My precious girl is covered in blood, bruises, dirt, and tears. A piece of me dies at seeing her like this, knowing I contributed.

"I'm so sorry," I whisper again before leaning over and untying one wrist and then the other.

My fingers find the edges of the tape on her mouth, and I apologize again for the pain I know it's going to cause. Tessa bravely nods even as tears spill out onto her cheeks. Ripping the tape off, I cover her mouth with my hand, muffling the whimper while trying to soothe the ache.

"Can you walk?" I murmur, helping her sit up.

"Hawk," she squeaks out, trembling from head to toe. "It's not what it looks like."

Christ, she's killing me. How could I have doubted her? More importantly, how could she ever forgive me for letting her father hurt her like this?

"I believe you," I assure her. "We'll have time to sort it all out later. Right now, I need to get you out of here."

She nods her head and lets me help her up. Tessa leans into me, every muscle tensing with pain as I half carry her to the open window. I let her rest against the wall while I climb out, then turn and offer my hand for her to take. My girl gathers all of her strength and reaches for me, letting me lift her out of the window.

I fold her into my arms, savoring the feeling of her pressed against me. Nuzzling into the top of her head, I breathe her in and kiss her there.

"Let's get you cleaned up, okay, love? Can you ride with me on my bike?"

Tessa nods, and I lead us around the back of the cabin to avoid her father, circling back to our bikes once we're hidden in the woods.

Rider nods in acknowledgment, though he doesn't leave his position. "Blade and the boys will be here soon. We'll handle it." His eyes flit from me to Tessa, and I understand what he's trying to communicate. They're going to fuck him up, but he doesn't want to go into detail in front of Tessa. I appreciate it.

"Leave some fun for me," I whisper to Rider. He grunts and nods.

I get on my bike, helping Tessa to do the same. She wraps her arms around my torso, clinging to me while she trembles out a sob.

"I've got you," I tell her, walking the bike a little way down the path before starting her up and getting the fuck away from this nightmare.

CHAPTER TWELVE

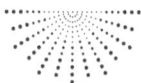

TESSA

I blink my eyes open and try looking around the dimly lit room, but my head throbs, sending a sharp pain slicing through my skull.

"Take it easy, love," comes a familiar, soothing voice.

I wake up a little more, my senses taking in the soft sheets I'm wrapped in. I recognize that voice, but I must be making it up. There's no way my beastly biker would be here after what I did to him. Still, I have to ask.

"Hawk?" I whisper.

"I'm right here, love. You're safe." The way he says it makes me think this isn't the first time I've woken up tonight.

Turning my head, I see Hawk sitting in a chair next to the bed, which I finally recognize as Hawk's. His hand gently rests on top of mine as if he's afraid to touch me.

"How did I get here?" I ask, my voice rough and scratchy. "I was taking out the trash, and then..."

I squeeze my eyes shut, trying to block the memory of my father slapping me. It's no use. Images of his hands around my neck flood my mind, and it's becoming more difficult to breathe. He shoved me in the car and…

My hand automatically goes to my forehead, my fingers finding a large gauze pad covering a lump on the side of my forehead. I wince, replaying the moment my father smashed my head against the window.

"You're safe, Tessa," Hawk says again, brushing his thumb over my knuckles. "I got you back to my place a few hours ago, and you passed out in my arms as soon as we stepped inside. It…"

Hawk clears his throat and rubs the back of his neck, looking away from me before capturing my eyes once more.

"It was the scariest fucking moment of my life," he admits softly. "I thought you were…" The pain in his eyes cuts through me, and I know what he was going to say without him finishing his thought. "Well, anyway. You were still breathing, still had a strong pulse, so I carried you in here and called the MC doc. He patched you up and left you with some pain meds."

"Thank you," I tell him sincerely. "After what I put you through, I wasn't expecting you to save me."

"Tessa… God, I'm so sorry," he whispers.

I slowly sit up in bed, furrowing my brow in confusion. Ignoring the sharp pain in my neck, I focus my attention on Hawk. "You have nothing to apologize for," I tell him, flipping my hand over so I can lace my fingers through his. "I should have said something. I should have told you who my father was. I promise, I would never betray you or the Savage Saints—"

"Slow down, love," Hawk soothes, leaning forward to tuck some of my hair behind my ear. His eyes flit my forehead, a look of sadness and shame reflected in his deep blue irises. Hawk cups my face so tenderly that tears spring to my eyes. I never thought he'd look at me again, let alone touch me.

"I'm sorry," I choke out, nuzzling further into his hand. I never want him to let go.

"Tessa, please don't apologize. I believe you. I trust you. I should have trusted you all along. I was just…" He trails off, shaking his head in disgust. "Fuck, I was shocked. Hurt. I needed a minute to process. But by that time, you were already being hauled away by the devil himself."

"I know it looks bad, but I swear I have no idea what he was talking about. Trackers or something?" I continue, getting worked up now. Hawk drops his hand from my cheek, placing it on my thigh over the blanket.

"Tessa–"

"And I only came to the Savage Saints clubhouse for a job because my father loathes the MC, and I thought he'd never come looking for me," I rush to say.

"Tessa, I–"

"But I just needed a job. One that paid under the table, in a place my dad wouldn't find me." I know I'm rambling, but I can't help it. I need to get all of it out, everything I've held back. If I want a second chance with Hawk, I have to be completely honest with him. "At first, I was only going to work until I made enough money to get a car and leave this town. My only goal was to get away from my horrible father. But then…"

I pause, gasping for air. Hawk has stopped trying to interrupt me, sensing that I need this moment to confess. He squeezes my thigh softly with the hand still placed there, then starts rubbing calming circles with the pad of his thumb, encouraging me to continue.

"But then?" he asks softly.

"But then I met you," I finish, my eyes finding his. Deep blue orbs stare back at me, and I can't quite place the look he's giving me. Disbelief? Disgust? "And I'm pretty sure I love you," I blurt out. "And the deeper I fell under your spell, the more I believed your kind words. I'm not stupid or worth-less. I'm not a burden. No one's ever..." my voice catches in my throat, and I sniffle rather unattractively. Hawk doesn't seem to care.

"I'm right here," Hawk reminds me, his steady presence keeping me grounded.

"No one's ever made me feel so special or got past my defenses with a single smile. And then it felt too late to confess, like I was going to ruin everything between us. But I had no idea the club had a rat. I didn't know the extent of your involvement with my dad. I just..."

I'm unsure how to finish, so I shrug and look away from the man who ruined me for all other men.

Hawk crooks his finger under my chin, gently drawing my face toward him until we're eye to eye. "Say it again," he murmurs. I tilt my head to the side, unsure of what he wants me to repeat. "Tell me you love me," he clarifies.

I can't hide the smile overtaking my face. After all of that, he only cares if I love him?

"I love you, Hawk. I don't know how it happened or when, but when I woke up in your bed this morning, I just knew. I wanted to stay here forever and spend my life being as good to you as you are to me."

"God, Tessa," Hawk exhales, standing from his chair and kneeling on the bed next to me. He carefully readjusts us so he's propped up on the headboard and I'm curled against his chest. "I love you with every goddamn thing in me. Never, ever apologize, especially for your father. Jesus, sweetheart. I can't imagine what it was like growing up with him. Was he this horrible to your mother?"

I take a deep breath, preparing myself for what's next. I want to share everything with Hawk, but some memories are still raw.

"She was an addict," I murmur. "She got clean while she

was pregnant and for several years after I was born. I remember playing in the backyard with her, laughing as she pushed me on the swing." A small smile tugs at the corners of my mouth, even though my heart is breaking open. There really were good memories of her before everything imploded.

Hawk doesn't say anything, he just tilts his head down and kisses the top of my head.

"One day, when I was five, my dad was at work, and Mom and I were home. She had been acting weird all morning. Jittery and irritated. So unlike the mother I knew. I remember she warmed up some soup for me for lunch, even though it was only a little after ten. She said she had some errands to run, and she wanted to make sure I had some food."

"Did she leave you alone like that very often?" Hawk asks. I shake my head no.

"Not at all. I was a little scared to be home alone, but I trusted her to be back soon."

My throat constricts, making my breaths choppy and shallow.

"You're safe right here, love," he reminds me.

"She never came back," I whisper.

"God, Tessa…"

"I didn't understand until years later what actually happened. She had relapsed in her sobriety and took off to find a new supplier." I take a calming breath, leaning into Hawk for his strength. "When she found her guy, they both shot up and overdosed within minutes. Something to do with how the heroine was cut with something else…? I don't know. I didn't care to research the details."

"I'm so sorry, Tessa. God, I had no idea."

"My father didn't handle it too well. He was a deputy at the time, and having his wife found at a known drug den was shameful. We didn't even have a funeral for her. All that anger and bitterness turned toward me once I started to look more and more like my mom."

I pause, reflecting on when the tides turned. My father was never a very involved parent, even when my mom was around, and after she passed, he did the bare minimum to keep me fed, clothed, and healthy. But then something flipped.

"I still don't understand him," I say, thinking out loud. "He resented my presence and called me stupid and worthless, yet he wouldn't let me leave. I tried once, but…" I shudder, trying to block out that terrible incident. "I ended up in the hospital."

"Jesus fucking Christ." Hawk tenses, a deep, dark rumble sounding from the pit of his chest. I place my hand there, hoping to calm him down. Hawk peers down at me, his features turning soft once more as he rests his hand on mine.

"As soon as I healed, I started making plans again, only this time, I had Sutton. She had recently moved to town, and we became instant friends. She helped me plan an escape and even offered to have me move in with her to her grandmother's house that she just inherited. Like I said earlier, I just need a job under the table to make some money. I didn't mean to lead my father straight to your clubhouse. It's no excuse, but I'm… I'm so sorry, Hawk."

"There's nothing for you to be sorry for, love. You did nothing wrong. I wish I'd known about your father earlier, but I understand your hesitation. Without knowing the details, I could see the signs of abuse and gaslighting. I should have ripped the fucker away from you the moment I came out to the alley. I should have never doubted you. I should have–"

I reach up, covering his mouth with my hand. Hawk's eyes go comically wide, making me smile. "No more apologies from either of us," I say, raising an eyebrow at him. Hawk nods, and I let my hand slip from his face.

Without another word, Hawk and I lean toward each other, our noses brushing before our lips meet. Hawk kisses me in slow, deep, almost reverent strokes like he's cherishing every part of me.

When we break apart, Hawk tucks me into his side, guiding me to lay my head on his chest. I close my eyes, listening to the calming, steady beat of his heart, knowing it belongs to me.

"Get some rest, beautiful," Hawk whispers. "I'll be right here when you wake up."

"Promise?" I murmur as I stifle a yawn.

"Promise," he confirms, placing a kiss on the top of my head. It's the last thing I remember before drifting off to sleep.

CHAPTER THIRTEEN

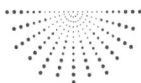

HAWK

"Yeah, she's doing a lot better," I tell Blade over the phone as I adjust the pillows on my couch.

It's been almost a month since everything went down at the clubhouse with Tessa and her father. The bruises have faded, and the cuts have healed, but my girl still wakes up in the middle of the night, sweating and crying from nightmares about her degenerate father.

"Madge is going crazy with worry. Any chance you can swing by with Tessa to show her proof of life?"

"She's not going back to work," I instantly reply.

"I think that's more her decision than yours, but that's not what I was saying," Blade corrects. "You know Madge. She's a mother hen to all of the staff."

"And bikers," I add. Blade chuckles.

"That, too," he agrees. "She just wants to know you two are okay. What's it been? Three weeks?"

"Four."

"Plenty of time for Tessa to heal up."

I grunt, knowing I'm being overprotective. It would be good for Tessa to get out and spend time with Madge, but

I'm having a hard time letting her out of my sight. In fact, I'm having a hard time not wrapping her up in a blanket and making her rest in bed forever with me by her side.

"How's our favorite Sheriff?" I ask, wanting to change the subject.

"A miserable fuck," he grunts, making me smirk. I'm sure he is, after how we handled the situation.

While I was taking care of Tessa, Blade, Rider, and a few other Savage Saints surrounded the cabin and got the jump on old Sheriff Huxley. Tied him up and interrogated him, not only about Tessa but about Rider's prison time, as well as a myriad of other misdeeds and miscarriages of justice.

Axel was back at the clubhouse the whole time, working behind the scenes. He had the brilliant idea of checking the security cam footage from the camera we keep trained on the back door and alley. Not only did that give us proof of the monster assaulting his daughter, but it also recorded a nice little sound clip of him talking about putting away Savage Saints when they get in the way and threatening to blow up the clubhouse.

I don't care how corrupt the police are in this town; that evidence alone was enough to lock him up. Not before we got a couple of hits in, however. I went back the next day to give him a piece of my mind as well. Along with a few good swings to his face and abdomen. He deserves much worse for the hell he put Tessa through.

"Hawk? You there?"

"Yeah, just thinking about that day," I tell him truthfully.

Blade grunts again. "You know they won't keep him locked up forever."

"They fucking should," I growl. "What more do they need? He's a menace to society, and he never should have been put in a position of authority."

"I know that, and you know that, but the law doesn't give

a shit. He lawyered up to drop the conspiracy to commit crime charges, and it seems like he has a pretty solid case, according to our intel."

"But the assault. I mean, Jesus!" I say a little more forcefully than I meant. I can't help it. I only saw the video footage once, and it nearly made me throw up. The way he talked to her, yelled at her, and put his grubby hands around her neck–

"You know how these things go," Blade says, cutting off my downward spiral. Good thing, too. I don't want to get all worked up. Not while Tessa is around. "They gave him five years and slapped a fine in his face. He'll probably be out in one year, maybe six months if his lawyer is any good at his job."

"We'll be ready if and when he comes around again," I tell Blade. He's the Prez and calls the shots, but I'm guessing he'll be on my side with this demand.

"Fucking right we will be," he confirms.

Just then, Tessa steps into the living room, wearing tiny pajama shorts and a sports bra. She's killing me with her outfit. Teasing me with her curves all on display. I've been hesitant to take things much further than making out since the incident, not wanting to hurt her in any way.

Tessa has other ideas, however.

She straddles my lap and runs her hands up my chest. Fuck, my dick springs to life almost painfully as my girl leans forward and gives me an incredible view of her tits squeezed together in her bra.

"Gotta go," I choke out over the phone. Blade mutters something, but I hang up and toss my phone somewhere behind me, my hands immediately finding Tessa's hips.

I groan as I squeeze her soft flesh and grind her against my lap. She rests her forehead on mine, her breath tickling my lips. I can't hold back.

My lips find hers, and I lead us in a drugging, desperate kiss, my hands sliding down to her juicy ass and gripping it tightly. Tessa whimpers into my mouth, making me growl in return.

We eventually break apart, panting for air in the wake of our devastating kiss.

Tessa nuzzles her head into the crook of my shoulder, and I hold her close, letting the rhythm of her heart and the warmth of her skin ground me.

I don't know how long we stay like that, but eventually, I feel Tessa stir in my arms. I reluctantly let her go, and she stands, holding out her hand to me. "Come take a shower with me?" she asks, biting her lip nervously.

"Tessa, love, I don't want to hurt you."

She shakes her head. "You won't. I'm all healed. The doctor said it himself last week at my check-up."

"He doesn't know shit," I mutter.

Tessa rolls her eyes. "You trusted his opinion before, so I think you owe it to him to trust it now, too," she counters. "Besides. I miss you."

She looks away from me, her cheeks turning pink at her confession. *Shit.* I didn't mean to neglect her or make her feel unwanted.

"I miss you too, beautiful," I murmur before standing and facing her.

Tessa's green eyes shine bright with joy, and I want to kick myself for waiting a whole week to give my woman the attention she desires.

She holds her hand out for me again, but instead of taking it, I scoop her up in my arms, smiling when she giggles.

"Love that sound," I murmur before kissing her nose and heading toward the bathroom.

Once inside, I close the door, turn on the water, and begin stripping us out of our clothes. I desperately need to feel her skin against mine and every inch of her beneath my fingertips. When we're both naked, Tessa steps forward and cups my face in her hands, pulling me down so we're mere inches apart.

"I need to feel you. Please make everything go away until it's just us. Please?"

"I love you, Tessa." I breathe the words into her mouth before kissing her with all my strength.

She drops her hands from my face to my neck, holding tight and deepening our kiss. I press us closer together, feeling her soft curves pour into the slats of my muscles. I pick her up with one arm under her waist and carry her into the warm water, pinning her against the tiled wall. Our lips never part, our kiss growing more desperate by the second.

Tessa wraps her legs around me, her hands trickling over my arms, my chest, around my neck down my back. My tongue rakes across the roof of her mouth, and she shivers against me, pressing against my body as I wrap my fingers around her silky locks. I want to hear more of her. Have more of her. Taste more of her.

Tessa rolls her hips, brushing her wet little cunt against my raging hard dick. She moans into my mouth, causing me to jerk my hips and hit her clit.

"God, yes," she whimpers, spurring me on.

With a contained roar, I thrust forward, her mouth opening in a silent scream as I split her open in one hard stroke. I slide back and into her again, swallowing her desperate cries until her fingers grip my back and score my flesh. Her hips press forward, taking another few inches until I'm bound to her, root to tip, as her pussy practically chokes me at the base.

"You feel so good, baby. Like coming home," I whisper into the shell of her ear before kissing down her neck.

Tessa bows her back off the wall and presses her tits

forward, practically begging me to suck on them, which I do, hungrily. I take her breast into my mouth, licking her pebbled nipple and grazing my teeth over her soft flesh, loving how she shudders in my arms and drips more of her sweet juices down my dick.

I feel her tight little pussy flutter around me, her breath growing shallow as her chest rises and falls rapidly. Tessa's muscles tense, and her pussy gushes for me, throbbing around my cock as her body tightens and squeezes me, hurting me so fucking good.

I piston in and out of her, building her up, up, up, tapping her clit with the base of my cock on every stroke. "That's it, love, come for me, baby, come for me and show me you're mine, only mine," I growl into the side of her neck before licking a line up to her jaw and nipping her there.

She goes still in my arms, her body wrapped around mine while her head tips back and her mouth hangs open. I lean over her, hovering my open mouth above hers as her orgasm ravages her soft body. I breathe in her little whimpers and moans that come with every wave of pleasure.

Her nails dig into my shoulders, making me grunt and thrust inside of her so fucking hard, once, twice, three times, and I bury my head in the side of her neck as I empty myself inside of her still-convulsing cunt.

I continue to rock in and out of her, prolonging our pleasure as long as possible. Tessa shudders and jerks and then knots her pussy around my thick dick as she fucking comes again. I hold her shivering body up and keep her pressed against the wall, in absolute awe of this goddess in my arms.

Gently, I pull out of her and set her down on the floor, pulling her into my chest and kissing the top of her head. Silently, I grab the body wash, pour some in my hand, and massage the soap into every inch of her body. I knead away the tension in her back and shoulders and then wash her hair, marveling at its color and texture. Every single thing about her is perfect.

When I'm done, Tessa soaps me up and lets her hands wander over my body like she's admiring me too. We rinse off, and I wrap her up in a fluffy towel and carry her off to bed, where I crawl in next to her and turn so we're face to face.

"Love everything about you," I tell her, combing my fingers through her wet hair. "Your smile, your bravery, and your pure heart." I lean over and press a kiss to her forehead and nose, hovering over her lips before whispering, "Love your sexy fucking body, your addictive kisses, and the way you get completely lost in pleasure when I make you come."

Tessa closes the distance between us, her tongue slipping into my mouth and coaxing me to kiss her back with the same intensity. I give my woman everything she asks, rolling on top of her and diving into her sweetness.

Reluctantly, I pull back after a few moments to give us some air. Nuzzling into the side of her neck, I place gentle kisses along her pulse point, loving how her heartbeat jumps whenever I put my lips on her skin.

"I love everything about you too. How protective you are, how patient and gentle you've been with me. You taught me to value myself for who I am, and..." she sniffles, and I look up from where I was kissing her neck. Wiping away the single tear that fell, I press my lips to her cheek, hating to see her cry. Tessa takes a deep breath, calming herself down. "And your hard, sexy body is also appreciated," she adds, a mischievous sparkle in her eyes. I love it.

"Thanks, beautiful. It's all for you."

My woman grins at me, her hands trailing down my chest, lower, lower, Christ... She wraps her hand around my dick, which is already half hard for her.

"We need to make up for lost time, don't you think?"

"Fuck, yes," I growl, ghosting my lips down her neck and chest, pausing to lick and suck on one nipple and then the other.

Tessa moans and wraps her legs around my hips, urging me forward. My girl is insatiable, and I can't wait to fulfill every single one of her desires.

Starting right the fuck now.

EPILOGUE

TESSA

"Careful! Don't go too fast!" I call out to Hawk as he slowly turns his motorcycle around in the clubhouse parking lot.

Our eight year old, Nathan, is perched on the front of the bike, his hands gripping the handlebars. Hawk has his hands covering Nathan's steering while letting him think he's the one in control.

They're only going five miles an hour, but my mother's heart can't help but worry.

"No! Faster!" Nathan shouts, the excitement in his voice making me smile.

Hawk revs the engine but doesn't pick up his speed. Our son squeals in delight, and I just smile and shake my head, watching the two of them do figure-eights in the parking lot.

The last ten years were nothing like I thought they would be when I stepped into the Savage Saints clubhouse looking for a job. They've been infinitely better.

Hawk and I waited a whole month before tying the knot. Our wedding was small and intimate and perfect, and I wouldn't trade it for anything in the world.

Two years later, Nathan came along, bringing so much joy to our lives. I'll admit I was a little worried about raising kids around the MC, but all of my fears were completely unfounded. The family we have here is generous and caring, if not a little gruff and stubborn. I've found that all the best people are.

Blade, Rider, Axel, Madge, and all the other members love playing with Nathan and humoring him when he wants to "help" with the bikes or "work" in the restaurant. The whole MC family really stepped up their game when Stephanie was born three years later. They treat her like a princess, and spoil her more than Hawk does, which is saying something. That kid has her father wrapped around her little finger.

Speaking of…

I peer around the parking lot in search of my sassy little five year old. I hear her bubbly laughter, and turn my head in that direction, smiling when I see Sutton tickling her. My bestie scoops Stephanie up and spins her around before setting her back on the ground. I'm beyond happy that she found herself a big burly grizzly bear of a biker to protect her and take care of her every need.

Taking a sip from my water bottle, I look around at the familiar faces of Savage Saints. I never would have pictured my life turning out this way, but I wouldn't trade it for anything.

Hawk and Nathan pull up in front of me, parking the bike. Hawk slips off the bike and helps Nathan down, taking the helmet off his head.

"Thanks, dad! When can we do it again?" our son asks.

"Why don't you get some water and food in you first," Hawk says. "We've been out riding all morning. Even Blade has to stop to refuel after a long day on the road."

Nathan looks over at Blade, who is standing to his full height, arms crossed, a stern look in his eyes. The Prez nods his head once, and Nathan widens his eyes. The next second, Blade cracks a grin, making my son erupt in giggles.

"Hey, beautiful," Hawk says, wrapping an arm around my waist and pulling me into his side.

"Hey yourself," I murmur, loving the way his blue eyes light up whenever he looks at me.

Hawk kisses the side of my neck, then cups my face, turning me toward him for a real kiss. Just like every time our lips meet, I get lost in the way he kisses me, the way he explores me like everything is still new and exciting. With Hawk, it is.

"Ewww," Nathan whines.

Hawk ruffles his hair without breaking our kiss, which makes me laugh. Hawk grunts when I pull away from him, his arm never leaving my waist.

"Go on and find Uncle Rider," I tell Nathan. "He'll fix you a plate of food." Our feisty little kid rolls his eyes and shakes his head as if we're embarrassing him. Still, he heads inside the clubhouse, leaving me with my handsy husband.

"Can't wait to get you home and under me tonight," he whispers into the shell of my ear, his hand sliding down my back to palm my ass.

"Yeah? Is it my yoga pants and ratty band t-shirt that are doing it for you?" I tease.

"Everything you do winds me up," he counters, his voice low as he presses a line of kisses from my shoulder up to my ear.

I grin at him, playfully swatting him away. Hawk frowns, which is just as adorable as it always is. "Keep it in your pants while we're at the clubhouse. So inappropriate!" I joke.

"Then we better get home. Think Sutton and Rider will take the kids for the night? They can have a sleepover with their cousins."

I look over my shoulder at Sutton, who's still playing with

Stephanie. She smirks at me and wags her eyebrows, making me laugh.

"Yeah, that should work out just fine."

"Good," my husband growls, walking me a few steps backward until I'm pressed against the side of the clubhouse. He pins me to the wall, ghosting his nose and lips up my throat, nipping at my pulse point. "God, I love you, Tessa," he says in a softer tone.

"Love you too, Hawk," I tell him, matching his tone.

"Still can't believe you're mine and that I have everything I've ever wanted."

I rest my forehead on his, combing my fingers through his hair. "Believe it," I whisper. "We're living our happily ever after."

"Hell yeah we are, beautiful," he responds, taking my lips in a searing kiss.

I can taste his happiness, his need, his promises of love and joy. I can't wait to see what the future holds for us.

* * *

THE END

Curious about Rider & Sutton? Get their story here!

Want to know more about Titan? Watch this grump find his sunshine here!

RIDER

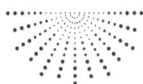

RIDER

Sutton is like a delicate wildflower sprouting up between cracks in the cement. She's beautiful, unexpected, and life-giving, especially after spending the last five years in prison.

The first time I saw her at the clubhouse, my knees buckled and I grew so lightheaded I thought I would faint. She's skittish, however. I don't know what she's been through, but my girl can barely look at her own shadow without shrinking away from the darkness.

Little by little, I draw Sutton out of her shell, showing her how strong and brave she is all on her own. When she finds out about my past, all the progress we made is undone.

Can my wildflower forgive me and see past my flaws? I hope so, because I know I can't live without her...

CHAPTER ONE

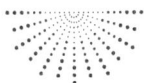

SUTTON

"There you are," Hawk says as he comes up behind Tessa.

He wraps his arms around her hips, and my best friend spins in his embrace, her dreamy smile matching his.

I look down at the bar top while they kiss, trying not to feel like a third wheel. Grabbing a napkin from the dispenser next to me, I twist it in my hands in a familiar, anxious gesture. I've been to the Savage Saints MC clubhouse a dozen times to visit Tessa at work, but my nerves still get the best of me if I'm here longer than ten minutes.

It's not just the clubhouse, though. I get panic attacks if I'm in the grocery store and someone is blocking an aisle I need to go down or if I'm waiting in line and someone steps up a little too close behind me.

Basically, I'm a pathetic mess.

The air around me grows heavy, and a spark of awareness shoots down my spine. *Rider is here.* I get the same feeling every time the tall, muscled, mysterious man is around me.

Turning slightly, I see Rider's large silhouette sitting on

the barstool on the other side of Hawk and Tessa. My eyes trace the sharp lines of his nose and chin, then wander down to his bulging biceps and thick, corded forearms covered in ink. I imagine what it would be like to curl up in his lap and have those arms wrapped around me, protecting me from everything. Maybe my anxiety wouldn't be so crippling if I knew I had someone like Rider by my side.

I tear my gaze away from Rider, but not before capturing his chocolate brown eyes. He's so intense, yet I don't feel like he's scrutinizing or objectifying me. No, when Rider's attention is on me, I feel… safe. Seen. Protected. All things I had been sorely lacking in my life until recently.

A yawn sneaks up on me. I close my eyes, breaking eye contact with Rider as I lift my hand to cover my mouth. I haven't stopped yawning since I stepped into the clubhouse an hour ago to visit Tessa while she finished her bartending shift.

"Why are you so tired, Sutton?" Tessa asks.

"Oh, you know," I say vaguely as I shrug. "Working on a big design project."

It's not a lie, but it's not the whole truth. I *am* working on a big design project I hope to finish soon. The client paid half up-front, and I get the other half once everything is complete. As for the rest…

"You need to rest and take care of yourself," my friend gently reminds me. Tessa rests her hand on my shoulder, squeezing slightly. "You have people who care about you now. It's not about survival anymore. We get to decide how we live our lives."

I nod, smiling at Tessa. I know she means well, but I'm not done operating in survival mode. It's not her fault she doesn't know. I haven't had the heart to tell her about my dreadful trip back to my hometown a few weeks ago that changed everything. How could I? She's finally safe and happy and living her best life with Hawk. The last thing I want to do is burden her with my family drama and living situation.

"Thanks for the reminder," I say before another yawn creeps up on me.

Tessa furrows her brow, and I catch Rider doing the same behind her. His eyes haven't left me once since he sat down, but I don't mind.

My friend opens her mouth to say something, but she's cut off by someone slamming their beer mug down on the bar top. Every muscle in my body tenses and I gasp, trying unsuccessfully to hide my whimper.

A second later, I regain control, telling myself I'm not in danger. It was just a loud noise. With each steady breath, I remind myself I'm not back in my childhood home, listening to my parents fight or scream at me for being in the way.

When I open my eyes again, Tessa has a worried look. I notice that Rider is gone, his drink untouched on the counter.

"I'm okay," I tell Tess with a reassuring smile. "Still working on my jump-scare reflexes," I say with a weak chuckle.

My bestie is unimpressed by my attempt at a joke, but she doesn't say anything else.

"Let's get you home, beautiful," Hawk tells Tessa before kissing her on the temple. She leans into his touch, that same dreamy smile spreading across her face.

Loneliness threatens to consume me, but I swallow past the lump in my throat. I'm happy for my friend. Ecstatic. No one deserves a happily ever after more than Tessa after everything she's been through. Her horrible, abusive father finally got what was coming to him, thanks to the Savage Saints MC.

Hawk takes Tessa's hand and leads her toward the door. I hop off my stool and follow them out into the parking lot.

"Thanks for visiting me at work tonight," Tessa says as they approach Hawk's motorcycle.

"Of course," I tell her, giving my friend a hug. "I don't get to see you as often these days, so I'll jump on any chance to hang out."

I meant for my comment to be sweet, but Tessa frowns slightly. "I know I kind of dropped off the face of the earth for a bit—"

I hold my hands up to stop her. "I didn't mean to guilt-trip you."

Tessa takes my hand in hers, squeezing slightly. "You're not guilt-tripping me. I've been meaning to stop by the house and see you, but I just..." She trails off, looking over her shoulder at Hawk.

I grin at Tessa, whose cheeks are slightly pink.

"No worries. Seriously. I'd rather see you here or at Hawk's," I tell her.

Tessa lifts an eyebrow at me, and I realize I may have been less subtle than I had hoped.

Thankfully, Hawk hands Tessa her helmet, distracting her enough not to ask follow-up questions. Good thing, too. I'm unsure what I'd tell her if she asked why I don't want her coming to the house.

"We'll talk later!" Tessa calls out as Hawk starts up his bike.

I nod and wave, watching them ride off into the night. With a fortifying breath, I straighten my shoulders and walk to my car, hopping inside and starting the engine.

When I reach the end of the parking lot, I don't turn left toward the house Tessa and I lived in together. Instead, I turn right, taking the gravel road further away from town. After a few blocks, I pull off to the side and ease my car under a large tree close to the edge of the road.

Turning off the car, I heave out a breath and sink further into the seat, resting my forehead on the steering wheel. This is not how I thought my life would turn out. Twenty-two and homeless.

Feeling sorry for myself isn't going to fix anything, however.

I dig around in my glove compartment for a granola bar I stashed there yesterday, but I can't find it. My stomach growls, and I try to ignore it. *I'll pick something up in the morning*, I tell myself, even though I'll have the same amount of money tomorrow as I do now. None.

Throwing open the driver's side door, I quickly get out and settle into the back seat, where I'll have more room to stretch out. Not much, but more than the front seat.

I grab the blanket I keep folded up against the back window and spread it out on top of me, using my purse as a pillow. As I curl up into a ball in the back seat of my car, I try not to let the tears break through. If I cry now, I might never stop. Besides, what good will tears do?

Even as I tell myself that, my eyes start to sting. I sniffle as the first tear falls, squeezing my eyes shut until the world around me is nothing but darkness. A pit opens in my chest, an endless void of loneliness that I fear may never leave me. I struggle to get a full breath in as rivers of despair pour from my eyes.

Eventually, I cry myself out. My eyes are swollen, and my throat is raw, but I have nothing left. At least now I'll finally be exhausted enough to sleep.

Pulling the thin blanket around my chin, I try to get more comfortable, only to be stabbed in the hip by a seatbelt holder. I'm sure I'll have a bruise in the morning, but right now, I'm too numb to feel anything.

Tomorrow will be better, I tell myself, even though the last fourteen days have seemed to get sequentially worse until I ended up sleeping in my car. Still, I have to hang on to that hope. One day, it will get better. Right?

CHAPTER TWO

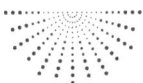

RIDER

*W*hat the fuck am I looking at?

I circle the decades-old Toyota Corolla for the third time since finding it partially hidden on the side of the road. I couldn't sleep, so I decided to head to the Savage Saints clubhouse to see if there was anything to clean or fix up. That's when I stumbled upon Sutton's car.

Peering in through the back window, I still can't believe what's right in front of my eyes. At first, I thought the car had broken down, and Sutton abandoned it. Upon further inspection, I discovered the woman herself curled up in the back seat.

Looking down on her now, I can see her curvy little body covered in a tattered and worn blanket. Sutton is shivering slightly, her inky black hair tangled around the strap of her purse, which she's using as a pillow. Her eyes flutter slightly, and I notice her nose and cheeks are red. Has she been crying?

My gut twists into a knot just thinking about this precious woman sleeping in her goddamn car. Why didn't she tell anyone? Why didn't I figure it out sooner? I saw how tired she was at the clubhouse last night, but never in a million years did I think it was because she didn't have anywhere to sleep.

Fuck, I should have caught her before she left. I had to deal with Slinger slamming his glass down on the bar. He scared my woman, and I won't stand for that.

My woman. I have to stop thinking about Sutton that way. She's not mine, even though I want her with every cell in my body. God, I can still remember the first time I saw her. I stumbled over my words, grunting at her like a caveman before shoving my giant, meaty paw in her face.

Sutton blinked at me, and those teal eyes reached into my very being and rearranged my chest to make room for her right next to my heart. When she didn't respond in any way, I realized what a fool I was.

Of course, she's not interested in someone like me. I'm a solid decade or so older than her, I've served hard time, and my presence alone is intimidating, especially to my sweet Sutton. I don't know what she's been through in her short life, but the mysterious, teal-eyed goddess can't even look at her own shadow without cowering away from the darkness.

With all of that stacked against me, I'm under no delusions that Sutton could ever be mine. That doesn't mean I won't do everything in my power to ensure she's safe.

My eyes drift to the door handles on her beat-up car, and I clench my fists, thinking about how easy it would be for someone to pry them open even if they were locked. Hell, it wouldn't take much to smash the goddamn window.

A growl escapes before I can suppress it. I ball my fists at my sides, every muscle tensing as I try to block out thoughts of what could have happened to Sutton if anyone else found her.

Jesus, she's so vulnerable out here. Anything could have happened...

Another growl is pulled from the pit of my stomach, and Sutton jerks awake, her eyes wide with fear. I can't fucking breathe when she looks at me like that. I never want her to be afraid of me, even if I tower over her and grunt like a neanderthal.

I hold my hands up, palms out, in a sign of surrender. As soon as she recognizes me, her shoulders relax slightly. She even graces me with a small smile, though it quickly disappears when she realizes I've caught her sleeping in her car.

Sutton untangles herself from the scrap of a blanket and pats her hair down before scooting over in the seat and opening the door. She slowly climbs out of the back seat, her eyes immediately focusing on the ground while she twists her hands in front of her.

"Um..." she starts, trailing off as she nibbles her bottom lip.

"What were you doing sleeping in your car?" I grunt more harshly than I meant. Sutton's shoulders rise to her ears, and I want to kick myself for being gruff. "You could have gotten hurt," I try again, though my tone is still sharp.

"Well, I... The house... and then my parents... I just..." Sutton can hardly say more than a few words at a time before she gets flustered and starts over. When the first tear falls, my knees give out.

Kneeling in front of her, I reach for her delicate little hands, taking both of them in one of mine. Her skin is so soft, so creamy and pure. It only serves to highlight the differences between us. My hands are weathered and worn from long days working and riding in the sun. My knuckles have scars from the violence I've inflicted on others over the years. My fingertips are rough, too rough to handle the broken angel standing in front of me.

"Breathe for me, little flower," I tell her.

Sutton gasps softly, her ethereal eyes finally meeting

mine. I'm not sure where the endearment came from, but it fits. My Sutton is exactly like a little wildflower: beautiful, unexpected, and life-giving.

She closes her eyes and takes a shaky breath before slowly exhaling.

"That's good," I encourage. "Take another one for me."

Sutton nods, her hands squeezing mine as she takes a steadier breath this time. God, I can feel her trembling. It takes everything in me to stay kneeling on the ground instead of scooping up this precious woman in my arms and hauling her back to my place so I can tuck her into my bed and ensure she never has to experience another night of homelessness again.

"I... I'm sorry," she finally whispers.

I furrow my brow, tilting my head to look into those blue-green eyes. "There's nothing to apologize for. I was worried about you. It's not safe here."

Sutton nods but doesn't say anything else. I want to ask her a million questions, including but not limited to her thoughts on a summer wedding and how many kids she wants. However, that will have to wait.

I have to be careful with Sutton. She doesn't trust easily, and asking her to tell me how she found herself in this position might be overstepping. My priority is to get her back to my place, back to a safe environment. Once she's rested, we can talk about the next steps, whatever they may be.

"How about you crash at my place for a bit?" I ask, slowly standing from my position on the ground.

Sutton keeps her left hand securely locked in mine, making my heart flip inside my chest. On some level, this woman feels comfortable around me. I'll take whatever I can get.

"Oh, no. I couldn't inconvenience you like that," she says

automatically, standing beside me. I don't like how rehearsed her response is.

"You're not an inconvenience," I assure her. I get the sense she doesn't believe me, but she will.

Soon, Sutton will know she's not a burden. She's the reason I wake up every day, hoping to steal a glance into her eyes or sit near her while she visits Tessa. She has no idea how obsessed I am with her, and part of me is worried it'll be too much. I don't want to suffocate my little flower. All I want to do is give her room to flourish in a safe environment. Without knowing anything about her past, I know Sutton hasn't had many safe places in her life. That ends today.

"How about just a nap, then?" I offer. "I have a guest bedroom. And, not to brag, but my couch is amazing."

Sutton's lips turn up into a slight smile. Fuckin' adorable.

"Is that right?" she asks softly as I guide her to the passenger side of her car. She stifles a yawn, and I open the door for her, grunting when I realize it was unlocked this whole time.

"Yes," I reply, hoping to cover the hitch in my voice. "When I got out… er, when I moved back into my house, the first thing I bought was a huge-ass couch that could fit my six-and-a-half-foot frame."

Shit. I almost said *when I got out of prison.* I don't want to lie to Sutton, but I don't think now is the appropriate time to broach that subject. I just got her to trust me. I can't ruin that by talking about my time behind bars.

"That sounds lovely," Sutton says before another yawn overtakes her.

It's on the tip of my tongue to tell her *she's* lovely, but I reel it in. I don't know where this cheesy, flowery romance shit came from, but when I'm around Sutton, I can't help it. I want to give her endless compliments to make up for the obvious lack of love she's had in her life.

She relaxes into the seat, and I put her seatbelt on for her, not even stopping to consider how overprotective that might come across. I look at her over my shoulder as I click the belt in place, her teal eyes wide and filled with... disbelief? Longing? Whatever it is, she seems surprised that anyone would go the extra mile for her.

Jogging around to the other side of the car, I hop in the driver's seat, adjusting everything so I can wedge my massive body inside. I fuckin' hate being in a cage, aka a car. Undoubtedly, a result of being cooped up in a tiny cell for s the last few years.

For Sutton, however, I'll drive this goddamn clown car across the country if it makes her happy.

Sutton digs around in her purse for the keys, handing them to me without a word. She can barely keep her eyes open, and my heart clenches in my chest.

I ease the old car back onto the road and take the quickest route to my place. It's nothing fancy, but it's a place to cook a few meals, wash up, and lay my head at night. That's all I need.

Will Sutton want a bigger house? I can make that happen. We'll probably need more rooms anyway once she gets pregnant.

Reel it in, I chastise myself. Just because she agreed to take a nap at my place doesn't mean she's suddenly in love with me.

But God, wouldn't that be incredible?

A few minutes later, I pull into my driveway and shut off the car. Sutton's head rests against the window, and I hear her soft little snores for the first time. This woman is killing me.

I unbuckle her seatbelt, careful not to jostle her too much, then get out of the car and jog over to her side. Slowly, I open the door and slide one arm behind her back while the other hooks under her knees.

Standing with my precious cargo, I close the door with my foot and head inside, carrying my princess into her new home.

CHAPTER THREE

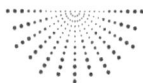

SUTTON

I roll over in the softest bed I've ever been in, burying my face into the nearest pillow, which smells like cedar and cinnamon.

Hold up.

I know that smell. It's warm and familiar and makes my stomach swoop. *Rider?*

Memories of this morning come flooding into my mind, and I flop over on my back, covering my face with the pillow. My cheeks heat in embarrassment as I remember waking up to Rider's growl. God, I can't believe the one person I never wanted to look weak and pathetic in front of found me.

At first, I thought he was angry with me. That's the default reaction to my presence.

Not anymore, I try to remind myself. Not since leaving my parents. My mom and dad weren't planning on having kids, so to say they weren't prepared or excited would be an understatement.

I learned from an early age to stay out of the way. If they couldn't see me, they couldn't be mad at me. At least, that was my logic. It worked about two-thirds of the time. The other third…

I shake off those thoughts, not wanting to relive the past. I escaped from my childhood home as soon as I had an opportunity. Unfortunately, that opportunity just got blown to smithereens, thanks to my parental units.

Groaning into the pillow over my face, I push all that aside and focus on the present. I have enough to worry about with trying to figure out what to tell Rider. I can't stay here. That's way too much to ask of him. More importantly, I need to convince him not to tell Tessa about my current living situation.

Finally gathering the strength to crawl out of the comfiest bed in the world, I toss the pillow aside and pull the blankets off, swinging my legs over the side of the bed. It occurs to me that I don't remember this room or walking from the car to the house.

Oh god. Did Rider carry me?

My hands immediately cover my rounded stomach, then slide to my extra wide hips. Shame courses through me at the thought of anyone having to carry me, let alone the sexiest, most chiseled man I've ever encountered.

How embarrassing! He must be disgusted.

New plan. Sneak out of Rider's house and drive my car off the nearest bridge.

Tiptoeing to the closed door, I slowly turn the knob, careful not to make a single sound. Years of living in the shadows and not drawing attention to myself have served me well. With the knob turned all the way, I inch the door open, peering my head out far enough to take in my surroundings.

Looking to the left, I don't see anything—just an empty hallway leading to more rooms. Looking to the right, I see…

"Sutton," Rider says, sounding equal parts relieved and

surprised. He rushes over to me, stopping a few feet away. He reaches out for me, then changes his mind, running his hands through his hair.

"Oh. Uh, um, hey," I stutter out like an idiot. "How long have I been asleep?"

"Three hours and fourteen minutes," he answers matter-of-factly.

"And you've been out here the whole time?"

"No," he says with a shake of his head. "After tucking you in, I paced around the hall and kept checking on you every ten minutes, but I didn't want to risk waking you up, so I started pacing in the living room to give you some space." His eyes never leave mine as he recounts his whereabouts all morning. It's kind of cute that he wants to get every detail right. "After an hour, I cleaned the kitchen and did a lap around the outside of the house to check on some projects I'm working on. Then I prepared lunch and resumed pacing in the hallway because I needed to be here the moment you woke up."

I stare at the dark-haired, dark-eyed beast of a man in front of me, watching as the tips of his ears turn red. Is he... blushing? After admitting he was so concerned about me he kept checking in while I was asleep?

A mix of overwhelming emotions slam into me, and I throw my arms around Rider before I can think better of it. He freezes, his muscles tensing the longer I hold onto his torso. I'm about to step away and run out the front door to resume my plan of driving my car off a bridge when Rider engulfs me in his embrace. His strong arms cover me completely, and I'm wrapped up in the warmest, safest hug in the universe.

I snuggle deeper into Rider, soaking up every single thing about this moment. Breathing his warm, earthy scent, I squeeze him harder, still not quite believing this is happening.

Suddenly, my feet aren't on the ground anymore. I'm lifted in the air, and Rider adjusts his grip to steady me. I gasp, then giggle as he spins me around. It's silly and sweet and so unexpected, and God, I find myself wanting to stay in his arms forever.

The moment is over when Rider sets me back down, taking a step away from me. I crane my neck to look up at the man curiously, taking in his deep brown eyes with a few crinkles in the corners. I love that he's older and has experienced more of life than I have. It's such a ridiculous thought, but if Rider were mine, his maturity would make me feel protected. Safe to explore my life, knowing I had Rider in my corner.

"Your laugh," Rider murmurs, his eyes searching mine as if I'm a rare treasure. "I've never heard it before." He pauses, his gaze wandering down my face in what can't possibly be awe. "It's magical." I'm unsure who is more shocked at his words, me, or Rider. "Uh, what I meant was…"

"Thank you," I whisper, not wanting him to be flustered. "No one's ever… Well, thanks." I give him an awkward smile, then stare down at my feet.

Rider clears his throat and claps his hands, apparently signaling a scene change. I grin at his tactic, then full-on smile when he takes my hand.

"Lunchtime," he announces, tugging me down the hall and into the kitchen.

"Oh my gosh, what is all of this?" I gasp, walking forward as I take in all the food set out on the table.

There are bowls of fresh-cut fruit, a container of something creamy and delicious-looking, some egg salad, all manner of bread, including a loaf that looks homemade, a giant tray of deli meats, an equally large tray of cheese, and five bags of varying chip brands.

"Just a few things for sandwiches," Rider says. I peer over my shoulder at him, one eyebrow lifted. "Okay, well, it started out as a few sandwich things, but then I realized you might be hungrier, so I whipped up some egg salad and a batch of my almond chicken salad with grapes. Then I thought grapes wouldn't be nearly enough fruit, and, well, I may have gotten a bit carried away when I started chopping up the pineapple…"

He trails off, breaking eye contact with me as he rubs the back of his neck in a nervous gesture. I still can't wrap my head around what is happening here.

"Wait. So all of this is for… me?" I thought maybe he had a bunch of leftovers he wanted to get rid of, but he made all of this. For me. Because he wanted to make sure I wasn't hungry.

"Of course," he responds as if it's obvious. "But if you want something else, I think I have all the ingredients for enchiladas. Or we can order in. I just thought something homemade would be nice."

"Rider, I don't even know what to say," I whisper, turning to face him. "It's too much." I'm not sure if I'm referring to the amount of food, which is undoubtedly more than I could eat in a week, or the act of this near-stranger going out of his way to provide for me.

"Then I guess you'll have to stay with me until we finish it all," he answers smoothly. Rider's lips pull to one side in the smallest, sexiest grin.

God. *Swoon.* How can I say no to that?

"Let's get through lunch first," I say, though I return his smile. It's not like I have anywhere else to go, and if Rider is content to have me here for now, I'll soak up every minute of being under his roof.

Rider hands me a plate and goes through the options again, each one more mouth-watering than the last. I make a chicken salad sandwich on the fresh-baked honey-wheat bread and an egg salad sandwich on a delectable-looking croissant. I scoop some strawberries and pineapple chunks onto my plate, and Rider adds a handful of blueberries and blackberries.

"High in antioxidants," he explains. His tone is so serious, I can't help but let out a tiny laugh.

"Thank you," I tell him sincerely.

Rider's eyes catch mine, sending my heart fluttering and my stomach somersaulting.

I sit at the breakfast bar since the kitchen table is covered in food. Rider joins me a moment later, his plate piled high with three sandwiches. He's also grabbed a bag of BBQ chips and sour cream and onion chips, setting them down in front of me like the proud hunter/gatherer he is.

This man just keeps getting more adorable and perfect with each passing second. There has to be a catch, right? When is the other shoe going to drop? Good things don't last for me.

"Oh, *wow*," I groan after taking my first bite of the chicken salad sandwich. "Rider, this is incredible. Like… really freaking delicious," I add after shoving another bite in my mouth.

He grunts, which I'm starting to understand is Rider's preferred method of communication.

"Where did you learn to cook like this?" I ask, hoping to get some kind of conversation going. If we talk about him, maybe we won't have time to talk about me and why I was sleeping in my car.

"My mother," he says softly. The way the words are spoken with equal parts fondness and sadness lets me know she's no longer with us.

"When did she pass?" I hold my hands up when Rider cuts a glance at me. "We don't have to talk about it—"

"How did you know?" he asks, interrupting my spiral.

"Your tone. I can tell you love and miss her, but not the same way someone misses family that lives far away. It's a deeper, more permanent loss."

Rider furrows his brow, those dark eyes piercing me right down to my soul. He nods slowly, and for a moment, I think the conversation is over.

Good job, I tell myself. *Way to bring up a painful subject the first time you have an actual conversation with the man.*

"Two years ago," Rider finally says. "I guess I haven't processed it yet."

My hand moves on its own, covering Rider's. He flips his hand over, weaving our fingers together as he stares at where we're connected. When he doesn't say anything else, I take a chance by continuing.

"Tell me about her," I whisper.

Rider takes a deep breath and closes his eyes. "The only thing she loved more than cooking was gardening. Wild roses, daffodils, gardenia bushes, and, of course, her herbs and spices. Ma always had fresh spearmint, basil, parsley, and dill."

"She sounds amazing," I say quietly, not wanting to disturb this moment.

"She is. *Was,*" he corrects himself. I squeeze his hand, and he squeezes mine right back. "And she did it all on her own. Raised me, taught me how to work hard and treat people with respect. All while working her ass off at the local diner. I don't know how she had time for it all while maintaining her garden and cooking for me most nights." Rider pauses, shaking his head slightly. "As soon as I could safely operate the stove and oven, I had Ma show me her favorite recipes. I started with one meal a week, then two, until I took over cooking for her altogether."

I never would have guessed the man sitting next to me loved his mama so much and could cook up a storm. Rider is one mystery after another, and I can't wait to find out more.

"And now you're using your cooking skills to feed the homeless," I joke. Rider frowns. "For real, though, your mom would be proud of the man you've become," I tell him sincerely.

He looks away from me, mumbling something that sounds like, "I failed her in the end."

I want to ask a dozen questions but now isn't the time. Especially since I can tell Rider is about to turn the tables on me and ask about my personal life.

"So, are we going to talk about your living situation?"

"I was hoping to skip that topic," I say lightly as I take a huge bite of the egg salad sandwich. It's also the stuff of dreams, for the record.

Rider waits patiently for me to finish chewing, but I take another bite, hoping to stall a bit more. He narrows his eyes at me, though his lip twitches with the slightest hint of a smile.

"All done?" he asks after I finish both sandwiches, the fruit, and a handful of chips.

"Yup. Just in time for a siesta."

Rider grunts out a laugh, which makes me unreasonably happy.

"You don't have to tell me everything, Sutton," he says, the sudden seriousness in his tone making me pay attention.

Rider stands from his seat and moves closer, stepping in between my parted thighs. I tilt my head back to look into those deep brown eyes. Rider gently, so gently cups my cheek, the rough pad of his thumb brushing against my skin in the lightest touch. I can't help but lean into him, loving the contact far more than I should.

"I need to know how I can keep you safe," he continues in a hushed tone. "Are you running from anything?" Rider's jaw clenches, though I'm not sure why. Is he that upset at the mere *thought* of someone threatening me?

"Just bad luck," I say with a tiny smile. Rider's eyes never leave mine, letting me know it's not the time to joke or be cute. "No, I'm not in danger or anything, just…" I sigh, shrugging my shoulders dismissively. "Just struggling," I finish, unsure what else to say.

"It's okay to struggle, Sutton. You don't have to go through it alone. Let me help."

"Why?" I'm not sure he can even hear me, my voice is so soft.

"Princess, it kills me that you even have to ask."

Princess. Did he really just call me that? *Me?* Lord, this man is ruining me.

"It doesn't make any sense. You're like this freaking Roman god with your muscles, tanned skin, and dark, broody eyes. You have a tight-knit family with the Savage Saints, a beautiful home, and I'm… me," I end pathetically, turning my head away from him.

Rider doesn't let me get very far. With one finger under my chin, he nudges my head up to look at him again. When I do, I can hardly breathe with the way his eyes are boring into mine.

"You, Sutton, are worthy of a safe place to land. You're worthy of good things and people who care about you. Tessa is a good friend, right?" I nod, barely able to move as I drink in every word he's saying. "Do you feel like you owe her for being your friend?"

I shrug. Truthfully, I still don't know why Tessa wants to

be my friend. She's this brave, incredible, kind woman with a fierce heart and gentle spirit.

"Sutton," he murmurs, brushing a few stray hairs out of my face and tucking them behind my ear. I close my eyes, memorizing how it feels to have someone like Rider care for me. "I don't know everything about you or your past, but I promise you, relationships aren't supposed to be transactional. I want to show you that. Prove that you're worthy of good things because of who you are."

"I..." My voice gets caught in my throat as tears threaten to spill down my cheeks. I shake my head no, unable to accept that, especially coming from Rider.

"Yes," he soothes, his voice both commanding and gentle. "All you have to do is let me show you. Can you do that for me?"

"But..."

Rider lifts an eyebrow, transforming his usually stoic features into a more playful look. I love it. I love every new thing I discover about him. I'm still unsure why Rider seems determined to be so nice to me, but I decide to trust it. For now.

"Okay," I finally whisper.

"Really? You'll stay here?" He says it like a kid on Christmas morning, which is the most adorable thing he's done yet.

"At least until all this food is eaten," I remind him with a grin.

Rider returns it, and lordy, what that does to me. "I guess I'll just have to keep cooking for you. Maybe I can get you to stay forever." My eyes widen, but Rider just winks as he steps back from me. "I heard you have a big design project you're working on. Why don't you set up shop out here in the living room while I do some yard work? I'm trying to wrestle the overgrown and sorely neglected garden beds into shape, but it's a bigger project than I anticipated."

I nod, smiling as Rider gathers the plates from breakfast. I know it won't last forever, but sleeping in, having food served up, and working on our separate projects sounds awfully domestic. Almost like we do this every Saturday.

Crazy, I know. But for now, I can pretend I have everything I've ever wanted.

CHAPTER FOUR

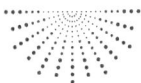

RIDER

"So that shithead thinks he can get the charges dropped?" Axel exclaims, his indignant tone echoing around the room.

Blade, the President of Savage Saints MC, called church about thirty minutes ago. After a check-in on current assignments and a briefing on upcoming runs, Prez gave us the bad news that Darren, the dirty sheriff we put away a few months ago, is trying to get out of prison on a technicality.

"Fuckin' low-life," one member grumbles.

"Shoulda put him six feet under instead of handing him over to the authorities," another man grunts.

"*Enough*," Blade roars, slamming his fist on the podium in front of him. "Slick, do you want to share your opinion of how I handled the situation again? Louder this time so everyone can hear?" The prez stares down the man who suggested killing Darren, daring him to say it to his face. "Didn't think so."

Slick at least has the decency to bow his head and shut the fuck up. Yeah, we're all pissed off and frustrated, but questioning Blade is about the stupidest response there is. Savage

Saints are loyal. We have each other's back. We don't fuck around with clubhouse drama, and that includes giving Blade shit.

"As we already know, Sheriff Darren is about as corrupt as they come. He has no moral compass and will do whatever it takes to maintain control over his police force and this town."

"Even lay his filthy fucking hands on his daughter," Hawk spits out.

I clap him on the shoulder and squeeze, letting my friend know I'm there for him. I understand why he hates that bastard.

Tessa, Hawk's girl, has the unfortunate luck of being Darren's daughter. She escaped the abusive piece of shit only to have him find her and drag her back into his clutches. Hawk, Axel, and I found her and brought her back to safety. Then we beat the ever-living shit out of him and threw him to the FBI after showing them evidence of the sheriff falsifying charges and assaulting his daughter.

I have a different reason for hating that despicable excuse for a human. Dirty fucking Sheriff Darren stole five years of my life. His false statement sent me straight to the slammer.

"Like I said, no moral compass," Blade affirms. "According to our source on the inside, he's trying to build a case for obstruction of justice against the FBI agents who arrested him. Seems flimsy, but I wouldn't put it past him to manipulate the system. He's been doing it for decades."

Heads nod around the room, the air thick with frustration and restless energy. We're all itching for a way to keep that man behind bars forever. And if not, we can discuss... *alternative* ways of taking care of the problem.

"Hawk," Blade says, staring at my friend. "I'm sure you won't mind the assignment of sticking close to Tessa until we know for sure the sheriff isn't going to get out on bail."

Hawk nods, and the prez continues.

"Axel has eyes and ears around the police station and other locations in the form of cameras, mics, and several informants. We'll take shifts monitoring everything, starting tonight. I'll take the first shift, and Axel will replace me at six a.m. You can sign up for your slot on the sheet of paper by the door."

Thirty heads turn to the table next to the exit. Sure enough, there's a clipboard with a pen attached and a sheet of paper with lines and times.

"Now get out of here," Prez growls, like he does at the end of every church meeting. "Rider and Axel, hold back."

The two of us slowly stand, walking up to the front of the room. I hope this doesn't take up too much time. I told Hawk I'd grab a beer with him after church, but what I want to do is go back home to Sutton.

She's been with me for two days now. Two blissful days of seeing her around the kitchen making coffee in the morning. Two days of cooking for her and watching her teal eyes light up with each new dish. Two days of longing for her with every breath, yet never getting close enough to touch her the way I want. The way I need.

"New mission time?" Axel asks with a bit too much enthusiasm, jarring me out of my thoughts.

He's calmed down quite a bit in the last month or so, but he still has moments of being an excited little puppy. As our newest member, I know he's trying to prove himself. We give him shit, but it's only because he's family now. Besides, Axel has already proven his worth with his hacking skills and technological know-how. He's also a talented mechanic, but we've been relying more on his cyber skills recently.

"Yes," Blade answers, his tone flat. There's a good-natured spark in his dark eyes, however, and I know he finds Axel amusing. "I would have brought Hawk in as well, but he's going to be distracted and busy enough watching out for Tessa." We both nod. "Axel is already in on this, so I'll have him explain it to you."

I turn to Axel, who is practically vibrating out of his skin. I can tell he's thrilled to take the lead on something, and honestly, I'm happy for the kid. He's earned it.

"So, while setting up the surveillance equipment around the station, I picked up on a lead for missing narcotics. At first, I thought it was gang activity or a rival club moving in on our territory. But then I listened more carefully and followed the clues… right back to the cops."

"Of fucking course," I grunt, not the least bit surprised.

"It gets worse," Blade warns.

I turn my attention back to Axel and nod for him to continue.

"Get this. The drugs in question are all confiscated narcotics from police raids over the years. Apparently, there are several warehouses nearby housing everything. The street value for the amount they've got…" Axel whistles and shakes his head. "Millions."

"Jesus," I grunt, though I'm not surprised.

"While everyone else is working on taking the sheriff down, I want you two to follow this intel," Blade says. "I have a feeling it all leads back to Darren, but I'm not sure how yet. Besides, we need to keep a lockdown on drugs in our town anyway, so two birds and all that shit."

I nod, waiting for the next instruction.

"I'll monitor the feeds from the clubhouse," Axel jumps in. "And you'll do some groundwork, meet with some of our less reputable contacts."

I nod, knowing my recent prison time will help ingratiate me with the right people. Or, rather, the wrong people.

"Be careful out there," Blade says, resting a hand on my shoulder.

I grunt, asking a few more details before we're dismissed. Axel follows me out to the bar section of the clubhouse, waving at Hawk, who is leaning against the bar top.

"Join us for a drink?" I ask Axel, making my way toward my friend.

"Another time. I only have some surveillance to do, then I should sleep while I can before my next shift starts."

"I'll hold you to that, kid."

Axel rolls his eyes every time I call him *kid*, which makes me smirk. He's not much younger than me in the grand perspective of things, but he's... less jaded. I know Axel hasn't had the easiest life—no one ends up in the Savage Saints because their childhood was great and they had all the opportunities in the world.

What's the opposite of an old soul? A new soul? Either way, Axel has an eternal optimism and motivation I associate with youth.

On the other hand, I've seen my fair share of gruesome crimes and experienced far more grisly horrors than I'd like to remember. If Axel sees the proverbial water glass as half full, I'm likely to assume it was once filled to the top with poison and is only half empty because the poor bastard who drank it died.

Until Sutton came into my life. My precious, brave little flower.

My life was filled with darkness long before I was locked away, and being in prison only hardened me more. I didn't think I was capable of feeling the warmth of the sun. Then Sutton smiled at me, her light piercing through the darkness and shining down on all the broken pieces of my soul.

"I know that look," Hawk says, startling me out of my thoughts. "Who is she?"

My eyes widen before I remember to school my expression. *How the hell did he figure it out so quickly?*

"Uh, what? What are you talking about? She?" I ramble.

Hawk grins at me and takes a swig of his beer. The bartender working tonight hands me a beer without me having to ask. I give him a nod and lay down a five-dollar bill, thankful for something to do other than look at Hawk's stupid smirk.

"Let me rephrase that. How are things going with Sutton?" I blink, unable to think of a response. "Rider, You could *not* be more obvious, my friend. And you weren't subtle the first time you met her."

I narrow my eyes at Hawk, not liking how quickly he's piecing everything together. I don't want to keep a secret from my friend, but truthfully, there isn't anything to say. It's not like Sutton and I are together. I'm just helping her out during a rough patch. And sure, I hope she falls for me, and I can convince her to stay for good as my wife and partner, but he doesn't need to know that yet.

Plus, Sutton asked me to keep her living arrangements private for now. I initially encouraged her to talk to Tessa about it, but she's hesitant to give her friend any bad news. As much as I wanted to make her see that Tessa loves her, I know my girl needs time. She needs consistency. Sutton was brave enough to let me into her struggle and to let me help. That has to be enough, at least for a few days.

It's not like I can judge her for wanting to keep a secret. I still haven't told her about the arrest or my time in prison.

"Well, it's just... I mean, there's nothing..." I trail off with a sigh and take a long swig of beer. "Sutton and I have been hanging out," I finally settle on. It's not a total lie. Between my duties to the club and Sutton's design projects, we've been getting to know each other more and more.

"And...?" Hawk asks, dragging out the word.

"And that's all. You know how shy she is. I can't push for anything she's not ready for."

"But you think *you* might be? Ready for a relationship."

"With anyone else, fuck no," I grunt. Women were never on my priorities list. No bitterness or terrible relationship experience, it just never felt right. Or worth it. Women were never the point and certainly never the most important thing in my life. Until my wildflower.

"But Sutton?"

I take a deep breath in, nodding yes on the exhale. "Yeah. She's… it. Everything. It's intense," I admit.

"Sure is," Hawk agrees. I know he's thinking about when he and Tessa first met.

"Not you, too," Blade says from behind me. Hawk and I turn slightly to make room for him. I give him a questioning look. "Found a woman to distract you, just like Hawk here."

"Tessa isn't a distraction," Hawk grumbles. Blade shoots him an incredulous look, which makes Hawk roll his eyes. "Fine. A tiny bit of a distraction. But more than that, she gives me a reason to be better and work harder. I want her to be proud of me."

Blade scoffs while I listen intently. Yes, that's exactly how I feel about Sutton. She makes me want to be a better man. The kind of man worthy of taking care of such a precious gift.

"Yeah, yeah," Blade says dismissively. "Whatever you say."

"What about you, Prez?" Hawk asks. "How is it that Rider spent the last five years locked up, yet he has a better love life than you?"

This startles a chuckle out of me, and a few others join in. Blade flips all of us off, though he's smirking beneath his scowl.

"It's called self-preservation, boys," he says, grabbing a bottle of whiskey from behind the bar. Blade backs away, then turns on his heel, bottle in hand. "Women are crazy," he hollers over his shoulder. "Every last fuckin' one of 'em."

"Can't wait to see the day you fall hard and fast for someone!" Hawk calls out.

"Never gonna happen!" comes Blade's response. He throws a final middle finger in the air as he takes a long draw from the whiskey bottle, then shoves his way to the back room, presumably to start his surveillance shift.

Hawk is still grinning when he turns back to me. "So, when are you seeing her again?"

"Uh…"

"Is it now?" he asks excitedly.

"I mean, after this," I answer cautiously. I'm not lying. I just don't want to mess up and say the wrong thing.

"Well, then go on, man!" he insists. "Seriously, I understand. We'll catch up later."

I'm about to protest, but it's been nearly four hours since I've seen Sutton. I'm feeling restless without her near me. I need to know how she's doing, if she's comfortable, and if she needs anything.

I nod, clapping my friend on the shoulder. "See you tomorrow," I tell him. I don't wait for his reply, which must amuse him.

Hawk's laughter follows me to the parking lot, where I hop on my bike and rev the engine, more than ready to return home to my woman.

CHAPTER FIVE

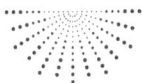

SUTTON

*J*finish polishing the stainless-steel fridge, smiling at my reflection in the freshly cleaned metal. Taking a step back, I look around the kitchen at my handiwork.

The dishes have been cleaned and put away from lunch this afternoon before Rider left for the clubhouse. I cleaned off the counters, organized the fridge and cupboards, swept, mopped, and polished all the appliances. I would have prepped something for dinner, but Rider is a much better chef than I could ever hope to be. I don't want to insult him by making him choke down something I made when we could enjoy whatever he cooks up.

My eye catches on a scuff mark on the stove, and I dash over there, rag and polish in hand.

"There," I say under my breath. "Spotless."

It's not a lot, but I need to start helping out more. There's no way I can ever repay Rider for his kindness, but this is a start. A clean house and yard. I can do that much, at least.

The now familiar sound of Rider's motorcycle gets closer and closer until I feel the vibrations of the powerful engine rumbling through the ground, into the floorboards, and up my legs, landing between my thighs. My core throbs as I listen for Rider's footsteps on the front porch. The closer he gets, the worse the ache blooming in my lower belly.

What the heck is happening to me? Can someone die of being too turned on? The man isn't even in the same room as me, and I'm about to melt into a puddle on the kitchen floor.

The front door swings open, and I rub my sweaty palms on my leggings, excited and anxious to see Rider again. His large frame fills the doorway as he strides inside, his shoulders barely fitting through the entryway.

Just like every time I see Rider, I'm struck by the depth in his espresso-brown eyes. Coupled with his strong brow, straight nose, and dark stubble, the man is so gorgeous it hurts.

When he grins at me, I nearly fall over from swooning so damn hard. Even after knowing Tessa for over a year, I'm still not used to people being happy to see me. And no one has ever looked at me like Rider does.

"Hi, princess," he says, his voice warm and raspy. I love all of his pet names for me. They make me feel special like we're a real couple.

"Hi," I stutter, wringing my hands in front of me. My heart is pumping faster than a hummingbird's wings, the sound deafening in my ears. Anxiety floods in, followed by my parent's voices.

"What did I say about being out here when I get home from work? I don't want to see you until after I've had a drink."

"If I wanted to talk to you, I'd come find you. Until then, shut the hell up."

I try blocking out my father's hurtful words and my mother's shrill tone, focusing on the present. They aren't here. They don't have any power over me anymore.

"Um, so I cleaned while you were away," I start, gesturing

vaguely around the house. "Swept, mopped, vacuumed, dusted. Oh, and I organized the fridge and cupboards in a way that I think will be more efficient for how you use things. Although, now I think about it, maybe that was intrusive. Shoot. I, uh…"

Rider steps closer to me, his eyes never leaving mine. I can't tell if he's upset, annoyed, or some other emotion. I should stop talking since that's what usually set my parents off, but I can't seem to hold back the words pouring from my mouth.

"And the yard!" I exclaim. "You said the garden beds were giving you trouble. I went through and pulled the weeds, then I found a garden hoe and tilled the soil. You'll probably need to mix in some new topsoil, depending on what you want to…"

I trail off, staring at the determined look in Rider's dark eyes. I watch as he steps into my personal space, still unsure if he's going to yell at me or…

His arms are around me in the next second, and I collapse into his comforting embrace.

"You're shaking, little flower," he whispers.

I don't say anything. I just nod. Rider somehow knows what I need. He tucks my head under his chin, and I rest against his chest, my ear pressed against his heart. The steady beat tethers my soul back to reality. Back to him.

Rider trails his fingertips up and down my spine with one hand while the other cups the back of my head, keeping me close. We stay wrapped up in each other for long moments, Rider rocking me back and forth while whispering that I'm safe.

Eventually, my beastly biker peels me off his chest. A wave of vulnerability washes over me, leaving me cold and raw. I feel exposed without Rider touching me in some way. Then he cups my cheek, tilting my face up to meet his.

"Sutton," he starts, his voice hardly above a whisper. It's like he knows I can't handle anything louder right now. "I appreciate all of your hard work today. This place looks incredible, and I can't believe you fixed up the garden beds for me."

I nod, giving him a tentative smile. "I can do more," I murmur, loving his praise. I didn't realize how starved for attention, for human contact I've been, until Rider showed up and gave me both.

"I want you to be safe and happy here, Sutton. You don't have to prove yourself or earn your keep. You give me everything by being here when I get home. You have no idea how much I love seeing you as soon as I walk in from a long day with the Savage Saints."

"Me?" I squeak, tears clogging my throat. I can't believe what he's telling me, but his brown eyes shine with sincerity.

"Yes. You, princess." I shake my head no, but Rider nods his head yes until I grin at him. "Come here. Let's talk."

My stomach sinks, but I follow Rider to the living room. He sits on the couch, and I move to sit next to him, only to be redirected by Rider's hands on my hips. He guides me to sit on his lap, and despite all my insecurities about my weight, I fall against him and curl up on his chest.

Rider adjusts me so my legs are off to one side and holds me close, nuzzling into the side of my neck. I breathe in everything about this moment, wanting to stay here forever.

"Who made you feel unworthy of being loved?" he murmurs against my skin. I can feel his whispered words echo throughout my body.

I shrug at first, but Rider grunts and gives me a stern look before pressing the sweetest, softest kiss to my forehead.

"I guess… I've always felt like a burden. My parents didn't plan on me and didn't want me after I was born."

"I want you," Rider growls as he tightens his hold on me.

Despite the emotion choking me at my childhood memory, I smile at my growly possessive biker. I want him, too. More than anything. I just hope he wants me in the same way.

"I was always in the way," I continue in a hushed tone. "As soon as I could contribute to the family, I started doing chores to try and make my parents… I don't know. Love me? It sounds so dumb now."

"Sutton," Rider whispers. "It's not dumb. You didn't have an example of what a family is supposed to be. You were trying your best to survive."

I nod as the first tear falls. I've never felt so completely seen. "I was trying my best to survive," I repeat, letting that truth sink into the marrow of my bones.

"But you don't need to try so hard anymore," Rider continues. "You're safe here, with me. You can be whoever you want, do whatever makes you happy. I'll be here to support you no matter what."

"How can you possibly mean that?" I ask, blinking away a few tears.

Rider wipes my cheeks, catching my tears on the pads of his thumbs. He cups my face, framing it in his hands as he looks into my eyes. "Remember the first day we met?"

I nod, thinking over how surprised I was that someone as sexy and ripped as Rider would want to introduce himself to me.

"I was a nervous wreck."

"What?" I gasp, furrowing my brow. "Why?"

"Why?" he echoes. "Because you're the most gorgeous, precious woman I've ever seen. Because I'm not always great with communicating, but I couldn't *not* talk to you, even if I knew it was going to end in disaster." I blink at him a few times, seeing him in a new light. "I've been at the clubhouse every damn day since, hoping to get a glimpse of your teal eyes and silky black hair. I've lived off your smiles for weeks, but I never imagined I'd be lucky enough to hold you, let alone take care of you."

"Lucky enough... to take care of... me," I repeat, the words not making sense.

"Yes," he confirms. "And one day, that won't be shocking to hear. One day, you'll trust that all I want is your happiness."

"Rider, I don't even know what to say," I breathe, leaning forward to rest my forehead on his.

Rider slides his hands from my cheeks down to my neck, resting his hands lightly there. "You could start by telling me why I found you sleeping in your car."

I nod, knowing I can't put this conversation off any longer.

CHAPTER SIX

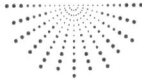

RIDER

*S*utton straightens in my lap, tucking her hair behind her ear before taking a deep breath. I keep one arm around the small of her back, holding her close, while the other lightly caresses her legs stretched out over me.

This woman is killing me with her tears and tender, bruised heart. I knew my Sutton didn't have much confidence in herself, but seeing her scramble to tell me all of the things she did while I was away broke me. She wants to be loved so damn bad, but doesn't she know I already do?

"My parents always told me we didn't have any other family," Sutton starts, her voice barely above a whisper. "Both of their parents had died, and no one had siblings or grandparents. It was just us."

I nod, unsure where this is going but relieved she's finally giving me another piece of her story.

"But last year," she continues, "I got a very official-looking letter telling me someone left me something in their will. A big something that needed to be discussed in person. Turns out, my dad's mom, my grandma, had been alive this whole time. I'm still not sure why they didn't tell me about her. Maybe I could have lived with my grandma growing up, you know? If they didn't want me, maybe my grandma would. I don't know."

I lean forward, pressing my lips to her forehead as she shrugs. I hate that she has no idea how valuable she is, how bright, beautiful, and caring her soul is. I'm more than happy to be the one to show her, to build her up and remind her how incredible she is for surviving.

"Anyway, my grandma lived here in this town for twenty years, I guess. She left me her entire house and everything in it. Crazy, right? I never met her, never knew a single thing about her, and suddenly, I owned her home. It was my chance to move, to change, to *exist*. I don't think I felt like a real person until I walked into my grandma's house. Does that make any sense?"

"Yeah," I say softly as I trace patterns on the palm of her open hand. I ache for everything she's been through, but I know there's more.

"I met Tessa the first weekend I was in town to sign the papers. She was so open and friendly, so kind and welcoming, even to me. She moved in with me shortly after, and things were going great. Tessa met Hawk at just the right time, and I'm so thankful she practically moved in with him after a week."

Sutton pauses, and I can feel her muscles tense and tighten as she thinks about what she's going to tell me next. I cover her hands with one of mine, squeezing gently to encourage her to continue.

"I started getting calls from the estate lawyer saying my parents were trying to contest the will. At first, the lawyer assured me they had no case. The will was cut and dry, and never mentioned my father or mother once. My dad kept hounding the lawyer, and eventually got his own legal team to come in and dismantle my grandma's will, rearranging it so *he* is the rightful owner of the house."

"Fucker," I spit out, startling Sutton. I'm about to apologize, but then she nods, a tiny smile playing at the corner of her lips.

"Yeah, I feel the same way. Especially since he won in the end and immediately evicted me. Not even a week later, the house was sold to the highest bidder, thus making me homeless and shit out of luck," she finishes.

My girl deflates in my arms, and I gather her up, cradling her against my chest. "Thank you for trusting me," I murmur.

What I really want to do is demand her father's name and address so I can wrap my hand around his throat and choke him until he pisses his pants. How the hell could a parent do that to their child? Take away her home, knowing she has nothing and nowhere to go? I shove those thoughts aside before I get too worked up. I can deal with that low life later.

"Thank you for… everything," she says with a sigh, snuggling even closer. "For listening to me, for taking me in, for making me feel…"

I perk up at her words, curious how I make my little flower feel. Looking down at her, I see her cheeks glow with the most adorable shade of pink.

"How do I make you feel, Sutton?" I ask, brushing my lips across her temple and pressing a kiss there. Her eyes flutter closed as she leans into my touch.

"Like I'm, I don't know. Like I'm special," she whispers.

"You are. What else?"

"You make me feel… important. Like my thoughts matter."

"They do, princess. What else?"

"You make me feel safe. I feel like I can, I don't know, explore more of who I am. More of who I want to be."

"And who do you want to be, little flower?" I rasp the

words against the sensitive skin of her neck, tickling her with my stubble. Her breath catches in her throat, and my sexy little vixen wiggles her hips, causing me to bite back a groan.

"I…"

My teeth catch on the tender flesh below her ear and lick away the sting, placing a kiss there.

"I-I…" my girl stutters, her back arching and body crying out for more of my touch.

"Tell me," I demand.

"I want to be yours," she finishes, her words catching me by surprise.

"Yeah?" I grunt. She nods. "Good. Cuz that's exactly what you are."

Her pink cheeks turn crimson, but her eyes never leave mine. "How is it possible to want you this much? After not even knowing you that long?"

"Time doesn't matter when you've found your person."

"And I'm your person?"

"Damn right, you are. And I'm yours," I inform her. She grins, and God, I don't know if I can hold off much longer.

"Is that so?"

"Yes," I growl. "Need me to prove our connection, Sutton?" I murmur into the shell of her ear before trailing my lips down her neck. I'm playing a dangerous game. Every second my lips are on her flesh, I want more, more, *more*.

She nods, and I grunt in approval, though I pull myself away at the last second. "Need your words, princess. Tell me what you want."

Sutton nods again, and I lift an eyebrow at her. She rolls her eyes, that little sassy spark making my dick impossibly harder. "I want… I want everything," she says tentatively. "I'm just, um, a little lost here."

"Lost?"

Sutton sighs, then rubs her lips together as if deciding what to say next. "Er, maybe *inexperienced* is a better word."

It takes me a second to realize what she's saying. "Princess, are you telling me I'll be your first?" I choke out. She nods, but that's not good enough for me. "Words," I grunt, nearly feral at the thought. Never thought I'd care about that shit, but when it comes to Sutton... goddamn right I'm possessive. I'm glad I'm the first person to see her like this. Touch her like this. I don't deserve this gift, but I'm taking it anyway.

"Yes, okay?" she says rather forcefully. "I've never done anything, even kissing, so I guess the joke's on you if you thought I'd be better or more mature or—"

I curl my fingers around the back of her neck and pull my angel closer, sealing my lips over hers. Fire shoots down my spine when I get my first taste, and I already know I'll never get enough. Sutton gasps, opening up for me in invitation.

Sliding my tongue between her juicy lips, I groan and let my other hand wander down her throat and chest until I'm squeezing her big, round breast. I find her nipple and brush my thumb over the hard little peak.

I pull Sutton into my lap so she's straddling me, my hands immediately gripping her hips and helping her rock against my aching cock.

"Rider," she breathes, tipping her head back to break our kiss.

I attach my lips to her exposed neck, sucking my mark on her. I don't give a single fuck about being a caveman around my woman. Soon, I hope to have my baby in her belly and my ring on her finger.

"Yes, sweetheart?"

"M-More..."

I grunt, then lift her, sliding my hands around to her ass and holding her close as I stomp to the bathroom. When I set

Sutton down, she looks up at me in confusion. Despite my raging dick and overwhelming lust, I lean down and kiss the tip of her nose.

"Let me explore you," I tell her, stripping off her shirt, followed by her bra. Bending forward, I lick one nipple, then suck on the other, grinning when my girl whimpers for me. "The shower will relax you, and then we can talk about what you want to do next."

Do I want to toss Sutton down on my bed and rut into her savagely? Fuck yes. But not for her first time. She deserves so much better. I don't have roses and champagne, but I can give my woman something else. An orgasm or five sounds like a good trade-off.

I make quick work of my clothing after helping Sutton out of her pants and little white panties. As soon as we step in the shower, I circle Sutton's round hips and back her into the shower wall, kissing the breath from her lungs. She wiggles against me, gasping when my cock rubs her hip.

"All for you, Sutton," I rasp, grinding my solid length against her soft skin.

I grunt and pin her to the wall, ravishing her mouth before kissing my way down her body. I lick her neck, suck on her collarbone, bite her nipples, and kiss the soft skin underneath her breasts. I lick down her tummy, kneeling before her, bowing before my queen.

I grab her hips and guide one leg over my shoulder, kissing the inside of her thigh. "Gonna lick this little pussy right up," I grunt. Brushing my lips up her inner thigh, I grip Sutton's hips, pinning her in place as she writhes with antici-pation. "I've got you, Sutton," I murmur before parting her pussy lips and dragging my tongue over her swollen, sensi-tive clit.

"Ohhhh! Oh, my *god*, Rider," she moans.

Oh my god is right. Her juicy little cunt is sweet and musky, her pink lips glistening with need.

I dip my tongue in her hole and massage the walls of her tight channel. Then, I flatten my tongue and drag it up her slit until I get to the bundle of nerves that controls her pleasure.

I feel her tense underneath me. She's close. I lick her up and down, landing on her clit. Sucking it in my mouth, she begins to shake in my hands. I bite down softly, and Sutton erupts in my mouth, gushing her release, trembling, and mumbling my name over and over.

I feel like the king of the fucking world, knowing I gave her that pleasure. I lick her through her orgasm until she pushes my head away, too sensitive from all the attention.

"Sorry," I grunt. "You're so damn delicious." I stand and pull her in my arms, kissing her soundly.

Sutton pulls away from me, a wicked glint in her ethereal eyes.

"You look like you have some very dirty thoughts for such a sweet angel," I tease, kissing the side of her neck.

Sutton nods and nibbles on her bottom lip. "I do. Would you like me to show you?"

Fuck. Yes.

CHAPTER SEVEN

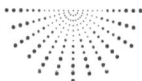

SUTTON

"*F*uck," he mutters under his breath before crashing his lips down on mine once more.

Something I said flipped a switch in my usually sweet and gentle giant. Rider is all beast as his tongue invades my mouth, demanding me to feel the strength and urgency behind his need for me. I'm right there with him. No one has ever made me feel the way Rider does. Not just physically but emotionally. I'm all wrapped up in Rider, and I know he's as caught up as I am.

"Fuck," he says again, sounding almost tortured as he buries his face into my neck, licking and kissing me there.

The next thing I know, he has me in his arms, carrying me across the hall to his bedroom. We're naked and dripping wet, but none of that matters.

Rider slides me down his body, setting me at the foot of his bed. He reluctantly pulls his mouth from mine. I automatically follow him, seeking more of his lips, taste, and tongue. He brings his hands up, cupping the sides of my neck and resting his forehead on mine. Both of us are breathing heavily, sharing the same air, and savoring the tension crackling between us.

"Be very sure you want this, my beautiful girl. Once I have you, I'm not letting you go."

"Same," I breathe before tilting my head and kissing him again. "Just tell me what to do. I… I don't know how to do any of this," I confess.

"Touch me," he groans. "Touch me everywhere. Anywhere. Just please… I need you to touch me right fucking now."

My hands find his torso, my fingertips gliding along the packed muscles of his abs and chest. A shiver runs through him as he flexes and tenses beneath my touch. I trace the swirling ink across his flesh, followed by my lips, pressing kisses to his heated skin.

"You're too good to me," he murmurs, taking my lips once again.

"Oh, god," I moan as his hands cover my breasts, kneading my soft flesh and plucking my nipples. I bow my back and thrust my chest further into his hands.

He slowly trails his fingertips down my torso, feeling every inch of my skin along the way. I don't have time to feel self-conscious about the extra weight around my hips and belly. Not when Rider is growling softly and massaging everywhere he can reach.

I tilt my head back and surrender to his touch, gasping when his lips connect with the sensitive skin of my neck. He blazes a trail of kisses over my collarbone and down my chest, sucking on one nipple and then the other.

My pussy clenches, and more of my arousal leaks out. I don't know how he knows, but Rider growls, almost like he can *smell* how turned on I am. He runs his hands back up my body, resting them on my shoulders and shoving me lightly. I giggle when my back hits the mattress, then gasp as Rider kneels before me.

He grips my knees and spreads my legs apart, staring right into my throbbing core.

"Again?" I gasp, unable to keep my hips from lifting and pressing my center closer to him.

Rider looks up from between my thighs, his brown eyes locking on mine. *God,* I swear I could come again if he keeps looking at me like that. "Better get used to it," he says with a smirk.

"Do you... Do you like doing that? T-tasting m-me?" I stutter. I know I shouldn't ask many questions, but I can't help it. I want to know if he's as crazy about me as I am about him.

Rider grins, a hint of mischievousness and darkness behind his gaze. "Yes, Sutton. I like doing that to you very much. You want to please me, don't you, sweetheart?"

"More than anything," I whisper, opening my legs wider for him, offering myself up to let him do whatever he wants to me.

He growls and guides my legs over his shoulders. Slowly, slowly, he drags his tongue through my folds. When he reaches my clit, Rider stops licking, merely flexing his tongue there, rolling it like a wave as pleasure breaks over my body.

I writhe under him as he licks and nips at my pussy, devouring me like he said he would. Rider reaches my entrance, circling his tongue around my throbbing opening before dipping it inside. We groan as I clench around him. He sips from my center, drinking my juices and massaging the walls of my tight channel.

I buck my hips, but Rider spreads one large hand over my stomach, stilling my motions and creating a delicious pressure in my core. His other hand slides underneath me, gripping my ass in a punishing hold. He has me locked in place, forcing me to feel every teasing lick, every slow stroke, every light scrape of his teeth over my sensitive bundle of nerves.

My back shoots off the bed as pleasure rockets through me. He slides his hands down to my hips, pinning me to the bed and growling into my pussy. I teeter on the edge, curling my toes, fisting his hair, and crying out.

I scream his name and thrash as a brutal orgasm rips through me. I feel unhinged, fucking his face like a wild animal, but he holds me in place, licking me clean.

"Goddamn," he grunts, as out of breath as I am. He stands, his hand wrapping around his massive dick. It's intimidatingly large, much like the rest of him. "Touch yourself," he grits.

"W-What?" I whisper.

Rider groans and fists his cock, pumping his hand up and down. "Spread those legs, pretty girl, and play with your cunt. Fuck, do it now."

My body responds to his command before my brain can catch up. I slide my hand down my torso and dip my fingers into my throbbing pussy, circling my clit.

"Jesus Christ, you're perfect. So beautiful. My sweet, sexy girl."

My chest swells with pride at his praise, and I feel warm liquid spill over my fingers. "I need you," I whimper, blurring my fingers over my bundle of nerves. My other hand moves to my breast, pinching my nipple like Rider did. I squeeze my eyes shut and bow my back off the bed, nearly coming undone again. Knowing he's watching me is so freaking hot, even more so when he swears under his breath like he's barely hanging on too.

"Enough," he grits out. Rider swats my hand away from my center, replacing it with his. "So hot and wet for me.

Gonna make this pussy feel so good, Sutton. Promise to take care of you. Do you trust me?"

"Always."

Rider climbs onto the bed, scooting me up before settling between my thighs. I feel his thickness slide up and down my cunt, coating himself in my cream and tapping the head of his cock against my sensitive clit.

"I'm the first one to see you like this, and I'm sure as hell going to be the last," he murmurs, taking my lips in a searing kiss. "Ready to be mine?" Rider whispers into my lips.

"So ready," I nod, kissing him again.

The head of his cock nudges my entrance, and then he thrusts his hips, filling me up in one long stroke. I cry out and cling to him as he stretches me and then holds still, buried inside me.

"I'm sorry, sweet girl. It won't hurt after this. I'll make it up to you, I promise," he whispers into the shell of my ear before placing soft kisses up and down my neck. He slides his hand between us, the rough pad of his thumb circling my clit. I let out a shuddering breath as my pussy pulses around him. "Fuck, you feel so good," he grits out.

"We fit," I murmur, wiggling my hips. "I know it's supposed to hurt, but it just feels…" I gasp when he pinches my clit, my core clenching and trying to suck him further inside.

"How does it feel?" Rider asks, starting to move inside me with shallow thrusts.

"Perfect. It feels perfect."

He growls in approval and pulls out almost all the way before snapping his hips and wedging his thick dick even deeper inside me.

"Fuck me back, baby," he grits, hitting the end of me with each stroke.

I plant my feet on the mattress and spread my legs, lifting my hips and meeting him thrust for thrust. Rider lets out a tortured groan and kisses down my neck and chest, swirling his tongue over one nipple and then the other.

We get lost in our rhythm, stroke after stroke, kiss after kiss, again and again, until we're both sweating and shaking. I'm almost there, almost to my breaking point. My sopping wet pussy grips his cock, trying to keep him inside me, needing that closeness.

Rider senses my urgent need and grinds down, hitting me so, *so* deep. "Yes! Oh, God, there, *right there*, right…" I suck in a breath and hold it as my muscles tense and lock up, preparing for my release.

All at once, my orgasm seizes my body, making me convulse underneath him and claw at his back. I come around his cock, each spasm of my pussy setting off another wave of bliss. Rider fucks me through it, never giving me a chance to recover as he pounds into me.

"Again," he demands, hooking a hand under my left knee and bringing it up so he can change the angle. His dick scrapes along my front wall with each thrust, hitting a super sensitive spot.

I gasp for air as another orgasm ravishes my body, tearing a guttural scream from the very depths of me.

"R-Ri-Ri-der…" I stutter, twisting and trembling as he hammers into me and wrings out every drop of pleasure from my bones.

He grunts in response, fucking me so hard, so good, I feel like I'm going to explode into a million pieces. My limbs shake and then go numb, but Rider doesn't let up. He thrusts into me over and over, rutting into me and seeking his end.

I can hardly move, my body is completely spent and blissed out, but I manage to clench my pussy around him each time he pulls out. His hips jerk and he shoves his cock so far into me I come again, taking him with me over the edge.

Rider snarls into the side of my neck as his release spills into my spasming cunt. He fills me with his hot, sticky cum, so much so it leaks out of me, trickling over my sensitive skin and making me moan.

He collapses on top of me, his sweat mingling with mine as we come back down. I comb my fingers through his damp hair and rub my cheek against his. This is the most perfect moment of my life.

"Mine too," Rider whispers.

I must have said that last part out loud. I smile at his mumbled agreement, loving that I wore him out as much as he did me.

We stay wrapped up in each other for long moments, our racing hearts eventually slowing down and finding the same rhythm. And then my stomach growls obnoxiously, breaking through the romantic afterglow.

I'm about to apologize profusely and jump out the nearest window, but Rider chuckles and tickles my belly. "Need some food, little flower?" he asks, though he already knows the answer. "I've been slacking in my duties. Please forgive me."

"I suppose I'll let it slip this time," I tell him, a playful grin on my lips. "But only because you gave me so many orgasms, I don't think I can move. You'll have to hand feed me and tuck me in."

"Deal." Rider kisses me on the forehead and then untangles himself from me, hopping out of bed before I realize what's happening.

"I was kidding!" I insist.

"I wasn't." Rider gives me the sexiest little grin, and I can't help but return it. "Stay here. Dinner in bed for the princess, coming right up."

I can't keep the cheesy smile off my face as I watch my beastly biker throw on a pair of joggers and race out of the room toward the kitchen. Yeah, a girl could get used to this kind of life.

CHAPTER EIGHT

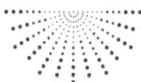

RIDER

I stir awake in the early hours of the morning, squinting against the orange glow from the rising sun streaming through the window. Sutton's floral scent wraps around me, and I turn to see my goddess on her back, the sheet pulled down and exposing her breasts.

Groaning, I brush my knuckles over her nipples, reveling in the pebbled peaks and the soft flesh surrounding them. My dick is solid granite, and when Sutton squeezes her thighs together while letting out a breathy moan, I know she's as desperate for another hit as I am.

Without wasting another second, I lean down and suck on her breast, teasing her with little bites and soft licks. Sutton moans softly and bows her back, offering herself up to me, even in her sleep.

I switch to her other breast, giving it the same attention. I can fucking feel her heart pounding in her chest. I swear I smell her getting wet for me. The thought makes me groan as I play with her other nipple. Each swipe of my tongue elicits a breathy moan, making my dick ache and leak precum.

Fuck, I want to be inside her tight little pussy, but I'll go at her pace.

"Rider?" Sutton's confused, sexy little voice fills the room. She whimpers for me as I pinch one nipple and bite down on the other. "*Yes*! Oh, God, yes…"

I look up at her, grunting with satisfaction when I see her eyes closed and her face scrunched up in pure pleasure. Sutton's lips part as she sucks down air. She rocks her hips, rubbing her wet heat against me. I don't think she's even aware she's doing it.

"You like when I play with your tits?"

"Mmhm," she moans, finally opening her eyes.

I bite the inside of my cheek to keep from coming. Her eyes are deep and dark, glazed over with lust.

She licks her lips and winds her fingers through my hair, pulling me toward her. "I think I'll like anything you do to me," she whispers before sealing her lips over mine.

Sutton dominates this kiss, taking what she needs from me. Her tongue tangles with mine as I swallow her passion and greedy little moans. She pulls back, gasping for air. I nuzzle into the side of her neck, breathing in her sweet, wildflower scent. I can't help but lick her skin, wanting her taste on my tongue.

"Rider," Sutton breathes out. "I need you. Please?"

"Need me to do what, baby?" I trail kisses down her neck before sucking on the sensitive spot beneath her ear.

"I-I ache for you. I feel so empty."

"Need me to fill you up?" I ask, my lips brushing up against the shell of her ear.

"Yes, I need it. Need your cock."

I growl and pin her to the mattress, devouring her sweet, filthy mouth. "Jesus, woman," I grunt before kissing her again.

Sutton wiggles beneath me and spreads her legs wide,

letting me settle between them. My heavy cock glides through her folds, making us both groan.

She clutches my biceps, digging her nails into my skin as I suck on her pulse point. "R-Rider…" she whimpers. "Don't tease me."

The last thread of my tentative sanity snaps, and I sink into her tight, wet little cunt one inch at a time, feeling her pulse around my thickness.

"More," Sutton whispers, wrapping her legs around my hips. "Deeper. I want it all."

"Fuck," I growl, pulling out and slamming my dick back inside. She feels so damn good, so warm and wet.

Sutton inhales sharply and then exhales a breathy moan. Her pussy ripples around me, sucking me in deeper, deeper, so fucking deep I see stars behind my eyes. I grit my teeth, hanging on to my orgasm by a thread. Sutton clings to me as I rock in and out of her. My thrusts become more forceful, and my needy girl loves it. She plants her feet on the bed and lifts her hips, meeting me brutal thrust for brutal thrust.

I scrape my cock along her front wall, searching for that spot…

"Fuck!" Sutton cries out as she spasms around me, her muscles flexing and releasing, squeezing my dick so damn tight as she comes around me like a goddess.

I fucking lose all control.

I hammer into her, hitting her G-spot over and over, grunting as I fuck her right through her first orgasm and into another. Sutton screams my name and claws at my back, tearing up my skin. It hurts so damn good.

"Again," I growl, burying my head into the side of her neck. I know I should slow down, but the way my woman is moaning and writhing beneath me, I don't think she minds.

My spine tingles with the first signs of my orgasm. My muscles flex and tense as I try to shove it back down. I'm not ready for this to end yet. White hot bliss courses through me, but I need her to come again before I give up the fight.

I sit back on my heels and pull her legs up to rest them against my chest, changing the angle. Her already tight pussy squeezes my cock like a vise, pulling a growl from somewhere deep in my chest as I thrust harder, faster, deeper inside her. Sutton's glazed-over eyes roll to the back of her head and her mouth hangs open, rewarding my rough strokes with greedy little whimpers as I bring us closer and closer to our climax.

"Oh, God. I think I'm..."

"Yes, baby. That's right. Come for me. I want to feel you come all over my hard fucking cock."

Her body responds to me immediately, that sweet pussy massaging me as I lean in for another kiss. She arches her back, and I know she's close. Just a little more. Fuck, I'm going to come, but I need her to get there first.

"Yes," she whispers. "Yes, yes, yes..."

"Who does this pussy belong to?" I snarl, unable to hold back the beast inside me.

"You," she cries out.

"Say my fucking name, Sutton. Say my name when you come for me."

"Rider! Fuck, Rider, Rider, R—"

I feel her climax as it rushes through her, overwhelming her curvy body as she clamps down on my thick dick over and over. I pound into her spasming cunt, losing a little more of myself with each rough stroke until I'm nothing more than a wild animal rutting inside my mate.

Sutton tenses for a heartbeat then claws my chest as a raw scream is ripped from her throat. I roar her name as we shatter together, our old selves breaking apart, making way for the new life we're going to build together.

I reluctantly pull out of my woman and collapse beside

her, draping her limp, sweaty body over mine. Her heart slams against her chest as she gasps for air. I rub her back in calming circles, letting her know she's safe with me, even in this vulnerable state.

My beautiful girl finally looks up at me, her teal eyes filled with satisfaction and awe. Yeah, I'm going to put that look on her face every chance I get.

"Holy shit," she finally says, making me chuckle.

I tuck some of her hair behind her ear, drawing her up for a kiss. "My thought exactly," I whisper before pressing my lips against her forehead and breathing her in.

Sutton hums contentedly and snuggles closer to me. I tuck her head under my chin and continue to rub her back.

"When did you join Savage Saints?" Sutton asks quietly after a few moments of comfortable silence.

"Right after college."

Sutton perks her head up, her eyes bright with curiosity as she props herself up on my chest. "You went to college?"

"Surprised?" I ask, lifting an eyebrow at my adorable princess.

"What was your major?"

"Business financing."

Her eyebrows disappear into her hairline while her teal eyes grow wide with shock. "Seriously?!"

"I dropped out after a month and haven't stepped foot on a college campus since," I tell her with a grin.

Sutton laughs, her entire body shaking with joy. "Now *that* sounds more like it," she says between giggles.

"My mom wanted me to go to college, so I gave it a shot. Signed up for classes, bought the books, even tried making a few friends in the dorm. It was miserable, and each day felt like ten years. I couldn't imagine doing that for another four years, only to graduate and get an equally awful job for the next fifty years."

Sutton nods, settling back on my chest and curling up like a cat. She even purrs like one as I continue rubbing her back and combing my fingers through her hair.

"Initially, Ma wasn't happy about my decision, but she agreed I hadn't been the same since going to school. I told her I would still make her proud, even if it wasn't with a college degree."

"Did she approve of the MC?"

I chuckle, thinking back to our conversation about me being a prospect for the Savage Saints. "Not at first. The night I told her, she grabbed her trusty wooden spoon and threatened to beat some sense into me. Of course, even back then, I was double her size, so it was an empty threat. Still, she didn't like the idea of her son being a *thug*. Her words, not mine."

"But she came around to the idea?"

I nod. "Once she saw how loyal the club was and the good we do for the community, Ma eventually gave me her blessing. She even came with me to the clubhouse on occasion to throw back a few beers." My cheeks are sore from smiling so wide. "Once she accepted that I was a Savage Saint for life, my mom was supportive and along for the ride."

"I wish I could have met her," Sutton whispers.

"Me, too." I swallow past the unexpected emotion in my throat. "She would have loved you." I can feel my girl smiling into the side of my neck, and I know it means a lot to her to have my mother's approval. She's the sweetest fucking woman in the world, and it pisses me off that her parents ever made her feel like a burden.

"How did she... Never mind." Sutton starts and stops her question, but I know what she was going to ask.

"Cancer," I choke out before clearing my throat. "By the time we caught it, there weren't many options other than trying to make her comfortable in the end. I wish I could have... If I was there when..."

I trail off, bringing my free hand to my eyes and rubbing them, trying to wipe away the pesky moisture that seems to be gathering there.

"We don't have to talk about it," Sutton murmurs, pressing the softest kiss to my cheek.

I want to tell her everything. I want Sutton to know my greatest failure in life was not being there for my mom during her final days. She was my biggest supporter, and she always believed that I was wrongfully put in prison. Still, being trapped in a cage while my mom wasted away into nothing is a special kind of hell and shame.

The words are on the tip of my tongue, but I can't seem to put my voice behind them. Sutton needs to know I spent the last five years behind bars. I can't hide it forever. I don't want to, yet every time I think about telling her, I picture the hurt and betrayal in her eyes. I've waited too long now, and it's going to be a whole thing once I finally confess what happened.

"I want to," I start. "I just... I need some time." *Coward*, I growl at myself.

"Of course. No pressure," my girl says soothingly. Of course, she's understanding and perfect. Which only makes me feel like more of an ass.

My phone rings, making us jump. I groan while Sutton giggles, and I can't help but lean forward and kiss the tip of her nose.

"The real world is calling," I whisper. "Want me to tell whoever it is to fuck off?"

Sutton laughs but shakes her head no. "It's okay. I'm almost done with this design project, and I'd like to finish today. So go ahead and do your thing."

Another ring from my annoying phone, and I grunt, rolling my eyes. "Fiiiine," I huff dramatically.

I answer the call while Sutton climbs out of bed and heads toward the bathroom. Blade is rattling off my mission for the day, and I calculate how long I think it will take before I can reasonably make it back home to my woman.

"Rider, you got it?" Blade snaps.

"Yeah, Prez. See you at the clubhouse in fifteen."

The sooner I get my club duties out of the way, the sooner I can have Sutton back in my arms.

CHAPTER NINE

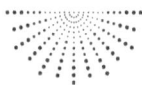

SUTTON

I finished my design project a few hours ago and emailed the files to my client for approval. Hopefully, there won't be any major edits needed, and I can get the last payment soon. It won't be enough to pay Rider back for everything he's done for me these last few days, but it's a start.

Rider said he'd be back before dinner, but it's almost six, and I still haven't heard anything from him. I get up from my spot on the couch and pace in front of the window overlooking the yard and driveway, pushing down thoughts of him abandoning me after our night and morning together.

He's not that kind of guy. If Rider is late, he has a good reason.

Plus, he can't exactly abandon me while I'm staying at his house. He'll have to come back eventually.

After a few more minutes of stress-pacing, I turn my attention to the living room and kitchen, picking things up here and there to keep myself busy. When seven-thirty comes and goes, my anxiety finally gets the best of me.

I'm not sure who to contact. I have Rider's number, of

course, but he hasn't answered my calls or texts all afternoon. I could ask Tessa to ask Hawk if he knows where Rider is, but then I would have to explain why I need to contact him, which would lead to me telling her about the house, and I just... I just don't have it in me right now.

Guilt twists my gut into a pretzel. I feel like a terrible friend for keeping something like this from my bestie, but I'm trying to protect her. That's how I'm justifying it, at least.

The only other thing I can think of is to go to the Savage Saints clubhouse and see if he's there. If not, maybe someone there will have information.

Wiping my sweaty palms on my jeans, I take a deep breath and go over the plan again in my mind. A few months ago, the thought of showing up at a biker bar alone would have terrified me. I'm still anxious, but visiting Tessa since she started working there as a bartender has helped. She's been working fewer hours lately, and I know she doesn't have a shift tonight, which is for the best.

Gathering up my purse, phone, and keys, I head out the front door and make my way to the Savage Saints clubhouse. Gravel crunches under my tires as I pull into the parking lot and come to a stop, my heart hammering against my ribcage.

I inhale deeply, reminding myself that I'm safe. This isn't about me right now. I need to find Rider and make sure he's okay. What if something happened to him while he was out on club business? Rider told me he can't give any specifics, but I'm not stupid. I know the Savage Saints are involved in dangerous endeavors.

That's all the motivation I need to kick open my car door and walk up to the clubhouse. I slip inside, inching along the wall until I reach my familiar spot in the corner of the bar top. I don't know that I'll ever truly be comfortable in a room filled with so many hulking men, but I've been doing better ever since Rider came into my life.

Now, I feel more vulnerable than ever. I'm lost without Rider, unsure of who to talk to or what to say. Luckily, no one seems to notice me. I fade into the background, observing the people around me as they throw back beers and joke around with their MC brothers.

Maybe Rider lost track of time while hanging out with his friends. That would make sense. I've taken up most of his afternoons and evenings this week, and I'm sure Rider wants some time with other people. I can't be selfish with him.

Deep down, though, I know he's not here. I can't feel his warmth. Plus, a part of me knows Rider would choose me over anyone here. As crazy as it is, he's nearly convinced me I'm the most important person in his life.

Still, I allow myself this tiny scrap of hope for a moment. Scanning the crowd, I don't see my Rider's kind brown eyes or hear his deep timbre.

"The fuck?" someone shouts.

Every muscle in my body tenses, and I barely hold back a whimper. Tessa isn't here to check on me, and Rider isn't here to reassure me with his steady gaze, but I'm able to calm myself down with a few deep breaths.

"How the hell… Yeah, yeah, of course. You know we have your back, Rider."

My ears perk up, and I hop out of my seat, drawn toward the sound of his name. Peering around a table of bikers, I see Blade, the President of Savage Saints. I haven't met him in person, but I know him from hanging around the clubhouse. The man is covered in tattoos, his dark olive skin barely visible through all the ink.

Blade has his phone to his ear, and he's gripping it so hard his hand is shaking. "Goddamn right, we're gonna get you outta there. We're not letting this happen again, brother. Hang tight, and don't lose faith."

Blade hangs up and runs a hand down his face, rolling his

massive shoulders as he sighs. All eyes are on him, and the clubhouse goes eerily silent as every single soul waits for whatever bombshell the prez is about to drop.

"Church!" he snarls as his head snaps up. "Fuckin' cops got Rider on some bullshit drug charges. Need all hands on deck to ensure he doesn't spend another five years in prison."

Men shout in outrage around the room as chairs scrape against the concrete floor. The bar empties as most of the patrons head to the back where church is held. I float toward the exit, everything in me numb as I climb into my car and buckle my seatbelt.

It isn't until I start the engine that everything comes crashing down.

Drug charges. Prison. Five years. Again.

It's that last one that sends me headfirst into a panic attack.

Blade said *another five years*, as in Rider *already* spent five years in prison? For drug charges? Something else? Something *worse*?

My breathing grows shallow, and for a moment, I think I might be sick to my stomach. Why didn't he tell me? Was he going to keep this from me forever?

Another thought flashes through my mind. Maybe he didn't tell me because he wasn't planning on having me around long enough for it to matter.

Rider said I was his. He held me so tenderly after consuming me, body and soul. Was that all fake? It couldn't be. Right?

God, I have no idea. I have nothing to compare this to. No past relationship or any kind of experience whatsoever. Was everything a lie?

I don't even realize I'm crying until tears drip down my chin and tickle my neck before soaking my shirt collar. My throat swells and nearly closes, each breath painful as it saws in and out of my lungs.

I wrap my shaking hands around the steering wheel, gripping the smooth surface tighter and tighter until my fingers cramp and my knuckles pop. It's still not enough. With no more tears left, I heave a dry sob, fearing I may crumble apart completely.

It *hurts.* Everything hurts. The agony of Rider's betrayal cuts me through and through until I'm flayed wide open.

I finally loosen my grip on the steering wheel and dig through my purse until I find my phone. With trembling hands, I look up the local women's shelter and call, asking about a bed.

Fifteen minutes later, I'm checked in and curled up on my side in the last available bed for the night. Pulling the thin blanket over my shoulders, I block everything out and let sleep drag me under. Maybe then I'll get some peace. When I wake up, I'll have a plan. I just need to sleep…

"Hey," comes a groggy female voice. "Wake up, girlie," the person says, a little sharper this time. I must have fallen asleep, though I have no idea how long I've been out. "Your phone keeps ringing. Answer it or shut the damn thing off."

Right on cue, my phone chirps with an incoming call. "Sorry," I mumble as I grab it from my purse. Tessa's name flashes across the screen, and I consider ignoring the call. One final ring, and I decide to answer. It's time to tell my friend what's been going on. It's not like things can get much worse.

"Tessa," I say once I've stepped out of the room with the other women staying here for the evening.

"Oh, my god, Sutton. Where are you? Some things went down at the club, and Rider and I went to find you at the house, but–"

"I know," I whisper, my shoulders heavy with shame.

"What happened? There's a giant sign out front saying the house is sold."

"Yeah, I, uh–"

"Where have you been staying?"

"Um, I…" My voice cracks, and I lean against the wall to support myself. My knees give out, and I slide down the wall, curling up into a ball on the floor as tears overwhelm me once more.

"Oh, Sutton," Tessa exclaims, her voice filled with worry. "Just tell me where you are. I'll come to get you. Please, let me help."

"I… I'm sorry," I squeak.

"Sutton, I love you. I want to help. Please tell me where you are."

"I've been staying with Rider, but I'm at the women's shelter on Walter Road right now."

I expect Tessa to ask about Rider and why I didn't say anything about him, but she thanks me and says she'll be here soon. Every limb feels like a lead weight, but I drag my weary bones and soul back into the room to gather my things, trying to figure out how to tell Tessa everything that's happened the last few weeks.

CHAPTER TEN

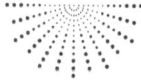

RIDER

I can't fucking believe it.

I stare down at my hands, grimacing when I see ink stains on the tips of my thumbs from when they brought me in and booked me last night. Balling my hands into fists, I push off the hard metal bench in the holding cell and resume pacing from one wall to the other. It takes me all of four steps before I have to turn around again.

Two blocks from home. I was two fucking blocks away from Sutton when Officer Pete Towe pulled me over. He claimed I was speeding, which is bullshit. Not saying I haven't had my fair share of joy rides that got the speedometer up in the triple digits. Last night, however, I was simply on my way home, going the speed limit.

I was prepared to bite the bullet and pay the damn ticket to get Pete out of my hair, not thinking much of it. The police give us Savage Saints more shit than we deserve and always try to pin ridiculous petty traffic violations on us when we're riding in town. Usually, I'd fight it, but I didn't want to make a scene. The only thing on my mind was getting home so I could finally tell Sutton everything.

What a fucking idiot I turned out to be.

I knew the cops here were dirtier than the toilet in the corner of my cell, and fuck, this isn't the first time I've been wrongfully arrested. Still, I wasn't expecting Officer Towe to plant drugs in my bike's saddlebags.

I growl as flashes of yesterday play over in my mind. Officer Towe ordered me off my bike and had his partner frisk me for weapons. As a convicted felon, I'm not allowed to own or carry firearms, blades of a certain length, or any other weapon. When I'm out on a mission, I say fuck it to all that and pack heat. I also have my club around me, ready to fight on my behalf if we run into trouble.

That day, like I said, I was going home. I wasn't armed.

While receiving the pat-down from his partner, Pete dug around in my saddlebags and pulled out enough meth to send me away for a long damn time. Forever, if the cops have anything to say about it.

"Fuck," I grunt, pausing my frantic pacing to rest my forehead against the concrete wall.

I should have told Sutton. I should have been honest with her from the start. She asked me about my past multiple times, but I always managed to steer clear of my time in prison. Sutton knows about my mom, my time in college, and what drove me to join the Savage Saints. She gave me every opportunity to share, yet I found an excuse every damn time not to go there.

And now I may have lost her forever.

"Fuck," I growl again. Self-loathing pours over me like tar; slow and suffocating.

"Aye, shut up in there," one of the guards shouts from his desk at the end of the hall of holding cells.

I snarl and pound my fist against the wall, not giving him the satisfaction.

"They said I can't shoot you, but I'm itching to try out my

brand-new police-issued taser," the guard informs me. "Might need to turn it up to twenty watts for you, big guy."

"I'd like to see you try," I grunt, though I'm not sure he heard me. I don't give a shit either way. What is one measly guard going to do when I'm at the mercy of a corrupt, careless, and cold system wrought with power-hungry sociopaths?

Turning to rest my back against the wall, I take a deep breath and try to let the cool concrete calm me down. My one call after booking wasn't to a sleazy lawyer, it was to Blade. He said he'd find a way to get me out. I want to trust him, but there's only so much the prez of an outlaw biker gang can do when up against a corrupt police department.

I slide down the wall, sitting on the hard ground with my elbows resting on my knees. Light from the small window twelve feet up shines into the cell, unaware of my life imploding around me. There's something oddly comforting about the indifference of nature. The same sun is shining down on my Sutton.

I watch the sunlight move from one side of the cell to the other before fading into night. No word from anyone, not Savage Saints nor the arresting officers. I thought I would have had some answers by now, some direction so I know what to prepare for. I'm unsure if the silence is good or bad, but from how things have been going lately, I'm going with bad.

"Get up!" a guard yells at me through the bars.

I startle a bit from my position on the floor, my muscles protesting as I stand. I haven't moved in hours, simply letting myself wallow in regret and misery.

"Bail posted?" I ask when the guard slides the door to my cell open.

He shakes his head no.

"I don't understand."

"You want to stay in here? Fine by me," he says with a shrug.

I glare at him as I walk through the door, not liking his attitude. The man is no more than five foot ten, and his arms are about as thick as my pinky finger. He might feel big and tough when he's looking in from the outside, but now I'm in front of him without a protective shield, the man cowers slightly. His posture changes from entitled and annoyed to submissive.

I step toward him, smirking when he winces. The guard scurries ahead of me, unlocking several doors with his key card until I'm finally back out in the precinct lobby, where Blade is waiting.

He gives me a nod, handing me the all-too-familiar brown paper bag of everything that was confiscated when I was arrested.

"Got your bike out of the impound lot and had Axel bring it to your place," he informs me as we walk out of the building. I roll my shoulders, the tension breaking up only slightly now I'm not in a cell. That's only part of what has me so damn anxious. The majority of my nerves are from facing Sutton. "My car is parked right here."

As soon as we're inside, I ask how the hell he got me out of jail.

"All charges have been dropped," Blade tells me as he starts the car and peels into the street.

"Say it again?" I ask, wanting to make sure I heard him right.

Blade looks over at me, a slight smirk on his otherwise impassive features. "Axel has been coming in clutch for us since the day he patched in, and today was no exception. He did some research and found that most of the drugs confiscated by police are tagged with invisible ink so they don't get redistributed in the community."

185

"Lot of good that did," I mutter.

"It took a little time, but the invisible ink did come in handy. The police here have been doing deals across state lines, where they have different policies and procedures, aka, they won't check for invisible ink since it's not in their training."

I nod, encouraging him to continue as we wind our way through town.

"Axel figured the shit planted on you came from confiscated evidence. He proved his case to the interim chief of police, and instead of turning Officer Towe into internal affairs or calling down the FBI again, we were able to negotiate your release."

I grunt, and I know Blade can read my thoughts.

"I hate that Pete fucking Towe will still have his job," he concedes without me having to say a word. "But now we know to keep an eye on him. His time will come, just like the rest of those dirty fuckers. What's important is that you're free."

"You're right," I tell him, still trying to wrap my brain around everything that's happened in the last twenty-four hours. "Thanks for having my back."

"Always. You're not going back in lock-up, Rider. Not while the Savage Saints are on your side."

I nod, and we ride in silence for a few moments before I ask the other question burning in my gut.

"Sutton?" I choke out.

When I called Blade from jail, I told him Sutton had been staying with me, and she was probably worried and scared. I expected the jaded prez to make fun of me or give me shit for thinking about a woman, but instead, he agreed to talk to Hawk and Tessa and have them go over to my place and talk with Sutton.

"She's with Hawk and Tessa," he assures me.

"Good." I'm unsure how else to respond or even what to think. What is going on in my sweet girl's head? Is she hurt? Angry? Can she ever trust me again? Did I lose her forever?

"Listen, I know I'm the last person on the face of this god-forsaken planet who should be giving relationship advice, but Sutton might need some space. She's safe with her friend for the night, so maybe you should hang back at your place tonight. Clean up and get some rest."

I narrow my eyes at Blade, who shrugs as he pulls into my driveway.

"Or storm over there and declare your love for her with a big boom box over your head," he adds.

This pulls a chuckle from some hidden reserve locked away in my chest. "I think the second one is more my style," I say as I open my door and hop out. "Thanks again for everything."

"Go get your girl," he tells me, rolling his eyes. "Still don't get how you and Hawk were taken down without so much as a fight," he mumbles under his breath.

"Can't wait until you meet the woman who bowls you over when you least expect it," I joke, slamming the door shut before he can respond.

Blade gives me the middle finger, and I grin, shaking my head as he backs out of the driveway.

Ten seconds later, I'm on my bike, racing toward town to make things right with Sutton. I have to find a way to make her forgive me, to make her understand. Now that I know what life can be like with Sutton by my side and in my bed, I refuse to go back to my pitiful existence without her grace and warmth.

Get ready, little flower. I'm not coming back home without you.

CHAPTER ELEVEN

SUTTON

"So you were living out of your car for two weeks?!" Tessa exclaims, her eyes wide with concern. "And you didn't tell me?"

My friend sounds hurt, which kills me. Not all that long ago, the thought of someone being upset that I *didn't* tell them my problems would have been ridiculous. I'm starting to get used to it, though it will take some time to fully accept that I have a friend who will support me no matter what.

"I wasn't in my car the whole time," I tell her, sipping the hot chocolate she made for me when we got back to her place. Tessa and I have been curled up on the couch under a blanket for the last few hours, drinking hot chocolate and finally catching up.

My friend gives me a look, and I know she needs more details.

"After everything with my parents contesting the will and selling the house, I scraped up enough money for a motel for a few nights. Then I called the shelter, which is on a first-come, first-served basis. I got a bed for two nights, then had to stay in my car for a night, then back to the shelter. Rider found me last week after I spent a few nights in my car."

Tessa's hand covers mine, and tears sting my eyes from whatever kind thing she's going to say.

"I'm so sorry you were dealing with all of this and I had no idea. If I thought for a second you were homeless–"

"I know. You would have insisted I stay with you and Hawk or set up a spot for me at the Savage Saints clubhouse," I finish for her.

Tessa nods. "So why didn't you say anything?"

I shrug, staring down into my hot chocolate. "It's one thing to *know* someone will theoretically help you when times are tough, and another thing entirely to *trust* them." I realize how that must sound, and immediately backtrack. "Not that I don't trust you," I rush to say. "It's me. I'm broken. I can't… I can't trust anything. It doesn't make sense to get something for nothing, especially when I'm such a burden."

"Sutton, I'm not mad at you," she reminds me gently. "I'm worried because I care. It's not a burden to be there for you or to share my resources. You're not a burden for simply existing."

I sniffle back a few tears and nod. She's right. I know she's right. Rider has told me the same thing over the last few days.

Oof, just thinking his name has my stomach churning and my breath catching in my throat. As if sensing my shift in thoughts, Tessa readjusts in her seat to face me, letting the blanket fall from her lap. I gather it up, needing this little protective shield for the question I know she's about to ask.

"So, Rider, huh?"

My cheeks heat, and I shrug, unsure what else to say.

"You know, he's been into you since he first introduced himself."

A smile spreads across my lips despite the pain tearing at

my heart. "He told me the same thing," I murmur. Then I remember hearing Blade shout about Rider being thrown in jail, where he's already spent some time. "But he lied to me. Why didn't he tell me he spent time in prison?"

"Why didn't you tell me about the house?" Tessa counters.

I blink at her, not expecting that question. "That's not the same thing at all," I start.

"Maybe not, but do you know why he went away the first time? Or if it was his fault?"

I continue to stare at my friend. That thought never crossed my mind.

"You know how awful my dad is," Tessa continues. "And he was the sheriff. Can you imagine what all of his little cronies are like, especially now that there's a power shift?"

"Not his fault," I repeat. "Like, he was set up?"

Tessa shrugs. "I don't know all of the details, but yeah. My father confessed to putting several Savage Saints in prison for simply being in the wrong place at the wrong time."

"Still, he didn't tell me. We shared so many things, and he knows my greatest vulnerabilities, so why couldn't he trust me with his?"

"Why couldn't you trust me with yours?" Tessa asks, flipping the tables on me once more. My shoulders drop, and my stomach twists. My friend scoots closer to me on the couch, taking the empty hot chocolate mug from my hands and setting it on the table before resting her arm around my shoulders. "I didn't mean that to shame you. I simply wanted to remind you what you told me a few minutes ago. You said it wasn't because of *me* but because you struggle to trust anyone or anything. Could Rider have the same feelings? The same insecurities?"

"Well…" I trail off, knowing she's right.

"I'm always on team Sutton," Tessa tells me, giving my shoulder a squeeze. "Whatever you want to do about Rider,

I'm here for you. If you want, I can probably get Hawk to punch Rider in the balls if that would make you feel better."

I snort out a laugh at my bestie's suggestion.

"But I wanted to give you a different perspective," Tessa says, more softly this time. "Other than finding out about Rider's past in the worst way possible, how have you felt being with him the last few days? Is he good to you? Does he make you feel safe?"

"Yeah," I say with a nod. "He's so sweet to me, and he makes me feel like I'm this precious gift. He told me he looks forward to coming home to me and my smile. I've never had that before," I tell her, my voice cracking at the end.

"Rider sounds like a good man to me," Tessa says. "Stubborn and a bit of an idiot when it comes to communicating, but all the best men are." My friend winks at me, and I can't help but return her smile.

Just then, we hear a commotion coming from the front entryway.

"Maybe just give her some—"

"Time? Yeah, I don't think so," comes the familiar deep, gravelly voice of my Rider.

"Rider," Hawk calls out.

Heavy footsteps draw closer to where Tessa and I are in the living room. A second later, my beastly biker steps into view, his massive frame silhouetted against the bay window as he strides toward me. I'm still confused, hurt, and a little angry, but mostly, I'm overwhelmingly relieved that he's here.

Tears spring to my eyes as Rider closes the distance between us, his brown gaze locking on mine. Before I can register what is happening, Rider scoops me up in his arms and tosses me over his shoulder.

I'm so stunned at the turn of events, I don't so much as

squeak when he promptly turns and stomps back down the hall toward the front door.

"Tell me everything the second you're done making up!" Tessa shouts from her spot on the couch.

Rider grunts and tightens his hold on me.

"You good?" Hawk asks.

"I am now," Rider says.

"I was asking Sutton, you brute."

"I-I'm good," I manage to say. "Confused. What exactly is happening?"

"I'm doing what I should have done from the start," Rider grunts. "Sitting you down and telling you the truth."

"And why can't we do that here?" I push myself up from where he has me flung against his back.

Rider takes the hint and sets me down, though he circles his arms around my hips to keep me close. "Because if all goes according to plan, my sweet flower, we're going to need some privacy."

It takes a second for his meaning to set in, and when it does, my face heats with a blush.

Rider takes my hand and guides me outside, stopping in front of his bike. He turns to me once more, cupping my cheek so tenderly as he tilts my head toward his. "You're safe with me, Sutton. I'm not... I'm sorry I didn't tell you any of this shit sooner. I'm not the criminal they've made me out to be. I'd never hurt you, and it would kill me if you ever felt uncomfortable or unsafe with me. I'll explain everything, I promise, just please... Please let me know I haven't lost you for good. Tell me I don't scare you."

This man. The genuine fear in his eyes swallows any last doubt I had about him. After everything he's been through, his biggest concern is if I'm afraid of him now that I know he's been in prison.

"You don't scare me, Rider. No one has ever made me feel safer than when I'm with you."

He releases all the tension in his muscles and rests his forehead on mine. "Thank you," he murmurs, though I'm unsure why he's thanking me. "Let's get home so I can grovel and explain everything."

I nod, and Rider steps away, placing his helmet on my head. I've never been on a motorcycle before. Never considered it before meeting Rider. The noise, the vibrations, the attention bikes draw from the general public... no, thank you. But now, seeing the sleek machine through Rider's eyes, I get it.

It's freedom. And he wants to take me along for the ride.

Rider climbs on his bike and directs me to get on behind him. "Hang on tight, princess. I'll get you home safely."

"Home," I whisper, though I know he can't hear me over the roar of the engine. We're going home.

CHAPTER TWELVE

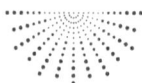

RIDER

*S*tep one of winning Sutton back went better than planned. I expected more resistance, but my girl agreed to come with me without a fight. Not that I gave her much of a choice by throwing her over my shoulder, but still. That has to be a good sign.

Sutton tightens her hold around my torso as I ease my motorcycle around a corner and straighten out. Her legs squeeze around mine, and it takes everything in me not to pull the damn bike over, strip her down, and kiss every inch of her body until she forgives me and tells me she loves me as much as I love her.

Soon. For now, I need to focus on getting my girl home and telling her the truth about everything. If she can still look at me when all of my shame is out in the open, I'll work on giving her enough orgasms so she can barely walk, let alone run away.

Who the fuck am I right now? These possessive thoughts have plagued me since laying eyes on Sutton all those weeks ago, but now I've had her and stand to lose her... they're more intense than ever.

I pull into my driveway and cut the engine, helping Sutton off before swinging my leg over and standing next to her. She's shaking, though I'm unsure if it's from the bike ride or all the anxiety and emotions I've caused her.

"You okay?" I ask softly, resting a hand on the small of her back to steady her.

"Yes," she says, though she shakes her head no.

I lift an eyebrow at her confusing answer.

"I-I mean, no, not really," she tries again, though her head nods yes this time. "Sorry, I'm just…"

Sutton shrugs, and I pull her into my arms, holding her trembling body against mine. "Never apologize to me," I whisper. "It's all my fault. Everything. I should have said something. I should have told you about my past and the danger that comes with someone like me."

"So tell me now," Sutton says, stepping back from my embrace. A bitter chill runs through me at the loss, but then she holds her hand out for me to take.

I curl my massive hand around her delicate one and lead her inside. We walk through the living room, past the kitchen, and down the hall, only stopping when we get to the bedroom. Sutton looks up at me with a curious expression.

"Need to hold you," I explain, my voice scratchy. Emotion clogs my throat, and I'd think I was about to cry if I didn't know any better.

Sutton nods and climbs into bed, scooting over and patting the space next to her. I yank my shirt off, grinning when her bright eyes widen and skim down my torso. My girl likes what she sees.

"Not fair," she mumbles as I crawl in next to her and turn her to face me.

"I need to feel you," I tell her truthfully. "And if the abs help distract, then all the better," I joke.

Sutton rolls her eyes, then smiles so sweetly. God, I don't

deserve her. When the light in her eyes dims, I know she's thinking about everything I put her through in the last twenty-four hours.

"I was pulled over on my way home to you," I start.

Rolling over on my back, I open my arm, satisfied beyond belief when Sutton curls up on my chest and lets me hold her. My fingers find the hem of her shirt, and I trace the edge of the fabric before tickling my fingertips across her bare skin.

"Dirty cops in this town planted drugs on me and hauled me into jail. Thankfully, Axel and my brothers at Savage Saints figured out a way to leverage my release. I won't be going away ever again."

Sutton nods, her hand tracing the stubble across my jaw. She's not looking me in the eye, seemingly fixated on where she's touching me. I know what she's going to ask before the words leave her lips.

"What about the last time you were in prison? Five years, was it?"

Teal eyes flick up to mine, and I hold her gaze as I confess everything to the only woman who matters to me.

"Yes. I was in prison for five years. Sheriff Darren, Tessa's dad, fucked me over with assault charges and carrying illegal substances, both of which were false. It didn't matter, though. Nothing Blade or any of the Savage Saints tried made a difference. The lawyer we hired got my sentence down from ten years to five, but... Well, anyway. I got out a few weeks before I met you." I pause, letting this information sink in.

Sutton blinks a few times, her pulse pounding in the side of her neck. "You've only been out for a little over a month?"

I nod, hoping I didn't just ruin my last chance with her.

"When I saw you sitting on the barstool at the club-house... I knew I didn't deserve to breathe the same air as you, let alone touch you. Then I found you in your car, and things between us escalated so quickly. I had everything I ever wanted with you in my arms, and I couldn't risk losing the best thing that ever happened to me and–"

"Breathe," Sutton whispers, cupping the side of my cheek.

I turn and kiss her palm, soaking up as many of her gentle touches as she'll give me. "All of my excuses burned into a pile of ash as soon as the cuffs slapped against my wrists," I continue. "I'm so sorry for keeping this secret from you. I was terrified you wouldn't trust me to take care of you if you knew I was a convicted felon. And then I fucked it all up by not telling you and causing you to lose trust in me anyway."

"You deserve to be loved," Sutton says, surprising the hell out of me. After everything I just told her, that's her first reaction?

"You don't know everything yet," I tell her, unable to process her response. "While I was in prison, my ma… fuck, she got cancer. I wasn't there for her. I failed her like I failed you, and I…"

"You deserve to be loved," she says again, her soothing voice rolling over me. "Your mom getting sick wasn't your fault, and neither was not being there. It was a horrible consequence of a broken, corrupt system."

"Sutton, you can't mean that."

"I do," she insists, pressing her lips to my temple in the sweetest gesture anyone has ever shown me. "From what you've said about your mom, I know she believed you were wrongfully convicted. I know she loved you and was proud of you. She would have wanted you to be happy and accept that you can be loved and forgiven."

"But… what?"

"You've been showing me every day since I moved in that I'm worthy of taking up space and asking for what I need and want. But what about you? You deserve to have good things in your life. You deserve love."

"But I... What?" I ask again.

"I forgive you," Sutton says. "I was surprised when I found out, and yeah, I was hurt that there was a whole part of your life you didn't share with me. But I get it. Tessa reminded me that I also kept secrets from her. I didn't want to burden her with my baggage, but in the end, it hurt her to know she could have helped, but I didn't let her in. So, will you let me in?"

"Let you in?" I whisper, hardly able to comprehend her words.

"Let me love you," she clarifies.

"Love me?"

Sutton's lips curl up into the cutest grin. "Are you going to repeat everything I say?"

"You love me?"

"That's what I'm trying to tell you, yes," she says with a spark in her eyes.

"I love you so goddamn much," I reply, my forehead resting on hers. "Love your tender heart and sweet kisses. Love how brave you are and how you push yourself to grow and be a better person. It makes me want to be better, to be the best because that's what you deserve."

"Can... Can you say it again?" Sutton murmurs. "The part about loving me?"

I smile at her, my heart growing impossibly bigger at her request. "I love you, Sutton. I love every single thing about you."

"Show me," Sutton says, her teal eyes pleading with me to prove my words.

I lean forward, taking her lips with mine and leading us in a slow, drugging kiss. Sutton's hands curl against my bare chest as I pull her closer, consuming her with each swipe of my tongue.

My girl wiggles out of my embrace and removes her shirt, making me groan. I'm on her in the next second, unhooking her bra and moving down her body, peeling her leggings and panties off.

"Beautiful," I rasp as I drag my eyes up and down her naked body. "Gonna kiss you and make everything all better," I promise, catching her eye before scooting down the bed and spreading her thighs.

I trail my lips up the inside of her right leg, pausing briefly to kiss behind her knee. Sutton inhales sharply, making me grin wickedly at how well I can read her. I continue placing featherlight kisses up her thigh, nuzzling into her soaking wet pussy.

"Jesus," I groan, unable to resist the urge to lick her from bottom to top. My girl is fucking delicious, and I'll never get enough of her.

"More," she whimpers. "I need more. I need it all."

I growl into her cunt and scrape my teeth along her clit. She lifts her hips and spreads her legs wider. I press my tongue against her tight-as-fuck entrance, groaning when I feel her little hole pulse and release a shot of cream into my mouth.

Sutton lets out a pained cry as she rubs her cunt against my face, coating me in her juices. That's my tipping point. Knowing she marked me, that she's as desperate and needy as I am, and I'm the only one who can satisfy her, has me ridding myself of my jeans and boxers in a split second, eliminating every piece of clothing between us.

My greedy girl whimpers and reaches for me as I crawl up her sexy-as-fuck body. I groan when I feel her delicate fingers trail over my shoulders, chest, abs, and lower.

Resting my forehead on hers, I hiss a breath when she

wraps her hand around my cock and strokes me up and down. "Fuck, Sutton. You feel so good, baby. So damn good."

I let her touch me and explore what now belongs to her. She shocks the hell out of me by guiding me to her entrance and rocking her hips. My eyes snap open, and I groan when I see her gaze burning with lust. "Need me to show you what it means to be mine, Sutton?"

"Yes," she whispers. Her eyes are blazing, barely containing the raging fire within.

I push the tip of my thickness inside her snug hole. Her pussy spasms, massaging the head of my cock.

"Need me to show you how much I love you?" I ask, pushing in a little further.

"Please," she moans, her fingers curling around my biceps as she spreads her legs wider for me.

"Need me to make this pussy come? Need me to fill you up so you can fucking come all over me again and again?"

"Yes!" Sutton cries out, thrusting her hips up, taking more of me.

I grunt and pull out, swallowing her whimpers before shoving my cock all the way inside her tight little channel. I pull out, looking down between us as I set a steady pace. "Look at us, Sutton. Fucking look at your little pussy stretching around me, taking my cock like a good girl." I don't know where these filthy words are coming from, but I can't seem to keep them in my head. She doesn't seem to mind.

Sutton whimpers and squeezes her inner muscles, making me growl as every part of my dick throbs in torturous pleasure. "More," she cries out, her lips seeking mine. She totally owns this kiss, nipping at me and sucking my tongue inside her mouth as her pussy sucks my cock deeper, deeper, so damn deep.

I pull out and slam back inside her. God, I can feel her

channel stretch and clench around me as I pick up speed. Her legs wrap around my torso, her heels digging into my ass, urging me on.

"Fuck, Sutton. I don't want to hurt you," I grit, though I don't slow down. Not for a second. I keep hammering into her over and over, tilting my hips and scraping my cock along her front wall in search of...

"Rider!" Sutton shouts and claws at my back, clinging to me as I tear her apart.

I can't stop. I know I should slow down, but I no longer have control over anything. My hands slip under her back and slide up, my fingers curling around her shoulders, giving me more leverage to fuck that tight little pussy.

Every time I hit the end of her, Sutton jerks beneath me, letting out the sexiest whimper. I keep pounding into her as I bury my face in her neck, sucking on her soft skin. I feel her entire body tighten around me, her muscles tensing, her pussy throbbing, pulsing, gushing for me.

I grunt with each savage stroke, more beast than man. Sutton breaks apart for me, her jagged cries and desperate moans growing louder by the second. She bows her back and digs her fingernails into my shoulders, sucking in a huge breath of air. She freezes, tenses, trembles...

And then fucking shatters so beautifully for me.

Her cries of pleasure echo around the room as her cunt snaps around me over and over. I sit back and grip her hips, fucking myself with her spasming pussy. Sutton fists the comforter and thrashes her head back and forth as another orgasm rips through her body, leaving her breathless.

"Goddamn," I snarl, shoving my cock deep inside her and staying still. I tip my head back and feel, just fucking feel every ounce of her pleasure ripple around me.

She's still twitching and whimpering out the last of her release when I pull out of her and grab my dick, stroking myself roughly. The need to mark her is such a primal, caveman thing, but it can't be denied. It won't.

My orgasm slams into me, and I roar as I paint her tits and pussy with my cum. I grunt something unintelligible, squeezing my dick so damn hard as it jerks and empties more of my release all over her.

I'm about to collapse, but then my dirty fucking girl rubs my seed into her skin. She cups her breast, pinching her nipple as her other hand trails lower, gathering my cum before she dips her fingers into her pussy.

"Jesus Christ," I growl, my body shaking with how turned on I still am despite my intense, all-consuming orgasm.

"Rider," Sutton cries out. "God, Rider, I can't stop, I can't stop."

Christ, she fucks her hand while I hover over her, taking in this goddess. Her mouth opens in a silent scream, all the breath leaving her lungs as she nearly comes again.

I swat her hand away, sliding down her body and prying her legs open. Flattening my tongue, I lick her up and down in frantic, feral strokes before spearing my tongue inside her entrance, scooping out more of her cream.

Sutton winds her fingers in my hair, holding me still as she rubs her pussy against my lips and tongue. Her scream carves through the air as a fierce orgasm overwhelms her curvy body. I grip her thighs, pinning them to the mattress as I drink down every last drop of her release.

I only stop when she goes completely limp. Looking up from between her legs, I see her head loll to the side as her chest heaves. I crawl up her body, placing kisses on her stomach, her breasts, her neck, and finally, her lips.

Collapsing beside her, I drape my Sutton over my chest and hold her trembling body close. We're both breathing heavily, our bodies slick with sweat as we cling to each other.

I comb my fingers through her damp hair and place a kiss on top of her head.

"You okay, princess?" I whisper, tugging on her hair slightly to tilt her head up.

"Hmm?" Sutton asks in a daze, her eyelids barely fluttering open as a sleepy, contented smile stretches across her lips.

I grin and kiss the tip of her nose. "Never mind. I've got you," I murmur, tucking her head under my chin. I hold her for long moments, listening to her breathing slowly return to normal.

We need to wash up and talk about other details of our new lives together, but there will be time for that later. Right now, I'm content knowing my Sutton is safe and happy here in my arms, where she belongs.

CHAPTER THIRTEEN

SUTTON

*R*ider and I walk into the Savage Saints clubhouse and are greeted with a round of cheers and applause. Rider squeezes my hand, letting me know he's right here if I get overwhelmed or panicky. I squeeze his back, letting him know I'm okay. This is different than other times. This is important, and I can't wait.

"Fuckin' hell. Almost lost ya to the law again," one man says as he claps Rider on the shoulder.

"Let me buy you a beer," another calls out as he makes his way through the crowd of bikers to get to us.

"Who's your lady?" someone asks off to one side. "She need a beer, too?"

"Rider, we need to–"

"Enough!" Rider yells, surprising everyone in the club-house, including me. My beastly biker looks down at me, his brown eyes twinkling and letting me know he's not upset. He's excited. "Yes, I survived another scrape with the dirty cops in this town, but that's not important."

"If that's not important, what is?" Blade asks.

"This," Rider answers seconds before lifting me into his

arms.

His lips are on mine in the next second, his tongue stroking inside my mouth and claiming me from the inside out. I kiss him back with every ounce of gratitude I have for this man who has healed me in more ways than one. We get lost in each other, only coming back to reality when the hoots and hollers of the crowd filter in around us.

"Mine," Rider growls as he sets me back on my feet. "My woman," he says again, addressing everyone staring at us.

The heat of a blush covers my face and travels down my body, but I can't deny that I like the attention. I like everyone knowing I belong to Rider.

"Okay, okay, we get it. Another one bites the dust," Blade says.

Rider grunts while a few of the patrons in the clubhouse chuckle. Blade grins, and I know he's happy for his friend. I hope he finds someone someday who keeps that smile on his face.

"A round of shots on me to celebrate the new couple," he announces as he lifts his beer glass.

Rider nods and lifts me in his arms.

I shriek and giggle, giving my man a questioning look. "I thought the point of this was to claim me in front of your MC brothers or whatever."

"Just did that. Now, I need to claim you in private." He's so serious as he carries me through the bar area and into a separate hallway.

"Um, as in...?"

"As in need to be inside you, need to feel that connection, need you wrapped around me as I remind you how much I love you."

"Okay, then," I say breathlessly as he darts into one of the empty rooms used for members who need a place to crash for the night.

Rider sets me down in front of the bed and strips me of my clothes so reverently despite his obvious need. He tears at his clothes, making me giggle with his intensity.

My laughter dies on my lips as he steps closer, erasing the distance between us. He runs his hands up and down my naked body, caressing my hips, breasts, and even my throat and lips. His strong, capable hands leave a throbbing, warm blaze in their wake.

His hand wraps around the back of my neck, pulling me into him for a punishing kiss. I'm his. He owns every part of me. That's what he's telling me with each stroke of his tongue, each anguished groan that travels through his body and into mine. I feel his kiss everywhere, and I need more.

"Please," I whimper, not even caring that I sound desperate. I am. He's right there with me.

"I've got you, baby. I've got you," he murmurs, gripping my hips and guiding me backward until the edge of the mattress hits the back of my legs.

Rider gently lays me on the bed, then stands in front of me, looking down at my body. It's all for him. I spread my legs, moaning when he growls and clenches his fist.

"Please," I whisper again, my hands trailing up my torso to cup my breasts. My skin is so sensitive, every light touch seems to go straight to my clit, making it throb in anticipation.

Rider tears his eyes away from where they were locked on my pussy, and he grunts again when he sees me playing with my nipples.

"Fuck, Sutton. You're so damn sexy." He's on me in the next instant, covering my body with open-mouthed kisses, sucking on my skin and leaving little love bites up my torso and on my breasts.

I jerk and twist beneath him, gasping for air and whimpering with each lingering touch and kiss. When Rider finally reaches my mouth, he slants his lips over mine and leads us in a slow, drugging kiss.

My legs automatically spread wider so he can settle between them. His long, thick cock glides against my pussy, collecting my juices and driving me crazy. He's *so close* to where I need him, and I nearly cry in frustration.

Rider sits back slightly and gathers my wrists in one of his massive hands. He raises my hands over my hand and pins them to the mattress before nuzzling into the side of my neck. "Fuckin' love seeing you stretched out for me," he says into my skin, his voice low, gravelly, and desperate. He drags his lips down my neck and across my collarbone, then nips at the tops of my breasts, grinning wickedly when I jump and gasp. "Gonna fuck this sweet little pussy now, Sutton. Are you ready for me?"

I nod and tilt my hips, nudging the swollen head of his cock against my entrance. Rider growls and reaches between us to guide himself inside in one smooth stroke. Fire spreads through my veins, and heat pulses from my core, overwhelming my body.

I wiggle my hips, making sparks sizzle and burn across my skin. Rider groans, leaning over me, one hand still holding my wrists above my head while the other trails up my side. He squeezes my breast, pinching my hardened, sensitive nipple before sucking it into his mouth.

My back bows off the bed, and he takes the opportunity to slip his hand between my back and the mattress, pushing my chest up so he can feast on me. Rider grinds his cock into me, filling me up before pulling back and slamming into me roughly.

My breasts jiggle with every thrust as he sets a relentless pace. I wrap my legs around him and dig my heels into his sculpted ass, crying out when he hits that spot inside me that pushes me right to the edge.

My muscles tense as my pussy tightens around his thickness. He lifts his head from my chest and studies my face, no doubt sensing how close I am. My thighs shake, and a shiver runs up my spine, seizing my lungs and forcing out a scream as I come around his cock.

Rivulets of pleasure course through my body, making every nerve ending spark to life. Rider fucks me through it, never letting up. He still has my wrists secured in his grasp despite all my writhing and trying to twist away from the intense pressure and sharp ecstasy he's creating deep inside me.

I swear I'm about to come again, but suddenly Rider isn't on top of me anymore. I hardly have time to register his absence before his large hands grasp my hips firmly. Rider flips me over effortlessly, then pulls my hips back so I'm on all fours.

"Fuck, yes," he grunts, gripping my ass cheeks and spreading them wide. "Jesus Christ, I've pictured you like this too many damn times."

Rider thrusts into me, growling when he bottoms out. I let out a broken cry as I unravel for him, my orgasm ricocheting through my body but never leaving me completely. I'm so fucking sensitive, so raw as he pounds into me.

"I-I-I ca-ca-n't…" I stutter, unable to take a full breath.

"You can, baby. Trust me, you can. Feel this with me. *Fuck*, feel it, Sutton."

I whimper and nod, staying right here with him in the moment, struggling to hold myself up on shaky arms while my pussy knots around him over and over. Incoherent words and strangled, almost tormented sounds fall from my lips as Rider tears me apart, fucks me so good, so hard, so damn rough. He's branding me with each savage stroke, claiming all of me, body and soul.

Rider slides his hand around to my front, spreading his

fingers over my stomach and pulling me even closer as he ruts into me. His hand creates more pressure. I swear I feel his dick rearrange my organs, he's fucking me so damn deep.

My fingers curl into the sheets, fisting them as I try desperately to hold myself up. When he brushes the tips of his fingers over my clit, my knees wobble and my arms give out. I face plant into the pillow, my ass still in the air, Rider still pounding away. He pinches my clit, and I sob out yet another orgasm. My pleasure spikes as white-hot bliss fills my veins. When it fades away, I'm completely limp. Boneless. Held up only by Rider's punishing grip on my hips.

"Gonna come inside you, love," he growls as he holds himself deep inside me.

His words make my pussy contract one last time, and that's his breaking point.

Rider lets out a feral roar as his cum fills me. He pulls back and enters me again as more of his release shoots out of him. There's so much that it drips down my thighs, the tickling sensation making me moan and involuntarily tremble in his arms.

The last of his orgasm drains from him, and Rider collapses on top of me. He's sweaty and panting for air as he rests his forehead between my shoulder blades. I feel his hot breath on my skin, the weight of his body on top of mine, his sweat mixing with mine.

Rider rolls off me and pulls me into his arms, draping my still boneless body across his chest. We don't say anything, and we don't need to. Rider combs his fingers through my hair and kisses the top of my head, his breathing finally returning to normal.

I tilt my head and smile, getting lost in his loving gaze. Those chocolatey brown eyes get me every time. "I'm yours," I whisper, brushing my lips against his.

"And I'm yours, Sutton. So fucking yours."

EPILOGUE

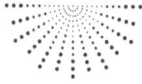

RIDER

"One... two... three... four. Four tires!" Laura, our three-year-old, exclaims, turning in my lap to smile up at me.

"That's right, sweetheart. That car has four tires. How about my bike over there?" I ask, pointing to my motorcycle parked outside in the driveway.

"Two," she says without counting. "That was too easy."

I grin at my youngest, then stand with her in my arms, swinging her up and over my head so she's sitting on my shoulders. Laura giggles, her joyful laugh almost as life-giving as her mother's.

"And what are you up to?" Sutton asks from behind us. I spin, giving my gorgeous wife a grin.

"Counting!" Laura says excitedly.

"Oh, yeah?" Sutton tickles Laura's little feet, making our daughter laugh. "Maybe you can help your brother with his homework. I give up."

I chuckle and lean down to kiss my wife on the temple. "What's Simon's homework this week?"

"Fractions," she says with a weary sigh, making me laugh

again. "I'm an artist, okay? The only time I work with numbers is when charging clients," she mumbles as she reties one of Laura's shoes.

"Switch?" I ask, lifting my little girl off my shoulders and handing her to Sutton.

"How about we go outside and play for a bit? I could use a homework break," Sutton says.

"Homework break?" Simon calls out from his spot at the dining room table where he's been plugging away at his fractions worksheet. He's next to us in a second, and I swear I can see a trail of dust he kicked up from moving so fast.

"Let's go," I tell him, leading my family out to the backyard.

Simon takes Laura's hand, and they run off to the playground while Sutton and I hang back on the porch.

My beautiful wife rests her elbows against the railing while I step up behind her and wrap my arms around her waist. She leans against me, letting me cradle her in my embrace.

"Love our family," I whisper, pressing a kiss to her temple.

She smiles, turning her head to kiss the side of my neck. "We love you," she murmurs, snuggling deeper against me.

We stay wrapped up in each other while watching our kids play in the yard. I never knew I wanted this: the family, the wife, the crazy kids, and the picket fence. Not that we have a picket fence. Yet. It's on backorder.

But now? I couldn't picture my life any other way.

Sutton is wildly successful with her design business, and it's been a joy to see her grow in her skillset and as a person. She has confidence in herself and her abilities, and she's not afraid to set boundaries and take up space. She's not afraid to be loved, and neither am I.

Every day with my Sutton is better than the last, which isn't to say we've always had it easy. I just know deep down in my soul that we'll make it through anything as long as we choose each other every time.

"Thank you for giving me a second chance all those years ago," I tell her, tightening my hold around her waist.

"Thank you for showing me how to love and be loved," she replies, her voice soft and sweet like the rest of her.

"You're too good to me, princess."

"We're good to each other," she counters, resting her head against my shoulder as I rock her back and forth.

"That we are, little flower. That we are."

* * *

THE END

Curious about Blade's story? Watch the grumpy Prez fall for his sunshine here!

BLADE

A GRUMPY/SUNSHINE MC ROMANCE

BLADE

I was out on a ride to clear my mind when I saw her on the side of the road, frowning at the black smoke pouring out of the engine. I wasn't looking for trouble, and I certainly wasn't looking for a blonde-haired, blue-eyed damsel in distress, but I couldn't just leave her stranded.

With nowhere to stay while her piece of garbage car is getting fixed at our shop, I begrudgingly let Sonya crash in one of the empty rooms in the clubhouse. Despite her current situation and uncomfortable accommodations, Sonya is all smiles, rainbows, and butterflies.

I should find it annoying. Off-putting. Unnatural. Instead, I'm addicted to her laughter. I live for her next corny joke. I could survive off of her smiles alone.

Our enemies discover my new obsession and try using her as leverage. They'll find out in no uncertain terms what happens when someone messes with the President of the Savage Saints.

CHAPTER ONE

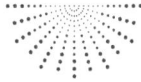

SONYA

"*Y*ou, you, you, oughta *knooooow*!"

I belt out the lyrics to my favorite Alanis Morissette song as I cruise down the highway, heading nowhere. I still remember the day my sister snuck the old CD into our house when we were little. Such heathen music was banned under our parents' roof as a direct order from Pastor Wellington.

A grin pulls at my lips as I remember hiding the cherished contraband in my pillow case for years. It survived many a book-and-music bonfire held at First Assembly of God's Chosen. I can't say the same for the N*SYNC album I secretly bought or my copies of To Kill a Mockingbird and 1984.

I shove those thoughts to the back of my mind and pick up the lyrics as Alanis begins on the chorus again.

My car jerks forward and sputters a bit before returning to normal. I hold my breath, waiting to see if that's a bad sign or just usual car stuff. This is my first real experience driving, and I fear I may have bitten off more than I can chew, so to speak. Three days straight of driving across the country after only a few driving lessons and a YouTube tutorial might have been a risky choice, but I had no other options. None that I could live with, anyway.

Another jolt from my car has me gripping the steering wheel tighter as if that will somehow calm it down. No such luck. The vehicle shakes and sputters, and no matter how hard I press the gas pedal, it slows until it rolls to a stop on the side of the road, completely dead.

Frick. Now what?

Taking a deep breath, I unbuckle my seatbelt and climb out of my car. I walk around to the front, where I stare at the hood. There's a latch around here somewhere…

"Aha!" I exclaim to myself when I see it.

The hood pops open, letting out a hiss and stream of smoke. I back away, coughing and waving my hands to clear the smoke. As it dissipates, I make my way closer to the car, resting my hands on my hips as I lean over the engine to inspect it.

Unsurprisingly, I have no idea what I'm looking at. Aren't engines supposed to be, like, metal? This one seems like it's made entirely of grease and dirt. That can't be good, right?

Stupid, silly girl. You really think you can make it on your own? Without the protection of The Chosen? The Devil will have your soul within a week.

"No," I whisper, shutting my eyes against my father's last words before I left home for good. "I can do this. I can do this," I repeat under my breath.

Do what, exactly? Fix the engine? Hitchhike? I don't even have a destination in mind. I just took off, needing to be anywhere but with my family and their oppressive religion. Even my older sister finally let go of her "rebellious youth" and settled down with one of the pastor's sons last year.

Something catches my attention. A low rumble in the distance, growing closer, louder, louder…

I whip my head up from where I was leaning over the hood in time to see a man on a motorcycle pull up behind my car. I watch him swing his leg over the bike and stand to his full height, which has to be nearly a foot taller than my five foot four.

I scan his muscular body, taking in his corded arms and bulging biceps covered in swirling ink. The beast of a man walks toward me, his long strides eating up the distance between us.

Brown eyes lock with mine, and I forget how to breathe for a second. No one at church or my small private school had tattoos. They're forbidden, of course. I've always secretly thought they looked… sexy.

A blush creeps into my cheeks as I think that word. It's silly, I know. At twenty-two, I shouldn't squirm at merely thinking of the word "sexy," but that's where I'm at.

When the massive, muscled, tatted-up biker stops in front of me, I crane my neck to maintain eye contact. I should probably be wary of this man. Instead, I'm insanely curious.

What do his tattoos mean? Does he have more on his chest? His back? What does his home look like? What does this man do in his free time? Probably competitive staring contests…

I blink, breaking the trance he's put me in. "Um, hi," I squeak.

He grunts, which is somehow… adorable. I know I should hop in my car and lock the doors. I may have lived an extremely sheltered life, but I'm not so naive that I don't recognize my vulnerable situation. Still, something about him feels… I don't know. He feels safe.

"So, do you come here often?" I tease, hoping to see what his smile looks like.

The man furrows his brow and tilts his head to the side.

217

"Do you speak English?"

He rolls his eyes, which makes me grin. "Yes," comes the grunted response.

"Oh, good. I was beginning to worry we had a communication barrier."

Another blank stare from the biker.

"Do you happen to know anything about cars? Are car engines anything like motorcycle engines? Like maybe the motorcycle engine is half a car engine or something? Is that what horsepower is?"

The monosyllabic man blinks, no doubt overwhelmed with my barrage of questions. "Yes, no, no, and no."

It takes me a second to realize he answered all my questions in order. I smile at his adorableness and step aside so he can look at my car. He leans over the engine and grabs a dirty bandana from his back pocket. The man uses it to poke and open a few valves and lids or whatever else an engine is composed of. I stand beside him, trying not to gawk at how the muscles tighten and flex in his arms.

"What's with the bandana?" I inquire, shuffling a little closer to him. It's so I can see what he's doing and *not* because I want to smell him. After all, I should learn about this stuff while I have an expert here. Next time this happens, I might not be so lucky.

"Engine's hot. And dirty," comes his muttered response.

"Oh, so it protects your hands?"

A grunt and a nod is all I get in return.

I give the good Samaritan a little peace and quiet while he continues his inspection. Anxiety eats away at my nerves the longer the silence stretches between us. *This can't be good. If it was an easy fix, wouldn't he have found it by now?*

"It's blown," he states, straightening to his full height.

"Um, that's not a good thing, I'm guessing?" My throat

gets tight as I swallow past the lump of emotion. *Don't cry, don't cry, don't you dare cry!*

"It means the damn thing is dead. When's the last time you changed the oil?"

"Uh…"

"And what kind of gas have you been putting in this thing? It's ancient, so it should be getting unleaded, not anything diluted with ethanol."

"There are different gas options?" I whisper, feeling stupid and childish. "I put in whatever was cheapest."

Another grunt. "That's probably what did it. Not sure it's worth saving."

"What? What do you mean? Like… no more car?"

What am I going to do without a car? This stupid hunk of junk is the only thing I have, aside from a duffle bag of clothes, what little I could pack of my shoe collection, and my contraband Alanis Morissette CD.

I'm vaguely aware of the man rattling off some car mumbo-jumbo, but it makes no sense to me. His voice fades into the background, replaced by my father's cruel taunting.

This is why God made men to rule over women. They can make better choices and be better leaders. This wouldn't have happened if you had a deacon with you.

I squeeze my eyes shut, trying to block out his nasty words. My breath grows shaky and uneven while my eyes burn with unshed tears.

Weak. Stupid. Gullible. Incapable.

The first sob breaks free, opening the floodgates. I gasp for air as tears stream down my cheeks.

"Uh, what… oh," the man stutters, his eyes wide with shock.

I open my mouth to apologize for my outburst, but another sob rolls out of me, followed by more tears.

"Um… it's… going to be… okay," he says, awkwardly

reaching toward me. He hovers his hand over my shoulder, then pats me twice before shoving his hands in his pocket.

I nod, but my entire body shivers as I cry my eyes out.

"Here," the biker grunts, shoving his bandana in my direction. I take it without thinking and swipe it across one cheek and then the other. "Oh, you, uh…"

He points to my face and then back to the bandana. It has grease all over it, and I assume I now have grease on my cheeks. Great. Just wonderful.

"I'll make it better," he rushes to say. "Just stop crying."

"S-s-sorry," I say pathetically.

"No, I didn't mean… Fuck," he mutters, running a hand through his short black hair. "I'm sure I have something else you can use."

The man looks around frantically, then whips off his leather vest with patches covering it, followed by his black T-shirt. I'm so shocked, I stop crying. My mouth drops open as my eyes glide over the dips and curves of his packed abs and sculpted chest. Yup, it appears that every square inch of him has intricate tattoos.

"Here." He tosses me his shirt, but I'm too distracted to catch it. The shirt lands on my head, and I grab it, wiping my face on the cotton.

Oh, gosh, it smells amazing. Pine trees and mint and the ocean.

When I'm done subtly huffing the biker's T-shirt, I busy myself with folding it up nice and neat.

"Thank you, mister…?"

"Blade."

"Thanks, Mr. Blade."

"Just Blade."

"Oh." I sniffle, holding the shirt out for him to take. I try not to gawk at his glorious body on display, but I'm fascinated. "I'm Sonya."

"Sonya," he repeats, finally taking the shirt. He stares at the neat and tidy folded edges, then unfolds it and puts the shirt back on. Shame. "Look, my club owns a repair shop. We can tow your car there, but I don't know if there's much we can do to save it."

My eyes fill with tears once more at the mention of my stupid car.

"But we'll try," he says, holding his hands out in front of him. "Just... no more tears. It makes my chest hurt for some reason."

I don't think he meant to say that last part out loud, and I'm not sure what it means. From the look on his face, he's confused as well.

"I don't have any money to pay you. I don't have... anything. Do you like Alanis Morissette?"

He tilts his head to the side, those dark eyes narrowing at me.

I sigh. "Never mind."

"We'll work out the details later. Let me make a call and get the tow truck out here. I'll give you a ride into town."

"That's very generous of you, but like I said, I don't have much money. Not for a car repair, not for a hotel. I was going to get a job wherever I ended up, but..." I shrug, letting the rest of the thought hang in the air.

Blade crosses his arms over his chest and looks at the sky as if searching for a solution among the clouds. After a few moments, he lowers his head and looks directly at me. "It seems as though you ended up here. You can stay in one of the spare rooms at the clubhouse while you get back on your feet."

Something strange washes over me, and I feel like a hot piece of coal is stuck in my gut. All the hairs on the back of my neck stand up, and I square my shoulders as I cross my arms over my chest, matching his stance. "I don't need a man to take care of me," I inform him.

"Clearly," he deadpans.

"I'm capable of doing stuff all on my own."

"I'm sure you are."

"I can make my own decisions," I tell him through clenched teeth. I'm unsure who I'm trying to convince, myself or Blade.

The mysterious man uncrosses his arms, letting them rest at his sides. His shoulders relax slightly, and this time, when his eyes rest on mine, they're a little softer. Blade furrows his brow, though not in annoyance like before. It's more like he's studying me the same way I've been studying him this whole time. Like he's trying to figure out what my story is.

Finally, he breaks the silence. "And what is your decision, Sonya?"

Oh, wow. Why do I like hearing him say my name?

"I…" Taking a deep breath, I straighten my spine and attempt to project confidence. "I'm deciding to accept your job offer, but only until I pay off the car. Then I'll be on my way."

"Sounds good."

"But I'm doing it for me. Not because you're some knight in shining armor coming to save the day."

Blade coughs out what I think is a laugh. "Never been accused of that, so you have nothing to worry about there."

"Right. So. We have a deal?"

I hold out my hand for him to shake. Blade stares at it, and his eyes flicker up to meet mine. We never break eye contact as he wraps his massive hand around mine. Instead of shaking it, however, Blade just holds my hand.

I can't look away, and for some reason, neither can he. I'm drawn toward him, my body swaying forward like a flower turning toward the sun.

Blade snaps out of whatever hold we were in, dropping my hand as if it burned him. "I'll make the call. Grab whatever you need from your car and wait by my bike."

"Sir, yes, sir," I tell him, saluting the six-and-a-half-foot beast.

Something dark passes over his features, but it's gone before I figure out why.

As I grab my duffel bag from the back seat, I remember my father's last words.

The Devil will have your soul within a week.

Looking over my shoulder at Blade, I think my dad may have been right for once. But I trust this devil more than my own flesh and blood. I can only hope I'm not making a huge mistake.

CHAPTER TWO

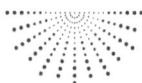

BLADE

*W*hat the hell am I doing?

I've been asking myself that for the last five minutes as I work out the details of the tow truck with Axel over the phone.

I did what any decent human would do when seeing someone stranded on the side of the road. I was going to stop, call a tow truck, and be on my way. That was before I saw Sonya.

I mean, what the hell is a curvy little blonde bombshell doing out here on this relatively deserted highway? What was she thinking, driving her piece of shit car into the ground with no destination and no means to fix it when it inevitably broke down?

But those eyes. Goddamn, if they didn't knock the fuckin' air from my lungs the moment I saw them. Paired with golden blonde hair, a slender nose, rounded cheeks, and a smile that could break a man weaker than myself, she's a lethal little package.

"Yo, Prez? You still there?"

"Yeah," I grunt over the phone. "All repairs will be charged to me. It's going to be a beast to fix, and honestly, we might not be able to salvage it."

"I'm up for the challenge," Axel assures me. He's our newest patched-in member of the Savage Saints and eager to take on any task I hand him. Love his enthusiasm, even if I can't match it. It's been good for the club to have some fresh blood.

"Good," I reply before hanging up.

I inhale deeply, rolling out my shoulders and preparing to be in Sonya's presence. I hope to God and everything holy that she's stopped crying. She burst into tears when I told her about her engine being blown. Unfortunately, I've been around crying women before, but I've never had the reaction I did with Sonya.

It was the strangest fucking thing. My heart lurched, making my chest tight. Felt like someone reached right into my ribcage and tore the damn thing out. Then I snapped at her, and she apologized…

Fuck me. I rub the heel of my hand over my heart, trying to ease the tension.

I need to set Sonya up in one of the rooms at the club-house before I slam down a bottle of whiskey with my MC brothers. I'm probably stressed from all the bullshit with the dirty cops in this town. That's why I'm having chest pain. It can't possibly be from one woman. One gorgeous, curvy, heartbreaking woman.

Dammit.

I shove my phone in my pocket and make my way over to my bike. I try keeping my gaze on the ground, but my eyes are drawn to hers. Blue eyes watch me approach, and I see her tense ever so slightly. I hope I don't frighten her, which is another new feeling for me.

"Ever been on a motorcycle?" I ask her as I mount the bike.

The golden strands of her hair catch the rays of the setting sun as she shakes her head no. I should have guessed. Pretty little thing like her was probably warned about guys like me.

"No, but I've always wanted to," she replies, her light blue eyes sparkling.

Why can't I look away from her? "Put your bag in that back compartment," I grunt a little more harshly than I meant. I can't help it. Everything about this woman is throwing me off my game. I clear my throat and try to be more civil. "Now, swing your leg over the bike and scoot up behind me. Use my shoulders for balance if you need."

Sonya looks at me, the bike, then me again. She nibbles on her bottom lip and nods. All the tension drains from my body when her soft little hand rests on my shoulder. Sonya sits and adjusts herself, but she's too far away. For riding purposes, that is. Not anything else.

"Closer," I tell her, trying not to growl. "Wrap your arms around my waist to keep you steady."

"Okay," comes her quiet reply.

The confounding woman does as I say, pressing her body against mine and clinging to my torso. Her thighs squeeze mine, and it takes a considerable amount of energy not to picture her thighs wrapped around me in a different way.

Fuck. So not appropriate.

"Ready?" I ask.

Sonya nods, and I start the engine. It roars to life, and Sonya tightens her hold on me.

"I'll go slow," I tell her.

"No!" she shouts over the sound of the engine. "Don't you dare. I might not get this chance again, and I want to enjoy every minute."

Huh. That was unexpected, but I'm not complaining.

Who would have thought the first woman I've ever had on the back of my bike would be this little ray of sunshine?

I rev the engine and pull onto the highway, getting up to speed in no time.

"Woo! *Yeaaaah!*" Sonya exclaims as we tear down the road.

I'm only doing the speed limit, but I'm sure it feels like a hundred miles an hour from her perspective. I remember my first time on a motorcycle. The rush of adrenaline. The vibration of the engine as it rocketed me forward. The wind whipping my face and bringing me back into my body after a stressful and exhausting fight with my father. One ride, and I was hooked. I knew what I wanted to do with my life.

When was the last time I felt that free? That sure of myself?

"This… is… *incredible!*" Sonya shouts.

I feel her laughing, her entire body shaking as she wraps herself tighter around my back. A grin tugs at my lips, which is odd. I can't seem to help it around this woman. She's crying about her car one minute, then throwing caution to the wind and hopping on the back of a bike with a stranger the next. I get the sense that whatever Sonya does, she does it with her whole heart and all of her energy.

Eventually, we pull into the Savage Saints clubhouse, though I admit I took the long way. Not because I like having Sonya on the back of my bike or anything. She was so excited about the ride, and I wanted to ensure she got the most out of it. She said it herself; she might not get another chance.

I park the bike and help Sonya off before swinging my leg over and standing up. Sonya's hair is wild, and her eyes are bright and excited. I get the insane urge to brush my fingers across her rosy cheeks, glowing from her first time on a motorcycle. She gives me the most radiant smile, and damn if I don't return it. Kind of. Mine's a bit rusty, and I think it came out as a grimace.

"Th-th-thank-k you," she stutters, her body still shaking.

She stumbles a bit, and I reach out to steady her with a hand on her hip. "Careful," I rasp, my voice not working for some reason. Certainly not because I'm holding onto this woman's ample curves. "First ride can take a bit to come down from."

Sonya nods and leans into my touch, snuggling against my side. I tense, not sure what to do. My arm moves on its own, coming to rest on her shoulders. The woman sighs, relaxing even more, though the occasional tremor still runs down her spine.

It's too much. I don't know what to do with these… feelings. Warmth. Longing. Concern. Everything is all jumbled up, and I need space to clear my mind.

Straightening up, I take a small step away from Sonya, dropping my arm from her shoulders. She takes the hint and turns on her heel to grab her bag from the back compartment.

Jesus, get it together. You're helping someone in a tough spot, not proposing marriage.

When Sonya has her things collected, I nod toward the front door. As soon as we step inside, I regret not taking her around the back.

A dozen pairs of eyes land on us, most of them sizing up Sonya. Out of nowhere, a possessive rage fills my lungs, pushing out every other thought and sensation.

I loop my arm around her waist and tuck her into my side as I take long strides toward the back rooms. My men know me well enough to get the hell out of my way, but I know they'll be talking about me when I leave the room. I'll have to come back out here and set the record straight.

Sonya's not mine, but she's sure as hell not theirs.

"Um, it's hard to keep up with you," she whispers at my side.

I tighten my hold on her and press her curvy little body closer to mine as I lift her, half carrying, half dragging her to the back.

"Oof, that's not exactly what I had in mind," she says once I set her down in the furthest room from the bar.

"Here's your room," I inform her, keeping my tone even. Detached. I don't think it's working.

"Thank you again. For everything."

I nod in acknowledgment.

"Are you always this intense?" she asks, throwing me off guard yet again. "I can't picture you making your bed with the same gruffness. Or brushing your teeth. Do you frown at yourself in the mirror?"

Dimples pop out on her adorable cheeks because, of course, she has fucking dimples. Smiles, sparkling eyes, and dimples. Sonya is all rainbows and butterflies, and I'm a hardened MC President with a black heart and a stained soul.

But something shifts as I look into those endless eyes. I move forward, unable to stay away from her light. Sonya peers up at me, holding her breath as I lean down and brush my lips against the side of her neck.

This is dangerous. I shouldn't know that her skin tastes like sugar and sunshine. Yet, I'm unable to stop.

When I reach the shell of her ear, I whisper, "I'm intense about the things that matter. My club. My bike. My woman… who I found on the side of the road," I finish before taking two huge steps backward.

Shit. Not my woman. Sonya is not my woman. I've known her for less than an hour. So what if she's unlike anyone I've ever met and elicits emotions I've buried for decades? It's too risky. Women are never who they say they are. I have a lifetime of watching my dad go through wives and girlfriends to back me up on that.

"Oh," is all Sonya says.

She lifts a hand to the side of her neck where my lips were. She traces the line with her fingertips, drawing my attention there.

I rip my eyes away from the siren and give her my back. "We'll get started on your car tomorrow."

"Okay," comes her response.

She seems confused, and I don't blame her. I don't have any answers for her. I have no idea what just happened, only that it can't happen again.

Even as I shut the door and walk back to the bar, I know I'm full of shit.

CHAPTER THREE

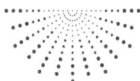

SONYA

I tuck the last corner of the bed sheet under the mattress, spread out the comforter, and turn it down at the top. Next, I place the pillow in its spot, smoothing out the wrinkles from the pillowcase.

I've been on the road and away from my family for five days, but the morning ritual of making my bed and having it inspection-ready will take some time to wear off. When I woke up this morning, I half expected my mother to come bursting through the door at any moment, yelling at me for sleeping in so late.

Back at home, my sister and I were up before the sun. With endless cooking and cleaning to do, we were taught at a young age that, as women, our chores completed us as we completed them.

Looking back down at the pristinely made bed, I get a wicked idea. One that's too tempting to pass up.

I spin around and flop down on the bed, splaying my arms and legs out and making a snow angel in the blankets. The neatly tucked-in sheets come loose on one corner, then the other, while the comforter twists around my limbs. I grab the pillow and toss it in the air, watching it sail up, up, up… and back down into Blade's large, tattooed hands.

He raises an eyebrow at me, and lordy, he's as devastatingly handsome and broody as I remember. I sit up in bed, blowing a few loose strands of hair from my face before smiling at him.

"What's this about?" he grunts, shaking the pillow. "And why is your door unlocked?"

"Good morning to you, too, Mr. Grumpy Pants," I tease.

He blinks at me, apparently not amused at my nickname for him.

"For your information, my door was locked all night. I only recently unlocked it since you said you were stopping by this morning."

Blade nods, which is about as much approval as I can hope from him at this point. "And throwing the pillow?"

"I'm enjoying that I don't have to make my bed anymore," I tell him.

The man stares at me, tilting his head to the side. He looks at me like that a lot, and I wonder if I'm as interesting to him as he is to me.

"Thrilling," he says flatly.

I grin and hop off the bed, sliding into my pink ballerina flats. They match my light pink sundress, which my mom told me was "inappropriate for my body type." That was her sanitized way of telling me I was fat and no one wanted to see all that skin.

But today is a new day, and I no longer have to listen to that crap. She doesn't define me, nor does my father or the men my parents tried to match me up with.

"I agree. It's not as freeing as riding on a motorcycle, but it's a little piece of freedom for me, you know?"

Blade furrows his brow, his eyes darkening slightly as he

stares a hole right through my brain. I'm unsure what he's thinking, but his ever-serious, stoic eyes soften slightly.

"Good," he declares. "Never make the bed again. Fuck sheets and pillows."

I giggle at his over-the-top reaction, and Blade freezes. The laughter dies on my lips, and I worry I've offended him. "Is everything okay?"

He grunts because of course he does. "Your laugh... I like it."

I'm unsure who's more shocked at his words, but I'm the first to recover.

"Thanks," I whisper. "I'm sure I'll like yours, too."

Blade grunts again, and I narrow my eyes at him playfully. He eyes me right back, but I see the barest inkling of a smirk on his lips. Everything about this man is hard and prickly, but I'm determined to find a soft spot. After all, he can't be all bad. He helped me on the side of the road and offered me a place to stay.

"Let's go check on your car," he says, quickly changing the subject. Blade spins on his heel, already halfway down the hall by the time I get to the door.

"Hey! Short person over here!" I call after him.

Blade stops in his tracks and stands stock still as I jog up beside him. Without a word, he takes a smaller step forward, watching me and matching my steps.

"Much better," I tell him with a smile.

Blade hums, the sound low and gravelly and not unlike his grunt. There's a slight difference, though, and I probably shouldn't know that.

We walk in silence across the street from the clubhouse and down a few blocks until we get to the Savage Saints Repair Shop. Power tools, clanking metal, and engines revving fill the air, followed quickly by the smell of rubber and gasoline.

"Oh wow," I say softly as we walk past huge open garage doors, each containing projects in varying stages of completion. Up until earlier this week, I had never driven a car. Now I'm watching people take them apart.

"Never been to the mechanic?" Blade asks, breaking the silence between us.

"I haven't been to a lot of places," I answer truthfully.

Blade peers down at me, that same concerned, slightly confused look in his eyes as earlier.

Thankfully, we're interrupted before Blade can ask any more questions. It's not that I want to hide anything from him, but I don't want to burden him with my sob story. Besides, it's irrelevant to my car, so I'm sure he doesn't care.

"Yo, Prez! I have you over here," someone says, pulling our attention in that direction.

"Thanks, Axel," Blade replies as he heads to the last stall in the garage.

"Prez?" I ask as I scurry to keep up with the tall men and their long strides.

As if remembering I'm short, Blade stops and waits for me to catch up, then matches my steps. "That's my title," comes his simple and inadequate response.

"As in... president?"

A single nod is all I get in confirmation.

Axel speaks up before I can ask what he's the president of. "I've got some unfortunate news about the car," he starts as he opens the hood of my red Toyota circa 1999. "We flushed out all the ethanol from the engine and cleaned her up a bit, but we're going to need a replacement. Might take a while to find the right parts with this being an older vehicle..."

Axel's voice fades into the background as I stare at the now shiny but worthless engine.

"Sonya?" Blade asks, his tone indicating this isn't the first time he's said my name. "Do you have somewhere to be? A deadline or anything?"

I shake my head no, swallowing past the lump in my throat.

"Where did you drive this thing from?" Axel asks.

"Um… Pennsylvania," I whisper, unsure if I should be giving out that information.

"Where are you headed after this? Maybe you can take a loaner car?"

"I… I don't know. I don't… I don't have a plan," I admit softly.

Tears well up, but I blink them away, not wanting to upset Blade or look stupid in front of Axel. Not that any of that matters at this point. I'm a failure, like my father told me. Alone, broke, and homeless.

My head spins, and I grip the side of the car to steady myself. I'm vaguely aware of Blade thanking Axel before his hand rests on the small of my back, guiding me through the back door and into the lobby. He leads me into an office in the back and encourages me to sit on the couch. He joins me a second later, leaning forward with his elbows on his knees.

"We'll fix your car," he says, his gaze as serious as ever.

"It's not just the car," I say miserably. I can't look at him while I'm feeling like a foolish child. "I don't… I don't have any money. No plan. Nothing. What was I thinking? Stupid, right? Silly, stupid Sonya, thinking she could make it alone."

"Sonya, you're not stupid."

"Stranded, then."

Blade huffs out a grunt. "Can't be stranded if you don't know where you're going," he counters.

A smile replaces my frown at his response. He's trying to make me feel better in his own way.

"Furthermore, I don't need a car if I have no destination,

right? So the problem solves itself!" I joke. The intense, tatted-up biker frowns at me, and I can't help but laugh.

"That's not what I was saying," he sighs.

"When's the last time you smiled?" I blurt.

Blade's brow tips up. His mouth opens and closes before he frowns. "When's the last time you got angry?"

It's my turn to raise my eyebrow. I wasn't expecting that question, and honestly, I don't know the answer. "I... I was always told that anger is a bad emotion. So I try to transform the anger into understanding and gaining a new perspective."

Blade stares at me for a beat, then shakes his head. "That's bullshit," he says matter-of-factly.

I can't help but giggle. He's so freaking serious about everything. He also hasn't answered my question about smiling, which breaks a little piece of my heart.

The corner of his lips twitch, and for a moment, I think he might reward me with a smile. It's short-lived, but he was trying. I hope I can bring that out in him.

"Look, how about you help out around the shop?" Blade offers.

"I'm not sure you want me poking around cars. Might be bad for business."

He gives me some side eye, but there's a glint of amusement in those dark depths. "You'll stick to the lobby area, making appointments, light filing, organizing, stuff like that." Suddenly, Blade's eyes widen, and he looks at me as if struck by a horrible realization. "Not that I think you're only good enough to be a secretary. But with the cars and my guys not having any manners, and..."

"Slow down there," I tell him, placing a hand on his massive shoulder.

Blade relaxes at my touch, and I want to curl up in his lap. I don't, of course, but I've never had an urge like that before.

"I'm not offended," I say with a smile. I don't blame him

for thinking I'd be sensitive, especially after I yelled at him yesterday that *I don't need no man*.

"Thank god," he says with a relieved sigh. "I just want to help. You'll be set up with a job and a place to stay while your car is being worked on."

"Why?"

Blade tilts his head again, searching my eyes for something.

"Why, what?"

"Why do you want to help? You don't even know me. I mean nothing to you. I'm just some random girl you found on the side of the road. I'm sure this isn't what you had in mind when you pulled over yesterday."

Blade moves closer on the couch until his knee touches mine. I look at where our legs make contact, then catch Blade's brown eyes with mine.

"It wasn't what I had in mind," he confirms, "but I don't regret a single thing. Do you?"

I shake my head no, swaying closer to him

Blade slides his hand over my cheek, then cups the back of my neck. My skin prickles with awareness as his fingertips weave through the hair on the back of my head.

"I think we're good for each other, don't you?"

I can't look away. I'm completely enraptured by his touch, his stare, every breath and beat of his heart. "Yes, sir," I whisper, my voice barely above a whisper.

"Love when you call me that," he rasps, dipping his head to ghost his lips over my temple. His voice is harsh, restrained almost, but his kiss is gentle, barely even there.

"Sir?" I question, ensuring I understood him. I'm a little light-headed from being this close to the sexiest man I've ever seen.

"Mmhmm," he grunts before backing away. Blade drops his hand from my neck, and I shiver as a cold breeze blows through me. "Now," he says, clapping his hands together as he stands. "You'll start work tomorrow afternoon. First, I need to take you somewhere in the morning."

"Oh?" I ask curiously, taking his offered hand.

He pulls me up, steadying me with a hand on my hip before stepping away. "You'll like it. I think. Either way, you need it."

"Okay, now I'm more confused than ever."

Blade gives me a mischievous look, and God help me, he's somehow even more lethal with that little spark in his eyes. "Do you trust me?"

I stare at him, holding his gaze for a moment before nodding. "I do."

"Good. Now that we have that settled, I need to get to work. Grab lunch at the clubhouse and ask around for Tessa. She's Hawk's old lady. Nice girl, I'm sure you two will get along."

I only understood half of what he said, but I nod, getting the gist. With a devious grin, I reply, "Yes, sir."

Spinning on my heel, I scurry out the door in time to hear Blade groan. I have no idea what that's about, but it makes my stomach dance and flip. I can't wait to see what else Blade likes.

CHAPTER FOUR

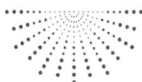

BLADE

"*I*s it true?" Rider asks as soon as I call church into session.

"How the fuck did this happen?" another man asks.

"We're not going to stand for this, right, Prez?"

"Silence!" I demand from my position at the front of the room. Every member seated in church shuts their mouth and turns their attention to me. "Yes, that fuck-wit of a sheriff, Darren, is out of prison."

The room erupts in a chorus of boos and grunts. I slam my hands down on the table in front of me, the sound echoing around the room and causing my men to focus back on me.

"He got off on a bullshit technicality that I'm sure his cronies helped him out with." More chatter and muttered curse words float around the room, and I know I'm losing them. I get it.

Sheriff Darren, the father of Hawk's old lady, Tessa, is about as corrupt as they come. Not only did he have Rider thrown in prison on false charges, but he was an abusive piece of shit to his daughter. And that's just a start. The man has ruled over this small California town for more than a decade with his police force of dirty cops ready to do his bidding.

Recently, we discovered the cops were reselling confiscated drugs across state lines. I mean, what the fuck? So much for serving and protecting. Ironic that the outlaw MC in town is cleaner than the actual law enforcement. This shit has to stop. Soon.

"Important takeaways from this," I shout over the muffled complaints and grunts. "The Sheriff is back with a vengeance. He's out for blood, and so are we. Be on the lookout and report anything suspicious. We'll find an opening, a weak spot, and exploit the hell out of it."

I look out across the room at the nodding heads, and I know my men are more determined than ever to wipe this fucker off the face of the earth. Not just him, either. It's not enough to take down the leader. We know that now. If it's war they want, we'll give it to them.

"Fuckin' right we will," Rider grunts.

I catch his eye and nod. This is far more personal for him and Hawk. Darren has pissed me the hell off and ruined my town, but Hawk and Rider have experienced his wrath firsthand. I'll ensure they get a few good swings in before I put the Sheriff six feet under.

"Dismissed!" I call out.

My men shuffle out of the back room, aside from Rider and Hawk. I figured they'd want more information and a more specific mission. There's a reason these two are my most trusted brothers.

"What do you have on him?" Rider jumps in, crossing his arms over his chest as he leans in a bit closer.

"Yeah, what can we do, Prez? I'll rip his goddamn head off if he dares to lay a finger on Tessa again. Hell, I'll rip it off anyway for the damage he's already done," Hawk adds.

"Can't go in guns blazing. You two know that, but I'm here to say it again to get it through your skulls. We're dealing with an entire police force."

"What about the FBI agents who originally arrested the sheriff? Can we get in contact with them? Surely they can't let this slide," Rider says.

"They've been on suspension since Darren's trial, but a contact I have informed me there may be a new officer investigating the charges and implications they have for the local police force."

"That's something, I guess," Rider grunts.

"It's too slow. Wait for an agent to fix everything? That's not our style," Hawk adds.

"Hell, no. We're not sitting back and letting the FBI handle this—if they follow up at all. I'm just saying we need leverage. Having a man on the inside wouldn't be the worst thing in the world."

"Axel can rig up surveillance shit again," Hawk interjects.

"And he has," I say, a warning in my tone. Hawk is all wrapped up in protecting Tessa, but that doesn't mean he gets to question me or demand that I do something. "We need more. Better info than tracking squad cars and audio recordings from the lobby. We need to be in planning meetings and back alley deals. Someone on the inside has access that we'll never have."

Hawk nods but wisely shuts up.

After a beat of silence, Rider changes the subject unexpectedly. "So, you got yourself a woman now?"

Hawk's eyebrows shoot up to his hairline, his mood instantly changing. "Blondie?"

"No. What? We're not... it's not... she's in a rough spot and needs a place to crash."

"And a job?" Rider inquires.

"And a car repair?" Hawk unhelpfully adds.

"Yes, and those things," I grunt. "It's not a big deal."

"Maybe not to some, but it's certainly notable for a man with an *all-women-are-crazy*-sized chip on his shoulder."

I glare at Hawk, who has a stupid smirk on his face. Looking over at Rider, I narrow my eyes at him as well when I see the same smirk on his face.

"Whatever," I mutter, pushing past them. "I have somewhere to be," I tell them over my shoulder.

"Going to see Blondie?" Hawk calls out.

"Fuck you," I grunt.

They bust up laughing, and though they're annoying, they're not wrong. Sonya is certainly notable.

I make my way down the hall to the spare rooms, my steps slowing the closer I get to Sonya's. I don't know why I'm so nervous. It's not like I'm picking her up for a date or anything. *Then why are my hands so sweaty? And why is my heart stuttering and stopping the longer I stand in front of her closed door?*

Shoving those thoughts aside, I take a deep breath and knock on the door. I realized yesterday I invaded her space by walking right in, but I truly wasn't expecting the door to be unlocked.

A second later, it swings open, revealing the object of my obsession in a yellow dress. It has lacy sleeves and hits just below her knees. She's radiant, as always. The sun shining through the window behind her lights her up like an angel.

"Hey," she says with a smile.

I try greeting her, but all that comes out is a half cough, half grunt. She doesn't mind. In fact, I'm rewarded with an even bigger smile. Why does she do that? I've been told my gruff demeanor can be off-putting, and truthfully, that always suited me fine. Sonya seems to find my grunts entertaining.

"So, where are we going? Am I dressed appropriately?"

The little siren spins, and the hem of her dress lifts enough for me to get a peek at her thick thighs and smooth, creamy skin. I tear my eyes from her legs, focusing instead on her hair. I'm mesmerized by the sun sparking in the waves of her golden hair and the strands brushing across her cheeks and lips as she spins.

"You're perfect," I say without thinking.

Sonya stops spinning. Her hair falls around her shoulders, framing her round cheeks and wide blue eyes. "You're not too bad yourself," comes her cheeky response. "Now, are you going to tell me where we're going or what?" she asks, her hands on her hips. She narrows her eyes at me, but she's about as intimidating as a fluffy kitten.

"It's a surprise," I tell her, stepping aside so she can join me in the hallway.

I wait until Sonya takes a step, consciously trying to match her pace. After a few steps, she shocks the hell out of me by looping her arm through mine. I stop and look down at our connection, causing Sonya to jerk backward. I quickly recover and resume walking, but I swear I feel her touch every-fucking-where in my body.

This woman is going to be the death of me.

Once we're settled on my bike, I peel out of the parking lot, loving how Sonya cheers and clings to me as we race down the road. We wind around back roads that take us to the edge of town and further into the desert country. I pull over and park the bike close to my favorite lookout spot, hidden amongst the brush and cacti.

"Uh, is this the part where you bury my body in the desert where no one will find me?" Sonya asks with a nervous laugh as she dismounts.

I follow, coming around to stand in front of her. "No," I answer, holding out my hand. Sonya hits me with those damn blue eyes of hers, an intoxicating mix of vulnerability and strength shining up at me. "Do you trust me?"

"Yes," she says softly, much like when I asked her yesterday.

I can't explain the rush it gives me to know this precious woman trusts me. She places her delicate hand in my much rougher one, and I wrap my fingers around it and lead her to the edge of the lookout point.

"Wow," Sonya breathes. "It's like the sea, only... sand."

I nod, guiding her to stand in front of me. I hold Sonya by the hips, keeping her steady as I lean down and brush my lips against the shell of her ear. "There's no one here to judge you," I whisper. "No one will punish you for not making your bed or speaking out of turn. You're completely free here. Can you feel it?"

Sonya inhales sharply, holding her breath for a beat before exhaling everything. She nods and looks at me over her shoulder. "Yeah," she murmurs.

"Free to do whatever the fuck you want. Free to say whatever you've been keeping locked up inside."

"How do you...?"

She doesn't have to finish the question for me to know what she wanted to ask. "How do I know you have something burning you up from the inside?"

Sonya nods.

"Everyone gets angry. From what little you've shared of your life, I think your anger is justified. Someone told you to behave under threat of punishment. They made you feel like you had to be perfect to be accepted. Am I close to the truth?"

"Too close," Sonya whispers. "It wasn't all my parents' fault. They were doing what the church commanded. What the pastor commanded."

"Then get angry at them, too."

"So much negativity won't solve anything. I'm on my own path now, away from all of that. There's no use dwelling on the past."

"Then there's no healing from it, either."

Sonya blinks and turns her attention back to the desert spread in front of her. She leans back, resting her head on my shoulder as I wrap my arms around her from behind.

"You have to feel it," I continue.

"What if… what if it consumes me?" Her voice is so soft, I barely hear her words.

"Then I'll be right here to bring you back."

"Promise?"

I nuzzle into the side of her neck, loving how she smells and how smooth her skin feels against my stubble.

"Promise, baby. Now, shout it out."

"Uh, what?" Sonya looks at me over her shoulder again, the cutest confused expression on her face.

"Scream into the void. Feel the rage, the injustice, the years of lies and bullshit, and shout out the pain."

"What do I say?"

"Whatever you want."

"I… I honestly can't remember the last time I shouted. I've never screamed, or at least not since I was a baby. It's not attractive or ladylike."

"Yeah, fuck that shit, baby girl."

Sonya laughs, the sweetest little burst of joy sparkling in her eyes. "You're right. I know you are, I just… It feels silly."

"Want me to go first?"

She nods.

I grin and clear my throat, then holler, "FUCK!"

Sonya jumps in my arms, then snorts a laugh.

"Now, you go," I encourage.

"I don't think I can say the F word," she says, though the fire in her eyes lets me know she can.

"Start with something smaller, but it has to be rebellious."

"Okay… Um… Ass crack!" she says in a normal voice.

I narrow my eyes at her, though her choice of expletive is amusing. She rolls her eyes, then says it a little louder.

"Come on, Sonya. That's nowhere near shouting, let alone screaming. Let me hear what you can do."

"Fricking cow-*dung*!" she bellows out.

"You've got the volume. Now let's work on content," I tell her, still grinning down at her. "It's fun. And cathartic. Give it a try."

Sonya nods, standing up a little straighter. She takes a deep breath, then shouts, "Fuck you and your fucking oppressive rules!"

"That's it, baby," I tell her, spreading a hand over her stomach to keep her close.

"I can wear *whatever the hell* I want," she continues. "My body isn't yours, and it's nothing to be ashamed of! I get to decide who I marry, *not you*."

I grit my teeth against her shouted confession. I hate whoever told her this shit. I mean, what the fuck?

My girl heaves in a huge breath, then screams nonsense words until she's shaking with the effort. Another inhale, and she lets out a shrill screech, the sound ripping open my heart as I hold her through the storm of emotions bearing down on her.

Finally, Sonya is out of breath, and she collapses against me, silent tears streaming down her face.

"I'm right here," I tell her, gently turning her so we're facing each other. She buries her head into my chest, and I cradle her in my embrace, protecting her from every damn thing. "I've got you, baby girl. Let it out."

"I-I-I…" she stutters. "It's too much."

"It's what you need. I don't know everything about your

past, but you've got some chains that need to be broken, yeah? It hurts, but it's worth it to be free."

"Free," she whispers, nodding into my chest.

We stay wrapped up in each other for long moments. Sonya's breathing slowly returns to normal, her tears drying on my shirt the longer we hold each other.

Eventually, I peel Sonya off my chest, cupping her cheek in the palm of my hand. Blue eyes crash into mine, a little watery from crying but shining with gratitude and a strength I always knew was there.

I lean down as she rises to her toes, our lips meeting in the middle. Sonya melts into me as I sip from her sweetness, one kiss leading to another, another, deeper, more, more…

She opens up for me, and I slide my tongue between her lips, lapping at the roof of her mouth and then tangling my tongue with hers. Sonya gasps and tilts her head up, exposing her neck to me. I groan and nip at her sensitive skin, nearly losing my mind when she lets out a breathy little moan.

My hands move from her back to her hips, gliding up and down her curves before cupping her generous ass.

"Blade," she rasps. Her eyes are closed, her lips swollen and perfect. "Do that again."

"How do good girls ask?" I murmur into the side of her neck.

Sonya snaps her eyes open, glaring at me before a playful smirk spreads across her features. "Please do that again, *sir*."

"Fuck me. When you ask so nicely…"

This time, my lips fuse with hers as I lift her, capturing her startled gasp in my mouth while I continue to devour her. Sonya automatically wraps her legs around my hips, and I growl at how goddamn good it feels having her curves pressed against the hard slats of my muscles.

I walk a few steps back toward my bike and set her on the seat, facing me. Her hands crawl up my shirt, tugging at me to get me closer. I grin, loving that she's as eager and desperate for my touch as I am for hers. Without her telling me, I know my girl hasn't had much experience, if any. I'm all too happy to be the one to explore this side of her.

When our lips meet again, the pull is even stronger. I open my mouth wider, kiss her deeper, needing more, needing something, needing to consume her completely. Sonya moans again, her fingers digging into the back of my head as she takes what she wants from me.

"Fuck," I breathe once we break apart.

We're both out of breath, panting for air. Sonya wraps her arms around me and rests her head on my chest, suddenly shy.

I untangle her arms and kneel in front of her. "Hey," I say softly. "Was that okay? Did I…" Jesus, I couldn't live with myself if I pressured her into a physical relationship. I didn't even know it was going to happen. We just… we kissed, and I lost my damn mind.

"Okay? Um, yeah. Better than I ever could have hoped for." Her cheeks are flushed from our kiss, but they turn crimson at her confession.

The vise around my heart loosens, and I stand, crushing her in my arms again. "Good," I grunt, making Sonya laugh. I'll never get tired of hearing that sound.

"Thank you," she murmurs. "For everything. I wasn't expecting this when I woke up this morning, but I'm not complaining."

The most adorable smile stretches across her lips, and I can't help but lean down and taste it for myself. We get lost in each other once more, our breaths mingling, our hearts beating as one.

I'm the first to pull away, though it takes considerable effort not to lay her on the ground and lick up every inch of her curvy, delectable little body.

"Ready for your first day on the job?" I ask, changing the subject. I need to get my hard-as-fuck dick under control before getting back on my bike.

"Yes, sir," she purrs.

Well, that's not helping the situation any. "You're going to be trouble, aren't you?"

"Yes, sir."

I groan, then help her off the bike, pulling her against me. I swat her ass once, twice, then squeeze her there. Sonya squeals and giggles, then looks up at me with a faux indignant glare.

"Careful, baby girl," I warn. A shiver runs down her spine at my deep tone, and fuck me, she's perfect.

Sonya winks at me, which I like far too much, then spins out of my arms. "Come on, I don't want to be late for my first day. I heard my boss is kind of a growly beast."

I shake my head at her but can't help the grin pulling at my lips as I hop on my motorcycle. Sonya easily slides in behind me, and it occurs to me how natural it feels to have her here with me.

I rev the engine, which I know Sonya loves, and hit the road. My girl laughs as I gain speed, clutching onto me as the wind tangles her hair and carries her voice across the desert.

Hell, yeah. I could get used to this. Now I need to convince Sonya to stay here for good.

CHAPTER FIVE

SONYA

*M*y eyes fly open as I gasp for air, my mind still swimming with the remnants of a nightmare. I sit up, placing a hand over my heart to calm the frantic rhythm.

"What have we said about your weight, Sonya?"

My dad's voice echoes in my brain, and I squeeze my eyes shut, trying to block out the rest of the conversation. It's no use.

"I'm God's creation, and being fat is disrespecting God," comes my practiced answer.

"That's right. And since you're unable to lose the weight yourself, we need to enforce some rules."

"No," I whisper under my breath, breaking the spell of the nightmare. "No," I say again, louder this time. Blade was right —there's power in talking back, fighting the lies, and calling my past what it is… Bullshit.

Grinning to myself at my swear word, I find the strength to pull off the covers and climb out of bed. I've been working at the repair shop for the last four days, and today is my day off. Blade has been "on a mission," whatever that means, for three of those four days. I won't lie, I miss him. Especially after those kisses we shared…

My cheeks heat with the memory of his tongue sliding against mine and the warmth of his hands as he caressed my curves. As far as first kisses go, I think I might have had the best one in the history of the universe.

I go through my new morning routine of washing up, brushing my hair and teeth, and slipping on whatever clothes I want. After years of school uniforms and hand-me-downs from my older sister, I started buying my own clothes at sixteen with my babysitting money. Bright colors, pretty dresses, and shoes to match. My parents never understood, but they aren't here to judge me anymore.

I smile at my reflection in the bathroom mirror. Today, I'm in a blue polka-dotted dress. It's admittedly a little tighter than I remember, but I've probably gained a few pounds since I last wore it.

The material of the A-line dress stretches against my chest and squishes my boobs together, making for a rather scandalous amount of cleavage. Most people probably wouldn't bat an eyelash at my outfit, but I know I'd be called horrible names if I went to First Assembly of God's Chosen like this. Heck, my own mother would call me half of those names before telling me to take off my dress and burn it.

Screw it, I think to myself. This is exactly why I broke free —so I could live my life without the oppression and judgment I grew up with. I do a little shimmy in the mirror, giggling when my breasts shake. My mother would be mortified. Good.

I check the bedside clock, surprised to see it's nearly one in the afternoon. *I guess I needed that sleep.* Thinking back on the last few days, it makes sense. I had a week-long road trip followed by my car breaking down, immediately started a new job, and worked the rest of the week.

Looking over the selection of shoes I was able to pack and take with me, I decide on the blue strappy heels. It's only a two-inch heel, but I can use all the help I can get when it comes to height. Blade doesn't seem to mind that I'm short, but I'm that much closer to him in these shoes.

I roll my eyes at my cheesy thoughts, but they make butterflies swarm in my stomach, nonetheless. Blade should be coming back today. Maybe he's already at the clubhouse?

My heart thuds against my ribcage as my skin breaks out in goosebumps. Part of me is still convinced I made him up, or at the very least, made up that he kissed me. It could have been a dream. Everything about that day, that kiss, was perfect.

I guess there's only one way to find out.

Placing my hand on the doorknob, I turn it and step into the hallway, taking one last grounding breath. After locking the door, I make my way out to the bar area, scanning the tables and booths for my Blade.

I wind through the seating area, ignoring the pit opening in my stomach. He's not here, and the more I look for him, the more attention I attract. Gruff older men stare at me, their eyes wandering from my face to my chest.

Stumbling past the last few tables, I finally reach the bar top, where Tessa is pouring a beer. At least there's one friendly face here.

"Sonya!" Tessa greets as she finishes her pour and hands it to the man standing next to me. He gives me some serious side eye before ambling away. "I was about to go check on you and make sure you didn't slip into a coma," she teases.

"Sorry. I wasn't expecting to be out for that long," I tell her before nibbling on my bottom lip. I push away the voice in my head telling me I'm lazy.

"Hey, there's nothing to apologize for. As long as you're

safe and happy, that's all that matters. If you need sleep, then sleep. It's that simple."

I nod, absorbing Tessa's words. *As long as I'm safe and happy, that's all that matters.* Safe and happy. I honestly don't know if I've ever felt that way until coming here.

"Thanks," I whisper.

Tessa rests her hand on top of mine and gives it a little squeeze before flitting away to help the next customer.

Blade was right. Tessa is awesome, and we've become friends in the last few days. Her best friend, Sutton, has also been hanging around. They're both with members of Savage Saints. I want to ask them a thousand questions about the club and what it's like being the partner of someone with so many responsibilities.

I'm not sure Blade wants people to know we're together, though. If we're even together at all, that is. I'm still half convinced nothing happened between us, and he's going to show up and be his usual growly self.

"Hey, there," someone says from beside me

I startle a bit and turn to address the man. "Hi…" I trail off, not expecting the man to be so close.

I lean away from him and get my first good look at the man. He's on the short side, but he's bulging with muscles that stretch out his leather jacket. He has more than a few teeth missing, which I notice when he gives me what I think is supposed to be a seductive smile.

"You look like a lost little lamb," the man continues. His voice is scratchy and grates against my skin with each word he speaks.

"Um, no. I-I-I'm supposed to be here," I inform him, though my voice is wobbly.

"You sure about that? You don't sound convinced. Either way, I bet I could make you feel right at home. What do you think, little lamb?"

He scoots closer, crowding my space as his eyes roam up and down my body.

I haven't prayed since leaving home, but I start praying now, asking for the floor to open up and swallow me so I don't have to be in this man's presence for one second longer.

"N-no, I'm just waiting—"

"Waiting for Prince Charming? You're not gonna find him here. I can show you a good time, though."

Before I can react, the man lunges, his hand inches from my chest. I'm about to scream when he's suddenly pulled back. I watch wide-eyed as the creep is lifted from the chair by a tattooed hand wrapped around his neck.

Blade.

He tosses the other man to the floor and spits on him before stepping on his chest with his massive boot. "Stay there, fucker. I'll deal with you in a second."

I'm shaking from head to toe, frozen in place as I stare at Blade. As if sensing my gaze, he jerks his head up, and his deep brown eyes lock on mine.

My heart sinks to my stomach when I see anger and disgust staring right back at me. *Is he mad at me? What did I do? How can I make it better?*

"Go to your room," he commands me through gritted teeth. His nostrils flare as his jaw pops from clenching his teeth.

Something snaps in my brain. One minute, I'm in the bar, and the next, I'm floating out of my body. My mind flickers and flashes until all I can hear is my father screaming at me to go to my room.

I'm barely aware of my feet shuffling along the floor. I need to get to my room before I make things worse.

Don't cry. Father hates tears. Don't talk back. It's against God's rules, and Dad will have to punish me. Just be quiet, back against the wall, don't talk, don't flinch, don't breathe.

I burst into my room. I'm confused. It doesn't look like my bedroom at home, but I somehow know it's mine. The past mixes with the present, flashing lights, my father's voice, the crack of the Bible as he uses it to slap my face...

A shudder works its way down my spine, followed by another and another, until I'm trembling and nearly hyper-ventilating. Still, I press my back against the wall, standing as straight as possible and trying to make sure my heels, calves, butt, back, shoulders, and head are all touching the wall.

It's harder than one might think, but I've gotten some-what used to it. Until about minute twenty or so, anyway. That's when the muscles start to cramp.

I squeeze my eyes shut, the anticipation of my father walking in with his belt and his Bible making me sick to my stomach. How many lashes will I get this time? How long will his sermon on my sinful ways be? Last time, it was over an hour, and I had a muscle spasm in my leg from standing tense for so long. Not that my father believed me. It was just another way for me to rebel in his book.

The first tear falls, and I curse myself for being so weak.

I'm sorry. I'm so sorry. Please forgive me. Please...

CHAPTER SIX

BLADE

*A*s soon as Sonya is out of the bar, I grab Chains by the collar of his shirt and drag him outside, tossing him down on the gravel with a thud.

"What the hell?" Chains grunts as I hover over him.

"Women are to be protected, not assaulted!" I shout.

Chains tries to crawl away from me, but I pin him to the ground with my knee on his chest.

"She was showing off the goods," he protests. "She wanted it. She was just being a bitch and playing games with me."

I'm fucking livid. Does this man want to die? Crimson frames my vision, and I seriously consider stomping this asshole's face in. Sonya doesn't need to see that side of me, however. Instead, I punch Chains in the nose, grunting in satisfaction when it snaps.

Blood pours from his nose and mouth, but I'm not done yet. Standing, I wait until Chains tries to get up before sinking my boot in his stomach. A pathetic cry falls from his lips as he curls up into the fetal position.

"You're suspended until further notice. The officers and I

will meet in a few months to decide the fate of your membership."

"Are you fucking kidding–"

I lunge toward him, and he wisely shuts his mouth. "Get the fuck out of here before I change my mind and put you six feet under."

Chains struggles to get to his feet, limping across the parking lot to his bike. I watch as he shakily gets on his motorcycle and peels out.

Taking a deep breath, I wipe my bloody hands on my shirt and roll my shoulders. Goddamnit, that's not how I wanted to greet Sonya after not seeing her for four days.

My men and I got back from a run a few hours ago, and I immediately went to the clubhouse to check on Sonya. Her door was locked, which I knew meant she was still sleeping. As much as I wanted to beat down the door and crawl into bed with her, she needed her sleep.

I puttered around the shop for a while, then returned to the clubhouse to work on a few things in my office. By the time I made it back out to the bar, Sonya was there, and she was about to be assaulted by one of my men.

I fucking snapped. No one, *no one*, is going to violate my woman and get away with it. Just thinking about the scene I walked in on has my skin prickling and my feet itching to chase after Chains and put a bullet in his head after all.

But Sonya needs me. I was harsh with her when I told her to go to her room, but my mind was racing with all the ways I wanted to hurt Chains. Getting Sonya somewhere safe was my priority, and I knew she'd be safe in her room while I dealt with her attacker.

Sonya is in a vulnerable position. From what I've gathered of her past, she's had a lifetime of people yelling at her. I hate that I'm one more person to tell her what to do, and I need to ask for her forgiveness once I ensure she's okay.

I make my way back to the clubhouse, jogging around the back so I don't have to face questions from my men. Getting to Sonya is the only thing on my mind. Stopping quickly in the bathroom, I scrub the blood and sweat from my hands and face, then grab a clean shirt from my office and throw it on.

Standing in front of Sonya's door, I take a grounding breath as I think of what to say. When I hear a sniffle on the other side of the door, I burst through, not caring about the right words as long as I can see her and hold her.

I'm not prepared for the scene in front of me, however. I furrow my brow, unsure why Sonya is standing against the wall in the corner of the room. She's shaking as silent tears stream down her cheeks.

I rush over to her, but she flinches away from me as if I'm going to strike her. Jesus, that hurts. My chest feels like it's being ripped open at the thought of Sonya being afraid of me.

"I'm not going to hurt you," I tell her softly. Well, as softly as a gruff, bitter old biker can manage.

Sonya doesn't look up at me, instead fixing her eyes on the floor.

I kneel in front of her, my palms raised to show her I'm not a threat. "I'm sorry I yelled," I continue. "I wasn't mad at you. I just needed you to get to safety."

Sonya doesn't acknowledge my words or my presence. I look at the beautifully broken woman in front of me and realize she's not here with me. She's having a flashback, reliving part of her traumatic past.

My heart aches for whatever she's been through, and I vow to protect her from every damn thing from this day forward.

Swallowing past the lump in my throat, I find a deep well of peace and calm I didn't know existed. It's all because of

Sonya, and now she needs to draw from my strength. She can have it all.

"You're safe," I whisper to the terrified, trembling woman.

"No," comes her shaky response.

"Where are you, baby?" I hope if she's talking to me, she can tell me what's going on in her head so I can bring her back.

"Kitchen," she murmurs. "Father will b-be here s-soon." Her breath catches in her throat, and the fear in her blue eyes is palpable.

"What are you afraid of?"

Another shiver runs down her spine, but she keeps her back straight and her limbs pressed against the wall.

"If I keep my back against the wall like an obedient daughter, maybe he won't use the belt." She's talking more to herself than me, but I don't care as long as she's talking. I hate what I've heard so far.

"Do you have to stand against the wall often?"

"It's n-not so b-bad," she whispers, hardly able to get the words out. "After a while, all the muscle aches blend together, and I go numb."

I grit my teeth and look up at the ceiling, trying to rein in my anger at her father. "And if you slip out of position? Or get tired and collapse?" I almost don't want to know the answer.

"I just have to get through the sermon," she suddenly says.

"Sermon?"

"My father has to tell me what I did wrong and punish me accordingly. He's trying to save my soul."

Not this fucking bullshit. I'm fine with having faith and following a religion, but not when it's used to manipulate, gaslight, and abuse its members. If this is the god Sonya's father believes in, then I want nothing to do with it.

"Sonya, your father isn't here. He's not coming," I say soothingly.

"He's... not?"

"No, baby. You're safe right here with me."

"Safe?"

The way she says it, like she's never even considered it a possibility, breaks me. I reach toward her, moving slowly and giving her plenty of time to pull away. Thankfully, she doesn't. Sonya allows me to take her hands in mine. I squeeze her delicate fingers gently, still kneeling in front of her and trying to make myself as unintimidating as possible.

"Look at me, Sonya," I murmur, coaxing her to give me her eyes.

She blinks a few times, then trains her gaze on mine.

"That's it. Do you know who I am?"

Her eyes are still a little unfocused, but I see more awareness flooding into her blue gaze.

Sonya blinks again, this time recognizing me. "Blade," she whispers. "Oh, my god. I'm... I'm... I'm so sorry," she chokes.

I can't fucking stand it anymore. I gently pull her forward, and Sonya follows, letting out a heart-wrenching sob as she collapses into my lap. I wrap my arms around her and cradle my woman against my chest, absorbing her tears and painful memories.

We stay like that for long moments, Sonya clinging to me while I rock her back and forth and press my lips to the top of her head, breathing her in. Fuck if this doesn't feel like my new purpose in life.

CHAPTER SEVEN

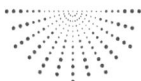

SONYA

I've never felt this safe, protected, and cherished in my whole life. I'm wrapped in the warmest hug from the most unexpected person. Then again, I always knew Blade's grunts were only to keep people away. I had a feeling once I got past that rough exterior, I'd find a kind and nurturing soul.

Blade kisses the top of my head, and I peel myself off his chest enough to look up at him. Brown eyes meet mine, concern swimming in their depths. "I..." What do I say? I have no idea what happened, only that Blade came in and made the demons disappear.

"It's okay," he whispers. "I'm right here."

I nod, resting my head on his shoulder. "That's never happened to me before," I say after a few moments. "It was like... like I was here, but I wasn't here. I was back home, and... the fear was so real," I murmur.

"I won't let anything bad happen to you," he promises.

I believe him. If anyone could fight off my father and the wrath of God's Chosen, it'd be Blade and the Savage Saints. "I know."

Blade grunts in satisfaction, and I smile. "Love seeing your smile, baby. Can't stand it when you cry."

"Sor–"

He cuts me off with a quick kiss on the lips. I'm stunned into silence. Blade gives me a hint of a grin, and God, I feel it sizzling all the way down to my bones.

"No apologies, Sonya. I'm sorry I yelled at you and sent you headfirst into a flashback. I didn't know, but that's no excuse."

"I didn't know either. What's wrong with me?"

"Nothing," comes his immediate response. "You're healing. It's a process."

"How do you know?"

Blade looks away from me, taking a deep breath as if searching for the right words. "Honestly? I've never had a reason to heal from my past. I ignored it, shoved it down deep, and forgot about my dysfunctional family. The thing is, I never really forgot. That anger, those feelings of rejection, loneliness, and pain... they never went away. I just got used to it and found a way to hide behind the trauma."

"Blade," I whisper, lifting a hand to cup his cheek. I draw him back to me, those deep brown eyes glassy with vulnerability.

"I never had a reason to be better, to work on my shit. Until you," he breathes, his lips inches from mine.

"Me?"

"You make me want to be the best version of myself so I can take care of you."

My heart stutters in my chest as I take in his words. How is it possible that this man wants to provide for me and protect me?

"Me?" I ask again.

Blade smiles softly, which melts everything in me as I fall a little more in love with him. "You," he confirms.

I'm unsure what to do with all of his attention, so I untangle myself from his embrace and stand, smoothing the skirt of my dress. Blade looks at me in confusion, like I've taken his favorite toy away. Adorable.

I hold out my hand for him to take, and Blade wraps his hand around mine, hopping to his feet and pulling me close. He closes his eyes and inhales deeply, letting the breath out with a contained growl. I lick my lips and tilt my head up in invitation.

Blade closes the distance between us, crashing his mouth down on mine. He pries my lips apart and pushes his tongue inside my mouth, licking and sucking on my tongue at a desperate, almost frantic pace.

All the emotions from the last hour have been racing around in my head, but as soon as Blade kisses me, everything stills. I focus solely on how he touches me, the heat of his body, and the steady strokes of his tongue.

I moan and press my thighs together to relieve the unbearable pressure building between my legs. Blade urges me to take a few steps backward, his lips never leaving mine. He presses me against the wall, one hand sliding around to my backside until he's squeezing my ass. I gasp into his mouth and automatically roll my hips against his.

He groans, continuing to trail his hand all over my body, cupping my breast and pinching my nipple through my thin dress and bra. I cry out, breaking our kiss as I tip my head back, exposing my throat to Blade's greedy mouth. He scrapes his teeth down my neck and sucks a super-sensitive spot below my ear.

"Fuck," he mutters into my skin, trailing kisses lower and lower until he's nipping at the tops of my breasts.

I glide my hands up his massive chest, and though it's covered with a tight t-shirt, I know he's covered in ink and scars. I want to hear the story behind each tattoo and scar on his skin. I still can't believe this is real. But the solid planes of muscles tensing and flexing under my fingers prove he's right here. Either that or this is the most vivid dream I've ever had.

"Can I make you come, baby?" he rasps as I unravel in his hands.

"I-I don't kn-know," I stutter out between heaving breaths. "Can you?"

Blade leans back slightly, his dark eyes nearly black with lust. "That a challenge, sassy little girl?"

"Yes, sir," I say softly.

He growls. "Fuckin' love when you call me that."

Blade grips my thighs and lifts me, pinning me to the wall with his massive, chiseled body. I feel his cock nestle between my thighs, causing my legs to tighten around his waist. His hardness grinds into me, sliding, pounding, playing right against the aching knot of my clit. I dig my nails into his rock-hard biceps and let him take control, let him bring me the pleasure only he can give. I surrender to his heat, his touch, his soft lips, and his greedy tongue.

Blade picks up speed, dry fucking me against the wall. He sucks on a tender spot between my neck and shoulder, catching my flesh between his teeth and biting down. I come in a vicious wave of ecstasy, my body trembling in his arms as pleasure pulls me under.

In one fluid motion, Blade sets me on the ground and falls to his knees in front of me, lifting my dress and pulling my panties off before I know what's happening. He pries my legs apart and buries his face between my thighs, lapping up my release.

I tangle my fingers in his hair as Blade grips my ass and holds me closer to his face. He alternates between long, languid licks up the seam of my pussy and tight little circles over my clit.

More of my juices leak out of me, and my inner muscles pulse and suck on air, aching to be filled with something. As if reading my mind—or, more accurately, my body, Blade shoves two fingers inside my entrance, stretching me to the point of pain. But it feels so, *so* good.

I come again, shouting his name as he pries me open, scissoring his fingers inside me and dipping his tongue into my tight tunnel. My body shakes and spasms in one long orgasm or maybe five small ones—I don't even know.

My vision is fuzzy and sweat coats my skin as my knees give out. Blade grips my hips and pins me to the wall. I lean forward and brace my hands on his shoulders. I can't stop coming, shaking, crying out. Blade continues to suck my clit and scrape his teeth over my folds.

Every part of me is tingling by the time Blade glides up my body, pulling my panties up as he goes. He kisses me and wraps his arms around the small of my back to keep me close.

I finally break the kiss, my vision blurry from lack of oxygen. Resting my forehead on his chest, I gulp down air and try to figure out what happens next. Blade combs his fingers through my hair, calming me and making me feel so safe. Precious. It's such a contrast to the way he devoured me, body and soul, only a few moments ago.

"You okay, Sonya?" he asks softly.

"So good," I breathe as I melt against him.

Blade's chuckle travels all the way through me.

A thought occurs, but I'm unsure what to do about it. "Um," I start, leaning back slightly to look at Blade. "Can I... return the favor?" I ask tentatively. I want to give him pleasure, too, but I'm painfully inexperienced and don't want to disappoint him.

Blade groans and lowers his head until it rests on mine.

"As incredible as that sounds, this wasn't about me. I wanted to make you feel good. Do you feel good, baby?"

"Yes," I answer emphatically.

My response elicits another rare grin from Blade. "Mission accomplished."

His phone beeps, and he grunts before taking it out of his pocket and staring at the screen. "Shit, I need to call church and give my men an update," he says as he taps the screen a few times.

"Oh. Yeah, of course. Do what you need to do," I reply, ignoring the sinking sensation in my stomach.

"I'll find you when I'm free. I'm not done with you yet, little Sonya." He gives me the sexiest smile, his eyes shining with lust.

"Yes, sir," I say with a grin, though the rock in my stomach is growing and making me nauseous.

He groans and kisses my forehead before leaving the room and shutting the door. I slump against the wall, one hand covering my mouth. That was the most intense experience of my life. My first orgasm—or five—and now... Blade is gone.

I hardly had a chance to catch my breath before the man who did this to me was gone.

He said he'd be back, but isn't that what all men say? That's what I was raised to believe. But if everything I was taught at home is false, then... I don't know. Can I trust Blade? Is it naive to throw myself into a relationship with the first man I've ever been attracted to?

I don't know. I just... don't know.

I plop down on my bed and wonder what the heck I've gotten myself into.

CHAPTER EIGHT

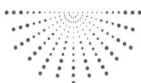

BLADE

"*H*ow long have we been out here?" Hawk asks anxiously, checking his watch.

Without saying it, I know he's thinking about being away from Tessa. One look at Rider confirms that he's thinking the same thing about Sutton.

I would've given Hawk and Rider shit a week ago for being distracted by their women, but now I get it. Leaving Sonya in her room, still panting from her first orgasm, was one of the hardest things I've ever done.

"Shit," I mutter, the realization of that last thought echoing in my brain.

I left her after I gave her an intense first sexual experience.

I told her I'd find her when I got back, but I thought this run would take two or three hours tops. Instead, we've patrolled the abandoned warehouses where we store our product and staked out the police station and Sheriff Darren's house for fourteen fucking hours.

"That's not exactly an answer," Hawk replies.

I glare at him, and he backs down.

What started as a typical run of exchanging goods for

cold hard cash turned into a stakeout when we realized we were being set up. Gotta hand it to the sheriff and his goons; this was one of their better ploys to take us down. They must have gotten some good intel with our client list, which means we'll need to revisit everyone we sell guns to.

But that will have to wait.

"Too damn long," I tell him, answering his earlier question. "We shouldn't be staking out shit. We should've vetted our client list better or picked up on red flags for the sale. Any amount of time spent out here is too long."

"Prez, it wasn't your fault we were set up," Rider says.

"Didn't say it was. Just stating facts."

Hawk and Rider nod while the other men around me grumble about being tired.

I close my eyes and wipe a hand down my face, releasing a sigh. I walk from one end of our lookout spot to the other, then wave the men away. "Go home. Get some sleep. It's nearly five in the morning. I'll call church when we have something more to go off."

Sighs of relief and grunts of acknowledgment fill the air, and in three minutes flat, almost everyone has cleared out. Surprisingly, Hawk and Rider remain, along with Axel. I catch the last part of a question as I approach the group.

"...Saturday night?" Hawk asks Rider.

"I'll check with Sutton. I know she'll love the idea of a grill out."

All three men look at me expectantly, as if I have a special mission for them. Not this time. I just don't know how to ask what I want to ask.

"Prez? Everything okay?" Hawk asks.

"Yeah," I say, coughing the word out. Jesus, when did I become so awkward? "Well, no. But it's not club business. It's... Sonya." I wait for the two of them to give me shit, but surprisingly, they simply nod and listen. "I think I screwed up already. I don't know how to… shit, I don't know how to do any of this. Be in a relationship. Trust someone. I don't know how to take care of someone like Sonya. I'm afraid I'm not good enough."

I clear my throat and train my gaze on the ground, rubbing the back of my neck anxiously. I didn't mean for all that to come out, but it's true. Every word. I know Hawk is going to have a great time poking fun at me for finally falling for a woman, but I'm not in the mood to hear it.

I'm shocked yet again when he gives me a serious answer.

"The fact that you're worried about not being good enough means you're on the right track," Hawk says.

"Does she feel safe around you?" Rider asks.

I think back to yesterday when I held her in my arms as she wept. "Yeah, she knows I'll protect her no matter what."

"How does she make you feel?" Axel pipes in.

"And what do you know about relationships?" I grunt.

He shrugs and gives me an easy smile. "About as much as you do."

"It's a valid question," Hawk adds.

"She makes me feel…" I trail off, trying to find the right words. "Like I can do anything, but the only thing I want to do is make her happy."

All three men stare at me. Rider's eyebrows float up by his hairline while Axel's jaw drops open in shock.

Hawk grins at me, the jerk. "Do you love her?"

I freeze, my brows furrowing as I think about his question. *Love.* Is that what this is? This obsession to be near her, the need to make her safe and happy, the way her pain calls to mine while her sunshine warms me up… *Love.* I love her. I fucking love Sonya.

"You three fuckers aren't going to be the first ones I tell that to," I rasp, reeling from my life-changing realization.

Rider chuckles while Hawk and Axel flat-out laugh. I don't give a shit. I need to get back to Sonya.

I'm vaguely aware of Hawk and Rider calling after me, but I'm already halfway to my bike and can't turn back now. Throwing my leg over the seat, I kick start the engine and tear out of there.

Fifteen minutes later, I pull into the clubhouse, which is empty. Of course it is. The bar doesn't open for another six hours. As much as I want to storm into the back where our rooms are, Sonya needs her sleep. Plus, I'm pretty sure I'd give her a panic attack if I pounded on her door this early in the morning.

Still, I can't bring myself to go back home. Not when my Sonya is so close.

Ultimately, I decide to park around the back and crash in one of the other spare rooms until a more reasonable hour to wake Sonya up. As soon as my head hits the pillow, every ache and pain from the last fourteen hours melts away. I'll close my eyes for a little bit.

I jerk awake, unsure what startled me. My vision is groggy, and I'm not in my own bed. I blink a few times, clearing the fog and squinting against the bright sunlight breaking through the crack in the curtains.

I'm at the clubhouse.

"Shit," I mutter to myself. "What time is it?"

I hop out of bed and dig through my pockets until I find my phone. It's a miracle I didn't crush the damn thing in my sleep. I wasn't expecting to sleep that hard. Or that long.

I groan when I see it's almost two in the afternoon. It's been a whole day since I've seen Sonya, tasted her lips, and felt her soft curves beneath my rough fingertips.

Heading to the small bathroom inside the micro-apartment, I rinse my face and run my fingers through my hair. It's time to find my woman.

Stepping into the hallway, I walk a few steps to Sonya's room, knocking on the door lightly. When I get no response, I try the doorknob, which turns. I open the door, poking my head inside, but not seeing Sonya.

My stomach sinks as I turn and make my way out to the bar. Only three patrons are inside, scattered at different tables, drinking alone. No Sonya in sight.

A rock sits heavy on my chest, and panic seeps in at the thought of losing her. I fucked up by leaving her yesterday, but she has to give me another chance. I can be better for her. I know I can.

I'm about to go outside and check the mechanic shop to see if she decided to go in over the weekend when I hear the most magical sound. Laughter. Not just any laughter. This sweet voice belongs to my Sonya. Everything in me relaxes knowing she's here.

I follow the sound to the kitchen, where Sonya stands beside Tessa, talking while making tea. Both women stop and turn toward me, staring as I stalk toward Sonya. Her blue eyes narrow, and I see confusion and hurt in their light blue swirls. It kills me that I made her doubt how I feel. That shit ends now.

The closer I get, the more her gaze changes. She's still confused, but that fire deep down is coming out. Her flushed cheeks and glassy eyes let me know she's been thinking about the last time we were together.

Without a word, I bend and toss Sonya over my shoulder, securing her with an arm around her thighs.

"Um, excuse me? What exactly are you doing?" she protests.

I lightly swat her round, juicy ass with my free hand, making her gasp in surprise.

"Don't you think this is a little caveman-ish?"

I grunt, which makes Sonya laugh. She's not all that upset

271

at the literal turn of events, which gives me hope.

"Have fun!" Tessa calls.

"Traitor!" Sonya says.

I spank her again, which causes her to giggle. She's going to be feisty. I fucking love it.

I burst through the back door and march to my bike, finally setting Sonya on her feet.

"Where were you? I thought you were done with me or–"

"Never," I rasp, stepping into her space and cupping her cheeks.

"Seriously, what are you doing?" she asks breathlessly.

"What I should have done yesterday," I whisper onto her lips.

"And what's that?" Her warm breath tickles my skin, and I can't hold back any longer.

I nip at her top lip, then her bottom lip, teasing my sweet girl before kissing her properly. I slide my tongue inside her mouth, needing more of her taste, more of her sexy sounds, more, more, *more.*

We break apart, gasping for air.

"I should have stayed with you," I whisper, resting my forehead on hers. "I didn't think… But that's no excuse. I'll do better. Please forgive me."

"Blade," she murmurs, leaning back to press her lips to my cheek. "I forgive you. This is all new to me as well."

"We'll learn together?" I ask, capturing her lips with mine in a kiss that ends too quickly.

"Together," she confirms, gifting me with another precious smile.

"Will you let me take you back to my place, baby?"

Sonya nods. "I'll let you do pretty much anything to me. Sir," the little siren adds.

I groan, rolling my forehead on hers. "You sure about

that? I don't know if I can control myself, and I don't want to scare you away."

"I'm not scared. I trust you. I want…" she trails off, her eyes shifting away.

"You want…?"

"I want to be yours. Completely. You already have my heart. I want you to have my body, too."

I kiss her lips, then trail soft kisses down her neck, nuzzling into the sensitive spot below her ear. "You have my heart and soul, baby girl. I can't wait to share everything else with you."

I've never meant anything more.

CHAPTER NINE

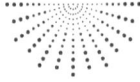

SONYA

*W*e somehow manage to untangle ourselves from each other and get on Blade's bike. I've ridden on his motorcycle several times now, but everything is more intense this time. My thighs vibrate as he revs the engine, the tremor rattling my core and making my clit pulse with each beat of my heart.

Blade races through town as I tighten my hold on him, digging my fingers into the hard slats of his muscles. He tenses beneath my touch, and I feel more than hear a deep growl clawing its way up his chest.

I find myself grinding against the seat and Blade's back, unable to stop as I climb higher and higher, the vibrations rolling through me like waves of prickly pleasure. Right as I'm about to hit my peak, the engine stops. I gasp in disappointment, but I'm lifted in the air before I can complain.

Blade scoops me up in his arms, fusing his lips to mine in a toe-curling, possessive kiss.

"The ride got you all worked up, didn't it, baby girl?" he growls as he walks up the front steps and unlocks the door.

He adjusts me so he can open the door, then carries me through his house. I guess I'll get a tour later.

"Yes, sir," I murmur, kissing his neck and cheek.

"You need me to make you come?"

"God, yes," I moan, clenching my thighs together.

"Yes, who?"

"Yes, sir," I practically whine as I squirm in Blade's arms. My skin is on fire, and he's the only one who can douse the flames. "Please, Blade. I need it. I need you."

"Love hearing you beg for me," he grunts.

I fall through the air before my back hits the soft mattress. Blade falls on top of me, pinning me with his weight, blanketing me in his strength. His lips are on mine, matching my need with his.

He holds himself up with one hand at the side of my head while his other slides down my body, cupping my breast. He squeezes lightly, groaning into my mouth. Then his hand moves lower, gripping my hip, sliding down my thigh until he reaches bare skin. Blade squeezes me there and groans again, pulling my leg to the side so he can settle between my legs.

"I need to see you naked, but I can't stop kissing these lips," he whispers, grinding his jean-covered cock against my core as he kisses me again.

I make a desperate sound in the back of my throat, tearing my mouth away from his and breathing fresh air into my burning lungs. Blade rests his forehead on mine, taking deep, ragged breaths. Knowing he's this wound up because of me is even more of a confidence booster.

I push on his chest, giving him a devious grin as he sits up. I follow him, standing in front of the ripped Greek god of a man. I tug at his shirt, silently demanding that he take it off. His eyes flash with wicked intentions that match mine as he pulls off his shirt.

My hands find his chest, my fingers teasing his skin in featherlight touches as I trace over his swirling tattoos. Lower, lower, lower my exploration goes, discovering the dips in his defined chest and abs. A shiver runs through his body and into mine, drawing us closer.

Blade tips my chin and kisses me soundly as he tangles his fingers in my hair and tugs at the strands. I moan softly when his other hand pulls down the zipper on the back of my dress. Slowly, so slowly, he peels it away, letting the fabric slide down my body.

His mouth finally leaves mine, his eyes roaming down my body. When Blade finally meets my gaze, he gives me a gentle, reverent look. He's letting me know he wants to cherish me as much as he wants to devour me. I feel the same.

"You're so beautiful, baby," Blade murmurs, unclasping my bra and tossing it aside.

He kisses my neck, my collarbone, and lower, licking one nipple and then the other. He kneels in front of me, blazing a trail of kisses down my torso. I'm trembling by the time his lips reach my mound. He places a sweet kiss there and looks up at me as if asking permission one last time.

"Please, sir," I whisper, tangling my fingers in his hair and urging him forward.

A low, guttural sound rumbles from deep in his chest as he hooks his fingers into the waistband of my panties and pulls them down. Balancing myself on his shoulders, I step out of my last piece of clothing, standing naked and unashamed before the man I love.

I gasp softly at that realization, then let it wash over me and sink deep into the core of my being. I love Blade. And I'm pretty sure he's half in love with me, too.

"You okay, baby?"

"More than okay," I reassure him. "But I think you need to be naked, too, for this to work."

Blade grins at me and stands. He leans in and nips at my mouth, pulling my bottom lip through his teeth. "Love that sassy mouth, Sonya. It might get you in trouble one of these days."

"Oh, yeah?"

"Yeah. But I think you'll like your punishment."

My pussy clenches and releases, making more of my arousal drip down my thighs. He's right. I think I'll like whatever he does to me.

I can't keep my eyes off his rough, tattooed hands working furiously to undo his belt and pants. As soon as he lowers the zipper, I reach out and tug his jeans and boxers down, eager, desperate, and hungry for more. For everything.

Blade helps me before gripping my hips and walking me backward until my knees hit the edge of the mattress. He cups my face in his hands and brushes his nose along mine in the lightest touch.

"I don't know everything that happened in your past, Sonya, but I need you to know I'm your future. Do you trust me?"

"With all of me," I don't hesitate to answer.

We share a tender moment, and so many unspoken words pass back and forth with one look. His hard dick grazes against my center, and just like that, I ache for his touch.

Blade tips his head back and groans when I grab his cock and rub the tip with my thumb, spreading his precum. "Fuck you feel so good. I'm clean, Sonya. I haven't been anyone in longer than I can remember. I want inside this pussy with nothing between us, but I'll put a condom on if you want."

I know I should tell him I've never done this before, but instead, I say, "I'm clean, too." He grunts in approval. "I can't wait anymore. Please, sir."

"Goddamn," he growls, pushing me down on the bed.

I expect Blade to join me, but he sinks to his knees. He grips my thighs in his large hands and pries my legs apart. I cry out and bow my back off the bed when he presses his thumb over my clit. A sudden, powerful burst of pleasure slices through me and rattles me to my core.

My pleasure grows more intense when his tongue slides through my dripping folds, licking me and nipping at my sensitive flesh. He nudges my clit with his nose and spears his tongue into my little hole, scooping out my juices and drinking them down.

Blade drags his tongue lower, lower, lower until it's teasing my back entrance. I gasp at the filthiness of it all, but the forbidden nature makes me even wetter. He licks around the tight ring of muscles and growls.

"Holy fuck," I whisper. "Ohmygod, Blade, oh…"

My whisper becomes a loud moan when the very tip of his tongue pushes inside. He rubs my clit in furious circles, and I grip the sheets, twisting them in my fists as my body expands and contracts.

"I'm…" I shatter before I finish my sentence.

My orgasm rushes through me with such intensity that I shoot up off the bed, trying to escape the overwhelming pleasure. Blade shoves me back down with a hand spread out over my stomach. He holds me there, making me feel all of it, every last drop of bliss.

He grunts in satisfaction, crawling up my body and crashing his mouth to mine in a passionate kiss. "Needed your taste on my tongue before I fuck this tight little pussy for the first time."

Leaning back slightly, he gathers my hands and guides them over my head. Pinning my wrists, Blade drags his cock through my folds, coating himself in my cream before lining up with my entrance.

"Ready?"

"So ready," I breathe.

He kisses me as he thrusts inside, tearing through the last barrier between us. I tense at the slight pinch deep in my core, holding my breath until it passes.

"Holy shit, baby. I didn't know…"

I open my eyes and stare into his deep, dark irises. He looks so pained it nearly breaks my heart. "I'm okay," I promise him. "I wanted it to be you. I want you so badly. Please don't stop."

"I'm gonna make you feel so good. I'll take care of you, Sonya. Always."

I nod and clench around his hard length, making him groan. I'm so full, stretched to the point of pain, but in the best way possible. It heightens my pleasure, sparks my nerves, and makes me thrust my hips to take him deeper.

"Then do it, already," I practically growl at him.

Blade chuckles, and I feel the vibrations inside and out.

He leans down and kisses my neck, biting down gently on my pulse point. I writhe beneath him, pleasure taking over the pain. Blade pulls out almost all the way, hovering above me and driving me crazy.

Blade gives me a dark, delicious look before thrusting back inside me. His thickness scrapes along my walls, the friction like striking a match as instant, overwhelming heat engulfs me. I bow my back and push against the hand still holding my wrists, grateful for an anchor in the raging storm of sensations.

He pulls my leg higher on his hip, changing the angle. I

whimper as his cock slides against some magical place inside me, sobbing his name louder with each thrust. He snaps his hips against mine, grinding his pelvis against my clit while hitting that spot over and over.

Blade grunts my name every time his balls slap my ass. I feel him losing control as his strokes become deeper, harder, and so damn rough. I love it. I convulse as he thrusts into me relentlessly. The exquisite pleasure bordering on pain builds and builds, higher and higher, one more, one more, again, again...until I break. Shards of pleasure cut and heal me as I cry out for him.

My orgasm rips through me, holding my body hostage, forcing me to feel every wave of bliss until tears drip down my face and I'm a sweaty, soaking mess beneath him. Blade stays still, buried deep inside my spasming pussy.

When the last of my pleasure leaves me, Blade growls and slams into me, letting go of my wrists and sliding his hand down my body. He squeezes my breast, leaning down and bringing the nipple to his mouth and lavishing it with attention until I'm shaking beneath him.

"Oh, God, Blade," I choke.

I claw at his back as he rips me apart in the best way possible. Each gut-twisting stroke winds me higher until I'm right on the precipice, teetering on the edge.

Blade's hips stutter as he loses his rhythm and ruts into me. His fingers dig into my hips as my nails bite into his skin, both of us clinging to this tension-filled pleasure. A shiver runs through me, followed by another and another until I'm shaking violently.

We cry out as his hot seed spills into me. Wave after wave of his cum splashes into my cunt and drips out, and still, there's more. My pussy snaps around him as I sob out my climax.

I gasp for air as I float back down to earth, the oxygen

burning my lungs yet somehow sending jolts of pleasure to my clit. Blade buries his face in my neck, and I wrap my arms around his torso, keeping him on top of me while we catch our breath.

"You're perfect," he whispers. "You're all mine."

I nod and pull him closer until most of his weight is resting on top of me.

Blade seems to understand my need better than I do. He surrounds me with his strength, blanketing me in his warmth. "I'm right here, sweet girl. I've got you."

I nod again, running my fingers through his short hair as he lays his head on my shoulder, placing soft kisses there.

"Thank you," I say, my cheeks immediately heating at my stupid response to having sex for the first time. "I mean… Never mind."

Blade lifts his head and readjusts us so we're on our sides, facing each other. "You never have to be embarrassed around me. What are you thinking about, baby girl?" he asks, reaching out to tuck my hair behind my ear. "Do you feel okay? Was I too rough or–"

"It was… everything. I feel so wanted and special. Is that dumb?"

Blade rolls onto his back and urges me to lie across his chest. I curl up into his side, and he lifts me, draping my body over his. I let out a breathy laugh at his insistence, but I don't mind. I love that he can't seem to get enough of me.

"Nothing you say or think is dumb," Blade reassures me, kissing my forehead. "Promise me you'll always tell me what's on your mind."

"Yes, sir," I say with a little grin. The dark glint in his eyes sparks an insatiable need, but I'm too tired to move.

Blade chuckles, tucking my head under his chin and gliding his fingertips along my spine until I'm nearly asleep.

"I've got you," he whispers again. "I'll be right here when you wake up."

I'm about to tell him I'm not tired, but a yawn escapes. The last thing I remember is Blade smiling at me sweetly, almost adoringly. My life is officially complete.

CHAPTER TEN

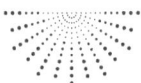

BLADE

I love everything about waking up with Sonya in my arms. Love the way her hair spreads over the pillow, the golden strands sparkling in the early morning light. Love her warm, soft, curvy little body pressed against mine. I love each and every steady breath she takes, knowing they give her life and sustain her. I hope she knows I'll do the same. I'll be her everything.

Never thought I'd be a romantic sap with flowery thoughts, but my woman brings it out in me. Sonya deserves flowers, chocolates, sonnets, a trip to Paris, and every other cliché thing her heart desires. She doesn't want any of that, though. She just wants me.

I still can't believe it.

Sonya stirs slightly, her ass pressing against my morning wood. I bite back a groan but can't stop my hand from sliding down her torso to cup her bare pussy. This time, I can't hold in my groan. She's fucking *drenched* for me. My dirty girl must be having some good dreams.

Sonya sighs so sweetly and grinds into me as I massage her little bundle of nerves. She moans softly, though I don't think she's awake yet. My lips find the side of her neck, and I kiss her there, breathing her in.

I dip one finger into her entrance and then two, slowly thrusting in and out, massaging her walls as I grind the heel of my palm into her clit. Sonya gasps and tenses in my arms, and I know she's awake.

"Blade…" she cries out, bucking her hips and taking more of me. She raises her arm over her head and tangles her fingers in my hair, pulling me down and urging me to kiss her neck. I gladly do, licking and nipping at her sensitive skin. "So good…"

I growl at her sexy, needy little whimper and guide her top leg over mine. I wedge my aching cock in between her ass cheeks, seeking some relief but not entering her. "What were you dreaming about, firefly? You were so fucking wet, I couldn't resist."

"I-I… I dreamed…" she gasps as a wave of her arousal gushes over my fingers, still buried deep inside her swollen channel. "Y-you were…"

I withdraw my hand and pinch her clit hard enough to sting. Her broken cry and pulsing pussy let me know she likes a little pain with her pleasure. "Tell me," I grunt, caging her clit in with a finger on either side. I rub up and down, keeping her aching but not touching her where she needs me most.

"Oh, God, please… please *fuck* me," she whines, her whole body shaking with desire.

I chuckle at hearing her swear. My angel is as sweet and polite as they come, but I'm teaching her to let go of her old life and embrace a new one with me. "Tell me what you were dreaming about. Tell me, and I'll make it come true."

"You were… making love to me," she says softly. "Slowly, at first. I felt… cherished."

It's not what I expected, but I love that she's opening up

to me. "You are, baby," I whisper into the shell of her ear before kissing the sensitive spot underneath it. I pump my fingers in and out of her like she's describing. "What else, love?"

"You picked up speed but still took your time, driving me insane," she murmurs.

"Like this?" I ask, thrusting into her faster as I place open-mouthed kisses over her shoulder.

"Yes," Sonya moans. "You went faster with each thrust like you couldn't control yourself."

"I can't," I grunt, adding a third finger and fucking her hard and fast.

I curl my fingers and tap her G-spot over and over. Sonya tightens her hold on my hair, tugging at the strands to the point of pain. I fucking love it. She's so close, so goddamn close. Her cream drips out of her as she writhes in my arms. I hold her there, keeping her orgasm just beneath the surface. I feel it claw at her insides, making her whimper with each breath.

Right before it hits, I take my hand away, moving it to her ass and spreading her cheeks. Without warning, I line up to her entrance and push her over the edge with one long, powerful thrust. She fucking falls headfirst into her climax, screaming my name and soaking my dick with her release.

I hold still inside her, growling as her orgasm ripples around my cock. Before she has a chance to recover, I hammer into her, setting a relentless pace. I grip her breast roughly, using them as leverage to fuck into her harder, hitting her so damn deep with each stroke.

"B-Blade… Blade, y-yes, yes," she chants.

I drop my hand from her breast and blur my fingers over her clit until her pussy clenches around me and soaks me with another orgasm. Pulling out, I flip her on her back, wrenching her legs apart and slamming home. Her back bows off the bed, and her legs wrap around me, holding me close. She digs her heels into my ass and claws my back, leaving her mark on me.

"Jesus, fuck," I snarl.

I claim her mouth, devouring her, biting at her lips, and spearing my tongue inside to lick every inch and suck on her tongue. It's a wild, messy kiss that matches how I'm fucking her like a goddamn animal.

I slide one hand down her body and grip her ass cheek, changing the angle of her hips and helping her meet me thrust for thrust. My cock scrapes against her most sensitive spot with each fierce stroke.

She's breaking apart for me; I can feel it. Every time I hit the end of her, she cracks a little more, the pressure of her orgasm building and pulsing and pushing her boundaries.

My balls draw up tight as my orgasm gathers in the base of my spine. My rhythm falters as I try to hold on, needing her to come with me. "Get there, baby. Fuck, please get there. Need one more from you."

"It's too much, too much…"

"I've got you, Sonya. Let go for me. I'm right here. Let go, love."

She sucks in a huge breath and holds it, her whole body trembling and then freezing. Every damn muscle is pulled tight as she clings to me with everything she has. With a last brutal thrust, we shatter.

Sonya floods my cock with her release, and I give her everything in return. My cum splashes into her throbbing pussy as she sucks in every last drop. We grunt, shaking and sweating as we ride the high together.

Sonya goes limp in my arms. I bury my face into the side of her neck and pump into her twice more before collapsing. Rolling to my back, I drape my freshly fucked little angel over my chest. I cup her face, tipping her head to kiss her closed eyelids and flushed cheeks.

She gasps and blinks her eyes open, her eyes darting around before landing on mine. "Woah," she breathes. "I think I passed out there for a second."

"Are you okay?" My brows furrow as I push the hair out of her face and look her over for damage.

"I'm so, so, good. I mean, I can't move, but I don't want to."

I take a deep breath, relieved she's not hurt, and chuckle at her response. "I don't want you to move either," I murmur, circling my arms around her and sliding a leg between hers. I want us tangled up forever.

After a few moments of peaceful silence, Sonya turns to face me, though I still keep her in my hold. Her teal eyes find mine, such love and contentment in their depths. "So, I feel like you know about my past, but what about you?" she asks softly, an adorable smile tugging at her lips.

"What would you like to know?"

"Everything," she sighs, curling up on my chest. "Start from the beginning."

I chuckle, which is still a new feeling, and prepare to break open my heart for this woman and her precious soul. "Well, I never knew my mother. I guess she kept me for a few months, then dropped me off with my dad, who didn't know I existed until I was placed in his arms."

"Was he happy to have a son?"

I snort a dark laugh. "No, not even a little bit."

Sonya pops her head up from where she was resting it, her eyes wide with concern.

"He wasn't abusive, just… well, neglectful, I suppose. That wasn't so bad. I made it through fourth grade without saying more than a handful of words to my old man. It's not that I was stupid or non-verbal. He just… he didn't have much to say to me."

"That's awful. You should've had a father who delighted in you and told you how special you are."

That concept is as foreign to me as learning Greek, but I love that my girl is calling out my father's shitty behavior. I know she'll be a great mom.

Holy shit. Did I just think that? I'm not nearly as shocked as I thought I would be. Having kids with Sonya feels natural. Of course we're going to have a family together.

"You should've had a father who did the same," I counter. "Not some asshole who physically assaulted you because his religion dictated he had to."

Sonya nods, her eyes softening. "We'll be better parents than them," she whispers.

I smile, loving that we're already on the same page.

"So, what happened after fourth grade? You said you made it that far without talking to your dad much."

I take a deep breath, trying to put all the pieces together for her. "The summer after fourth grade, my dad met his first wife. She was even less excited about me than my old man, and I guess they decided I was mature enough to take care of myself. My dad moved in with Cynthia and left me in our apartment. He stopped by once a week to drop off food and supplies, but he was done with me."

"That's awful," Sonya whispers.

I shrug and look up at the ceiling. I haven't thought about that summer in a long time.

"Honestly, that was probably the happiest time of my childhood. After the divorce, my dad moved back in and started drinking. His next wife only married him because he bought all the alcohol she could drink, which, unsurprisingly, ended horribly. Wife number three was bat-shit crazy. Any little thing would set her off, and when she was upset, she screeched like a damn banshee. After one particularly terrible fight, my father was left with a black eye and a broken nose. She never came back, and that was that."

"How many times was your dad married?"

"Seven. No, eight. No, I don't know if he married Lillian or if they just lived together. About seven or eight, but I'm sure that number is in the double digits by now. Moved out of that chaos when I was sixteen. Dropped out of school, hit the streets, and found myself running around with thugs and criminals. Eventually, I found Savage Saints and started hanging around as much as possible. Technically, I was too young to patch in, but they let it slide. Since then, the club has been my whole life."

Sonya sits up, leaning over me as her blue eyes capture mine. "I'm so proud of you for choosing your own path. You know you deserved better than the parents you had, right?" she asks me, her voice clear and strong.

God, she's beautiful. "You did, too," I remind her. "You deserved a family who loved and accepted you, who supported you instead of abusing you and tearing you down."

She smiles sadly but nods, her delicate hand cupping my cheek. "We'll be better for each other."

"We'll support each other," I add.

"And comfort each other."

"And love each other."

Sonya looks up at me, her eyes filling with tears. Shit, I thought she would be happy about–

"You love me?" comes her whispered response. She looks like she doesn't quite believe it.

"Is it too soon to say that?" My heart races, hoping I haven't fucked everything up again.

"I don't know, but I… I love you, too."

The tightness in my chest releases, and I let out a relieved sigh. "Thank fuck."

Sonya giggles, and I take the opportunity to flip her on her back and tickle her.

"Blade! Oh, my gosh!" Sonya squeals and tries to wiggle away from me, but I pin her down and rub my stubble over the smooth skin of her stomach. She writhes and laughs as she pushes me away.

I fall to my side, gathering my woman up in my arms. "I love you," I whisper, kissing her forehead.

"I love you, too," she murmurs, pressing her lips to mine.

Our sweet moment is interrupted by my phone. We both groan, but Sonya rolls away and grabs my phone from the nightstand, tossing it at me.

"I'll get dressed, and you can take me to work?" she asks as she hops off the bed, completely naked.

I scan her body, remembering how her curves felt pressed against me.

"Eyes up here, mister," she sasses.

I grunt and hop off the bed, circling her in my arms and pulling her close. "You're impossible to ignore under normal circumstances. How do you expect me not to look at you when you're naked?"

She smiles sweetly and gives me a chaste kiss before spinning out of my arms. I'm about to tug her back into my embrace when my phone rings again.

"Better get that!" Sonya calls as she makes her way to the bathroom.

"I'll drop you off at the shop, deal with club business, then pick you up at noon. We're having a half day. Your boss demands that you spend more time in bed."

Sonya giggles and nods. "Whatever you say, *sir*."

The little siren.

CHAPTER ELEVEN

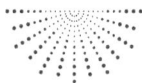

SONYA

J pour a little more flour into the pancake mixture to thicken it up, humming to myself as I work on breakfast. We've gotten into a nice routine the last four days, which usually includes sleeping in and Blade serving me breakfast in bed. But today, I was awake first, so I got to make breakfast for Blade and surprise him.

A shuffling sound catches my attention, followed by a grunt. I smile, knowing Blade will walk in here at any moment.

"There you are," he says in his gruff, scratchy morning voice. He's so adorably grumpy in the morning. Well, most of the time, but I love it. I love everything about my Blade.

"Can I help you, sir?" I ask him with a smile.

He narrows his eyes as he comes around to the other side of the breakfast bar and stands behind me. He wraps his arms around my waist and kisses his way up the back of my neck, pressing his hard cock into my ass.

"I can think of a few ways you can help me, love," he whispers in my ear.

A moan escapes my lips as he grinds into me, slipping his

hands up his oversized shirt I'm wearing and gripping my hips. Blade continues his exploration with his hands as he sucks and licks my neck. Before I know it, he has my shirt off and pushes me down on the counter so my ass sticks out.

Blade growls and palms my cheeks, spreading me wide open for him. He takes himself out and rubs his dick between my folds while I push back, trying to get him inside me again. I'm addicted to this man. I know he's the only one who will ever be able to satisfy my cravings.

I feel his lips on my lower back, slowly moving up my spine.

"Tell me what you want, beautiful," he whispers into my skin.

"You," I breathe.

"You have me. What do you want me to do to your gorgeous body?"

He continues to saw in and out of my folds, not penetrating me yet.

I moan loudly, my pussy squeezing nothing as it gushes over his cock.

"I want you to… fuck me, sir."

He growls. "Tell me again." He snaps his hips, bumping my clit.

"*Fuck me*, sir."

"Jesus, baby," he grunts. Blade pulls back and slams home, again and again, hitting me so deep I cry out with each thrust. "You like that? Like my thick cock stretching out your perfect little pussy?"

"Mmm…" I moan, pressing back into him, meeting him thrust for thrust. I squeeze my pussy each time he pulls out, which I know he likes based on how he groans and his breath hitches in his throat.

"Fuck, Sonya. Love being inside you. I'll never get enough. You're mine. *Mine*," he grunts as he picks up speed.

He pushes me closer and closer to the edge, and just when I'm about to fall into blinding pleasure, he pulls out.

"No!" I yell in frustration.

He chuckles and leans his huge, hard body over mine. "I'm not done with you yet, beautiful," he growls.

Blade walks us backward to one of the kitchen chairs and sits. He guides me onto his lap so my back faces his front and my legs are spread on either side of his. Slowly, he lowers me onto his hard shaft.

"Oh, Blade, this is…" I have no words.

Riding him backward feels so freaking good. As I bounce on his long, hard length, I find I like being in control of our pleasure. I reach my hands behind me and tangle them in his hair, urging his head forward so he can kiss my neck.

"That's it, beautiful. Ride my big dick. Fucking hell, you feel so good."

I lift up and impale myself on him again and again. Blade's large hands cup my breasts as he kneads the soft flesh and pinches my nipples. One hand slowly slides down my torso and rests on the mound of soft curls above my pussy. His fingers part my folds and circle my clit, bringing me right back to the edge of my orgasm.

"Blade, right there. Oh, god, I can't hold on…"

I grind down on him, loving how his cock fills me, stretching me and hitting every sensitive spot deep inside.

"Let go, love. I've got you," he whispers, biting my shoulder.

I throw my head back and grip his hair as my body locks up, every muscle and nerve pushed to the extreme, waiting for my permission to let go.

Blade pinches my clit, and I scream my release, my body curling up and pitching forward with the force of my orgasm. Blade holds me steady with one hand on my breast, the other cupping my pussy as he fucks into me from below.

"I'm coming too, baby. *Fuck!*" he roars.

One orgasm rolls into another and another until I'm a big ball of nerves, electrocuted with each thrust of Blade's hips. He spills his warm, sticky seed into me, the remnants of our orgasms dripping down my thighs.

Blade presses soft kisses up my shoulder and neck. He helps me to stand long enough to scoop me up in his arms. I look up at him in question, but he kisses the tip of my nose.

"Gotta wash you up before I drop you off at work."

"I can shower on my own, you know," I inform him.

"That won't be necessary."

I laugh as he sets me down in the shower and turns on the water.

An hour later, I'm in the back office of the mechanic shop, answering emails. When I started my escape road trip a few weeks ago, I never imagined it would end like this—staying with a big, growly biker who *loves* me and fulfills my every fantasy. Everything turned out better than I could have hoped…

Which is why something is about to go wrong. I just know it. After a lifetime of having rules and twisted morality beaten into me, it's hard to accept that walking away from God's Chosen was the best thing that ever happened. In a previous life, I would have been called a slut, a whore, an impure woman. My worth would have decreased by being with Blade, but in reality, Blade is the only person to ever truly show me how valuable I am.

But it can't be that easy, right?

The bell for the lobby entrance dings, and I quickly finish replying to the email before heading in that direction. I'm startled to see two police officers in uniform wandering around the lobby as if looking for something.

"Um, hello," I greet them.

Both men stop and turn, their eyes immediately latching

onto mine. Something sinister flashes across the cops' faces, and I instinctively step back.

"C-can I help you with something? A squad car or police motorcycle acting up?" I try for professional, but the quiver in my voice surely gives me away.

"What do you think, Officer Marc? Can she help us?"

The two exchange a look that has all the hairs standing up on the back of my neck. My stomach roils while I take another step toward the back office. I'll barricade myself in there if necessary.

"Oh, yeah. This has to be our girl. Thick, curvy, golden hair, blue eyes. Not who I pictured the President with, but hey. We've all got our kinks, right?"

The officers laugh, but not in a joyful way. It makes me feel gross like I'm the butt of their joke, but I can't figure out why.

"I think you must be mistaking me for–"

"Sonya?" Officer Marc finishes.

I nod automatically, regretting it when his eyes glint with satisfaction.

"Oh, yeah. You're our girl, all right. Are you going to come with us, or are you going to be difficult?"

"Go with you? Am I in trouble?" I ask in confusion.

"Not yet, but you will be. Hopefully, enough trouble for your boyfriend to come and save you. Then we'll get him, too."

"What? What are you–"

Officer Marc lunges toward me, and I reel back, only to run into the other officer behind me. He wraps an arm around my waist while the other covers my mouth with a cloth.

"The hard way it is, then," someone says, their voice fading into the distance.

It's the last thing I remember before darkness consumes me.

My brain pounds against my skull, and the sharp throbbing wakes me from my drugged sleep. Blinking a few times, I squint against the sunlight, rolling to the side as my world turns at a ninety-degree angle.

I slowly realize I'm handcuffed in the back of a car. *What the heck...?*

And then I remember.

Two cops showed up and were acting strange, and then... *Oh, my god.*

We take another sharp turn, and I roll to the other side of the seat, groaning when my shoulder bangs against the window. My arm spasms, sending pain shooting down my elbow into my wrist and causing the metal cuffs to scoot up my arm and dig into my skin. My right hand now has a little more wiggle room, and I don't have time to think. I see an opportunity and go for it.

Throwing myself backward, I clutches the door handle with my right hand and yank the damn thing with all my strength. To my surprise, the door is unlocked, and I roll out of the backseat and onto the gravel road with a bounce. Thankfully, the car was slowing down, so the impact wasn't too bad. I'm sure I'll have some scrapes and bruises, but I don't have time to worry because the vehicle stops and the driver is about to chase after me.

Adrenaline pumps through my veins, and my fight-or-flight instinct goes into overdrive. *I won't lie down and take it anymore,* I tell myself as I struggle to my feet. It's hard to maintain my balance with my hands still cuffed behind me, and I fall to my knees several times before getting a few steps in.

I'm not your prisoner. I'm no one's prisoner. One foot in front of the other, keep going...

My foot catches on a soft patch of grass on the side of the gravel road, and I pitch forward, rolling down a small embankment. My head bangs against something hard, but I don't waste time looking to see what it is. It doesn't matter. I need to keep moving.

Throwing my weight upward, I gain enough momentum to haul myself over the other side of the ditch and break into an awkward sprint across what appears to be a nicely mowed field. I'm unsure where I am, but the terrain is easy enough to navigate.

It's not until I nearly run smack into a giant gravestone that I realize I'm in a cemetery. I stop in of the six-foot tall memorial, peering around one side and then the other before deciding to hang a right and keep going. I don't know if the man driving the car is still chasing me, but I have to keep moving. I need to get back to Blade.

"Hey–oh!" comes a sweet, startled voice beside me.

I look to the left and trip over a small headstone.

"Oh, my god. Are you okay?"

I hit the ground with a thud, wincing at the pain in my shoulder.

The woman rushes to my side and looks me over, her eyes landing on the cuffs around my wrists. I worry she might get the wrong idea and call the cops about an escaped convict, but she pulls a bobby pin from her hair and a pocket knife from her purse and gets to work picking the lock on the cuffs. Thirty seconds later, they loosen and fall to the ground.

She backs away, and I sit up, rubbing the raw marks on my wrists. I look over my shoulder, searching for my captors, but I don't see anyone.

"Are you okay?" the woman asks again.

I jerk my head in her direction, taking in her black combat boots, torn fishnet tights, leather shorts, and black, lacy top. She has a cute little black and white top hat clipped to the side of her bun, making her look like an adorable goth princess.

"Um, I…" How do I answer that?

"Dumb question. Someone running through a cemetery with a gash on their forehead and handcuffs isn't having a good day."

I huff out a laugh, then suck in a breath at the sharp pain ricocheting around my skull.

"Here. I think I have some Aspirin or something," she says, digging through her bag. "I'm Gemma, by the way."

"Aren't you concerned that I had handcuffs on?" I blurt. Not sure why I thought that would help my situation, but here we are.

Gemma smiles at me. "Aren't you concerned I knew how to pick a lock?"

I grin, knowing we're going to be good friends. "Not even a little bit. I'm Sonya."

I hold out my hand for her to shake, but Gemma throws her arms around me instead. We're still crouching on the ground, so it's a little awkward, but the warmth and genuineness radiating from Gemma makes up for it.

"Do you have time to talk about your day, or do we need to get moving?"

"We?"

"Hell, yeah! This is the most exciting thing to happen to me since my true crime podcast hit number one-hundred-fifty-thousand in the Spotify store!"

I'm unsure if being number one-hundred-fifty-thousand is noteworthy or not, but Gemma is certainly pumped about it.

"I need to get back to Blade," I say as a shiver runs down my spine. I can feel myself crashing, and I know I'm not back to safety quite yet. I hope I haven't dragged Gemma into my mess.

"Blade. Got it," Gemma says with a nod as she stands. She holds out her hand, helping me to my feet. "Where do we find Blade?"

"Savage Saints clubhouse."

"No, shit?" Gemma's eyes are wide with fascination.

I chuckle at her response. "Yeah, he's the President."

"No fucking way," she whispers. "That... is... AWESOME! Yes, let's go to the clubhouse. That's so freaking cool. I mean, not that I'm happy you had to be in whatever position you were in to end up here or anything–"

"I get it," I tell her, hoping to ease her worry. "Can you point me in the right direction? The clubhouse is out on old highway–"

"Sixteen," Gemma finishes for me. "Sorry, I didn't mean to cut you off. I'm kind of weird about maps and geography." Her cheeks flush red.

I smile at her. "That's cool. I'm glad you know. I'm a little lost."

"Let's go. It's not too far. We can stick to the forest line along the road in case whoever is looking for you comes back."

I nod, and Gemma loops her arm in mine, helping to support my weight as I limp along beside her.

"Thank you," I murmur after a few moments of silence. "I don't know what I would've done if I hadn't run into you."

"Good thing we don't have to find out, huh?" Gemma squeezes my arm.

I swallow past the lump in my throat at her kindness. If I start now, I may never stop. I need to get to Blade first. He'll make everything better.

CHAPTER TWELVE

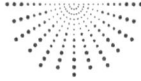

BLADE

"*W*hat the fuck happened here? Where was everyone? Who the hell let the fucking cops into our shop?" I yell at Hawk, though I know it's not his fault.

I swung by the shop to take Sonya to lunch a few minutes ago, but instead of finding my woman behind her desk, I discovered a note scrawled on an old carbon copy receipt.

It's about time you had someone worth using for blackmail. Want your woman back? Disband the Savage Saints once and for all.

They didn't have to sign it for me to know it was the fuckin' cops. Usually, they'd be the ones to call in a situation like this, but the police in this town are responsible for more crime than all of its civilians combined.

"Fuck!" I growl, pounding my fist against the cement wall.

The impact sends shockwaves of pain up and down my arm, but that's nothing compared to the gaping hole in my heart. I should've been here. I should never have left her side. I was so concerned by Sonya healing from her wounds that I didn't think to protect her from mine. Namely, the dirty, motherfucking pathetic excuse of a police force that has it out for the Savage Saints.

I stomp around the lobby like a rabid bear, worry and anger churning in my gut and making me sick to my stomach. Running a hand through my hair, I tug at the strands until it stings, then continue to pace.

"Prez, we can stake out–"

"No time to stake out. We need to *get* her. Right now," I spit out.

"Where–"

"Everywhere!"

I know I'm not making any sense. I've never had something so important ripped away from me, never cared about anyone enough for them to be a liability. It's my fault Sonya was taken, and I'll sure as fuck be the one to end this shit between the Savage Saints and the PD. After this, there won't be a war, only a king. Me.

My phone rings, and I answer it without looking at the screen. "What?"

"Prez, you need to get to the clubhouse."

"I'm busy, Axel. Need to get to–"

"Sonya's here. She just walked in with another woman."

"She's… there? Right there? With you? Now?" My heart stutters and stops, only beating again when I hear her voice on the other end of the line.

"B-Blade, I'm ok-kay," she whispers.

"I'm coming for you, baby. I'll be right there. God, I'm so sorry, Sonya. If they hurt you…"

"I'm okay," she says with a little more confidence.

"I'll be right there. Love you, baby girl. Hang tight."

I shove my phone in my pocket and tip my head at Hawk, who I assume heard the majority of the conversation. We hop on our bikes and speed out of the parking lot, eating up the few blocks between here and the clubhouse in no time.

I barely put my bike in park before stumbling off and sprinting inside. "Sonya? Sonya, where–"

"Blade!"

My woman has a blanket draped over her shoulders and a cut on her forehead, but she rushes toward me all the same. I meet her halfway, scooping her up and cradling her against my chest. She wraps the blanket around us, and I press my lips to her forehead, careful to avoid her wound.

"Sonya," I whisper, holding her close. "I'm so sorry I wasn't there to protect you. I should have told you the cops in this town are rotten and out to get us. I should have taken them out long before now, so they never had a chance to hurt you. God, I should have–"

My woman cuts me off with a kiss. The racing thoughts and gut-wrenching worries stop when her lips meet mine. I sip from her sweetness, giving her gentle strokes with my tongue and silently promising her I'll never let anything bad happen to her ever again.

Someone whistles behind us, and I tear my mouth from Sonya's long enough to grunt at them. She giggles, and Jesus, it loosens the vise that's been squeezing my heart for the last hour.

"Love that sound, baby. Love everything about you. How did you escape?"

"I woke up in the back of a car," she starts.

"A cop car?"

"No, I don't think so. It didn't have a metal divider. The doors were unlocked, so I rolled out of the back seat and ran for the nearest clearing, which happened to be a cemetery."

I grunt, knowing exactly which road she was on.

"That's when Gemma found me."

"Gemma?"

Sonya points to someone standing by the front door. I missed her completely on my way in.

"Thank you, Gemma," I tell her sincerely. "You kept my woman safe, so now you have the protection of the Savage Saints."

The little lady's eyes widen, and then she does the strangest thing. She curtsies. "Thank you, uh, Mr. Blade. I mean, Mr. President. President Blade? Oooh, that's a kickass villain name. Not that you're a villain. You have the sweetest girlfriend. And—" she cuts herself off, her cheeks bright red. "And anyway. Uh, thank you. I'll just... yup. I'll go." The odd woman spins and walks out the door. She pauses and looks at Sonya over her shoulder. "I wrote my number on a piece of paper and put it in your pocket. Call me when you feel better, and we can hang out without the handcuffs."

Sonya laughs and agrees, and the women wave at each other as Gemma skips out the door. I'll have to remember to ask Sonya about her new friend later. If she needs a motorcycle or a car or a fucking castle, I'll find a way to get it to her. She helped the love of my life when I couldn't, and I'll forever be in her debt.

"Let's get you home, love," I murmur to Sonya, finally setting her on her feet.

No sooner do I turn to leave than the front door swings open... revealing a goddamn police officer. My gun is trained on him in less than a second, along with every one of my men in the room. The bastard wants to finish the job? I'd like to see him try.

"Give me one good reason not to fill your head with bullets," I grit.

The officer holds his hands up in surrender, his eyes panning around the room and growing wider as he sees how many guns he's up against.

Sonya tugs on my arm, and I glance at her crouching behind me. "He's the one who was driving," she whispers.

I cock my gun, aiming for the fucker's forehead.

"Wait! I didn't know!" he protests. "This is my second week on the job. I just transferred from San Francisco. As the newest one on the force, I was assigned a lot of prison transfers since no one likes doing them. I was told she was another transfer."

"Bullshit," I growl, taking aim again. "You weren't in a cop car. Hard to miss that detail."

"I know. I was told the vehicle was going up for auction soon, so they stripped the identifying markers and dividers to get it ready to sell. It took me a bit too long to recognize what a dumb lie that was. In fact, I realized it as she woke up. I was slowing down and had the doors unlocked. She bailed before I had a chance to stop."

"You chased after me," Sonya says, peeking out from behind me.

"I wanted to make sure you weren't hurt, but then I saw you talking with another woman, and she was helping you out of the cuffs. I didn't want to scare you further, so I hung back a bit and followed you until you got to the Savage Saints clubhouse."

"She's safe here," I inform him, my tone icy.

"I can see that now, but I wasn't sure. She's been through a lot."

"Thanks to your brothers in blue," I spit out.

The man surprises me by nodding. "I figured that out as well." He turns to address Sonya, now standing at my side, her hand wrapped around mine. "Are you okay? Are you safe here? I'm sorry for my part."

Sonya narrows her eyes at him and squares her shoulders. "Why should we trust you?"

I grin at her, falling more in love with my woman by the second.

"Because I think we have a similar goal in mind. Weeding out the dirty cops in this town and reclaiming it. What do you say?"

"You want to team up?" Sonya asks.

The officer shrugs.

"You want to be our man on the inside," I correct.

He nods, his palms still facing out in surrender.

I stare into his green eyes, noting that he's shaking slightly, but his gaze is steady. The man can't be more than twenty-five, so his story about being a rookie checks out. If he were lying, it wouldn't make sense for him to show his face at the clubhouse. He took a huge risk stepping foot in here.

I reengage the safety on my gun and tuck it into my belt, nodding at my men to do the same. The officer sighs in relief, which makes me smirk. It's good that he's scared. It means he realizes the seriousness of the shit he's found himself tangled up in.

"You can handle cleaning this incident up with your co-workers? Get them off our back while we plan a takedown?"

"I'll say you guys caught up to me and jumped me."

"Might need a black eye to make that believable," I grunt.

He nods again. "And a split lip. Make it look good. I'll drive the car back to the same spot and slash the tires."

I look over at Hawk, then at Axel. With a slight dip of my chin, they know the plan.

"Deal." I step forward to shake his hand.

"I'm Officer Jake Cardell," he tells me as we shake hands.

"Blade." I jerk my head to the left, "That's Axel." I nod to the right. "And Hawk."

The two men step forward and follow Jake out to his car.

They'll handle it from here. Right now, I need to get my woman to safety.

"Ready to go home, baby?" I ask her.

Sonya nods and throws her arms around me as I pick her up and carry her to my bike. I don't know that I'll be able to leave her side ever again.

CHAPTER THIRTEEN

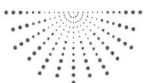

SONYA

"*N*o... *No, please...*"

"Sonya, love, wake up," comes a deep, calming voice. "You're having a bad dream, baby. Come back to me. I've got you."

Blinking my eyes open, the last of the dream fades into blackness as the moon's dim light bathes us in silver. "Sorry," I rasp, shaking my head of the remnants of fear stuck in the corners of my mind.

"No reason to apologize," Blade whispers. "You had a traumatic day. Can I do anything for you?"

"I'm okay," I assure him, snuggling against his chest. A few moments of silence pass, and I feel the guilt rolling off him in waves. I hate that he feels responsible for what happened. I got a little banged up, but nothing serious. No stitches, no broken bones. "The scariest part was thinking I'd never see you again," I admit.

"Sonya," he says softly, cupping the side of my face and turning my head so we're eye to eye. "I'm yours. I'll always come for you. Always protect you. I let you down today, but it won't happen again."

"Blade, it's not your fault. You've given me everything—a chance to start my life, a job, a way to pay for a car repair that we both know isn't worth all the work, a place to stay, a reason to get up in the morning, a reason to trust and love and–"

He cuts me off by taking my mouth. There's no build-up, only passion and heat from the very beginning. His tongue plunges into my mouth, tasting every inch of me like he owns me. He does.

He strokes the sensitive roof of my mouth, and I moan at the sensation, breaking the kiss. He nuzzles my neck and tightens his arms around me like I might bolt at any minute. Finally, he looks up at me.

"Sonya…" he starts, then trails off, trying to find the right words. "When we're together, it's like nothing I've ever experienced. It's not just physical with you, although that part is overwhelmingly incredible." He smirks, somehow putting me at ease.

Blade's gaze turns serious, his brown eyes begging me to listen to him. "I'm bound to you forever, Sonya. I want to feel all of you, all at once, and not just physically. I want to crawl inside you and figure out how you operate. I want to know how you hurt so I can fix it like you're already fixing me."

"Blade…" I whisper. This man keeps surprising me with his tenderness and sweet words. I think it's surprising to him, too.

"You're everything to me, my whole fucking world," Blade continues. "I love you, but love doesn't even feel like an adequate word. I…"

I rest my forehead on his, breathing him in. "I feel it, too, Blade. I want you with everything I am. You're a part of me, and being separated from you is like tearing myself in half. I need you more than my next breath."

His lips are on mine, his hands roaming all over me,

squeezing my breasts, stroking my back, tangling in my hair to guide my head as he deepens his kiss. He consumes me, each stroke of his tongue reminding me I'm his, each soft moan from our lips adding to the symphony of our love.

Blade quickly undresses us, hovering over my body as I stretch out beneath him. He kisses my nose, lips, and cheeks. Kneeling on the bed at my feet, he trails his fingers over my toes, up the arch of my foot, higher, until he's tickling the insides of my ankles.

Blade continues his teasing touches, bending to add soft kisses to the places his fingers just left. He works his hands higher up my legs, massaging my calves, knees, and thighs. When he gets to my center, he places a sweet kiss on top of my curls and continues moving up my body.

His hands slide reverently over the curve of my hips, and he places small kisses on my belly, nuzzling his head there. I wonder if I'm pregnant. The thought should scare me, but I find that I want it. I want everything with him.

He looks up at me, and a moment of understanding passes between us. "I want that too, Sonya. We'll make it happen, I promise."

He returns his focus to my body, kissing a trail up my torso and between my breasts. His knuckles brush my nipples, and he traces the round curve of my breasts with his tongue.

Blade worships my body, showing me how much I mean to him. His hands glide down my arms and he twines his fingers with mine, bringing my arms above my head and holding them in place with one of his large hands on my wrists.

He dips his head and sucks on my collarbone before licking the curve of my neck and placing a soft kiss on my pulse point. He kisses up my jaw and places sweet kisses on my temple, my forehead, my eyes, and my nose. He hovers above me, inches away. We share the same breath and get lost in the moment.

Finally, Blade kisses me. It's tender and reverent, full of promises. He reaches down and drags his throbbing cock up my slit, rubbing my juices all over him. He deepens the kiss and slowly slides into me. I feel every vein on his beautiful shaft as he presses himself into me, keeping his slow, steady pace.

We both groan when he's fully buried deep inside me. He stays there for a few seconds, bowing his head to rest on my chest. The hand not holding my wrist ghosts up and down the side of my body, from the curve of my hip to the side of my breast.

"This is everything. Everything. Mine. Mine. *Mine*," he whispers into my chest, more to himself than me.

Blade moves inside me, pulling out at the same slow pace. My walls pulse, wanting to suck him in and keep him inside me. Once he's fully out, he enters me again, excruciatingly slow. I need him, need his cock, need our release. But he's in control.

In and out, he never picks up speed, slowly thrusting and feeling every inch of my pussy. It's like he's memorizing me from the inside out, figuring out which places are sensitive, which ones make me flinch and buck and lose control.

The slow burn is killing me. The edge of the flame licks at my core, not quite there yet. His delicious torture is like nothing I've ever experienced. In and out, slow and steady. I wrap my legs around his hips and press him further into me so his cock hits my clit with each slow thrust.

He releases my hands and places his arms on either side of my head. I wind my fingers in his hair and pull him down for a kiss. His tongue twists with mine in a slow dance, the same pace as his thrusts.

The flames reach my core, and I'm so sensitive even

though I haven't come yet. He keeps me on the edge, and it's almost more than I can take. I grip his shoulders and try to move myself up, chasing my release.

His hand goes to my hip to still my movements. Blade rests his forehead on mine.

"Feel this with me, love. Feel me. Feel us…" he rasps as his hips buck, sending shockwaves throughout my body.

"Blade…" I whisper, not wanting to break whatever spell his body is casting over me.

He continues his slow pace, occasionally adding a quick, hard thrust that brings me right to the edge before he slows down again and pulls me back. My juices trickle out of me and pool on the sheets beneath me.

"Please…"

He thrusts again, harder this time.

"Oh! Oh. God. I'm right there, Blade…"

"Come for me, Sonya. I've got you. Look at me. I want to see you fall apart for me."

With a final thrust, my orgasm takes me. It's slow and all-consuming, starting in my core and squeezing my muscles one by one. I swear my heart stops. I can't take in air as wave after wave of delicious pleasure pulses through my body.

I stare into Blade's eyes. It's so intense, so vulnerable. He swells inside me as he empties deep into my womb. His jaw clenches and his nostrils flare as he comes, never breaking eye contact with me. He's shaking and panting as much as I am.

Blade collapses on top of me, and I savor his skin on mine, covering me, melting into me, as close as we can possibly be.

"Sorry," he mumbles as he rolls us over.

I lie on top of him, completely spent and content. I rest my cheek on his chest and throw a leg over his, tangled up in him. My arm stretches over his chest as I place my hand over his heart. "Mine," I whisper.

"So fucking mine, Sonya. My sweet, filthy, perfect baby girl."

I sigh contentedly when Blade presses his lips to the top of my head. This man has become my whole world in such a short amount of time. I can't wait to see what the future holds for me and my growly biker.

EPILOGUE

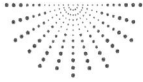

BLADE

"$\mathscr{C}$heers to ten years!" Axel calls out from across the bar. My men raise their glasses toward me and my old lady and say their congrats and well-wishes. Sonya waves and raises her wine glass, laughing when Tessa whistles at her.

I climb off my bar stool, standing to address everyone in the clubhouse. We closed down to the public about an hour ago to celebrate our tenth anniversary. It's hard to believe this woman has been in my life for a decade now. Then again, I can hardly remember who I was before Sonya came waltzing in with her sunshine and bright smiles.

"Thank you for joining us this evening," I start. "Ten years and two months ago, I was perfectly content to be a cold, jaded bastard. Then my Sonya showed up on the side of the road needing some assistance." I turn and face my beautiful woman, the love in her eyes reflected in my own. "I thought I was saving you that day, but truthfully, you were the one who rescued me from a lifetime of loneliness."

Sonya hops off of her seat and wraps her arms around

me, standing on her tiptoes and kissing my cheek. "When did you get so cheesy?" she teases.

"About the same time you cast your spell over me, my little siren," I whisper so only she can hear. I take her lips in mine, not able to resist her for one second longer.

Like every time we touch, the world fades away until it's just us. What starts out as a chaste kiss turns into something deeper as I sink into her sweetness. Sonya's hands crawl up my chest until she's fisting my shirt, pulling me closer.

Cat calls and hollers filter through my brain, and Sonya gasps once she remembers we're putting on a show. I smile against her soft lips and nip at her playfully before nuzzling into the side of her neck.

"Fuck off," I grunt at everyone. The room fills with chuckles and laughter, but none of that matters. Not when I bend down and toss my precious, sexy-as-hell woman over my shoulder and sprint toward the apartments in the back.

"Oh my god, Blade," Sonya says with a sigh, though I hear the amusement in her voice. "Such a caveman."

"You love it," I counter, bursting through one of the bedroom doors and tossing her down on the bed.

"Is that right?" she asks, her brow tilting up in the most adorably playful look.

I nod, then peel my shirt off as I stare down at Sonya, spread out before me. "Need me to remind you how much you love this caveman?"

Sonya nods, nibbling her bottom lip.

I smirk at her and drop to my knees, pulling her by her ankles until her ass is nearly hanging off the mattress. Without hesitation, I flip up the skirt of her dress and rip her little panties off. I dive in, licking the seam of her pussy and then plunging my tongue deeper inside.

"Oh, god," she breathes out, writhing around on the bed.

I steady her by spreading my palm out over her stomach, pinning her in place while increasing the pressure in her lower belly. Sonya snaps her thighs together when I scrape my teeth against her clit, then cries out as I suck her sensitive bundle of nerves.

Grunting in satisfaction, I switch my attention to her tight, wet entrance, dripping with her desire. I spear my tongue inside, groaning as her walls pulse against the invasion. Sonya gushes into my mouth, rocking against me and chasing her pleasure.

I slide my hands over her body, wrapping them around her thighs and prying them apart. I open her up for me, securing her legs on the mattress as I continue my assault on her juicy little cunt.

I alternate between fast and slow licks, taking my time to read my woman's body and give her what she needs, but never quite enough to push her over the edge.

"Blade, please..." she whines, the desperate sound spurring me on.

"Hold it, baby," I command.

Sliding two fingers into her entrance, I curl them up and search for her most sensitive spot. I know I hit it when Sonya jerks and floods my hand with more of her sweet, slick cum. Bending down, I resume sucking and nipping her clit while rubbing and tapping her G-spot, working her up into a frenzy.

Her breath hitches as every muscle locks tight... and then she shatters for me, coming hard and crying out her release. Sonya whimpers as I lap up her sweet honey, drinking it down like the sweet nectar it is.

When she's finally wrung dry, I crawl up her limp, sated body, placing kisses on her chin, nose, and cheeks before curling up next to her.

"I love you, baby girl," I whisper.

Sonya turns to face me, her eyes glassy and cheeks flushed.

"Love you forever," she murmurs, pressing a kiss to my forehead.

Just then, a knock sounds at the door.

"What?" I yell, not appreciating the interruption.

"Sutton wanted me to let you know the kids can spend the night at our place so you two can, uh, *celebrate*," Rider says. I can tell he feels awkward as hell, which makes me smirk.

"Thanks, we'll take you up on that. Call you in the morning."

He takes the hint and walks away, his footsteps fading into the background.

"Oh my god," Sonya says with a giggle, hiding her face in my chest. "Was I really loud?"

I grin at my gorgeous girl, thinking back to her shouting out her orgasm. "I hope everyone heard. They need to know you're mine."

"I think they already know that, Mr. Possessive-Biker-Pants."

I flip her on her back and tickle her, laughing when she shrieks and giggles again. "Never hurts to remind them. Plus, we got a free night of babysitting," I say with a shrug.

Sonya hits my chest playfully, then tugs me down on top of her. "Better take advantage of it then, hmm?"

I groan and nod my head as I tilt my head down to kiss my wife. Ten years and three kids later, she's still as addicting and perfect as the day I met her. I know the next ten years will be even better.

* * *

THE END

Want to know more about Gemma & Axel? Get their story here!

AXEL

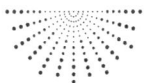

AXEL

Gemma is the strangest woman I've ever met. She spends her free time in graveyards and knows more about serial killers than any one person should. I can't afford a distraction right now, however.

I'm the newest member of Savage Saints MC and I need to prove the Prez made the right choice in letting me pledge and then initiating me. Despite my best efforts, my mind keeps wandering to the red-headed goddess who picnics in the graveyard.

The quirky yet enchanting woman is connected to the Savage Saints in a completely unexpected way. She's afraid I'll judge her for her family, but she has no idea how much I can relate to her past.

Now I have two things to prove; my loyalty to the club and my dedication to Gemma. I hope she's ready for a biker like me.

CHAPTER ONE

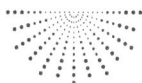

AXEL

*T*he rev of the motorcycle engine beneath me is music to my ears. I take the next turn a little faster than the last one, leaning in and feeling my adrenaline spike as I'm held in place by centripetal force alone.

Back on the straightaway, I correct my posture and breathe deeply, drinking in the cool air as it hits me in the face. Nothing feels like being on a motorcycle. Some people say it's the freedom of a bike on the open road, while others seek danger to fill a void in their lives. Not me.

Motorcycles were my way out of the hellscape I grew up in.

I learned to make myself useful at an early age, and something about engines and bikes clicked. Even more so when mods and digital upgrades became available on newer models. Working on computers, electronics, and kick-ass bike upgrades and repairs became my business plan from the time I left home at thirteen.

Last year, I fulfilled the only goal I've ever had—patching in as an official member of the Savage Saints MC. Since then,

I've been working my goddamn ass off to prove to my brothers I'm an asset to the club.

I slow down slightly as the highway meets the small California town where the Savage Saints are headquartered. Never would've guessed the outlaw biker gang would be straighter than the cops, but Sheriff Darren has a strong hold over the people here. His lackeys are as power-hungry and dirty as he is, and we've had enough of their oppressive control.

I take another breath and follow the curve of the road, letting the hum of the tires on asphalt calm me. As I take the next corner, I come upon the massive graveyard that's been around since this was a mining town during the gold rush back in the 1850s.

Elaborate headstones and monuments are scattered among more humble graves, the rows of plots going up one hill and disappearing down another. Something red catches my eye, and I slow even further as I get closer.

It's not blood-red, more of a fiery hue, like orange leaves in the fall. I realize it's *hair,* and it's attached to a body. The person is lying on the ground, not moving.

Without a second thought, I tear my bike off to the right and park it in a rush on the side of the road. Hopping off, I sprint up the slight embankment and come to a halt in front of the strangest sight.

A woman is flat on her back, resting on an old plaid blanket between two graves. Her bright red hair is spread around her, a shining, coppery beacon in the otherwise gray sea of headstones. Her eyes are closed, but she's still very much alive and breathing. For some odd reason, I note that her rosy lips are the same color as her flushed cheeks, no doubt red from the slight chill in the air.

My gaze travels lower, down her shoulders, over her generous breasts that I'm not allowing myself to stare at, and finally resting on her hands folded over her stomach. Her delicate fingers are wrapped around a bouquet of wildflowers, the tips painted neon pink and lime green. Something about that detail makes me grin.

I take in her black dress. It looks like a cross between a corset and a lacy fairy skirt, paired with fishnet tights and black combat boots at least two sizes too big for her. The napping punk rock princess suddenly opens her eyes, and I nearly fall on my ass and roll down the hill into oncoming traffic.

Green. Clear, twinkling, terrified green eyes stare back at me, knocking the air out of my lungs.

The woman sits straight up, her wide eyes darting around to assess for threats. "What's going on? Who are you? How long–"

"Gemma?" I ask, recognizing her as the one who helped the Prez's woman, Sonya, when she was hurt a few weeks ago. The wariness in her gaze turns into panic. What has her so frightened? "I'm a member of the Savage Saints."

As soon as the words leave my mouth, she relaxes. *Interesting.* That's not the typical response when someone hears I'm part of an outlaw biker gang.

"I do recognize you," she says softly, peering into my eyes as she clambers to her feet.

Gemma tilts her head to the side, and some of her long hair falls over her left shoulder. I notice a few twigs and leaves tangled in the strands and reach toward her automatically, picking out the debris.

Realizing I'm violating her space, I immediately drop my hand and step back. The red-headed rebel princess sways toward me but then catches herself. She stands with her shoulders straight and her hands behind her back. Those damn green eyes are filled with curiosity, and I get the sense she's about to explode with questions.

"How long have you been a member? What do your patches mean? Do you have to bring your own bike to join the club, or do they provide one for you?"

Gemma has another question on the tip of her tongue, but she seems to reel her excitement in a bit. Not too much. Not at all, really. She bounces slightly on the balls of her feet as if gearing up for something. It's kind of... adorable. I don't think anyone has ever been this excited to talk to me. Her energy is contagious, and I find myself grinning at the amusing woman.

"I'm the newest member of the MC."

Gemma nods and smiles, eating up every word. It's almost like no one talks to her, but I can't imagine anyone not instantly being friends with her.

"Really? What was that process like? Did you have to kill anyone?" Her eyes widen at her last question, and she looks over her shoulder to ensure no one else is around to hear. Fuckin' adorable. "You don't have to tell me. That's probably club business, right?"

I chuckle and run a hand through my hair. This woman is unlike anyone I've ever met, and I've only known her for two minutes. *What other surprises will I discover?*

"It was nothing as dramatic as murder," I tell her with a wink.

Her cheeks turn from dusky pink to berry red, and a wicked thought crosses my mind before I can stop it. *I wonder if I could get her to blush everywhere...*

"Just a good, old-fashioned maiming, then?" Gemma asks in all seriousness. Her cute little eyebrows furrow in concentration, and her jaw tenses as if bracing herself for the harsh truth.

"Sorry to disappoint, but no maiming, either."

Those green eyes sparkle with mischief, and fuck if my dick isn't twitching to life for the first time in God knows how long. What is it about Gemma that's pushing all the right buttons?

"Got it. No violence whatsoever," Gemma says, giving me an overdramatic wink. She bursts out laughing, which makes my chest feel funny. "But for real, what about the bike? I've always wondered. Does the club give you a bike?"

"No, you gotta bring your own," I say with a smile. She's kind of ridiculous with her questions and enthusiasm, but it's charming, and I find myself wanting to stretch this conversation on as long as possible.

"Shoot. So I'll need a bike first," she responds, nodding once.

"You want to join the Savage Saints?"

Gemma shrugs. "Just keeping my options open." She hits me with another brilliant smile, but something is off in her tone. It takes a second for me to realize what it is.

She's looking for options, aka, an escape. *What are you running from, princess?*

Before I can ask, her phone beeps. Gemma digs it out of a pocket hidden in her layers of lace and fabric, and the color drains from her face when she looks at the screen.

The hairs on the back of my neck stand up, and a long-dormant protective streak pushes to the surface. I want to wrap Gemma up in my arms and demand she tell me who put that fear in her eyes.

"I have to go," she rushes to say. "I I didn't realize how late it was. I lost track of time and... I need to go."

Gemma gathers up her blanket and shoves it into her backpack, along with a book, a notebook, and what looks like a recording device and lapel mic I didn't notice earlier.

"Wait, what's wrong? Who was that?"

Gemma doesn't answer at first, too focused on securing the snaps on her bag. "No one," she finally replies.

My look says it all. *Yeah, fucking right.*

Gemma dips her head, breaking eye contact with me. My heart drops to my stomach as I watch her fold in on herself. Where is the energetic, lively woman who wanted to know every detail of the MC? What is she hiding?

"It's a long story, but... thanks for, um, for this." She still won't look at me, and I hate it.

"Gemma," I say softly, taking a few steps closer to her.

She holds her backpack in front of her like a shield, and while I know it's not directed at me, her automatic response to protect herself kills me.

"I'm sorry. I have to go," she repeats.

"You're free to go. I'm not stopping you," I assure her. "I just want to make sure you're safe."

This gets her attention. Gemma blinks a few times, and her expressive eyes tear me apart like she can't quite believe her safety would be important to me. "I..." Green irises dart between mine as she struggles to find an answer. Anything other than an automatic yes is a red flag in my book. "I'm late. I have to go."

With that, she spins on her heel and weaves in and out of rows of headstones before disappearing down the hill. I'm left staring after her, holding the tiny bouquet of wildflowers she had wrapped in her hands.

What the hell was that? And when can I see her again?

CHAPTER TWO

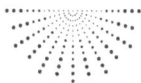

GEMMA

"*Y*ou can do this," I whisper to myself. "Just open the door, walk inside, and…"

Letting out a frustrated sigh, I cross my arms over my chest and resume my pacing in front of the Savage Saints Clubhouse. I've been here for ten minutes, trying to work up the courage to go inside and ask to speak to Blade.

Truthfully, this is the third time I've been here this week. I chicken out every time. I get all worked up, psych myself out, and then sprint the three blocks back to the graveyard—the only place I feel safe.

"Nothing changes if nothing changes," I say under my breath. Cliche words, I know, but they're what I need to hear right now.

I try again, gathering all my strength and wrapping my fingers around the door handle. I can't hear anything other than my heart pounding and blood pumping. This is it. If I do this, there's no going back.

Just open the door…

I drop my hand and spin around on my heel, continuing

my pacing a few feet further from the clubhouse than before. I can't seem to bring myself to go through with it. Grunting in frustration, I grab my long braid and begin twisting it around my fingers in a familiar, soothing gesture.

I thought maybe seeing Axel yesterday was a sign that I was ready to try again, ready to walk inside the clubhouse this time. Apparently not.

"Gemma?"

I let out a squeak and crouch, my automatic response to an unexpected intruder. Hide, stay quiet, don't ask for anything. If they don't notice me, I can't get into trouble for "not pulling my weight."

"Hey, it's okay," comes the voice I now recognize as Axel. "I'm not going to hurt you."

Embarrassment floods my system, and I know my face is bright red. There's no hiding my emotions with my light complexion. I pop up from where I'm cowering like a baby and attempt to give Axel a reassuring smile. From the concerned look in his deep blue eyes, I don't think I quite pull it off.

God, he's as gorgeous and chiseled as I remember from yesterday. More so, in fact. With black hair and ocean-blue eyes framed in long, dark lashes, his gaze is almost hypnotizing. And then there's his broad chest and strong arms, corded with muscles and decorated with tattoos.

I want to curl up in his embrace and ask him to keep me safe, but that's a ridiculous thought. He doesn't know me or my family. If he did, he might not be so friendly.

"Hey, there," I say with a little too much enthusiasm. My heart is still racing, though I don't know if it's from my earlier scare or being in Axel's presence. "I, um, was just…" I trail off, unsure what to say. Can I trust him with this? Am I naive for thinking Axel and his club can do anything about my situation?

Axel doesn't miss a beat. He sees how uncomfortable I am and gives me a charming smile, putting me at ease. "Stalking me already, huh?" He grins, running a hand through his dark hair. He did the same thing at the graveyard, and like then, I stare at the movement of his arm, mesmerized by the flex of his muscles.

"Awfully conceited of you to assume I'm here just to ogle you," I counter.

"Aha, I didn't say ogle, I said stalk. But yeah, you can ogle me too, princess." Another wink and wicked smirk has me blushing and my stomach swirling.

What is it about this man that makes me want to trust him? I feel... safe around him. I think that's what this is. Safety.

"Princess?" I ask, raising my eyebrow as I question his nickname for me.

"Short for punk-rock princess. Or goth princess. Oh, and princess of the graveyard. Take your pick."

I look down at my black A-line dress with dark purple polka dots that hits right above my knees. My dark purple tights match, and I've paired them with my favorite pair of Converse shoes I found while dumpster diving. I cleaned them up and drew little skulls and crossbones with neon fabric markers that pop against the black canvas.

Yeah, I'm guessing this look isn't exactly what he typically goes for in a woman. Not that Axel thinks about me that way. Obviously I have too many curves, a messed-up family, and nothing of value to offer anyone. There's no way this sexy biker beast has anything other than a passing curiosity about me. Or maybe he's being nice because he knows I helped Sonya when she needed it last month.

"Hey, where did you just go?" Axel whispers.

I finally stop staring at my feet and look up, meeting his gaze. "I'm right here," I reply in the same soft tone.

Axel steps in my direction, wrapping his hand around mine and tugging me closer so we're nearly chest-to-chest. "You went somewhere in your head. I get the sense you were saying mean things about yourself."

"I…" *How the hell did he know?*

"I wasn't making fun of you, I promise. I like your style. It's unique and very… you."

I furrow my brow, but Axel gives me the biggest grin. He looks down at me like I'm… amusing. No, that's not quite right. He looks at me like I'm adorable, and maybe, just maybe, I'm more than a curiosity to him.

"Uh, thanks. I think," I murmur awkwardly.

Axel untangles his hand from mine, sliding it up my arm and cupping my face. I can't help but lean into his touch, getting lost in those ocean-blue eyes. "One day, you won't doubt my compliments," he says softly. I blink, not sure I heard him correctly. "One day, you'll believe me when I tell you how beautiful you are."

Me? Beautiful? It's too much. Too good to be true. Too sweet, especially knowing what I'm going back to after this.

I step back, and a shiver runs down my spine as soon as his hand drops from my face. I like his touch. Far more than I should. I can't get used to gentle touches and kind words. They'll only make coming back to reality that much harsher.

"Now who's the one ogling?" I tease, giving Axel my best smirk. I'm still a little breathless from being so close to him, so I'm not sure I pull it off.

He smiles and wags his eyebrows, which makes me giggle. "So, are you going to tell me the real reason you're here?"

I rub my lips together nervously, deciding if I can tell him. Maybe I'll test the waters. Talking with Axel might be easier than going straight to Blade. I guess there's only one way to find out. "Well, uh, I was wondering…" I pause, breaking eye contact to look up to the sky. "What did Blade mean about me having the protection of the Savage Saints?" I ask in a rush.

I'm met with silence, so I peer back at Axel. His features have grown intense, his brow furrowed, his jaw tight with tension, and his blue eyes nearly black. "Who do you need protection from?" he asks, his tone serious.

"N-no one," I say in an unconvincing voice. He's not buying it, so I try again. "It was hypothetical. No big deal." I wave my hand in the air, dismissing the thought altogether.

Axel's face never changes. He scrutinizes me, and I don't know if I'll hold up under the pressure. I might break and confess everything, but I don't think I'm ready for that. Not yet. Axel won't look at me the same once he knows the truth.

"Anyway," I continue, taking a few steps backward. I look at my wrist as if checking my watch, only I don't have one. "Better get going. I forgot to... uh, forgot to turn off the oven," I ramble, groaning internally over the lamest excuse to leave in the history of the world.

"Gemma, wait," Axel calls as I turn. "You can't keep leaving–"

"Seems like that's exactly what I'm doing!" I joke as I break into a run. My only focus is getting the hell out of here before I give in to the urge to turn and run right back into Axel's arms.

"Gemma!"

I half expect him to chase after me. Lord knows he could catch me easily on his bike or on foot. One last look over my shoulder reveals he's debating letting me go. In the end, he stands at the end of the Savage Saints Clubhouse parking lot, watching me sprint away.

I run past the graveyard and down the next block, only stopping when I can no longer ignore the cramp in my side. Doubling over, I clutch my side while catching my breath. *Shit.* This isn't how I wanted today to end, and now I'm late.

My parents don't like it when I'm not home by dinner. It's not because we have a family meal planned or anything, although there's a lot of cooking—just not food.

Straightening, I walk the few blocks to the trailer park on the other side of the graveyard. I hear my mother and father screaming at each other before reaching the mostly broken door of our trailer.

My shoulders tense, and my heart rate spikes. Everything in me is on high alert. Instead of walking through the front door, I creep along the side of the trailer to my bedroom window. I usually leave it open a crack in case I need to sneak in. Suffice it to say, this isn't the first time I've come home to screaming matches. I've walked in on physical fights between my parents or three older brothers, drug use, and other questionable behavior.

I grip the window pane and shove it upward, opening it enough to wedge myself inside. Wrapping my fingers around the window ledge, I step on the cement cinder block I keep underneath the window and hoist myself up.

My bedroom door bursts open as I get my top half through the opening. My eldest brother, Randall, stomps inside, a sinister grin twisting his lips as he lunges toward me. I scramble away, but he grabs my arms and tugs hard, pulling me through the window and letting me fall to the ground with a thud. My left hip takes the brunt of the impact. Pain shoots down my back and leg as I try to catch my breath.

"Trying to sneak in and avoid your family, Gemma?" Randall spits out as he wraps his fingers around my forearm. He yanks me off the floor and tugs me forward, his grip tight enough to bruise.

"No, I–"

"Save it," he snaps, dragging me to my parents in the main room.

The two stop fighting and look at me, disgust and annoyance in their eyes. I should be used to it, but I'd be lying if I said their disdain for me didn't hurt every damn time. I know I was unplanned. Randall is almost thirty-nine, Carl is thirty-seven, and Nathan just turned thirty-six. I'm fifteen years younger than Nathan and nothing short of a total outcast in my family.

"Where the fuck were you?" my mother asks, making her way toward me. "You know your shift starts at six. We have orders to keep up. Product to push."

"I know, I just–"

"Unless you'd like to sell, instead?" my father grunts, approaching me.

I brace myself for whatever mood he's in. None of them are good. "N-no, I don't want–"

I hear the slap before I feel it. The sting follows a second later, quickly joined by a throbbing pain in my left cheek and temple.

"I don't give a fuck about what you want. You need to start pulling your weight around here. This is the family business. Got it?"

"Yes, I understand. I just thought maybe tonight I could–"

"No," comes the automatic response. "No more excuses. No more nights off. No more headaches or whatever other bullshit you say to get out of your responsibilities."

I nod, too scared to say anything else. My father's eyes are crazy tonight. He's been sampling his product again, and meth is a hell of a drug.

"Fuckin' useless waste," he mutters before stepping away from me.

I release the breath I was holding, hoping the worst is over. Before I have a chance to take another breath, something cracks against my face. Sharp pain almost blinds me as I stumble backward, unsure what just happened.

"Shut up and follow your brother to the kitchen. You're ruining my buzz."

It takes a second to register the voice as my mother's. The left side of my face throbs, sending agonizing bursts of pain ricocheting around my skull. It's not the first time I've had a black eye, but it's the first time I've been sucker-punched out of nowhere. Then again, when drugs and aggression are involved, I suppose I should expect violence at all times.

My mother turns and flops down on the broken, stained couch, grabbing a pipe and a lighter before getting settled. I peel myself off the wall, only to sway on my feet and catch myself with one hand on the opposite wall.

"Get yourself cleaned up and meet me in the kitchen," Randall grunts. He grips the back of my neck and pushes me toward the bathroom.

Once inside, I shut the door and brace myself on the small, rusted-out sink. Staring at my reflection in the cracked mirror, I gape at my swollen eye and cheek. It's going to be purple by tomorrow. I hope I'll still be able to see out of my left eye, but it wouldn't surprise me if it swells shut by morning.

"This is the last time," I whisper to myself. "I can't take this anymore. I *won't*."

Even as I say the words, my resolve is already fading. Where would I go? What would I do? This is all I know. All I'm good for. This is my life.

CHAPTER THREE

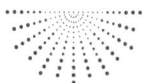

AXEL

"They've found another source," Officer Jake announces.

I straighten in my chair, as do my MC brothers. We've been in church for damn near an hour. I don't usually mind the long meetings, but I'm filled with restless, anxious energy today

I can't stop thinking about Gemma. She's run away from me twice now, leaving me more unsettled each time. I tossed and turned all night, thinking about her wide, green eyes filled with terror when her phone went off that first day. Images of my princess wringing her hands as she stood in front of the clubhouse flash through my mind, and I clench my fists at my sides when I remember her rushed words.

What did Blade mean about me having the protection of the Savage Saints?

"...thanks to Axel setting up the recording device, we know the new meth lab is in the Orchard Grove trailer park," Officer Jake continues.

I attempt to shove my thoughts about Gemma and why she needs protection to the back of my mind and focus on my club. The worry is still there, and I have a feeling that part of me will always be concerned about Gemma's well-being and happiness.

I nod at Jake to show him I'm paying attention. Mostly.

"Anything more specific?" Blade asks from his position next to Officer Jake at the front of the room.

"Not at this time. I've asked the interim sheriff to let me know about any special projects coming up. I think I'm getting close to being accepted into the inner circle."

The Prez nods and uncrosses his arms, clapping his big hand over Jake's shoulder. "Never thought I'd be saying this to a cop, but good work."

Officer Jake still looks a little rattled to be in a room filled with armed bikers who have a bad history with law enforcement, but he's come a long way in the last few weeks. A lot of my MC brothers were wary of working with the police after being betrayed by them again and again, but Jake has proven himself to be loyal so far. That's not to say I haven't been keeping tabs on him, too, however.

Blade says a few more words in closing, then dismisses us. Looking at my phone, I see it's almost four in the afternoon. Like every spare moment of my time over the last several days, my mind wanders to Gemma.

What's she up to? Is she safe? Where does she live? What is she so afraid of?

I don't even realize I'm on my bike until I exit the club-house parking lot. I didn't plan on going to the graveyard, but that's where I'm headed. Hopefully, I'll find the object of my obsession before I lose my damn mind altogether.

A few minutes later, I pull up at the bottom of the hill where I found Gemma resting. I see her bending to place something on a headstone, and it takes a second to realize it's a little bundle of wildflowers like she was holding the first day I found her.

So damn sweet.

When Gemma stands and continues walking down the row, I notice her limping slightly on her left side. Every protective urge rises in me, and I scramble up the side of the embankment to get to her.

"Gemma," I call out, hating myself when she tenses and crouches on the ground. *What has happened in her life to give her that instinct?* "Sorry, it's just me. Didn't mean to startle you."

"Oh, hey," comes her response. She's trying to play it off like no big deal, but I see her. I see how she holds herself as if everything is a threat.

Gemma stands slowly. I'm unsure if it's because she's a little shaken or hurting. God fucking help me if it's the latter.

"Everything okay?" I ask, taking a few steps closer.

She wobbles when she puts weight on her left side. I reach out, placing my hand on her hip to steady her. Gemma hisses at the contact and inhales sharply, turning away from me.

What the fuck?

"Did I hurt you?" I murmur, not wanting to scare her more than she already is.

"No, sorry, just, uh…" Gemma looks down, her fiery red hair hanging over the left side of her face like a curtain. "Just a little sore today," she finishes, wrapping her arms around her torso in a protective hold.

She looks so small, so heartbreakingly vulnerable. I wish I knew what to say to get her to trust me, but I'm at a loss for words.

Moving on instinct, I raise my hands in front of me, palms out, so she knows I'm not a threat. "You're okay, Gemma," I say softly. "You're safe here. You're safe with me. Do you know that?"

Still not lifting her head, Gemma whispers, "I... don't know what it means to be safe. But whatever I feel around you is safer than I've been in a long time."

Jesus, this woman is killing me. Would it send her into a panic attack if I scooped her up in my arms and carried her off to my apartment behind the clubhouse?

"You can talk to me," I encourage. "I can help. The Savage Saints can help. You don't have to go through this alone."

Please, please trust me. Let me in. Let me help, I silently beg.

When I hear her quiet sniffles, I can't stand not seeing her face anymore. Slowly, so slowly, I reach out and brush her silky red hair out of her face. My gaze immediately lands on the fucking black and blue bruise swelling up her left eye and cheekbone.

I want to curse and scream and hunt down whoever hurt my precious girl, but I swallow my rage and focus on taking care of Gemma.

"Sweetheart," I murmur, gently cupping her chin and tilting her head so I can examine the damage. Her poor skin is swollen and tender, with purple, blue, and black splashes of color pooling around her eye socket and cheekbone. Gemma's eyes are filled with tears, but she doesn't let them fall. "What happened?"

Gemma blinks a few times, the eyelid of her left eye almost swollen shut. She nibbles on her bottom lip nervously, breaking eye contact once more.

"You don't have to tell me right now," I whisper, dropping my hand from her chin and holding it out for her to take.

She rests her hand in mine, and I notice a set of angry, finger-sized bruises on her forearm as if someone yanked her or dragged her somewhere. The more I learn about Gemma's homelife, the less I like.

"Gemma—"

Before I can say anything else, she collapses into a pile of tears. I wrap my arms around her, holding her against me and soaking up a river of sadness as she pours out all her pain.

I'm not sure where else she's hurt, but I gently, so damn gently, cup the back of her neck and tuck her head under my chin. She fits perfectly in my embrace. She's right where she belongs, here in my arms, where I can protect her from the whole fucking world.

"I've got you," I whisper, trailing my fingertips down her spine. "Let it out, sweetheart."

Gut-wrenching sobs are pulled from the very depths of whatever trauma she's had to endure. They wrack her curvy little body, sending her into shaking fits. I hold her through it all, wishing I could take her pain away.

"I-I-I'm s-sorry," she cries, her voice muffled from where her face is buried in my chest.

"Shh, there's nothing to apologize for," I soothe. Never thought I was capable of saying tender things, but Gemma is pulling out all sorts of surprises from me. Fuck if I'm not going to keep her and cherish her forever. But first, I need her to trust me.

"I'm a mess," she says with a sniffle. Gemma peels herself off my chest and steps back. I bite back a grunt at the sudden separation. I don't like it. She should always be in my arms. "I'm... I'm just... I'm no good."

"No good? What do you mean?"

Her damn phone goes off, and she tenses and shuts down like last time. Not that she was very talkative before, but now I know I won't get an explanation.

"I have to go," she says, her voice barely above a whisper.

"You can stay. I can help. I can protect—"

Her phone chimes again, and Gemma winces like she knows she's in trouble before even reading the text message.

I know she's going to run away from me, but I'm not

letting her go this time. No way in hell am I walking away after discovering she's in danger.

Fuck, I never should have let her leave the clubhouse yesterday. I knew something was wrong but didn't want to press her for more information or scare her off. Guilt sits like a lead weight in my stomach. If I'd asked her a few more questions and been more aware, I could've saved her from the abuse she suffered last night.

"I have to go," Gemma whispers. "I'm sorry. I'm... I have to go."

"Please stay," I beg. "Let me help." I'm helping no matter what, but I want to give her a chance to choose it for herself.

Her green eyes meet mine, and her swollen face makes my stomach churn angrily. I see a storm of conflict raging inside her, but after a few moments, she shakes her head and gives me one last look.

She doesn't think she's worth saving.

I'm unsure how I know that, but something about her eyes, her fucking *soul*, reaches out to me.

Gemma takes off a little slower than usual with her limp but still clearly walking away from me. Again. I'm not letting her go this time.

Waiting until she's almost to the other side of the graveyard, I break into a jog down the main row leading to the exit. I watch as she turns left out of the exit, then take the same turn, following her from a distance.

A few minutes later, Gemma turns left again, veering off the sidewalk and heading down a well-worn footpath toward the old trailer park. The hairs on my neck stand up as pieces of the last few days fall into place.

Orchard Grove trailer park.

Keeping an eye on Gemma, I see her head for the plot of land in the back, facing the woods. She doesn't go through the front door but opts to go around to the side and hoists herself through a window.

I get closer, crouching to remain unseen. Is she breaking in? No, that doesn't sound like my Gemma. Not that I would judge her, but I can't see her committing a crime.

When I'm about ten feet from the side of the trailer, I smell it. There's no mistaking the chemical ammonia scent emanating from inside. *Meth.*

I hesitate momentarily, then take off into the woods, looking for a good hiding spot before pulling out my phone. Blade picks up on the first ring.

"Prez, you're never going to believe what I just found."

CHAPTER FOUR

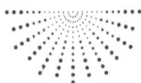

GEMMA

"*That's* all I have for this week's episode of Grave Secrets, your favorite true crime podcast bringing you stories from beyond the grave! Make sure to join me next week when we'll discuss the possible demon possession of Anneliese Michel... or was it a hoax? Find out–"

My voice cracks, and I curse under my breath, knowing I messed up another take. I already recorded the intro for this episode yesterday. I just need the outro, and I can edit the audio file and put my new episode of Grave Secrets up.

I can't seem to get this outro right, however. This is my eighth time recording it. The first two times, I couldn't stop my voice from shaking. The third time, I spaced the entire second half of the script. Five takes later, my mind is still scrambled from seeing Axel in the graveyard today.

Closing my eyes, I remember how he touched me so gently, his blue gaze mapping out my features as if cataloging my injuries so he could heal every single one. He can't, though. Not really. The bruises fade, but the fear grows stronger.

I allow myself one more moment to remember Axel's warm embrace and the beat of his heart as I lay my head on his solid chest. *Safe. Home.* That's what it felt like.

A loud banging on the trailer's screen door jars me out of my happy place. The damn door rattles on its hinges and squeaks obnoxiously as whoever is outside pulls it open.

Everything in me is on high alert. It could be a dealer coming for more product, a junkie looking for a fix, one of the women my father sleeps around with, or a neighbor wanting to get in on the business side of things.

I carefully and silently unfold myself from where I was sitting on my bed with my laptop and tiptoe the five and a half feet across my room to the door. Like every other door in this trailer, it doesn't fit the frame and hasn't been able to close all the way for the entire six years we've lived here.

Honestly, it served as a good lookout spot during that time. Not that there was ever much I could do about the bad, scary, and illegal things happening on the other side, but at least I knew to stay put. Stay quiet.

Peering through the splintered wood, I'm shocked at the three men standing in the living room. Of all the people who come and go in our trailer, I never would have guessed tonight's visitors would be cops.

Are they finally shutting us down?

My family has been cooking and selling meth since before I was born, but this is the longest we've ever stayed in one place. Six months couch surfing with a family friend, a few weeks renting out the cheapest hotel available, then off again to a new location when we got run out of town by the law or a competitor. We've somehow managed to fly under the radar of the local police for years in this small California town.

"How much?" one of the officers grunts.

I furrow my brow as I look at my dad, who has his arms

crossed over his chest. "And why should I trust you? Y'all are cops. You could be settin' me up. This ain't my first rodeo with the law," my father spits out at them.

The policeman in the middle of the trio looks to the officer on his left, then on his right. The sick smiles twisting their faces make my stomach churn. Nothing good will come from this.

"You think this is the first we've heard of your operation?" the middle officer, apparently their leader, asks. "We've known about you since the day you stepped foot into this town five, six years ago. Sheriff Darren knows about every shitty meth den in this town. We *let* you carry on your business because it's good for our business."

I blink a few times, not quite believing what I'm hearing.

"And now you're done *letting* me conduct my business?"

"No. Now we're changing the terms. You're our hookup. You sell exclusively to us at a wholesale price, we keep and push the product, pocketing the difference."

"Now why would I shoot my own business in the foot like that? Just to be shackled to the law? Why wouldn't I simply close up shop and move on to the next town?"

The men stare at one another, sizing up each other and calculating their next move. Finally, the officer breaks the silence.

"This isn't a courtesy call. This isn't us asking permission. This is the goddamn law coming to your door and telling you how it's going to be."

"You gonna shoot me if I refuse?"

The officer laughs, though it's hollow and haunted. Sinister.

"No. If you refuse, if you run, if you get some big idea to narc on us, I guarantee you'll be begging me for a bullet. Death would be too easy, though. For someone like you, a special fucker with an ego as big as his addiction, I'll pull out all the stops. You'll be in a straitjacket, rocking back and forth in a padded cell, unable to get your next fix. I'll ensure you have good enough healthcare to keep you in your new home for a long, long time."

This resonates with my dad. I know the threat hit home when he shifts on his feet and uncrosses and recrosses his arms. My father is never anxious because he's either high or punches whatever perceived threat comes his way. But right now? He looks like he might pee his pants.

"Well, hold on, now. No need to get graphic," my father says, changing his stance. He's softer this time, his shoulders curling in, his arms dropping to his sides. I've never seen him like this. "Now that I've had time to think about your offer, I agree that the terms are favorable."

What have you just gotten us into?

I can't stand to listen anymore. My heart can only take so much. Is there no justice in this world? No cosmic scale of right and wrong? How can so much evil exist without some sort of consequence?

Backing away from the crack in my door, I turn and plop down on my bed. It's just a mattress on the floor, but it's better than what I used to sleep on. As crazy as it may seem to others, my time in this shitty trailer is the most stable I've ever been.

I got to go to the same high school all four years, though that didn't help me make friends. It was difficult earning trust when I couldn't invite people over or tell them what my parents did for a living. When I showed up to class wearing long sleeves and long pants to cover my bruises, I was made fun of for being allergic to the sun.

Still, I knew I had someplace to come home to after school. That wasn't a luxury I was afforded in the past. On more than one occasion, the school bus dropped me off, and

I walked to the motel we were holed up in, only to find it empty. My mom always came to get me... eventually.

I shake my head of those thoughts and concentrate on the task at hand. My podcast. It's not much, but I make some money from my true crime blog and the podcast. I would love to start a YouTube channel, but there's no way I could record video footage here.

As I begin edits on my laptop, my bedroom door opens with a crash. I startle from my spot on the bed, scrambling away from the commotion on instinct.

"Come on, Gem. Time to cook. Got a big order, and they're gonna keep on coming." Randall takes two long strides to reach me and yanks me up by my arm. My laptop, headphones, and notebook fall from my lap as Randall half drags, half carries me into the living room.

I must be going crazy from all the stress, but I swear I hear the distant rumble of a motorcycle engine. Maybe I'm hallucinating about Axel and his bike as a way to comfort myself. Or, more accurately, as a way to mentally escape from what my family is forcing me to do.

The noise grows louder, closer, and then seemingly erupts all at once as if hundreds of bikes are revving their motors outside our trailer.

"What the fuck?" Randall mutters, releasing my arm so I stumble to the floor.

I remain crouched for a few moments, listening with the rest of my family.

"Who is that?" my mother asks no one in particular. She's been passed out in her recliner in nothing but a tank top and dirty underwear. Sometimes, she doesn't wake up for a whole day when she crashes. I'm surprised the noise got to her.

"Don't fuckin' know, but I'm about to find out," my father

grunts. He grabs his shotgun, slinging it over his shoulder as he opens the front door. "What the–"

Chaos breaks out on the front lawn, and the trailer windows shatter. A shot rings out, and I hit the floor, covering my head with my hands. More shots are fired, some outside, some inside, while my brothers race around the trailer in search of more weapons.

I crawl on my stomach to my bedroom, making it inside as a scream rends the air and an explosion detonates in the kitchen. *Shit, something must have caught fire in the lab...*

I don't have time to think or rationalize, moving on survival instinct. I can't go back to the living room with the fire raging and gunshots being exchanged. I toss the only things that matter to me, my laptop, recording mic, and headphones, into my backpack and shove my window open.

I peek outside. It seems to be quiet on this side of the trailer. Most of the action is happening in the front and other side of the trailer, giving me the perfect distraction to get the fuck out.

I carefully lower my backpack as far as possible, letting it drop the last foot and a half to the ground. Even though the mic and laptop are in padded cases, I still wince at the sound of the bag hitting gravel. I worked my ass off babysitting, cleaning houses, washing cars, and other odd jobs every spare moment until I earned enough to purchase all the equipment to start my blog and podcast.

None of that matters now, though. I need to survive tonight and figure out my next steps.

I take one last look around my bedroom, knowing I'll never be back here again. It was never comforting or safe, but it was familiar. In a life wrought with anarchy and turmoil, familiarity is the best you can hope for.

I'll need to find something else familiar. Maybe this will be my chance to find my true home.

I grip the window ledge and use the nightstand as leverage to hoist myself through. I've only used the window to sneak into the house, not out of it. When coming inside, I crash land on my bed. Out here, however, there's only dirt and gravel. Still better than meth and fire.

Closing my eyes, I shove myself the rest of the way out the window, bracing myself for impact. My back hits the ground, and I exhale sharply as the breath is stolen from my lungs. Bits of gravel bite into my skin, but I ignore the pain, rolling to my side and forcing myself to stand on shaky legs.

I throw my backpack on, take a deep breath, and peer around the corner to see the progress of whatever takedown is happening. My jaw drops open when I see Blade with his hand around my dad's neck. The rest of the Savage Saints appear to be raiding and dismantling anything that isn't on fire.

I can't wrap my head around everything that's happened this evening. First, the cops show up and want to make a deal with my family to buy meth. Then, the outlaw biker gang comes in swinging, wanting to shut down the operation for good, I assume.

My eyes land on Axel, and everything in me stills, aside from my racing heart. He's not looking at me, but just knowing he's here, seeing him pry apart my deepest secret and greatest shame...

I can't take it. What if he sees me? He'll know I'm trash. I'm no good. Not worth the help he and his club have so graciously offered me.

As if sensing me, Axel turns, and his far too perceptive blue gaze hones in on mine. I gasp and spin on my heel, sprinting in the opposite direction. My hip is still swollen and bruised from yesterday, and screams at me with each heavy step. My head throbs, and the pain in my left eye and cheek worsens with my increasing heartbeat.

I ignore all of it. The excruciating pain, the sting of the gravel still embedded in my skin, the stitch in my side that makes it hard to breathe. The only way I'll get through this is to focus on escaping. Axel will forget all about me in the excitement. I'm sure of it.

Too bad I'll never forget him or how I felt wrapped in his arms.

CHAPTER FIVE

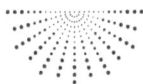

AXEL

Gemma. Thank fuck.

I lost my damn mind when her dumbass brothers lit a firework and shot it off in the wrong direction. I assume they were aiming for us and trying to scare us off, but instead, they shot their own fucking trailer.

And then her father opened fire, escalating the situation. One of my brothers, still not sure who, shot back, right into the trailer. Blade explicitly instructed everyone not to shoot at the trailer until I got Gemma to safety.

Then the fire broke out, and everything went to shit.

I see my girl take off toward the tree line, her red hair catching the light of the flickering flames. As I sprint after her, I'm more determined than ever to protect Gemma and ensure she never runs from me again.

"Gemma!" I call out when I'm about a dozen feet from her.

She looks over her shoulder, a heart-shattering look in her green eyes. She wants to be saved, but she's so convinced she's not worth it.

"I can't," she says breathlessly, holding back tears. "I'm–"

Gemma stumbles on a rough patch of grass and pitches forward. I reach her as she falls, sliding my arm around her waist and pulling her into my chest.

"I've got you," I whisper, holding her loosely against me. I don't know where she's hurt, and it would kill me if I caused her more pain.

It was hard enough leaving her in that filthy trailer once I figured out her family was the new hookup. I couldn't exactly walk up to the front door and demand Gemma come out. As someone who grew up with plenty of abusive people, I know firsthand that it doesn't take much to set them off, especially if drugs are involved. I needed the club's backing, but gathering the resources took too damn long.

"No," Gemma chokes, trying so hard not to cry. She pushes against me, though her protests are half-hearted at best. "I'm no good," she tries again, her voice a little stronger this time.

"I've got you," I whisper again, my hands spreading over her back and stroking gently. She doesn't want me to leave. She wants me to show her she's worth fighting for. "I'm not letting go."

"You d-don't understand," Gemma continues. "My family… they're not good people."

She tries pushing me away again, and I gently loop my fingers around her right wrist, bringing her hand to my lips to kiss her palm. Then, I place her hand over my heart and cover it with mine, letting her feel my steady heartbeat.

"Mine aren't either. Not my biological family, anyway."

"I've… I've done things. Things I'm not proud of." Gemma attempts to twist away as if looking at me is too much.

It hurts seeing her in so much anguish, but I'll stay here all damn night long, fighting her demons with her if that's what it takes. "Me too."

"I'm trailer trash, don't you get that?" she yells, her voice becoming scratchy. "And now I'm not even that. I'm homeless."

Gemma makes one last weak attempt to slip out of my arms, but I hold her steady, cupping the back of her neck and tucking her head under my chin. Like last time, I have an overwhelming sense of completeness. She fits perfectly right here. This is where my princess belongs.

"I've got you," I repeat softly. This time, my bruised and broken princess surrenders to my care, collapsing in my arms and letting me support her weight. "I'm never letting go."

Our hearts break and mend together as I cradle Gemma in my arms. She sobs silently, her curvy body shaking with the effort of holding everything in.

"Are you okay to ride with me?" I ask after a few moments.

Gemma unburies herself from my chest and peers up at me, her green eyes puffy and rimmed in red from her tears.

I reluctantly let her take a step away but keep her hand secured in mine. Can't take any risks with her running off again. "I'm taking you back to my place," I tell her. "Where you'll be safe. We can figure out what comes next, but first, you need a hot shower and a good night's sleep."

"But…"

"Do you trust me, princess?"

Her brow furrows, and she gives me an odd look. "You're still calling me princess? After all of this?"

Jesus, this woman. She has no idea how precious she is.

"Gemma," I murmur, cupping her chin and tilting her face toward mine. "This doesn't define you. Your family doesn't have to be your identity. You get to decide to be whoever you want to be." She doesn't quite believe me yet, but she wants to. That's a start. "You're my princess because you looked like Sleeping Beauty when I first saw you in the graveyard with your eyes closed and your hands clutching a bouquet of wildflowers. Every moment since then has only shown me more of your sweetness and light."

My girl smiles, and her eyes well up with tears, but I don't think she's sad. Gemma hasn't had much love in her life, but that shit ends here. I vow to remind her every day how valued and worthy she is.

"So, do you trust me?" I ask her once again.

Gemma nods, and I pull her toward me, wrapping my arm around her waist and tucking her into my side. I lean over and kiss her temple before leading her to my bike, parked beyond the tree line. I camped out there while waiting for my brothers to get here, keeping an eye on Gemma, and ensuring nothing happened to her before I could get her out.

I throw my leg over my bike and direct Gemma to climb on behind me. She's wearing ripped black skinny jeans tonight and a black lacy top that flows around her generous curves, making her look like a breathtaking gothic angel. I like Gemma in everything she wears, but I'm thankful she's wearing jeans for this bike ride. I'll need to get her some proper riding gear soon.

That thought brings a smile to my face despite the heart-wrenching last few minutes. I like the idea of Gemma being around long enough to need riding gear.

She scoots up behind me, her inner thighs pressing against the outsides of mine. I grit my teeth, trying to get my damn libido under control. Tonight isn't about that. I shouldn't be thinking about our bodies tangled up in other ways, but it's hard not to when Gemma's curves are right here, pressed against my back. When she wraps her arms around my torso, my dick twitches.

Not happening tonight, I silently tell the fucker. Gemma

needs to be taken care of in other ways first. Then, hopefully, when she trusts me enough, we can share everything.

"Hold on tight, princess," I call over my shoulder. She squeezes my abs and clenches her thighs together, and fuck me, I'm going to have to give my hardening cock another talking to when I get Gemma tucked into bed.

I take off into the night, rescuing my princess from the evil villains and bringing her back to my castle. And by castle, I mean my apartment behind the clubhouse. We have rooms for those who need a temporary place to stay, but there is a row of legit three-bedroom apartments in the back lot.

It's not long before we're pulling into the clubhouse parking lot. I pull my bike around back, holding my hand out to help Gemma dismount before doing the same.

"How was your first ride?" I ask. Gemma is shaking slightly, and I worry it was too much.

"Amazing," she says breathlessly. My girl hits me with the brightest smile, mending a little piece of my heart after the chaos and pain of the evening.

I grin and take Gemma's backpack before gathering her delicate hand in my much larger one. "I'll take you on a longer ride once you're all healed up," I promise, lifting her hand to kiss her knuckles. I can't help it. I always want to be touching her in some way.

Unlocking the door, I lead Gemma inside and set her bag down. She looks up at me, those green eyes shining with trust but also a bone-deep weariness.

"Let's get you cleaned up, yeah?" I ask softly. I can tell the excitement and adrenaline of the night are wearing off, and she's going to crash soon.

Gemma nods, and I lead her to the main bathroom in the hallway. I also have one in the main bedroom, but I don't want to freak her out or make her uncomfortable. Guiding her to sit on the edge of the tub, I grab a washcloth and the first aid kit from my medicine cabinet and get to work setting out the bandages, a cleansing wipe, and antibiotic cream.

I kneel in front of Gemma and take her hands in mine. She swallows thickly, and tears form in her emerald eyes. Without her saying a single word, I know what she's thinking. I can feel it with every cell in my body. Nobody has ever taken care of her like this. No one has ever been kind or gentle with her.

It kills me to know that, but it hardens my resolve to fill her life with enough love to drown out the darkness she's experienced.

Taking the damp washcloth, I wipe away the dirt and grime on her face in gentle circles. When she's cleaned up, I get a better look at her black eye. There's a slight cut on her cheek, and I get to work disinfecting the wound. I finish with a soothing ointment, then cover the cut with a small bandage.

"I'm so sorry, Gemma," I whisper, ghosting my fingers around the edges of her bruise.

"For what?" she asks, matching my soft tone.

"I knew something was wrong that day you showed up at the clubhouse, but I just… I let you leave. If I had any idea you were being abused…" I close my eyes and inhale sharply, the guilt twisting up my stomach.

Gemma places her hand on my chest, right over my heart. "It's not your fault," she murmurs.

I open my eyes and rest my hand on top of hers. "It's not yours either."

Gemma nods and nibbles her bottom lip as the first tear falls.

"Sweetheart," I whisper, careful to avoid her swollen bruise as I wipe her tears.

I stand, taking Gemma with me and wrapping her in my arms. I hold her for long moments, but eventually, we break apart. She needs a warm shower followed by sleep. I'm happy I can provide both for her.

After showing Gemma how to work the shower, I drop off towels and some of my clothes for her to change into. Black sweatpants and a black T-shirt, of course. Gemma wouldn't have it any other way.

I make a note to place an ice pack on her nightstand as well as vaseline to rub over the skin for discoloration. It's been a long time since I've had to tend to bruises, but I know the drill.

Ten minutes later, I've nearly worn a path in my hardwood floor from pacing around the living room. I stop when I hear the bathroom door open, holding my breath until Gemma tiptoes into the living room.

She's gorgeous with her red hair braided and slung over her right shoulder. I love seeing her in my clothes, and I grin when I notice she's rolled up the sweatpants to make them fit. She's adorable in my too-big shirt and pants, and it makes me want to curl up with her in my lap.

Soon.

"Feel a little better?"

"Yes, thank you," Gemma says quietly. She looks down at her feet, wringing her hands in front of her. I hate seeing her nervous like this.

"No need to thank me," I tell her, closing the distance between us. She looks up at me again, and I reach out, running my fingers over her neatly done braid. "Knowing you're safe is enough." Gemma tilts her head to the side and furrows her brow. I smile and kiss her temple. "Ready for bed?"

"Yes, please," she says with a yawn.

I chuckle and take her hand, showing her to the guest

room. I've never had anyone else over, but the place was already furnished with the basics when I moved in, and I never had another use for that room.

"I'll be right next door if you need anything," I tell her once we're standing next to the bed. I'm finding it hard to let go of her hand.

She looks down at where our fingers are laced together, then up at me. Gemma sways forward, her gaze locked on my lips.

Fuck, I know what she wants. I want it, too, but I don't want to overwhelm her.

When I see a slight hint of doubt and rejection in her eyes, I can't hold back. I'd never reject Gemma, and it's about time I show her exactly what it means to be mine.

Gently, so damn gently, I cup her uninjured cheek and tilt her head up a little more. Her breaths grow shallow as I lean down, brushing the tip of her nose with mine. "I'm going to kiss you now," I murmur against her slightly parted lips.

"Please," she begs so sweetly.

I press my lips to hers, sipping from her, teasing her top lip, then her bottom lip, before licking inside her mouth. Gemma gasps softly, her tongue tentatively sliding against mine. It shouldn't make me nearly feral that she's so inexperienced, but I won't lie; I love it. I love that I'm her first kiss. Her first everything. I'm sure as hell going to be her last.

Gemma moans, rolling her body against mine. I feel the kiss leading to something more, something deeper, but I pull away. Barely. My girl follows me as if our lips are connected by magnets. I smile and press a quick kiss to her lips and forehead.

"Can't wait to do that again," I whisper into the shell of her ear. "But right now, you need rest."

Gemma sighs, making me chuckle.

I pull back the covers for her, watching as she crawls

under them. I want to be in there with her so badly, but I don't want to move too fast.

"Goodnight, princess." I lean down to give her one last kiss on the forehead.

"Night," she whispers, her eyes already closed.

Good. I'm sure she's exhausted, and not just from tonight. Her whole life has been a battle, but I'm here now. Gemma will never be alone again.

CHAPTER SIX

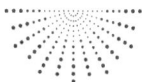

GEMMA

"*No. No, please. I can't...*"

I jerk awake, not sure what happened or where I am. My throat feels raw, like I've been crying or screaming. My heart pounds so fast that it's hard to catch my breath. Fear grips my muscles, each one tense to the point of shaking.

The door bursts open, and I scream, but all that comes out is a broken sob.

"Gemma," someone says, their voice laced with worry. "Gemma, what's wrong? I heard screaming."

It takes me a second to realize it's Axel. I'm in his guest room.

"N-nightm-mare," I stutter between heaving sobs. I can hardly remember what it was about, only that it ripped me from my sleep and left terror behind.

Axel climbs onto the bed, slowly reaching toward me and giving me plenty of time to pull away. I don't want to. All I want is to curl up with Axel and have him hold me and tell me everything will be okay.

Thankfully, he seems to want the same thing.

"You're safe," he whispers, cradling me in his arms. I tuck my head under his chin, loving how protected I feel when he holds me like this. "I've got you. I'll never let them touch you again."

I believe him.

Once my breathing has returned to normal and my tears have dried, I uncurl myself from Axel's embrace. He seems reluctant to let me go, which warms me. Is he as drawn to me as I am to him? It doesn't make sense. Then again, the way he kissed me like I was precious and irresistible...

"Can you stay here with me?" I blurt.

Axel doesn't say anything for a beat, and I'm about to pull the blankets over my head and never come out again. "I'll stay with you as long as you want. As long as you'll let me."

I smile at his sweet and sincere answer. Who knew a tatted-up biker could say such comforting things? Axel is kind of perfect.

I get settled back down in bed, and Axel crawls under the covers, scooting up behind me and spooning himself around me from behind.

"Is this okay?" he asks, his lips right next to my ear. "I'm not hurting you?" His breath tickles my skin, and I swear I can feel the sensation all the way down in my core.

"It's perfect," I whisper.

We stay like that for a while, but I can't seem to fall back asleep. Every time I start to doze off, the remnants of my nightmare jerk me awake.

"It's okay, Gemma," Axel murmurs, stroking my side in a soothing gesture.

"Sorry. I can't seem to relax. You can go back to your bed if I'm keeping you awake."

"Never leaving," he says, burying his face in the top of my head before kissing me there.

I smile at his ridiculousness, though I love how obsessed with me he seems.

"But I can help relax you," he whispers.

Like last time, the tickling of his breath against my ear is mirrored between my thighs. I squeeze my legs together to find some relief from the pressure, but it's not enough. "Oh, yeah?" I breathe out.

"If you want. I don't want to move too fast–" Axel breaks off into a groan as I press my ass against his growing erection.

"Please," I beg. "I want it."

Axel spreads his hand over my stomach, softly caressing my skin. That simple touch makes my pussy throb and my skin break out into goosebumps. I should be embarrassed about having a nightmare, but I can't think about anything except how Axel is touching me.

"You're so soft," Axel murmurs as he pulls me closer.

Every inch of his body is rock hard, from the defined muscles on his chest and abs to his thick cock digging into my ass. It feels so good being pressed against him while he continues to explore my body with gentle yet scorching touches.

I arch my back when he cups my breast and glides his thumb over my pebbled nipple. Axel growls softly and grinds his erection against me. He kisses the back of my neck and nips the sensitive spot below my ear. I whimper when he scrapes his teeth along the same spot like he wants to devour me. I want him to.

Axel tugs at my shirt, lifting it up and over my head with little to no help from me. He squeezes my breasts and pinches one nipple, then the other. He grunts something about perfect tits, but I hardly hear him over the over-whelming sensations he's causing in my body.

Axel slides his hand down my torso, his fingers dancing

along the edge of the pants of his I'm wearing. The featherlight touch drives me crazy. He's teasing me, making me squirm and want so much more. I've never been this needy, this desperate, this... wet. God, I'm so, so incredibly turned on right now. I *ache* for him.

He slips the tips of his fingers beneath the elastic waistband, making me gasp at the sudden rush of arousal shooting through me. Every nerve ending spikes with pleasure, causing more wetness to drip from my throbbing pussy.

"This okay, princess?" Axel asks softly, his voice tinged with the same desperate need I feel.

"Yes," I whimper. "Please."

He groans and wastes no time shoving the pants down my thighs. I wiggle and help him remove them completely as needy little whimpers fall from my lips, my desire growing with each second his fingers aren't inside me.

The aches and pains from my injuries melt away, and all I feel is anticipation for what's to come.

Once I'm completely naked, Axel runs his hand across my bare skin, leaving a trail of fire in its wake. Finally, *finally,* he dips one finger into my slit and strokes me. I cry out when he circles my clit with his calloused fingers. My cunt throbs and clenches, and I swear I'm already right at the edge of total bliss.

"Jesus, Gemma. So wet for me," he grunts, circling my opening with the pad of his finger.

I buck my hips and grind down on his hand, unable to control my movements. Axel teases my pulsing little hole, not quite entering me. How does that feel so good? I wiggle my hips, trying to get him to do... something. I don't know. I just need more.

He runs his fingers up and down my slit, gathering up my juices and rubbing my clit until I'm moaning uncontrollably. I'm right there. So close, I shake. So close, I squeeze my eyes shut and hold my breath. So close, I reach my arm behind me and fist his hair, needing something to hold onto.

And then his hand is gone. I gasp and grunt in frustration, my orgasm clawing to the surface but unable to break free. The pressure in my lower belly is almost painful with my pent-up release.

Axel chuckles and slides his hand down my thigh, gently lifting my top leg and guiding it to rest over his. This way, I'm open to him, giving him more access. "That's it, beautiful. God*damn*, you need to come, don't you?"

"So bad," I respond, my voice nothing but a breathy whimper.

Axel slowly eases his finger into my entrance, stretching me deliciously. "So tight," he grunts, sliding another inch inside me.

I clench around him, coating his hand in my juices as he fingerfucks me in a steady rhythm. He grinds the palm of his hand down on my little bundle of nerves, keeping me right on the edge, the pure bliss amplified by the slight sting of being stretched. *What's it going to feel like when he fucks me for real?* The thought has me thrusting my hips forward, trying to get him deeper.

An intense pressure builds low in my belly, throbbing outward with each steady stroke. I tighten my grip on his hair, pulling him toward me, letting him know I'm here with him and want this so, so bad.

He groans and sinks his teeth into my exposed shoulder, just enough to sting and cause a jolt of lighting to flash through my body. It weaves in and out of my cells, electrifying every inch of me, inside and out.

Axel adds a second finger, making me cry out with overwhelming pleasure. When he curls his fingers up, hitting some super sensitive spot, my entire body spasms, sending more electricity flowing through my veins.

CAMERON HART

"Axel," I moan. "Axel, fuck…"

Every muscle draws up tight as my joints lock, preparing for the onslaught of my release. My orgasm tears through my body, and pleasure cracks me open, vibrating through me. I cry out as I pulse, thrash, and claw at Axel's scalp, digging my fingers into his skin to anchor myself.

He doesn't stop, not for a second. My orgasm continues to devastate me to the point I see black dots clouding my vision. I gasp for air, nearly coming again as oxygen fills my lungs. With a final, shuddering breath, the last of my release drains from me.

"Holy shit," I barely whisper as I gulp down air. I'm still trembling, my muscles weak and worn out from how hard I came.

"Are you okay? Was that too much? Did I hurt–"

"That was incredible," I manage to say between breaths. "I don't feel anything except sleepy and…" I break off into a yawn, making Axel chuckle softly.

Axel kisses my temple, brushing his lips against mine so tenderly that I almost tear up. He rolls onto his back, lifting his arm in invitation. I smile and scoot closer, resting my head on his chest over his heart. Snuggling as close as possible, I relax even more when Axel runs the tips of his fingers along my spine like he's trying to memorize the sensation of my skin.

As I drift off to sleep, Axel whispers, "What else do you feel?"

"Hmm?" I reply, not bothering to open my eyes.

"Earlier, you said you feel sleepy and…?"

"Loved," I murmur, though it might have been too soft for him to hear.

"You are."

For the first time in my whole life, I go to sleep feeling safe.

CHAPTER SEVEN

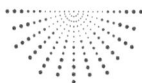

AXEL

*G*emma tightens her grip on my hand as we walk across the parking lot toward the clubhouse. She woke up about forty-five minutes ago after sleeping for nearly ten hours. My girl needed it after everything she's been through.

I meant every word I said last night while holding Gemma after her nightmare. I'll never let anyone lay their hands on my princess again. I think she's starting to trust me, thank God. She surrendered her body and her pleasure to me. Fuck, she's perfect. I hope she can trust me with her heart the same way.

My lungs expand and fill with fresh air as I take a deep breath. Everything feels lighter today. Warmer. I know it's because of Gemma. Last night, she told me she felt loved before she went to sleep. I don't know if she heard me, but I told her she was.

I've never meant anything more in my life. I love this beautifully broken princess and her kind heart. I love every inch of her, from her bright red hair to her lime green toenail polish. When she's ready, I'll tell her exactly how I feel. Until then, I'll have to be content to take care of her and show her I'll always be here.

I rub my thumb against Gemma's, hoping to calm her nerves. We talked this morning about telling Blade and the Savage Saints about her family's involvement in the meth business. I promised her that nobody would judge her and that everyone in the club has faced impossible choices. Most of us also came from fucked up families, and we know what it takes to survive day to day.

"You're not in danger," I remind her. "And you're not in trouble. The Prez already knows you were there, and now we're just filling in the details. We have to know how to protect you. That's all." I don't want to minimize her anxiety, but I hate that she's trembling the closer we get to the clubhouse.

"I know you're right," Gemma whispers.

She sighs and leans into me. I let go of her hand and wrap my arm around her waist, tucking her into my side. I'll be her strength when she's too tired to stand. I'll be her everything.

We stand in front of the back door, but before I open it, I turn to Gemma. "Do you trust me, princess?" I love how her cheeks turn the lightest shade of pink when I call her *princess*.

"I do," she says, her green eyes filled with sincerity. I'll ensure she never regrets it.

I open the door and guide her inside, keeping a hand on the small of her back to let her know I'm right here. Blade is already sitting in the back booth, waiting for us.

He's every bit as intense and scrutinizing as before he met his woman, Sonya, but she's softened him a little bit over the last month or so. Other people might not notice it, but the Prez has a little more empathy, thanks to Sonya. That's why I know he'll handle this in a sensitive way. It wasn't all that long ago his woman was in danger, and Gemma was the one to bring her back to safety.

"Axel," the Prez says as we approach. "Gemma…" he trails off when he sees her black eye, instant anger rising to the surface. His nostrils flare, and his teeth grind together, realizing the serious nature of our conversation. It's not only to fill him in on what she knows about the drug operation; it's to reaffirm our promise of protection. "…good to see you," he finishes.

Gemma nods, giving him a little smile.

We sit across from Blade, who immediately gets down to business. Resting his elbows on the table, the fearsome President of the Savage Saints focuses on Gemma. I gently lay my hand on her thigh and give her a reassuring squeeze.

"I promised you the protection of the club, and I'm a man of my word. Can't thank you enough for how you helped my Sonya. I just wish you'd come to us sooner."

Gemma's shoulders curl in, and she dips her head, breaking eye contact with Blade. "I know. I'm sorry. I didn't know you were going after my parents. I would have helped–"

Blade raises his hand, effectively cutting her off. "I only meant that I wish you felt comfortable enough to ask for help before things got so bad."

Gemma lifts her head, tilting it to the side as she stares at Blade. I can tell she doesn't know how to respond, and it kills me to know my woman has never been afforded kindness like this.

"This isn't even that bad," she murmurs, one hand gently touching her swollen eye. It's healing surprisingly well after we iced it again this morning and put on another layer of vaseline.

I tighten my hold around her thigh, then lean over and press a kiss to the side of her head. I loathe her family for doing this to her, for hurting this precious woman and taking advantage of her sweet nature.

"Still," Blade continues, "I don't like seeing battered women, no matter the context. I'm sorry you had to grow up like that."

"I promised I'd always protect her," I say, unable to stay quiet any longer.

Blade nods. "As will the club."

Gemma relaxes slightly, leaning against my side. I move my hand from her thigh to her back, holding her close while Blade launches into questions about her family and the operation.

My brave girl calmly answers everything, letting us know the ring leader is her father and the main organizers of distribution are her three older brothers. She tears up a bit when she admits to cooking for them on occasion, but Blade doesn't blink an eye. I hate that she was put in that position, but like I told her, every Savage Saint has shit in their past.

Gemma gives her version of events from last night, which we didn't get to. Between cleaning her up, the nightmare, and the orgasm, we didn't have a ton of time to go over the details. Plus, I didn't want her to relive it all so soon.

Blade grunts and nods as she tells us about the cops showing up earlier. *Dammit*, I must have missed that when I was hiding out in the woods. I left for ten minutes to meet with Blade and the guys before coming up with a plan to raid the place.

The Prez finishes up his questions and thanks Gemma for her honesty. He tells her again that she's safe and the Savage Saints have her back. I appreciate the gesture. Blade stands and tips his chin toward the back room, and I know he's about to call church.

"Be right there," I tell him.

I turn to Gemma once Blade is gone, cupping her chin

and guiding her to look at me. "I'm so proud of you," I tell her, gently rubbing my thumb along her jawline. "And I'm so sorry for everything you've been through. Not just last night, but your whole life."

"Don't apologize. You're saving me from all of that."

I take her lips in a gentle kiss, savoring her sweet flavor and the slide of her tongue against mine.

"We can finish that later," I whisper onto her lips. "I have to go to church."

Gemma pouts, which is the most damn adorable thing I've ever seen. I can't help but kiss her again, with a little more passion this time.

When I pull away, she follows me, just like last night. I love that she can't get enough. Lord knows I'll always crave Gemma and her curves.

"Sonya is up at the bar," I tell her, standing from the booth and offering my hand to help her up. "She has some clothes she said you could borrow until we can go shopping."

"What? No, that's totally not necessary."

"We like helping people who deserve it," I tell Gemma, making sure her eyes are fixed on mine. "And you, princess, deserve the whole world." My girl can't hide her smile. She's absolutely enchanting with the mid-morning sun streaming through the front window, making her emerald eyes twinkle with gold. "Sonya can introduce you to Rider's old lady, Sutton, and Hawk's old lady, Tessa."

Gemma raises an eyebrow at me, making me grin. "Old lady? Hawks are involved?"

"I'll explain everything when we get home," I answer with a chuckle.

"Home," she murmurs, her eyes going soft.

"Yeah, princess. You have a home now."

She nods and leans against me, wrapping her arms around my waist. I hug her back, hoping to infuse her with all the love and peace I'm going to provide for her in the future.

I reluctantly step back, pointing Gemma in the direction of the other girls. I know Sonya already loves my Gemma, and Tessa and Sutton are also sweet and friendly. I'm thankful she'll have friends built into her support system, along with me and the Savage Saints family.

Thirty excruciating minutes later, the guys are updated on the latest between the police and the drug operation. Officer Jake, our man on the inside, informed us that the cops are taking credit for busting the meth lab and arresting all five of Gemma's family members. Of course they are. No one would believe it was us anyway. That's fine; we don't do it for recognition. Giving the real monsters credit for doing good, however, is straight fucking bullshit.

We each get our missions. Mine is to use tracking software, recording devices, and my less-than-legitimate connections to underground resources to gather as much information as possible. Officer Jake is going to find out what their next plan is if they have one. The rest of the men will search for other drug dens and report what they find.

Usually, I stick around after church to shoot the shit with my brothers, but I have other things on my mind today. As soon as I step into the bar area of the clubhouse, my eyes land on Gemma. She's leaning against the bar top, laughing at something Tessa said.

God, she's gorgeous. Even after her horrible family tried to break her mentally and physically, Gemma still has warmth and light inside. She's too bright to be snuffed out, too strong to give up and follow in their footsteps.

I walk toward her in long strides, my eyes locked on her. As if sensing me, my woman turns and smiles when she sees me coming. Goddamn, I don't think anyone has ever been this happy to see me. It's addicting like the rest of her.

When I reach Gemma, the overwhelming urge to kiss her, claim her right here and now takes over. I weave my fingers into her hair, tilt her head up gently, and lean down to press my lips to hers.

My girl gasps, not expecting the public display. Her shock wears off, giving way to need. Gemma moans softly, spurring me on. I pry her lips open, tangling my tongue with hers. Her hands slide up my chest, fisting my shirt and pulling me closer.

Fuck, I can't hold back, even though I know everyone is watching. Screw it. I want them to see. I want them to know this woman is mine and mine alone.

I slide my hands down her body, careful to avoid her sore hip. Gripping her juicy ass, I lift her and set her on the nearest barstool, stepping between her legs and continuing to swallow her desperate whimpers. Gemma grinds her hot little core against me, and I grunt, ready to rip her shirt off and suck on her nipples to see if I can get her to come from that alone.

We're rudely interrupted by whistles and cat-calls, and Gemma buries her face into the side of my neck.

I chuckle and comb my fingers through her hair. "I'm glad they saw," I whisper. "Everyone needs to know you're mine."

She peels herself off my chest, hitting me with those sparkling green eyes. "Yours?"

"Yes, princess," I say with a nod. "Need me to show you what that means?"

"Yes, please," she murmurs, nibbling on her bottom lip.

"*Fuck me*," I groan, barely resisting the urge to kiss her breathless again.

Instead, I help Gemma off the stool and scoop her up in my arms. She giggles while Tessa and Sutton laugh good-naturedly.

"You're kind of ridiculous," she says as I burst through the

371

back door and stride across the parking lot toward my apartment.

"You love it," I respond, grinning down at her.

She nods as I reach the front door. Reluctantly setting her down, I fumble for my keys, nearly ripping the door off its hinges to get inside. I turn as soon as I shut the door, setting my sights on Gemma.

I close the distance between us and cup the back of her neck, drawing her in for a kiss. How is it possible to already be addicted to everything about her?

She moans into my mouth as my hands trace the curve of her hips and grip her thighs. I easily lift her onto the nearest flat surface, my kitchen table, and step between her legs. Gemma wraps her thighs around me and rocks her hips against my aching cock. Fuck, I can feel her heat, her need. I need it too. Need to taste her.

I break the kiss to nip and kiss her jaw, neck, and down her shoulder. I can't explain the need to sink my teeth into her soft flesh, to suck and mark her as mine. My dick grows impossibly harder when I picture her creamy skin red from how I've loved her.

"Axel... Axel..." She moans my name as I growl into her skin. My hands slip under the hem of her shirt and grip her soft curves before dipping below the waistband of her pants. "I need you."

"I've got you, beautiful. I'll always give you what you need."

I take her mouth again in a searing kiss as I tug down the sweatpants I gave her to wear. I pat her ass a few times and tell her to lift up for me.

"Good girl," I growl, the beast inside me clawing to get out and devour every inch of her. In one swift move, I have her pants pulled off her legs and thrown somewhere behind me. Her shoes must have come off at some point, which only makes it easier for me.

"Lie back, princess. Let me see what's mine."

She nods and leans back on the table, her trust in me as much of a turn-on as her curvy little body and sweet kisses. I gently pry her legs apart, placing her feet on the table. Gemma is spread out before me like a delicious meal. She's soft and pink and dripping for me. My thumbs part her folds, and I see her little clit, fucking throbbing for me, begging for my attention.

Before she has a chance to say anything, I dive into her sweet perfection.

Jesus, fuck.

Gemma gasps and moans for me as I lick her up and down. I suck on her folds, dipping my tongue into every crease, memorizing everything about her. Her legs twitch and snap around my head, but I place my hands on the insides of her thighs and spread her wide open for me again.

I dip my tongue into her tight hole, pulling out more of her sweet juices. My woman is fucking gushing for me.

"Axel, ohmygod, I-I… oh, *God*…"

Her voice is breathy and sexy as fuck. I love knowing I'm licking her senseless. I want to taste every inch of her. I force my tongue out of her entrance and pull her juices up, up, up to her clit, flicking my tongue over her tight bundle of nerves just once.

"Oh, shit!" she yells as her hips buck against my mouth.

"Fucking delicious, Gemma," I tell her when I come up for air.

"Mmhmm…" is all she can say.

I dive back in, sucking on her clit while she trembles at the tip of my tongue. Slowly, I slip a finger into her tight little hole. Her pussy squeezes me, and I'm barely inside her.

My balls draw up tight, imagining how her silk walls will feel around my thick cock.

Gemma grips the edge of the table as she hangs on for dear life. I curl my finger up, finding her G-spot while working my tongue over her clit, licking and sucking and bringing her higher and higher. I feel her tense, her body strung so fucking tight. I want to feel her snap.

"Come for me, sweet girl. Come all over my face," I growl.

When I add a second finger, Gemma screams my name and bows her back off the table, writhing and crying out her orgasm. Her pussy pulses, gripping my fingers and sucking them further inside. I continue to thrust my fingers in and out of her, and she keeps coming, her release filling my hand.

Gemma's mouth is open in a silent scream as her body trembles out the last of her orgasm. She gasps for air, flushed, sweating, and so goddamn gorgeous.

I remove my fingers, and she whimpers. I chuckle before licking my fingers clean, savoring the taste of her on my tongue. I stand and lean over to kiss Gemma, letting her taste herself. Her arms wrap around my neck as she tries to pull me closer.

Breaking the kiss, I rest my forehead on hers. We're both panting, sharing the same air.

"More," she whispers. "I want to feel you everywhere. I want to feel all of you."

CHAPTER EIGHT

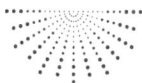

GEMMA

*A*xel stands with me in his arms, practically running down the hall. I giggle and kick my legs out, gasping when he sets me down in front of his bed. He strips the rest of my clothes off, then tears his clothes off in two seconds, his need matching mine.

Cupping my cheek, he slides his hand down my neck and over my chest until it rests over my heart. Our eyes meet, and his deep blue irises are filled with so many emotions.

He leans down, his lips brushing against mine in the softest kiss. "Are you ready for us, princess?"

"Ready when you are," I tell him with a playful grin.

He nips at my bottom lip, then gently pushes me backward so I'm spread out on the bed, completely naked. Axel groans, and his massive frame falls on top of me. He catches himself with a hand on either side of my head, and I automatically wrap my legs around his hips, moaning when I feel his thick, heavy cock across my slit.

"I need you, Axel," I murmur, leaning up for a kiss. He opens up for me, letting me take control. This one kiss says it all. Axel wants to take care of me, yes, but he also wants to give me confidence and space to grow.

"Fuck, I need you too, Gemma. Need you with every cell in my goddamn body."

I whimper and nod, spreading my legs wider. I brace for his monster cock, but Axel surprises me by flipping our positions. He grips my sides in his large hands, steadying me and getting me into position.

I look down into his stormy blue eyes, so deep and full of emotions that are new to both of us. I can't believe he wants me. The look of awe on his face lets me know he thinks the same about me. I think he loves me. I think I love him, too.

"Axel..." I whisper, unsure of how to voice my thoughts.

"I know, princess. I feel it. I feel you."

He lifts me, guiding me over his hard length. I sink down a little, gasping when the head of his cock spreads me wide open. My pussy spasms at that small contact, and a wave of wetness coats his dick, which helps me slide down a little more. Axel hisses and groans in pleasure, giving me the confidence to take all of him. I gasp as he fills me, stretches me, and breaks through the last barrier separating us.

"God, Gemma," he half whispers and half groans. "You feel so damn good, baby. Take it slow."

Axel cups the back of my neck and draws me down for a kiss. It starts sweetly, almost reverently. I rock against him, making him growl into my mouth and pull my bottom lip through his teeth. His hands slide up my bare back, his fingertips leaving a burning trail as they roam back down. He grips my ass, spreading me wider and helping me circle my hips.

"Fuck," I moan when the base of his shaft rubs against my clit. My pussy contracts as pleasure rockets through my body. Sitting up, I steady myself with two hands on his chest, clawing down his chiseled muscles as I lift on my knees. I circle my hips again and rub the head of his dick through my folds, using it to massage my clit.

"Gemma…" Axel grunts, tipping his head back as he slides his hands up my torso, cupping my breasts.

I cry out when he pinches my nipples, my entire pussy throbbing and gushing at the slight pain. I drop back down, needing more of him, more of this connection. Axel kneads one breast with his hand while the other leaves teasing little touches along my ribcage and tummy until he reaches my center. He slips one finger into my folds, rubbing my clit as I grind against him.

"Oh, God," I gasp, throwing my head back.

Axel grunts and pinches my clit, sending sharp currents of electricity throughout my body. "That's it. Jesus, that's so fucking it."

His words pull a moan from my lips as I lift my hands from his chest to tangle in my hair. Axel grunts in approval, rubbing furious circles around my clit while I ride him, taking him as deep as possible. Each time he hits the end of me, the breath is stolen from my lungs. I pant and writhe, so, *so* fucking close to falling apart.

My thighs tremble, and my muscles lock, bracing myself for what's to come. My entire body is strung tight, teetering on the sharp edge of ecstasy. Axel senses my need and wraps his hands around my upper thighs, keeping me pinned to him. He anchors me in place and fucks up into me in powerful strokes, taking control. I gladly let him.

Desperate, wanton whimpers fall from my lips as he tears me open with each rough stroke. I inhale sharply and hold my breath, the intense pressure in my core throbbing and consuming me, nearly choking me as my orgasm slams into me all at once.

I freeze and then spasm violently, collapsing on top of Axel as my climax tears through me. He growls and cups my ass, holding me in place while he fucks up into me, shoving his cock so damn deep, forcing me to feel every ounce of pleasure he's offering.

I'm a sweaty, shaky mess by the time I come back down, but Axel gives me no reprieve. He flips me onto my back and sinks into me, hooking his hand under my right knee and spreading me wide open.

It's impossible, but an orgasm fights to the surface, threatening to swallow me whole. I cry out, twisting the sheets in my fists and bowing my back. "I-I can't... can't come again..." I moan breathlessly.

"You can, princess. You can take it. Do you trust me?"

"Yes," I answer without hesitation.

Axel's eyes grow dark and determined at that one word. "Then take what I give you."

With that, he picks up his speed, stroking into me as I whimper and writhe beneath him. He's keeping me right there, so close, each thrust bringing more blissful agony than I thought possible.

Axel takes my lips in a searing kiss, licking into my mouth and taking control. I'm completely at his mercy as he fucks me with his tongue and huge cock. I love being taken by him, filled by him, ruined by him.

He growls into my mouth, the sound almost painful. "I'm gonna come. I'm gonna come so damn hard. Come with me. Come with-"

I cut him off with a scream as I splinter. I wrap my legs around his torso, locking my ankles behind his back. I cling to him as every nerve ending vibrates with deliciously sharp pleasure. Ecstasy courses through my veins and drips out of me as my pussy snaps around his cock.

He swells inside me, stretching me impossibly wider. He roars his release, his bulging muscles tensing and releasing as he fills me with his cum. Our combined orgasm stretches on for long moments as we hold each other close.

Axel holds himself deep inside me after we're completely spent. He buries his face in my neck, kissing me there and letting out a huge breath. I comb my fingers through his hair, loving this tender, almost fragile moment. He sighs and relaxes even more. I love the weight of his body on top of mine.

He lifts his head, resting his forehead against mine. I didn't think it was possible, but his cock is still hard. I whimper as he starts rolling his hips slowly. Aftershocks of my intense orgasms spark through me.

Axel cups the side of my face, gently stroking my cheek. He's making love to me. That's what this is. Slowly, so slowly, he enters me and pulls back out. I feel every ridge and vein of his thickness as he pushes inside me once more.

He rocks into me, his forehead never leaving mine, his hand never leaving my cheek. We come together silently, holding each other's gaze. I swear I see tears in his eyes, but Axel leans down to kiss me before they fall.

I feel so precious at this moment. Surrounded by his strength as my limp body melts into the mattress makes me feel so thoroughly loved and protected.

Axel gently rolls us over, draping me across his body. I drift in and out of sleep, each time waking up to Axel stroking my back or massaging my neck and shoulders. I'm unsure how long we've been lying here, but eventually, Axel breaks the silence.

"Can you tell me about your family?" he whispers.

I don't know what I thought he was going to say, but that wasn't it. "Um, well… I pretty much told you and Blade everything already."

"That was about the operation and drugs. I want to know your story, Gemma. I want to know everything about you."

I take a deep breath, letting it out as I rest my head over Axel's heart. The strong, steady beat tethers me to him, and I know Axel will be my anchor in the storm of emotions.

"My parents weren't planning on having another kid. They were happy with the three boys they already had. My mom thought she couldn't get pregnant anymore, but then, *surprise*," I say sarcastically. "There's fifteen years between me and the next sibling, so it often felt like I had five parents. Well, five angry, violent, often strung-out parents."

"That sounds rough," Axel whispers.

I shrug. "I've never known anything else. We moved around a lot, some places better than others."

Axel hums and I get the feeling he knows exactly what I mean. The "nice" places were grimy and smelled stale, while the not-so-nice places had infestations and smelled of feces.

"When my family set up shop here, we ended up staying. Like I told Blade earlier, we didn't get run out of town by the cops or even questioned by them in all five years we've been here. Now I know why."

I grow quiet, both of us resting in silence as we absorb everything I told him.

Axel nudges the top of my head with his nose, which makes me smile despite the sad memories. "Tell me about your podcast," he says with a big smile.

He looks so excited and sincerely interested, and I don't know what to do with it.

I surprise both of us by bursting into tears.

Axel's eyes widen with panic, but I wave him off and put my hand over his heart.

"Sorry, I don't know what came over me," I say once I've had a chance to calm down and take a few breaths. "I just... no one has ever asked me about it before. My parents didn't understand what a podcast was, and my brothers made fun of me all the time, saying it was stupid and a waste of time."

I look away from him, the vulnerability of this moment almost too much to bear. Axel cups my cheek, turning my head so we're facing each other. His blue eyes shine with something close to love. Or maybe I'm just projecting.

"I'm so sorry no one ever encouraged you or supported your dreams. I'm so fucking sorry you know what it's like to live with junkies. I…"

This time, it's Axel who breaks eye contact. I'm not letting him get away with that, though. I prop myself up on his chest, place my hand on his cheek, and turn him back toward me. He closes his eyes and leans into my touch.

"Do you trust me?" I ask softly. He's asked me that several times over the last few days, and now I want to know if he feels the same.

"Always," comes his automatic response.

"Then tell me your story. I want to support you, too."

Axel leans forward, capturing my lips in the most tender, reverent kiss. "You're too good to me, princess," he whispers as he guides me to rest my head on his shoulder while he wraps his arms around me and keeps me pressed close to his naked body. "My mom was an addict as well. Never knew my dad, but part of me doesn't hold it against him for ditching us. She never let me forget what a nuisance I was or that she could have gotten an abortion but didn't."

"What?" I gasp, lifting my head slightly.

Axel tilts his head down so our eyes meet. He shrugs. "She tried to sell me once for a fix. Ended up getting enough heroin to put her in a coma for three days. By the time she woke up, the dealer's girlfriend she pawned me off on had had enough of playing house. I was returned to my mother, who wasn't happy to see me. The only thing that calmed her down was that she didn't have to pay for the drugs retroactively."

I don't realize I'm crying until Axel stops talking and asks if I'm okay.

"Yeah," I say with a sniffle. "I'm just... I'm so glad you survived."

His eyes soften as he tucks a few strands of hair behind my ear. "Me, too, sweetheart. I didn't know it at the time, but I survived so I could meet you."

His words are everything to me. This incredible man is somehow gruff and tender, silly and sweet, and perfect in every way.

"Same," I whisper, leaning in to rest my forehead on his. It's on the tip of my tongue to tell him I love him, but I don't want to ruin what we already have by taking it too far or asking too much of our relationship so early on.

After a few moments, I break away to stifle a yawn.

Axel chuckles and kisses my temple. "I'll be right back," he says, kissing me again.

Before I can ask where he's going, Axel is already returning from the ensuite bathroom. He's holding a damp washcloth and surprises me by gently wiping between my legs, cleaning up the remnants of our first time together.

"Thank you," I murmur when he finishes and pulls the blankets over me.

"I love taking care of you, princess," he whispers.

God. *Swoon*.

The bed dips with his weight, and he curls up behind me, cocooning me in his warm embrace. For the second night in a row, I fall asleep feeling safer than I ever have.

CHAPTER NINE

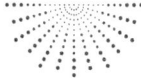

AXEL

*M*y phone rings right as I'm drying the last dish from breakfast. I can't cook worth shit, but Gemma is an incredible chef. She somehow made bacon, egg, and cheese breakfast sandwiches with homemade spicy aioli. I said I'd clean up while she got started on editing her latest podcast.

I dry my hands as my phone rings again. "All right, all right, I hear you," I mutter to myself. Reaching into my pocket, I'm surprised when I see who is calling. "Kingsley?" I ask once I've answered.

"Axel," comes his ever-professional voice. "Are you available for a job?"

I pull the phone away from my ear and check the number again. I haven't heard from Kingsley Bowman in... five years? Six? He was a client of mine back in the day when I was still working my way up and off the streets. Kingsley went to a prestigious college and hired me to work on his cars from time to time. He loves American muscle cars, which is the only reason I agreed. Well, that, and he paid a ridiculous amount of money for my services, claiming he'd rather have one mechanic he knows well than fifty he doesn't trust.

Didn't matter to me why, as long as he kept paying me.

When Kingsley discovered I also had a knack for computers and sleuthing, he hired me for different jobs. Less legit, but a bigger paycheck. The last job I did for him was when he was about to close a billion-dollar real estate deal with a large company that was merging with an even larger company.

I did some digging into the CEOs, CFOs, and other corporate alphabet job titles. Pulled some info on several civil suits against each company for shady practices. I ended up helping Kingsley raise the offer by twenty percent. He ensured it was reflected in my paycheck.

"Hello? Are you still there?"

"Yeah," I reply, his sharp tone pulling me from my thoughts.

"I need some info on an employee. Well, technically, she's a contract worker."

"I'm your guy."

Kingsley grunts something that sounds like "good," which is about all the confirmation I'll get from him. The successful real estate mogul might give Blade a run for his money when it comes to one-word responses and a general grouchy disposition. Then again, the Prez has gotten better since Sonya.

"Her name is Clementine Clarkson."

Down to business, as per usual. Kingsley Bowman doesn't have time for chit-chat.

I grab a pad of paper and a pen, jotting down the name as he spells it out for me. "Need a basic profile, or am I looking for something specific?"

"Basic profile to start. Well, maybe... Do you have access to medical records?"

"Uh, is someone sick?" I'm confident in my skills, but hacking into a medical database is a bit much.

"Yes. Maybe. I mean, there's no other reason for it," he mutters, more to himself than to me.

"It?"

"She's so damn… *happy*," he says, the disgust evident in his voice.

"And that's a medical condition?" I hold back my laughter, but only because Kingsley has the money and power to send someone down here to punch me in the face for making fun of him.

"She has no reason to be so cheery. It's unsettling."

"Okay…" I grin from ear to ear, loving how uncomfortable he seems with this woman's happiness.

"So, can you do it?"

"Look, I'll find out what I can, but I'm not breaking into a medical facility's mainframe."

Kingsley grunts and takes a deep breath. "Fine. Half up front, half after the information is delivered."

"I know the gig," I reassure him.

The billionaire doesn't bother with a thank you or a goodbye, which I'm used to with him.

I shake my head. What the hell was that about? I'll have to look up this Clementine later. I have a feeling this is personal for him. Interesting.

Setting my phone on the kitchen counter, I make my way to the living room, where Gemma is set up with her laptop, headphones, and mic. I stand in the doorway, leaning against the wall and watching my adorable woman work on her podcast. I love seeing her eyes light up when she gets something right and how she nibbles her bottom lip and squints her eyes when she's concentrating.

My girl senses my presence and peers up at me with green eyes and a bright smile.

I sit beside her on the couch, scooping her up and placing her in my lap. "That's better," I murmur as I bury my face into her and breathe deeply. I love her strawberries and cream scent mixed with something uniquely Gemma.

"You're ridiculous," she says, even as she melts against me.

"You love it."

Gemma nods, sighing so sweetly.

"How's the editing going?"

"So *slow*," she answers. "I've been trying to upload the audio from the outro I recorded, but it's taking forever."

"That's weird. How long is the clip?" I mentally go through all the reasons for a slow upload process or file expansion.

"That's the thing. It should be no more than thirty seconds. Maybe forty-five."

"Huh. Can I see it?"

Gemma leans over and grabs her laptop from its spot on the coffee table. I rearrange Gemma on my lap so she's holding the computer in front of us. I right-click on the file in question, surprised to see it's nearly twelve hundred megabytes instead of the ten I would expect from a clip that short.

She sees it, too, and her eyebrows furrow as she leans forward to examine the screen.

"Do you know why that file is so huge? Like, a hundred and twenty times larger than it should be?"

"I mean... the only thing I can think of is that I must have forgotten to shut the recording off after the last outro take?" Gemma chews on her bottom lip, concentrating on the time-line of events. Her narrowed gaze widens, and her green eyes pop out as she realizes something. "Oh my god," she whispers. "I think I recorded everything that happened during the raid."

It's so soft I almost don't hear her. "What?"

"I was recording my outro that night but kept messing it up. I thought I finally got a good one at the end, but now I remember it was still messed up. I was interrupted by something before getting the chance to record again."

"Okay, I'm tracking," I tell her, brushing some of her wild red hair behind her ear.

"I was interrupted by the cops banging on the door and demanding my father cook for them exclusively."

It takes me a second to realize what that means. "Holy shit," I whisper.

"Yeah," Gemma says, equally as hushed.

"You have proof. Everything you told Blade yesterday, all the incriminating evidence… you have a tape of it. Holy shit," I say again.

"So, that will help take the dirty cops down? For good?"

"I'd say it certainly doesn't help their case. I can export the audio file to a thumb drive and have Officer Jake listen. Maybe he can identify the voices."

"Good idea!"

Gemma sets the computer down and hops off my lap, making me irrationally upset. I don't like being in the same room as her without touching her in some way. I growl when I see her bend over and shuffle through her bag, presumably looking for a thumb drive.

That will have to wait.

I'm out of my seat and standing behind her before I'm even aware of what I'm doing. My dick is rock-hard, but the desire is deeper, the ache greater than needing to get off. I need to be inside her, to be connected to her, to prove to her and myself that we're still here despite the shit we've been through.

I smooth my hands over her round, juicy ass, and grip her hips, pulling her back into me so she can feel how hard I am for her. Gemma gasps and stands, leaning into me. I groan and kiss up and down her neck while she grinds against me, teasing me, driving me fucking crazy with her curvy body.

My hands slide underneath the hem of her shirt, spreading over her soft stomach and down to the waistband of the leggings she's wearing. She moans and lifts one arm behind her head, her hand fisting my hair and drawing me closer to her while her other hand rests on top of mine, guiding me down past the waistline of her panties.

"This what you need, princess?" I murmur, nipping at her pulse point and licking away the sting.

"Mmm... please," she moans.

I stroke her soaking wet slit, dragging our hands through her folds. Together, we rub her clit and thrust our fingers into her tight little opening. A warm wave of her cream pools in my hand, making me growl.

"Fuck, you're my dirty fucking princess, aren't you?"

"Yes..." she whimpers, rocking her hips into our joined hands, fucking herself with our fingers.

"Jesus," I grunt. I withdraw our hands and peel her pants and panties halfway down her thighs before unzipping my pants and pulling myself out. "Hands on the desk, Gemma. Need inside this pussy right fucking now."

She does as I say, bracing herself for my thickness. I grip her hips and slowly slide into her, feeling every inch of her silky heat squeeze around my cock. I pause when I'm fully seated inside her, taking a moment to be with her like this, buried in her dripping cunt, connected to her in the most intimate way. I nuzzle into her shoulder, pressing light kisses there and breathing her in.

Then I pull out and slam back into her, fucking the air out of her lungs with deep, steady strokes. I slide my hands underneath her shirt, gripping her large tits and using them as leverage to thrust into her deeper, pull her closer, grind against her harder.

Moans fall from her lips as I fill her over and over. She pushes against me, giving as good as she's getting. I love that about her.

I knead her breast with one hand and slide the other up her back. Wrapping her hair around my fist, I pull her head to the side. I crash my lips down on hers, prying her lips open for me so I can taste her while I fuck her.

She kisses me back with a wild frenzy that almost outmatches mine. I open my mouth wider, needing more, needing to get deeper, taste more of her, consume her completely. I swear to fucking God I could drown in her, fall right into her cleansing waters and never come up for air.

Gemma breaks our kiss, a jagged moan ripped from her core as she struggles to fill her lungs with oxygen. Her pussy tightens and flutters around me, letting me know she's close. I back off, thrusting into her slowly, keeping her on the edge without pushing her over.

She whines and wiggles her ass, but I laugh darkly and kiss her neck.

"Axel, please…"

"Please, what? Tell me what you want."

"I want you."

"You have me. All of me."

"Prove it."

God fucking damn. I love this woman.

I smack her ass and ram my fat cock into her, slicing into her juicy little cunt. I scrape my shaft against her front wall until she cries out, letting me know I found her most sensitive spot. I pound into it again and again, gripping her ass cheeks and spreading her apart so I can watch her pussy swallow all of me. I growl at the sight of us. A perfect fucking fit.

Gemma gasps for air and shakes in my arms. Her pussy throbs around me, coating my cock with more of her cream.

Her entire body freezes as she sucks in a huge breath of air and screams as her pussy snaps around me.

I'm sure everyone on the whole damn Savage Saints compound can hear her, but I don't care. I love that everyone will know how much pleasure I can bring my woman.

"Oh god, oh god, oh god," she repeats. "I-I can't, ohmygod, I can't… take… it…"

"You can, Gemma. You can take it."

I slap her ass again, making her squirt all over me.

"Axel! It hurts so good. Don't stop. Don't ever stop."

"Jesus Christ," I grit out, riding her ass hard with everything I am.

Sloppy, wet, smacking sounds fill the apartment, adding to the soundtrack of Gemma's breathy moans and my feral grunts. I wrap my arms around her hips right as her knees give out. Holding her up, I rut into her like a man possessed, driving us higher and higher, my muscles burning as I tense and flex and fuck her savagely.

The desk shakes, pens, books, and papers falling and scattering around us, but I can't stop. Sweat drips down my forehead, and my balls draw up tight, the sharp sting of ecstasy shooting through my body just as Gemma comes again. Her orgasm ignites mine. White-hot flames travel down my spine and shoot out of me into Gemma's ripe pussy. I come so hard my balls ache and my cock feels raw.

We collapse onto the floor. Gemma lands on my chest, and I wrap my arms around her, gently rolling us onto our sides so I'm spooning her. I bury my face in her hair, letting her familiar scent ground me.

We stay cuddled in silence for long moments before Gemma giggles. I feel the sound deep in my chest, making my heart lighter than it's ever been.

"What's so funny?" I murmur.

"That was… hot." Her cheeks turn from flushed pink to bright red.

I groan at her innocence mixed with the sex goddess I know she keeps hidden. I love that I'm the one to bring that out in her. "Hell, yeah, it was," I rasp, brushing my lips against her ear.

Gemma giggles again and relaxes into my embrace. My heart is full, and I know I need to tell her how I feel. I need her to know she's mine, and I love her more than I thought I was capable of. I'll love her better than anyone if she'll give me the chance.

CHAPTER TEN

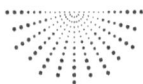

GEMMA

"hank you so much for agreeing to be interviewed for Grave Secrets!" I tell Ari, my special guest. She's on the other side of the country, but thanks to Zoom, I can interview anyone, anywhere, any time. "Your insights about traveling and ghost hunting were amazing and added a lot of context to some of the stories I tell. I think I have everything I need. It usually takes me about a week to edit. Then I'll send the file your way for final approval."

"That sounds great. This was so much fun! We should do more collaborations in the future after my next trip in a few months."

"I would love that. Maybe you can take me to one of your favorite haunted places, and we can do some paranormal experiments!"

"Yes!" Ari exclaims. Her enthusiasm is contagious, and my cheeks are sore from smiling and laughing so much. I can't wait to meet her in real life. "I'm gearing up for a hike in the Smoky Mountains. There's an old, abandoned town in a long-forgotten valley. Rumor has it, there's evidence of someone living there again, even though no one has been seen in the flesh."

"Are you going by yourself? That sounds a little scary and dangerous."

Ari waves her hand in front of the screen, dismissing my concerns. "I'll be fine. I've spent the night in the haunted Missouri State Penitentiary *and* the Winchester mansion."

"Don't your parents worry about you?"

The usually bright and bubbly Ari, aka Arizona, loses a bit of her light at the mention of her parents. When she looks at me again, her eyes are dim and subdued. "They passed away when I was a kid. The aunt who raised me doesn't talk to me much these days. She thinks I'm silly and stupid for being a travel blog writer, especially a paranormal one."

My heart goes out to her. "I'm sorry about your mom and dad," I say in a hushed tone. "And I'm sorry your aunt never believed in you. My family wasn't supportive of my podcast either, but screw 'em!"

This makes Ari smile. "Agreed. We're better off without the negativity."

"Exactly," I say with a nod. "But now that you have me, you officially have someone who's worried about you. So please check in with me on your travels and let me know you're safe."

Ari looks surprised, then a little teary. I get it. I didn't believe people cared just because they cared. Not until Axel swooped in and reminded me I'm worthy of good things and kindness.

"I will," she whispers before clearing her throat. "I promise," she says a little more clearly.

We say our goodbyes, and I lean back against the couch. I've been staying with Axel for a few days now, and I must admit, I could get used to life here. Especially when Axel walks around shirtless and gives me dark looks like he's doing right now.

"All done with work for the day?" he asks, stalking toward me.

"Not even close," I tell him, though I'm not so much looking at his eyes as I am his chest and sculpted abs.

Axel chuckles, though the sound is rough. "Maybe I can distract you for a bit?"

I squeeze my thighs together automatically, the ache blooming there already almost unbearable.

The sexy beast of a biker stands in front of me, then leans down, placing his hands on the backrest of the couch, one on each side of my head.

I look up at him, practically purring when I see the lust in his deep blue eyes. "Yes, please," I breathe, my gaze fixed on his lips. I've never needed anything or anyone the way I need Axel. One look and I'm a wet, whimpering mess.

"I know what you need," he murmurs. Before I can ask, he lifts me in his arms and carries me toward the bathroom, kissing me the whole way there.

He turns on the water and then faces me, gently peeling off my clothes. Axel guides me into the warm shower, stripping out of the rest of his clothes before joining me.

His fingertips follow the streams of water as they pour over my shoulders, breasts, torso, hips, and finally my throbbing pussy. I moan as his knuckles barely graze my mound before continuing down my inner thighs.

Axel's other hand wraps around the back of my neck, pulling me in for a punishing kiss. I open up for him, needing to taste and touch and feel him everywhere. He tugs my hair, pulling my head back to deepen the kiss. Two fingers dip into my slit and start circling my little bundle of nerves in slow, steady strokes.

I grip his biceps, digging my nails in as one finger pushes

into my entrance, then two. Axel thrusts his large digits in and out of me, slowly at first, and then faster, faster, faster, grinding the heel of his hand on my clit while devouring my lips.

Breaking the kiss, I bury my face between his neck and shoulders as I cry out. I'm *right* there, so close to my much-needed release. He keeps pumping his fingers, twisting and curling them to rub against my G-spot. Again, again, one more time...

Suddenly, his hand is gone. I nearly fall over at the loss of him, but I regain my composure and glare at his stupidly handsome face. Axel grins, which makes my pussy clench. God, this man. Frustrating, sweet, and sexy as hell.

"Not yet, princess. Patience."

With that, he spins me so my back is to his front and massages me everywhere. His large, calloused hands squeeze my breasts, my hips, and my soft, round belly that I've always been a little self-conscious of. Axel has made it clear that he loves every inch of me.

His hands trail lower, once again teasing my pussy lips. My clit throbs in time with my heartbeat, begging him to do something about the unbearable ache he's created.

"Axel..." I moan, wiggling my hips to get him to touch me where I need him most.

"Not yet," he murmurs again, licking the shell of my ear before trailing kisses down my neck and shoulder.

His hard cock digs into my ass, so I wiggle a bit more until his length nestles between my cheeks. Axel groans and rotates his hips, grinding his thick shaft against my ass.

"God, please, Axel," I beg. My legs shake, and I lean forward and brace myself against the wall.

A low growl rises from deep in Axel's chest. The sound vibrates through me, nearly making me come on the spot. He grips my left leg under my knee and lifts it so my foot rests on a bench in the corner of the shower.

"That's it. Fuck. Love it when you're spread out for me, Gemma." He touches every inch of me, caressing my thighs and widening my stance.

Axel gives me a satisfied grunt, which makes me giggle. My laughter is cut off when his cock slides along my slit. He taps my clit, nearly sending me over the edge. I'm so damn sensitive and ready to come that I think I might die if he doesn't get inside me this second.

"I've got you, Gemma," he murmurs, lining himself up with my entrance.

I expect him to thrust inside me and fuck me hard. I know he's as desperate for me as I am for him. But Axel slowly inches inside me, prolonging the sweet pain deep in my core. He grips my hips, holding me in place as he stretches me open. I hold my breath as he slides home, hitting the very end of me.

"Fucking Christ," he whispers.

Axel pulls out just as slowly, making me whine. I open my mouth to tell him to fuck me already, but then he slams his thick dick all the way inside, making me come instantly.

He wraps his arms around me, holding me up as I spasm around his cock. He fucks me through it, hammering into me over and over as I continue to convulse and cry out his name. He grips my inner thigh, spreading me wider and angling my hips so he hits my G-spot with every thrust.

"Y-y-yesss…" I hiss as I pound my fist against the wall and throw my head back against his shoulder.

Axel wraps his hand around my throat, tilting my head back as he splits me open with his dick. "So fucking tight for me, love," he grits.

I whimper in response as another orgasm rushes to the surface. Axel senses it, gripping my neck, which is hot as fuck, and trailing his other hand down my body to circle and pinch my clit.

My orgasm slams into me, hard and fast, ripping a scream from my lips. Axel growls and ruts into me, rubbing furious circles over my swollen, pulsing clit. A painful, delicious pleasure takes over every part of my body as I come again for him, sobbing his name.

Axel pulls out and spins me around, crashing his lips down on mine as he lifts and spears me with his cock. I wrap my legs around his hips and hang on for dear life as he pins me to the wall and fucks me like a man possessed.

"Mine, mine, fucking *mine*. Say it, Gemma. Tell me."

"Y-yours," I whisper, my voice scratchy from screaming his name.

"Louder," he growls.

"I'm yours!" I cry out, writhing in his arms.

Axel roars as he comes, burying his face in my neck to muffle the sound. I open my mouth in a silent scream as my entire body pulses, tenses, stretches... and collapses in on itself while my orgasm ravishes me from the inside out.

I swear I feel Axel come again, shooting his cum deep inside me in forceful bursts.

I drag air into my lungs in short breaths, trembling in his arms as he keeps me pinned to the wall. I comb my fingers through his hair while he nuzzles into my shoulder.

"You were right," I finally say once I've caught my breath.

"Oh?"

"I needed that."

Axel grins and kisses me again, wrapping me in his arms. Standing under the warm water with the steam curling around us and the remnants of my orgasm slowly fading, I know for certain that I love this man. Now, I need to figure out a way to tell him.

CHAPTER ELEVEN

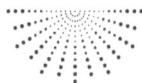

AXEL

*O*nce we cleaned up from our time in the shower, Gemma headed over to the clubhouse to hang out with Tessa, Sonya, and Sutton. I love that she's become close with them. My woman hasn't had many friends, and it warms me to know she now has friends and a family with the Savage Saints.

I told her I'd be right over after uploading the audio file to the thumb drive. Officer Jake agreed the recording was excellent and was enough to launch a full internal affairs investigation and take several cases to federal court.

Checking the progress bar, I nod when I see the estimated time is less than a minute. I throw on my Savage Saints cut and comb my fingers through my hair, which is as much of a morning routine as I've always had.

I grab the thumb drive after the file is complete, shoving it in my pocket as I head out the door. As soon as I step outside, I sense something is off. I scan the parking lot, but nothing is out of place. Still, I didn't get this far without listening to that gut feeling I get when I know things are about to go to shit.

My first thought is about Gemma. Did something happen to her? Tessa was kidnapped by her father, the former sheriff of this town and Sonya was almost stolen from Blade by the police for blackmail. Traditionally, our women are badasses, but that doesn't mean we like putting them in dangerous situations.

With that in mind, I startle out of my haze and focus on getting to the clubhouse to ensure Gemma is okay. What starts as a fast walk turns into an all-out sprint the more my brain comes up with worst-case scenarios.

Did the cops get her? Did they come back for retribution for the raid of their new meth hookup? Did her dad send someone after her?

My heart pounds against my ribcage, and panic courses through my veins. I pump my legs, pushing myself the last two hundred feet to the back door.

One minute, I'm running, and the next, I'm flat on my face in the gravel.

What the fuck? Did I trip?

And then a boot wedges in my side, and pain explodes across my torso. Rolling onto my back, I squint to see two officers leaning over me. Shit.

"We know you have something," one of them says.

I recognize his voice from the recording, but there's no way in hell he knows about that. Gemma didn't even know about it until a few days ago.

I don't say anything, opting to reel back and smash my head against the closest cop's face. Blood pours from his nose and mouth, and he stumbles back, clutching his ugly mug.

"Fuckin' degenerate," the man spits out. "We know about the daughter. The one shacking up with you."

"Where is she? What did you do to her? I swear to God–"

"God's got nothing to do with this," the second cop says. "It's not her we're after. Not yet, at least. Word on the street is the little goth freak has some recording equipment. It would be a shame if she picked up a certain conversation. Wouldn't want to hurt her unnecessarily."

I snarl at him, becoming more unhinged with each word from his mouth.

"We can avoid that, though, can't we? Just give us the laptop, and no one gets hurt."

"That's the biggest lie I've ever heard from the police, and that's saying something in this town. When was the last time no one was hurt on your watch? Every second your corrupt department is in charge hurts people."

The second cop fists my shirt and attempts to pull me from the ground. He only lifts me a few inches before dropping me. I'm sure the move would've been more effective if he had muscles instead of a beer belly.

I hop up, shoving him aside and settling into a fighting stance. I don't know their endgame, but I don't have time to call for backup. Injured Cop runs at me from the side. I move out of the way, only to back into Fat Cop. He grips my arms, pinning them behind my back while holding me still.

I jerk in his arms, almost breaking his hold on me. Injured Cop stomp-kicks my foot and knees me in the stomach. My steel-toed boots protect my feet from the feeble stomp, but the knee to the gut did some damage.

Doubling over, I cough and spit on the gravel before jerking my head back to smash Fat Cop's face. No such luck. He kicks the back of my right knee, sending me falling to the ground with a thud.

Injured Cop stands over me, his fist cocked back as rage fills his eyes. Fat Cop keeps me on the ground by pressing his boot to my throat and applying pressure. I can hardly get a breath in, but I'm determined to beat these fuckers to a pulp for threatening my woman.

Right as I'm about to be sucker punched, Injured Cop's eyes widen, and he topples to the side. Fat Cop is momentarily shocked, and while I have no idea what just happened, I'm happy to take advantage of the distraction. I wrap my hands around his ankle and rip it to the side, causing him to lose balance and fall, twisting his ankle.

Jumping to my feet, I whip my head around to see what made Injured Cop pass out. I don't know what I expected, but I'm speechless when I see Gemma with the old metal toaster from the clubhouse kitchen.

A grin spreads over my face, and my woman returns it. "The American serial killer, Belle Gunness, killed her second husband by hitting him in the head with a ten-pound meat grinder. I figured a toaster could do some damage as well."

"God, I love you," I tell her, closing the distance between us and scooping her up in my arms. My lips find hers, and I infuse all of my love and passion for this woman into the kiss.

We're interrupted when Fat Cop attempts to stand, shouting out a curse as his likely broken ankle gives out. Injured Cop was knocked out cold, thanks to my amazingly brave princess.

"Are you fuckin' kidding me?" I growl at the cop. "You're not going anywhere. In fact, I have a few friends at the FBI who want to talk to you and your friend here. The sheriff won't be too far behind, I imagine."

The back door of the clubhouse bursts open, and Rider and Hawk come sprinting toward the scene.

"What the hell happened?" Hawk asks.

"Dirty fucking cops playing dirty fucking games," I reply. Gemma squeezes me, and I hug her back, not wanting her to ever leave my arms.

"You okay?" Rider asks.

"Thanks to Gemma," I say, looking down at her with a grin.

"You still have the recording?" she asks.

I nod, kissing the top of her head. "Of course. They didn't get anything other than the ass-kicking they deserved."

She smiles, but I feel a slight tremor run down her spine. I'm sure she's still pumped full of adrenaline, and I know she'll crash soon. I want to get her home, take care of her, and thank her for coming to my rescue. She's kind of perfect, and she needs to hear it.

Turning to Hawk and Rider, I nod at the passed-out cop and Fat Cop, writhing on the ground and half-heartedly attempting to crawl away.

"We'll clean up," Rider says, understanding what I'm silently asking. "Officer Jake is on the way with some agents."

"Thanks," I tell them sincerely. Digging around in my pocket, I grab the thumb drive and hand it to Hawk. "Make sure he gets this. I'm taking the rest of the day to be with Gemma."

"Got it," Hawk confirms. "I'll let Blade know."

I shake his hand and nod at Rider, dragging Injured Cop's limp body to the side. I won't lie; I'm insanely proud that Gemma took him out. And insanely turned on.

"Ready to get back home?" I ask softly.

She nods. "Yeah, I think that's enough people-ing for the day," comes her sweet response. "Besides, we need to talk about the whole confessing-your-love-to-me thing."

"Whatever you want, princess. I'll tell you every damn day how much I love you."

I lean down to scoop her up, but Gemma spins out of my reach, giving me a playful look. "You can't carry me every-where. I have two working legs and two feet."

"And ten adorable toes." I grab her hand and pull her into

my arms. "Princesses often get carried to their next destination."

This time, Gemma doesn't fight me. She lets me pick her up and carry her, bridal style, through the door to our apartment.

CHAPTER TWELVE

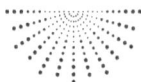

GEMMA

*W*e barely get inside the apartment before Axel sets me down and presses my back against the closed door. His lips are on mine in the next second, and I fall under his spell once more.

He breathes me in and swallows me down, possessing me, body and soul. I tear my mouth away from his and gulp down air, but Axel isn't finished with me yet.

His lips and tongue tease up and down my neck, and he nibbles at my pulse point, making me gasp softly. "Need to be inside you now, Gemma. Need to feel the woman I love from the inside out," he whispers, diving in for another kiss.

"Love," I repeat, my eyes finding his.

"I love you, sweetheart. Everything about you. Your kind heart, strong spirit, and sassy little mouth. I love how you pursue your creative passions and how brave you are in the face of pain and betrayal. I love your sense of humor and your adorable button nose. Your red hair, green eyes, neon-colored nails... there's nothing I don't love."

I blink back tears, trying to put my thoughts together in a coherent sentence. All that comes out is, "I love you so much.

I don't know what I did to deserve someone like you in my life."

"Gemma, you never have to earn my love. You have it just by existing."

"Same."

"Say it again," he rasps, closing his eyes.

"Same?"

"The other thing."

"I love you?"

"Now say it like you mean it instead of a question." He opens one eye and grins at me.

"I love you. I love you. I love you," I repeat.

"Marry me."

My eyes widen, but I'm not overwhelmed or shocked by his statement. It makes sense. Of course, we're going to get married. Still, I need to draw this out a little more. Make him work for it a tiny bit. Especially if he's going to do what I think he's going to do…

"Marry you?"

He nods.

"Is that a question or a demand?" I inquire with a raised eyebrow.

"Will you marry me?" he grunts, making me laugh.

"Hmm…" I tap my chin and look up as if trying to decide.

When I look down at Axel, his beautiful blue eyes flash with lust. The next thing I know, he throws me over his shoulder and carries me to the bedroom.

Axel claps his big, rough hand over my ass, making me squirm in his arms. "You took too long to answer," he says matter-of-factly. "Now you're mine."

We burst into the bedroom, and Axel tosses me onto the bed, making me giggle.

"I don't think that's how it works," I tease him, sitting up on the bed and quirking an eyebrow in challenge.

Axel stares at me and starts stripping. I watch his every move as I remove my clothes. Soon, we're both naked and gazing at each other. I'll never get used to this man's perfect body. The muscles in his arms tense and tighten as he squeezes his hands into fists. My man is gloriously naked, with his massive cock growing right in front of my eyes. I lick my lips as a bead of precum forms and drip down the head of his cock.

"Fine," Axel says with a grin, stroking his huge dick. "I'll have to see if there are a few other ways I can get you to say yes."

I tuck my legs underneath me and get on all fours, crawling toward him. "Maybe you just need to ask the right question," I murmur before sticking my tongue out and licking up his arousal. I never take my eyes off of his. I love seeing him get lost in his lust. Our lust.

Axel tips his head back and hisses out a breath. When he looks back down at me, I see a wild, feral glint behind his usually calm, tender gaze. Good. I love it when he loses control like this.

"What question is that?" he grits, reaching down and tucking my hair behind my ear.

"I think you know," I whisper, licking the head of his cock again and dipping my tongue in the little slit on top, just the way he likes. I moan when he fists my hair and tugs my head back.

"Do you want to suck my fat fucking cock, princess?"

"God, yes," I moan, licking my lips. He's still holding me tightly, my lips mere inches from what I want most at this moment.

"Then open up, baby. I'm gonna fuck your pretty mouth now," Axel growls.

I obey his command, opening my mouth wide for him as he holds my head in place and slides his dick past my lips, stretching me wide to accommodate his girth. I moan at his salty, earthy taste and eagerly suck more of him down until he hits the back of my throat. Axel pulls back and then enters me again, fucking my mouth nice and slowly.

But I don't want nice and slow. I want his passion, his dominance. Reaching out, I cup his balls in one hand and gently massage them, loving the shiver that runs through his huge, muscular body.

"Fuck," he grunts, bucking his hips more forcefully and shoving his big dick deeper into my mouth.

I breathe in through my nose, relax my throat, and dig my nails into his ass, pulling him closer to me.

"Jesus Christ," he growls, pumping in and out of me.

I moan around him and lick the sensitive vein on the underside of his cock with each thrust. My juices drip down my legs as my pussy throbs and aches for attention. Keeping one hand on Axel's sculpted ass, I move the other down my body until my fingers sink into my soaking slit.

"Fuck, baby. I feel you trembling. Does giving your man pleasure make you wet?"

I answer him by moaning and bobbing my head faster, taking him deeper and digging my nails further into his skin. I'm so close. My fingers rub furious circles around my clit while I work Axel over until we're in a frenzy of lust and ecstasy.

My muscles tighten. Axel's dick swells and twitches in my mouth. I know we're about to come together.

But then Axel swears and pulls me off his dick, pushing me back on the bed. An animalistic growl rises from deep in his chest as he crawls on top of me and slams his cock so deep, so fast, so roughly I come instantly.

"Axel!" I shriek, clawing at his back and hanging on for dear life as he fucks me through my orgasm and sucks on my neck. "Ohmygod, so good, so..." I scream again when his teeth sink into my shoulder, and another orgasm slams into me violently, rocking me to my very core. My pussy pulses and grips him, never wanting to be separated.

"Goddamn, so tight," Axel grunts before taking my lips in a wild, vicious kiss. He bites my bottom lip and sucks my tongue into his mouth, devouring every inch of me. "Give me another one. Need to watch you come again."

I shake my head no, even as my hips buck and my back bows off the bed. "I… can't…" I whimper.

"Yes, you can, and you will. Again and again. Swear to Christ, Gemma, I'm going to fuck this little pussy till we're too exhausted to move. So come for me like the good girl you are."

I shiver at his dirty words and dirtier promises. Axel grins wickedly. Sitting back on his heels, he grabs my hips and uses my body to jerk himself off. He picks up his pace, hammering into my G-spot at this new angle. My whole body convulses each time he hits the end of me.

It doesn't take much to send me flying over the edge again. My orgasm burns through me rapidly, stealing the air from my lungs as I thrash on the bed. Axel holds my body tightly against his, feeling me come around his dick.

My pussy is still throbbing when he pulls out and flips me over on my stomach. I get up on all fours, still trembling from my orgasm, and look at him over my shoulder. Axel slaps my ass as his big cock slams into me. I move back along him, bucking my ass and panting as his powerful strokes rattle me to my very bones.

He smirks, his ripped body tense. Sweat rolls down my skin as he works me, and pleasure floods me from every direction. I'm totally mindless, absolutely devastated by his cock, but loving every single inch of it.

He slides out, making me gasp, and rolls me back over. He spreads my legs wide and pushes himself inside me. I lean forward, kissing him as he grinds his cock into my pussy. He fucks me like that, legs spread wide, mouth against mine. It feels so good to have him deep between my legs. He grinds into me, fucking me hard, making me moan, making me say his name as I cream all over his thick dick.

My pussy feels raw and so, so sensitive. I feel every ridge and vein in his cock as he pounds into me again and again. Liquid fire shoots through my body, singeing my nerves and burning me up from the inside out.

I cling to Axel, locking my ankles behind his back and clutching and clawing at his shoulders. I bury my face in the side of his neck as I brace for the raging inferno he calls forth from deep within my core.

"Axel," I gasp, almost afraid of what will happen when I finally climax.

"I've got you, sweetheart," he assures me. "Just trust me and let go, Gemma. Let go for me."

All my muscles squeeze up tightly as I curl into Axel, and my whole world burns to the ground as I scream my orgasm. Axel roars and sinks so fucking deep inside me as his release ravages his massive, muscled body. We cry out and hold onto each other as we fall into the very depths of pleasure.

After an eternity of intense, sharp ecstasy, I finally open my eyes. Axel is lying on his side next to me, drawing a line with his fingertips from my sternum to my belly button and back again.

"There you are," he whispers, nuzzling into my neck and kissing me there. "How do you feel, baby? Are you okay?"

I inhale a shaky breath and try to get my heart to stop thrashing around in my chest. Axel drifts his fingers over my skin, bringing me back to reality with his touch.

"Breathe for me, love," he says gently, pressing his lips to my temple. "That's it. Good girl."

With my breathing and heart rate finally under control, I

turn my head toward Axel and take in his warm blue eyes, strong jaw with the perfect amount of sexy stubble, and soft lips pulling up into a gentle smile.

I return his smile and bite my bottom lip. Axel grasps my chin in between his thumb and forefinger, gently tugging my lip from the grasp of my teeth so he can kiss me. It's slow and tender, as if we have a lifetime of moments like this.

As if reading my thoughts, Axel pulls back and rubs his nose up and down mine. "What do you say, princess? Are you ready to spend forever with me?"

Tears immediately spring into my eyes as I smile with all the love and gratitude I have in my heart. I nod vigorously, my smile growing bigger by the second.

Axel grins. "I'm gonna need to hear you say it, love."

"Yes! Yes, I'll marry you!" The words are barely out of my mouth before Axel crashes his lips down on mine.

When we break apart, he chuckles and rolls onto his back, tucking me into his side. "Good to know I can get you to say yes to pretty much anything after giving you four orgasms."

I roll my eyes playfully, which makes Axel bend and kiss my eyelids. I sigh and snuggle closer to him, letting my fingers roam over the hard muscles in his chest and abs.

This princess can't wait for the happily ever after her prince has promised.

EPILOGUE

Axel

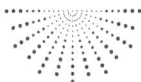

"Three, two, one… Here I come, ready or not!" I shout across the yard.

It takes less than ten seconds for me to spot every single one of the kids currently hiding in my backyard. Between Hawk and Rider's rugrats, Blade's three little hellions, and my two trouble makers, there are nine kids here who absolutely suck at hide-and-seek.

I'm a good sport though, taking a few steps toward the slide, where two little girls are huddled up. Gemma informed me several years ago that when kids play hide-and-seek, they don't want to be found right away. I told her they should find better spots, but she wasn't having any of that. Apparently, I'm supposed to be a mature adult and play the game so the kids can have fun. She then promised that we'd always play a fun game after where we both win.

God, I love her.

I didn't think it was possible, but I somehow love my princess more today than I did that first day we met in the graveyard nearly ten years ago. Gemma has refined her punk-rock style slightly, but her wardrobe is still mostly black and neon. She gets her nails professionally done these days, thanks to her hugely successful true crime YouTube channel, Grave Secrets.

She confided in me shortly after we got married that she always wanted to try a video format of her podcast, but she never wanted to film in her trailer. As soon as I heard that, I took her shopping for a camera and a new computer with enough RAM to run video editing software.

My gorgeous, talented, brilliant wife hit one million subscribers in less than a year, and she's expanded her brand into a whole network of true crime podcasts and shows. I couldn't be prouder of her and everything she's accomplished.

The girls hiding under the slide start to giggle, pulling me back into the moment. I feign looking everywhere but under the slide, scratching my chin and then shrugging before moving on to the bushes, where my son is fidgeting.

Brandon just turned five last month, and I swear the little man has enough energy to power a super computer. He can't sit still to save his life, thus making him one of the worst hide-and-seekers in the world. Love the kid.

Taking a few steps up and down the row of bushes, I notice Patricia, our eight-year-old, lying on her back on top of a dirt mound from a yard project I have yet to finish. I grin and shake my head, loving that my daughter is as unique as her mother.

I take the search party farther into the backyard, walking around the perimeter of my toolshed. When I get to the open door, I'm caught off-guard when a hand snakes out and grabs mine.

"What–"

Gemma's sweet strawberries and cream scent fills my

lungs, and I pull my wife into my arms as I walk us backward into the darkened shed.

"Found you," I whisper onto her lips before taking them as my own. Gemma sinks into my embrace, her hands sliding up my chest and wrapping around my neck.

"What are you going to do with me now that you have me?" she practically purrs.

Instead of telling her, I show her exactly what I want to do to her delectable, curvy little body. Lifting my woman up in my arms, I place her on the workbench and step between her thighs. My lips ghost up and down her neck, pausing to nip her pulse point before licking away the sting.

"Axel," she breathes out, her legs tightening around my hips.

"Yes, princess?"

She doesn't answer, instead opening her mouth in a silent moan as I palm her breast and grind my thick cock into her center. Her mouth crashes down on mine, and she totally owns this kiss, prying my lips open and drinking me down with untamed need.

I'm about to rip our clothes off and lay my woman out on the bench so I can devour every inch of her, but then she pulls away from me. I grunt, not liking the distance between us.

Gemma grins, leaning closer, closer, closer, her lips barely an inch from mine. "It's not time for us to play our game yet," she whispers.

I groan while Gemma giggles and wraps her arms around me in a hug. I hug her back and help her off of the workbench, setting her down on her feet.

"I believe there are still some children who need finding?" Gemma says, lifting an eyebrow at me.

"It's too hard. I need help finding them all," I say with a pout.

"Uh-huh, sure," Gemma responds, rolling her eyes. I smack her ass, making her shriek and glare at me, though she's smiling the whole time. "Rider and will be here soon with Blade and Hawk to pick up the kids. Think you can wait until after bath time for our fun?"

"No," I grumble. Gemma laughs as she heads out through the door, but I'm not quite done with her yet. Sliding my arm around her waist, I pull my princess back into me, her back pressed against my chest. "Love you, princess," I whisper into the shell of her ear.

"Love you more," she replies, resting her head on my shoulder.

Each and every moment with my Gemma is better than the last. She's made me happier than I ever knew possible, given me two kids I'm crazy about, and continues to amaze and surprise me with her creativity and strength.

Just like the first day I met Gemma, I vow to provide her with safety and happiness. I'd like to think I've made good on that promise so far. When my beautiful princess sighs sweetly and snuggles into my embrace, I know I must have done something right to have her right here with me after all these years.

I can't wait for a hundred more.

* * *

THE END
Curious about Kingsley and his too-happy assistant? Check out their story here!
*
Want to know more about Ari and her travels to the Smoky Mountains? Get her story here!

ABOUT THE AUTHOR

Cameron Hart is a USA Today bestselling author of contemporary romance. She writes books with lots of heat, plenty of sweet, and just enough drama to keep things interesting.

Want to meet me? Check out events and book signings I'll be attending across the US: https://www.cameronhart.net/meet-me-in-person/

Sign up for my newsletter and get a free novella!

ALSO BY CAMERON HART

1012 Curvy Way

Office Romance:

Boss Me Series

Beastly Brute

Executive Rule

Cowboy & Small Town Romance:

Roped in by Love Series

Sequoia Stud Farm

Small Town Love Boxset

Where I Belong

Seducing Sophia

Take Me Home

Forbidden Romance:

Secret Obsession

Secret Protector

Secret Desire

Holiday Romance:

Working for the Scrooge

Adored by Landon

Unwrapping His Package

Coming Down Her Chimney

His Christmas Angel

Hungry for Owen

Snow & Her Seven White Lies

Accidental Valentine

For Richer or Poorer

Made in United States
Cleveland, OH
31 May 2025

17398488R00233